I0818896

A PAIR OF ACES

Titles by
Marie Benedict and
Victoria Christopher Murray

The Personal Librarian

The First Ladies

A Pair of Aces

A PAIR OF ACES

MARIE BENEDICT AND
VICTORIA CHRISTOPHER MURRAY

BERKLEY
New York

BERKLEY
An imprint of Penguin Random House LLC
1745 Broadway, New York, NY 10019
penguinrandomhouse.com

Book design by Katy Riegel

Library of Congress Cataloging-in-Publication Data

Names: Benedict, Marie author | Murray, Victoria Christopher author
Title: A pair of aces / Marie Benedict and Victoria Christopher Murray.
Description: New York: Berkley, [2026]
Identifiers: LCCN 2025047616 (print) | LCCN 2025047617 (ebook) |
ISBN 9780593637937 hardcover | ISBN 9780593637944 ebook
Subjects: LCGFT: Historical fiction | Fiction | Novels
Classification: LCC PS3620.E75 P44 2026 (print) | LCC PS3620.E75 (ebook)
LC record available at https://lccn.loc.gov/2025047616
LC ebook record available at https://lccn.loc.gov/2025047617

Printed in the United States of America
1st Printing

The authorized representative in the EU for product safety and compliance is
Penguin Random House Ireland, Morrison Chambers,
32 Nassau Street, Dublin D02 YH68, Ireland,
https://eu-contact.penguin.ie.

For all of the Eunices and Pollys past, present, and yet to come. Women of different races and backgrounds who join together to make the world better for everyone. Women who understand that power is multiplied through allyship.

A PAIR OF ACES

PART I

CHAPTER ONE

POLLY ADLER

New York, New York
April 3, 1935

SOMETHING FEELS OFF. The sensation hits me the moment we step into the swanky Algonquin Hotel suite. As I glance around the mahogany-lined sitting room, all seems in order: Our host lifts up a gleaming cocktail shaker to welcome me and my girls; nearly all the gents relax in the royal-blue plush velvet armchairs arranged around the low-lit space; the warm hum of jazz from the phonograph drifts around the room. But in my line of business, I've learned the hard way to trust my instincts.

I turn toward my girls. Virginia, Kit, Rosalie, and Angelica stand behind me, dressed to the nines in glittering, figure-hugging gowns and heels so high they teeter alluringly as they walk. Hands on hips, they are busy sussing out the men, unbothered by whatever has gotten under my skin. Could I have misjudged the scene? Nothing to do about it now. I motion for the girls to start mingling.

"Polly Adler, welcome! Come have a martini!" Our host, Archie Elwyn, renowned owner of theaters up and down the East Coast, calls me over to the bar nestled into the corner of the room. As I sidle up, he gestures to the man facing him, the only one with his back to the room. "I'd like to introduce you to Mr. Brown."

The man swivels in his chair to face me. His face is sallow, and his rumpled gray suit hangs off him like a sack. He certainly doesn't resemble Archie's usual guests, well-heeled film studio executives and theater impresarios with whom Archie's trying to make deals. And whom my girls are meant to please. *Anything to keep my plays on the stage and the theaters full,* I've heard Archie say often enough. But this Mr. Brown doesn't look like he could afford a ticket to one of Archie's productions, let alone have the funds to produce one. Not to mention there's a barrel-chested man of enormous girth standing cross armed against a nearby wall, not partaking of the fun but certainly scrutinizing it. And I see the telltale bulge of a gun under his suit jacket.

"I hear a lot of talk about you, Polly. Word on the street is you're the best of the best. Aces, even, in the skirt trade," Mr. Brown says.

His voice is low and gravelly and his accent thick. As an immigrant always trying to polish up my own speech, I've become tuned in to others' pronunciations, and I'm guessing this man hails from the Bronx. Not the usual hometown of Archie's theater folks.

I'm not certain how to reply to Mr. Brown's remark, and I stare at the man for a beat too long. It's an unspoken rule that no one overtly mentions my business. Especially outside my house, the place where I typically conduct it. The walls have ears, after all, particularly hotel walls.

Archie's eyes are fixed on me; I don't think he's ever seen me speechless. Stepping into the awkward breach, he asks, "Polly, would you mind popping into the butler's pantry and grabbing me some olives for these martinis?"

I nod, happy to move away from this strange Mr. Brown. Opening the door to the small space outfitted with cabinetry and a brass sink, I fling open one cabinet door after another in the hunt for olives. And then I freeze.

Stacked inside a deep cabinet in the corner is a heaping pile of tommy guns. Definitely not the sort of thing men use to duck hunt, which Archie is known to brag about endlessly. These submachine guns are the signature weapons of criminals, and this qualifies as an arsenal.

What in the hell is going on here?

The butler's pantry door swings open, and I jump. I almost reach for one of the tommy guns to protect myself before I realize it's Archie. "These better be stage props, Archie," I hiss, my voice so quiet as to be nearly inaudible.

He places a hand on my arm in a futile effort to calm me. "Times are tough, Polly, and investors are scarce. I've had to expand my horizons." His volume is barely above a whisper.

"What do you mean?" I feel sick.

"Don't you know who the men out there are?" He looks genuinely surprised.

"Why should I? I mean, they don't look like your usual Hollywood honchos, but one john is as good as another as long as they pay what's due and don't hurt my girls."

"Mr. Brown is Dutch Schultz."

I feel like I've been slapped, and I lean against the wall of cabinets for support. Dutch Schultz? The man who's created an underworld domain so expansive he controls gambling and extortion and God knows what else in New York City? Dutch is one of the most powerful mobsters in town and notorious for the violence that earned him the position.

Suddenly I stand up straight and move to exit the butler's pantry. "Where are you going, Polly? You can't leave. You definitely can't take the girls." Archie's voice is tremulous.

"I'm not an idiot, Archie. I won't put myself or you in harm's way by pulling the girls and angering the men, although you deserve it. You played me for a sucker by inviting us here without telling me the truth." I pause for a deep breath, then say, "Excuse me. I need to check on my girls, to make sure they're all right."

Mustering all of my five feet—my height in three-inch heels, if I'm honest—I push past Archie and reenter the suite. I take a quick measure of the sitting room. The girls are perched on the men's chairs, flirting and sipping drinks. Using the private hand gestures and eye contact we employ, I check in with Virginia, Kit, Rosalie, and Angelica in turn, and all's well, according to the girls. But I observe this tableau with new eyes, and though the men seem jovial enough, I cannot unsee their roughness. I want to take the girls and run.

Just then the so-called Mr. Brown motions to me. My heart races as I force a smile onto my lips and walk toward him.

"Polly, I want to get your address. Me and my boys might like to stop in from time to time. I like the look of your girls, and I like the way you handle yourself." Dutch glances at me as if he's bestowed the compliment of a lifetime instead of a death sentence.

"Of course, Mr. Brown," I say, keeping the smile pasted on my lips. Although I mean the exact opposite. In the fifteen years I've been running my business, I've done everything I can to avoid connections with the upper levels of the Mob. Sure, I've had the occasional gangster visit my house in the company of one of my regulars, but I've fended off any opportunities for a regular relationship. On one occasion, a policeman friend offered to make an introduction to Dutch because, as my friend put it, *he's a good spender*, but I firmly declined. Why would I invite bloodshed into my house? There's trouble enough in my line of work.

"Can I get a card?" he asks when I don't immediately offer up the location of my secret house.

Here and now, how can I say anything but yes? Reaching into my bag with a trembling hand, I pass him one of my infamous calling cards. Printed in vibrant blue ink, the card features only my phone number and a line drawing of a parrot perched on a stand, a subtle nod to my name, as so many parrots are named Polly. No actual reference to my name or my address can be found anywhere on the card. I can't risk it ending up in the wrong hands.

"You won't see my address on the card, but my house is in the Majestic," I say, and he nods once.

"Mr. Brown" passes the card to the behemoth guarding the room, who slides it into the inner pocket of his jacket. And then he says, "You'll like being in my circle. I treat the people in it real good." Looking at Dutch—who allegedly murders as casually as he picks his teeth—I cannot breathe.

"Will you excuse me?" I ask, gesturing toward the powder room.

Lifting his hand in permission, Dutch turns back to his martini and to Archie, who's resumed his place behind the bar. I cross the room, trying my level best to keep my gait steady and my expression pleasant. As soon as I enter the marble-tiled powder room, I lock the door behind me and sink to the floor, my back against the door.

Fighting tears and trying to catch my breath, I wonder what I'm going to do. I've been given no choice but to invite the Devil to my doorstep, and I know all too well what happens to brothels that become the regular haunts for prominent mobsters. Should I move to another apartment, start over with a new name and a new house? Should I leave town altogether? But what would happen to my girls?

Just then, I hear two distinct voices outside the powder room door. They speak in low tones, but I'm sure one of them is Dutch. A phrase catches my attention: "Mad Dog." My shallow breathing grows even shallower at the mention of the violent former hit man currently at war with Dutch. Mad Dog Coll's quest for power has left the city on edge: Dozens of men are dead, including Coll's own brother; immeasurable numbers of buildings, shops, and automobiles have been destroyed; at least eight gangsters have been kidnapped; and, worst of all, a five-year-old Harlem boy, Michael Vengalli, was accidentally gunned down during a botched shooting of bootlegger Joey Rao. Even for the Mob, Mad Dog's path of destruction has been brutal.

I press my ear to the door. "Boss, I don't think we'll ever get a better shot at Coll."

Dutch's gravelly voice is barely audible, but I manage to hear him ask, "Where is the bastard?"

"In a phone booth at a drugstore on the corner of Eighth Avenue and 23rd Street in Manhattan. Our boys are at the scene."

"Order it," Dutch says.

"Do you want to do the deed yourself?"

"Nah, I don't want to dirty my hands with that scum." Dutch chuckles. "But I might want to watch. Or at least see the aftermath."

"Lulu, round up the men," the other man barks. Within seconds, a clatter of footsteps sounds in the hall, and the hotel suite front door slams shut.

I wait in the powder room for another painfully long minute until I hear my girls murmuring. Pushing myself to stand, I take a quick peek at my face in the mirror. With a shaking hand, I slide my compact from my bag, powder my blotched face, and reapply my crimson lipstick. No one has ever called Polly Adler pretty—my features are too blunt, my figure too plump, and my heritage too Jewish by popular standards—but no one will ever call me unpolished either. Or weak.

Squaring my shoulders, I unlock the powder room door and enter the suite. Except for Archie, the men are gone, and only my girls remain. Sipping on their Whiskey Slings and Gin Rickeys and Pink Ladies, they appear nonplussed at the disappearance of the men. And why should they be concerned? The girls are in the dark about the identity of the men, and I will do nothing to illuminate them. My job is to see nothing and hear nothing and do nothing. Because people who are blind and deaf and immobile can't be whacked on suspicion of snitching.

"Time to go, girls," I announce with a clap of my hands.

"Aw," Kit complains, drawing deeply from her Pink Lady. "Can't we stay a little longer? Archie's pouring some delicious cocktails. And maybe the men will come back."

Archie offers me an apologetic smile, but I don't return it. "No, Kit, the men are gone, and we should be, too. Archie, I wish I could thank you for a terrific evening."

Without waiting for the girls' acquiescence, I head toward the front door, knowing they will follow. When the elevator arrives, we all file inside and ride down to the lobby in silence. Just before the elevator doors slide open, I say, "I promise some killer cocktails when we get to the house."

They chatter excitedly as we stroll through the Algonquin lobby, elegantly decorated with English oak and marble and chockablock with palm trees and flowers. I'm familiar with it from many assignations like this one and the occasional pop in to drink with some of my regulars who haunt this place. But tonight, the hotel feels unusually empty, even for a Wednesday night, and I spot none of the literary types who toggle between this establishment and my own. Where is everyone? Are all the guests out on the town watching some big jazz band I don't know about or a Broadway debut I haven't heard of yet?

A lone doorman holds open the brass doors for us, and I ask him to hail us a cab. But as soon as we land on the sidewalk, we are swarmed by blue-uniformed New York City cops. My arms are pulled behind my back and cuffed, as are the girls'. An officer steps forward from the pack and, with a wide grin, announces, "Miss Polly Adler, you are under arrest."

CHAPTER TWO

EUNICE CARTER

New York, New York
April 4, 1935

I HURRY THROUGH the labyrinth of crisscrossing hallways, passing one frosted-paneled door after another until I reach a wide-open bullpen. The space hums with secretaries and stenographers, clerks and accountants. Standing watch over it all are the duty officers, stationed throughout this ten-thousand-square-foot office—and beyond—to protect Special Prosecutor Thomas Dewey and this team he's assembled to take on New York City's organized crime and one of its brazen and cold-blooded kingpins, Dutch Schultz.

A haze of cigarette smoke greets me the moment I enter the meeting room, and then I hear the low murmur of voices. The other nineteen assistant district attorneys are already crammed around the long oak table. Once again, I am the last attorney to arrive, but only because I was the last to be informed. At least this time Dewey saw fit to notify me.

No one glances up when I enter, a shift from the first weeks, when we were all brought together to be part of this prosecution team. Back then, every conversation ceased whenever I entered. The curiosity surrounding my appointment, it seems, has dulled.

Slivers of sunlight slip through the drawn venetian blinds. Every window throughout the office is covered—a layer of security against spying eyes from nearby windows and rooftops. Even here in the meeting room, we're watched. Two broad-shouldered men stand in the corners, their glares sharp as ice shards, with service revolvers resting on their hips; each would make any man blink once and think twice.

I spot Murray Gurfein peering at me over the top of his wire-rimmed glasses. He raises his hand, then points to the empty chair beside him. I exhale. Murray is the only colleague I consider a friend. From the first day, he's been my refuge in this sea of white men in dark suits.

"Thanks. Do you know why we've been gath—" Before I finish, Dewey strides into the room. Standing tall, he looms, not by height but by presence. He has a set jaw and piercing gaze, and his brown eyes study us as if he's taking the measure of a jury. Of course, we are no jury. We are his team. The twenty against the underworld, as the press calls us.

For the briefest moment, Dewey's eyes land on me—the only Negro, the only female he selected when he was appointed to this position with the singular objective to rid the city of racketeers, vice lords, and murderers. First up is Dutch Schultz.

Under the intensity of his stare, I sit up straighter, proud of my place among these men.

"Gentlemen," he begins, then glances at me. "Mrs. Carter. Last night, there was another murder in the city. It'll hit the newspapers this morning, but Vincent Coll was killed. He was gunned down in a telephone booth on 23rd and Eighth."

The room erupts.

Vincent—"Mad Dog"—Coll is dead?

My only thought—it didn't happen soon enough.

"Simmer down. While Coll wasn't the target of our investigation, his death may help us nail Schultz. His murder is the result of the war between the two. I want you all to mine your networks. Keep your eyes and ears open for anything linking Schultz to this murder. This is not the big, organized scheme we hope to bring him in for, but still, a conviction for the murder of Coll would put Schultz behind bars. Any questions?"

Not an eye strays from Dewey as we shake our heads.

"Now, one word of caution. Violence rarely ends with one bullet. Violence begets violence. And this killing may set off a chain of bloodshed. So be on the lookout. Mind your movements. Take good care of yourselves; remember these men kill with ease and without conscience." After a pause, he slaps his palms on the table. "All right, back to work."

Chair legs scrape against the polished oak floor, and we stand, the mood now somber. As we file from the meeting room, Murray steps in line with me. He shortens his stride so I can keep up with him.

"Things are heating up," he whispers.

"Yes," I say as my mind races, worrying about what this Coll situation means.

Murray follows me to my office. This isn't unusual. We have been friends from the day Dewey first gathered his team together, and at that meeting, I slipped into the chair beside Murray. At the end, the men, still buzzing with excitement, agreed to extend their conversation over lunch. But when one suggested Fraunces Tavern, a popular joint for the legal set, I gathered my things and started back to my office.

"Mrs. Carter, aren't you coming?"

I turned to Murray, but before I could speak, I caught the flicker of understanding in his eyes. He knew it was unlikely that I'd be welcomed at Fraunces Tavern. I was colored.

Without missing a beat, Murray told the others he'd join them the next day. Then, minutes later, he appeared in my office doorway with a bag from the corner deli.

"I hope you like liverwurst and Coca-Cola," he said, and we'd shared lunch and laughter.

We chatted about our families and where we'd attended school. I shared with him that I received my bachelor of arts and my master's of social work from Smith College and, a few years later, my law degree from Fordham University Law School. He told me about his years at Columbia University and then Harvard Law School—and his past five years at the US Attorney's office under Dewey. By the end of the hour, he was Murray, I was Eunice, and we were friends.

As I slip into my desk chair now, he says, "Something else happened last night. Something that will be of interest to you."

"Something more righteous than Coll being murdered?" My tone is heavy with the loathing I've long held for that man—the baby killer, as I've come to know him.

He settles into the chair across from my desk. "Polly Adler was arrested."

Polly Adler? The most infamous madam in New York? "At her brothel?" The location of her brothel has been a well-kept secret, and even uncovering that would be a coup.

"No. Outside of the Algonquin Hotel."

I nod slowly. In this war we've waged against the underworld, each assistant district attorney has been assigned a particular racket where the Mob reign through fear and bloodshed. We're up against everything from extortion to murder, in industries like construction, retail, and restaurants. As the only attorney from Harlem, I assumed I'd be assigned to the numbers racket—the illegal gambling game that costs players only pennies but funnels millions into the pockets of the "numbers men." The police have largely eradicated "the numbers" throughout the city, but in Harlem, it's allowed to thrive unchecked.

Schultz was gunning for control—both literally and figuratively—of this racket. But he was being thwarted by a colored woman, Stephanie St. Clair, the Queen of the Harlem Numbers. Given the prominence of Miss St. Clair and my station and connections in the Harlem community, that assignment should have fallen to me.

Instead, unlike the men, I hadn't been given a racket at all. Rather, I'd been assigned the task of fulfilling a promise Dewey made to the citizens of New York when he was first appointed special prosecutor: "We need your help in rooting out organized crime in this city," he'd said on a WOR broadcast. "Therefore, if you've seen, heard, or know of anything, we want to hear from you. We will investigate every complaint, and I have someone assigned specifically to this task."

That someone was me. I listened to every New Yorker who called, came to our office, or wrote a letter with a gripe about the Mob.

At first, I was far from pleased, certain this assignment was dismissive and kept me from the front lines. However, as I interviewed dozens of residents, I noticed that, while most complaints centered on prostitution, there was a familiar pattern forming, specifically with brothels the police seemed to ignore. It reminded me of my days working in Women's Court, when I'd noticed another pattern, that time also with the prostitutes.

These patterns, along with the citizens' complaints, had me wondering, Is there more here? Could there be Mob-connected corruption from which I might build a case? A case grounded in a racket of organized prostitution?

Of course it was a long shot, but I'd been determined to make something out of the nothing that had been handed to me. So I began combing through court records, sitting in on countless arraignments and trials, listening to the hollowed-out stories of the prostitutes. And I spent hours in the Manuscript and Archives Room of New York Public Library, poring over the records of the Committee of Fourteen, a group of wealthy New Yorkers who, through undercover investigations and interviews, had spent thirty years trying to understand prostitution and eradicate it from New York City streets.

And at last, my suspicions are beginning to bear fruit.

But Murray is the only one in the office who knows that I've gone far beyond the mandate I was given.

"I knew you'd be interested that Polly and a few of her girls were picked up on pandering charges," Murray says, snapping me back to the present.

"That *is* interesting," I finally say, a plan already forming in my mind.

"Isn't it?" Murray says. "Have you turned up anything from your observations in Women's Court?"

"No," I say, not ready to discuss what I've discovered. There are still too many unconnected dots. But this development with Polly Adler could springboard my investigation. "Where is Polly Adler being held?"

Rows of narrow, iron-barred windows flank the towering entrance of the 30th Precinct Station House. I've been here just a few times, but whenever I step inside, the gray walls, concrete floors, and overhead steel beams are as intimidating as they were during my first visit. Muffled chatter passes between two officers behind the partitioned counter, while another policeman pecks away on a Remington, barely glancing up as he types.

A fourth officer notices me. He stands and crosses his arms as I approach. His eyes narrow with reproach and recognition.

I stand strong against his glare, one that, in my nearly thirty-six years, is familiar to me. This policeman is aware of who I am. Not that I had many criminal cases during my short time in private practice. But I came here for a couple of clients. And since my appointment to Thomas Dewey's special prosecution team, my picture has been plastered across the newspapers.

"I'm Assistant District Attorney Eunice Hunton Carter," I say, and hand him my official credentials. "I'm here to see one of the ladies arrested last night. Polly Adler."

He takes his time filling in the registry, then points to the wooden bench behind me. "Take a seat."

I bristle. Any white lawyer would have been escorted to the small waiting room reserved for attorneys before seeing clients or witnesses.

Although irritated, I settle onto the bench and bide my time. Never did I imagine I'd find myself face-to-face with Polly Adler, the madam of all madams. I first heard her name last year when I volunteered in Women's Court. Back then, my private practice clients were so scarce, I feared my hard-earned Fordham law degree was a gamble I shouldn't have taken. So to fill up my time, I volunteered, helping magistrates clear their overflow. While the courts did handle child support and wife beating cases, the majority of the cases were prostitution and pandering charges.

It didn't take long to notice a pattern. Most girls were booked and arraigned, their fates sealed within minutes. But a handful walked free, their charges dismissed or their sentences suspended. The difference? Lawyers. The girls who walked were always represented by the same small circle of men. Most notable among the attorneys—Abe Karp, a lawyer whose fees were far beyond the means of any of these girls. So the question of how they were paying for Karp has stayed with me.

In recent weeks, I've returned to that same courtroom, this time as an observer. While the parade of prostitutes has continued, there are a couple of differences. First, the attorney of record for the girls who are set free is now Max Rachlin. While Abe Karp still appears in the courtroom alongside Rachlin, he was disbarred last year after the Seabury investigation—the same sweeping probe led by attorney Samuel Seabury into corruption in New York City Magistrates' Courts that forced Mayor Jimmy Walker to resign. Karp's role in bribing judges right here in the Magistrates' Courts was uncovered during the investigation.

And I also noticed that second, Max Rachlin represents a lot more girls than Karp ever did.

"Eunice!" the officer calls out. "You can go back now. She's in the first cell, and you have twenty minutes."

I stand and move toward him. "My name is Attorney Eunice Carter," I say, my eyes locked with his.

He stares but looks away first, and then I follow him toward the gate. The keys on his belt jingle as he inserts one that releases the lock. He hoists the lever and drags the heavy gate open.

Moving past him, I step onto the other side, and the gate crashes shut behind me. I flinch, but it's more than the sound that jolts me; it's the sense of confinement in the hands of this man who holds the keys to both my entrance and my escape.

CHAPTER THREE

POLLY

New York, New York
April 4, 1935

THE SHARP CLIP of heels on concrete echoes throughout my cell, growing louder with each step, and I brace myself. The fast tempo isn't the lazy thunk of a guard's boots or even the confident, slightly bored stride of a lawyer's dark tan Derby shoes. No, the staccato, metallic sound is unusual for the corridors of the 30th Precinct Station House, and yet, I should be able to identify it. After all, I've spent many a long hour listening to the clatter of shoes as they cross bedroom floors to engage in all manner of debauchery.

I start to get concerned, and then I have it. Only the heel of a woman's oxford pump could make that sort of solid but somehow dainty rat-a-tat-tat. With its elegant, womanly heel curving into a narrow point and its sensible perforated top designed to resemble a man's oxford dress shoe, the oxford pump is the shoe of a woman who stands between two worlds. The shoe of a woman who means business but hasn't entirely surrendered her femininity. Among other things.

But now I'm even more curious. Because it's strange that the sort of person who'd wear those shoes would be in this jail. The 30th

Precinct Station House is the place for the drug addicts and drunks and streetwalkers and thieves who've been hauled in; even I don't really belong here, and neither do my girls. *Unless*, it comes to me, the woman in the oxford pumps is a rare female lawyer. Who else would have access to jail cells in the 30th Precinct Station House?

With this thought, a new sort of worry sets in. Could she be here for me? When I was booked into the station, the charge was listed as pandering, or "facilitating prostitution." I've batted away this charge time and time again, but I haven't heard a peep from the cops or my lawyer since last night. Even when I asked to call my attorney. What if I'm being held here on pandering charges, but they're really planning on squeezing me for information on Dutch? Do the cops know that he and his thugs were in that hotel suite with us—just before Coll was murdered?

My heart begins thudding in time with her step. Not that an onlooker could tell. Should the unkempt detainee slouched against the cinder block wall in the cell abutting mine wake up and look in my direction, she'd see a petite, well-manicured, composed woman of an indeterminate age in sky-high heels. I'd seem out of place among the common criminals surrounding me, with the exception of my girls, of course. And they've been placed in cells scattered around the jail, so we aren't close enough to talk.

I pull my fur stole tight around my shoulders like a shield. I've worked long and hard to build up my business—traveled far from Russia with its poverty and its pogroms and endured far worse on the shores of this so-called Golden Land—and I have no intention of returning to a desultory existence. Just like I have no intention of a life without the regular feel of a fur stole on my cheek.

So when the clatter of heels grows louder and abruptly stops in front of my cell, I do not look up. Leaning against the hard steel bars that constitute one of the walls of my cell, I keep my eyes firmly fixed on the dingy gray cell floor before me as if there's no one there at all.

A long moment ensues. A powdery lemon scent drifts into my cell—could it be Charles of the Ritz's new Jean Naté?—and I learn something else about the woman outside my cage. Her fragrance, decidedly not floral or fussy, is worlds away from the heavy, spicy, sometimes musky perfumes my girls wear. Or the distinctive Chanel and Lanvin concoctions chosen by the few select grand dames who frequent my house. It is the scent chosen by a woman with means who intends to be taken seriously.

Neither of us speaks for a long moment. Finally, she clears her throat. "Miss Adler?"

There, between the steel-gray bars of my cell, I peer first at her shoes: two-toned oxford pumps. I have to suppress a self-satisfied smile. I knew it. Working my way upward, I take note of the sensible stockings and the navy worsted wool skirt, the coordinating jacket cinched at the waist with a cordovan leather belt that matches her shoes. All as I expected for a woman lawyer.

Then my eyes reach her attractive face with its symmetrical features, arched brows, and stern lips, and nothing is as I guessed. Because the woman standing before me is the rarest of creatures. Not only is she a woman in a man's world, but she's a colored woman in a white man's world. I've forged my way in a man's world, too, but nothing quite like this.

"Who's asking?" I answer when my eyes meet hers.

My tone is barbed, because I've got to be very, very careful to whom I speak and what I say. I'm no stranger to getting pinched, but the more I think about it, the odder this latest arrest seems. The timing on the heels of Dutch and his men rushing out to witness the shoot-up of Mad Dog Coll, for instance, which I know did happen, because I've heard the guards natter on about it. The way in which the Algonquin lobby had been cleared out and the cops ready for us, as another example. Either I'm being set up to turn on Dutch, maybe for the role he played in the murder of Mad Dog, or someone identified me as *the* Polly Adler on the way to an assignation with my girls at the Algonquin Hotel and really has it out for me. Regardless, I've got to protect myself, and that includes not becoming a rat.

"Assistant District Attorney Eunice Carter," the woman answers.

A colored female assistant district attorney? I thought I'd never see the day. In fact, it occurs to me that the only one I've ever heard of is the woman Dewey hired for his special group of lawyers dedicated to fighting the Mob. My stomach lurches at the thought that this Eunice Carter could be one of Dewey's and that she might be here specifically to get me to talk about Dutch. Why else would she come here *now*?

Even if this Eunice Carter doesn't know that I've interacted with Dutch, and even if she's not one of Dewey's special twenty, the fact that an assistant district attorney is here to talk to me isn't good news. It means that this was no normal police roundup. Or maybe that I'm no normal inmate.

I will myself to stay still, stay silent, and I remind myself that it isn't necessarily about Dutch. After all, the name Polly Adler is known in and of itself, and arresting me for pandering is a feather in the cap for any cop or assistant district attorney. I must wait for this unusual woman to play her cards.

She's patient and steely, though, and can play the waiting game, too. Our eyes are locked—hers deep, dark brown and mine a coppery shade. Just when I think I might break first, she says, "I'm here to talk to you about your work."

"And what work would that be?" I ask, trying to make my face the picture of innocence. I will give up nothing to this woman.

"I understand you run a house of prostitution," she says matter-of-factly, gesturing down the row of jail cells. "In fact, I think a few of your girls might have been brought in with you."

"I don't know what on earth you're talking about." I shake my head as if her comment is ludicrous.

"Actually, I've heard that you run the most prestigious house of prostitution in the city. Apparently, you're so famous that the phrase 'going to Polly's' has become a euphemism for engaging in the sort of illicit fun you offer."

I will not be lured in by her compliments; I wasn't born yesterday.

When I don't speak, she continues. "Miss Adler, I am not here to gather evidence for the pandering charges that have been lodged against you. I'm only interested in learning how your business operates. I promise."

She seems earnest, and honestly, I'm relieved that she's not asking any questions about Dutch or the Mob. But it's clear this Eunice Carter doesn't understand anything about me or my business if she thinks I'll roll over so easily. I keep my lips sealed.

"Miss Adler, I'd be grateful for any information you might be willing to share. It must be a thrill to run an establishment as well-known as Polly's, and quite exciting for the girls who work there." She pushes on, a pleading note in her voice.

Here she goes with the flattery again. I've got to shut this down. "Assistant District Attorney Carter," I say, enunciating every syllable. "I don't know a thing about running a 'house of prostitution.' My arrest is a big mistake. I'm just a lady who was out on the town for a few drinks with some friends. But I will tell you something for nothing. No girl wakes up in the morning wishing to spend her life as a whore."

CHAPTER FOUR

EUNICE

New York, New York
April 5, 1935

"EUNICE!"

It's barely a whisper, yet it steals into my sleep. My eyes flutter open. I blink to get my bearings in the darkness. A shadow looms beside me, shifting in the darkness, and my breath catches. But then I realize it's only Lisle.

Pushing myself upright, I click on the lamp. The light spills over my husband perched on the edge of the bed, still in his suit. His jacket is a bit rumpled, the creases in his pants no longer crisp, and his tie askew.

"I want to talk to you," he says.

I take a quick glance at the clock on the bedside table—a quarter till five.

I cross my arms. "Are you just getting home?"

"I was at the Forum," he says, referring to the private club for colored professionals. "Tonight was my night."

Lisle is the president of the Harlem Forum, and each night, one of the officers of the club is assigned to stay until the last member leaves. Still, I notice he didn't answer my question. "Well, what in the world do you want to discuss this early in the morning?" I ask.

"Did you hear that Vincent Coll was murdered?"

I draw back. *This* is what my husband wants to talk over *now*?

He continues. "Reverend Powell told us the moment he arrived at the Forum last night. And we raised our glasses in a toast."

I can imagine that Adam Clayton Powell Sr., the reformist pastor of Abyssinian Baptist Church, marked the moment this way. Acknowledging that no man will escape justice and judgment.

"Yes, the chief told us about Coll yesterday morning. But this is certainly not anything I want to discuss now," I say, scooting deeper beneath the blanket.

"Well, when do you want to discuss it, Eunice?" His tone hardens, and he springs from the bed. "In the mornings, you're busy with Junior, and then most nights, you don't drag yourself home until well after dinner."

Sitting up once again, I sigh, making no effort to hide my frustration. At least I'm home before midnight, which is more than I can say for my husband.

There are times when I wonder what happened to the Barbadian who set my heart ablaze back in '23, with his Bajan lilt, a smile that could warm every street from Lenox Avenue to the Hudson River, and charm as smooth as the finest bourbon poured neat.

As he eases back down onto the bed, I allow my mind to drift to that day when Lisle Carleton Carter strolled into my office. I was a social worker just two years out of college, organizing a free dental clinic for Harlem residents.

"Have you ever worked in a clinic like this?" I asked after he announced that he was there to volunteer his services.

"Not quite. Most don't run as tightly and gracefully as yours," he said, his accent rich with the rhythm of the Caribbean.

It had taken the better part of my self-control not to swoon. "Flattery, Mr. Carter?"

He shook his head. "Observation, Miss Hunton. I reserve flattery for lesser minds."

For a moment, I was disarmed. To cover my reaction, I asked, "May I ask why you chose dentistry?"

"Because good teeth lead to dignity, and our people deserve to walk with their heads high." I was touched by that sentiment, and then, with a quick smile, he added, "And I never could learn how to play the piano, so I had to find *something* to do."

I laughed, and within weeks we were courting. I came to love so much about Lisle: his intellect and the gentleness beneath his commanding confidence. And he was a sight to behold, with bronze skin kissed by the West Indian sun.

That was the man I married, but not the one perched on the bed now. "All right, Lisle. Let's talk."

His voice is low and tight. "Hearing Coll's name brought back all of those memories. Last night, every man in the Forum agreed that goon deserved worse than being shot down in a phone booth. The police should have turned him over to the father of that little boy he killed," he says. "Just for five minutes."

My heart softens. "Or, better yet, he should have been given to Michael's mother. Coll wouldn't have survived two minutes with me if he'd taken Junior away from us."

The strain between us eases, and Lisle reaches for my hand. In the silence, I know we're both thinking about Michael Vengalli, who, because of Coll's violence that day in July four years ago, will forever be five years old. Men with tommy guns and without conscience had opened fire, spraying bullets at a crowd. Michael, his seven-year-old brother, and three others were struck.

Michael didn't make it through the night.

I've tried to imagine how a mother survived burying her five-year-old son, a boy who was then the same age as mine.

Relations between Negroes and Italians in Harlem had always been fraught, but on that day—and for the weeks and months that followed—every stoop, every corner, every street mourned as one. Colored mothers cried openly, colored pastors offered prayers from the pulpit, neighbors passed the plate in barbershops and beauty parlors to raise money for Michael's family. Together, we demanded justice for that little Italian boy.

After a moment, Lisle says, "I'm concerned that Coll's murder may yield a new rash of violence."

I draw in a breath, already bracing, already dreading where Lisle will drag this conversation as he has so many times before.

When he says, "Sweetheart, you have to see that it's time to bow out," I pull my hand away from his, but he continues as if he doesn't notice. "You have to consider stepping away."

"I'm not doing that," I say, as I have every other time he's told me to leave the special prosecutor's office. "And there's not a single reason why I should."

"From the day you stepped into that office, there's been a reason," Lisle shoots back. "You're gunning for the most dangerous men in this city. Can't you see you're not safe because of that? No one is."

Even as I remember Dewey's words yesterday morning for us to be cautious, I say, "Lisle, how many times must I say this? We're the safest people in New York. Those men know that if they so much as lay a hand on anyone on Dewey's team, the law will flatten them."

"And what about our son, your mother, and me?" he asks.

"I'm talking about all of you. We're all under the protection of the special prosecutor."

He rises once again and paces. "I don't understand you, Eunice. You're staking your life on the reasonable judgment of gangsters, and that's utter madness. Why are you so set against leaving that office?" His tone is clipped with the same exasperation I hear from him every time. "It's not as if you'll be home twiddling your thumbs. Between caring for Junior, your work with the Harlem Commission," he says, referring to the commission established by Mayor La Guardia after the recent riots, "and keeping our household in order, you'll have more than enough to occupy your time." He stops moving and stares straight at me. "You could even lend a hand in my practice."

I tamp down my rising fury. I have three hard-earned degrees, and Lisle wants me to clean his dental tools? "I love our family and my work on the commission to help Harlem thrive, but the work I'm doing with Dewey is in conjunction with that. When we take down the Mob, we'll be reclaiming our city, making our streets safer, especially here in Harlem. I can't walk away and leave the hard work to someone else."

Lisle shakes his head and stomps toward our bedroom door. His tone is as cold as steel when he says, "I hope this grand crusade of yours doesn't get you . . . and everyone in your family shot down in the middle of one of these *safer* Harlem streets." He slams the door behind him.

I sit in my bed, eyes fixed on the door. *Surely*, I think, Lisle will come back, offer an apology, and speak to me like a reasonable man. But in the dozens of quarrels we've had over my hard-won position with Dewey, reason has seldom been Lisle's way.

Exhaustion settles deep into my bones as I close my eyes and sink back against the mattress. As I drift into sleep, I can no longer ignore the truth—after eleven years, it is apparent that my marriage is coming undone. All because I have finally found my calling. I spent the first decade of our life together wandering, searching for my place beyond being the wife of Harlem's most successful dentist and part of the glittering Uptown social scene. From social work to dabbling as a writer, and then finally deciding to accept the challenge of law school, it was a winding, restless road.

Then came the news: Thomas Dewey had been appointed the special prosecutor by Governor Lehman to wage war against organized crime, and he was assembling a group of the best prosecutors in New York.

I told no one when I applied for one of the positions. Told no one when I was granted an interview. I guarded the secret until the night I hurried home with the letter naming me as one of Dewey's select corps of prosecutors. My mother bubbled over with excitement.

But that was the first time I'd ever seen my husband's face go still.

The aroma of the percolated coffee rouses me, and I breathe a long sigh of relief. I wrap myself in my housecoat, then pad across the parquet floor through the hallway and into the parlor. The rising sun glows through the opened drapes of the massive windows, and I cross the room to the kitchen. It isn't Lisle there, though; it's my mother.

"Mama, what are you doing up so early?"

"It's not that early," she says, handing me a cup of coffee.

"This is early for you," I say. "When I smelled the coffee, I thought it was Lisle." I take a sip, hoping to hide my disappointment.

"Making coffee?" She chuckles. "You know your husband can't find forks in the kitchen drawer." Her tone carries the same affection she's had for Lisle since the day they met and she learned he was a graduate of Columbia Dental School. "He left a little while ago."

"Left? This early?" I frown as we slide onto the upholstered chairs at our mahogany dining room table. I didn't hear him in the bath, nor his return to our bedroom.

"You two had quite a discussion this morning," she says.

My eyebrows lift. Lisle and I weren't speaking loudly, but my mother could catch a whisper through a brick wall.

I sip my coffee. "He's upset with me."

A beat passes, then, "Do you want to talk about it?"

That's not the question my mother wants to ask. She wants me to repeat our conversation from the first word to the last—in case she missed anything.

"No." I shake my head.

When my mother says "All right" far too easily, I squint at her over the rim of my cup. Has she spiked our coffee?

Addie Waites Hunton—the woman *The Amsterdam News* declared one of the greatest women of our race for her work with the YMCA, the NAACP, the National Association of Colored Women, and countless other causes—has been here with Lisle and me for just over a year. Living in the family brownstone on Greene Avenue in Brooklyn became too much once her rheumatism crept into her joints and weakened her limbs. So Lisle and I invited her into our home. That was the only choice, because she would never leave New York for Washington, DC, where my brother, Alphaeus, works as a professor at Howard University.

While the rheumatism may have slowed her body, it hasn't touched her mind. She's as sharp as ever—whether she was born in 1866 . . . or 1867 . . . or 1875 . . . depending on which year she claims on any day. Whatever year she settles on, one thing about my mother has never changed: She has never had a thought she didn't speak or encountered a piece of information she didn't want.

So I'm not surprised when she adds, "It always helps to talk to your mother."

"It's the same thing, Mama. Lisle wants me to quit. He *says* it's because he doesn't think it's safe to be part of Dewey's team."

My mother tilts her head. "That's what he always tells you. But it sounds like now you think it's something more."

I shrug. "I don't know. Sometimes I think back to the day when

I told you and Lisle about this new job. You were so excited, but Lisle . . ."

"What you have to understand, sugar, is that the news was everywhere, on the radio, in the newspapers, in the beauty shop, in churches. Thomas Dewey was hiring a team of prosecutors. The whole city was abuzz, certain that Dewey and his men would wipe out crime in the city. So do you know what it was like to find out that one of Dewey's *men* was *you*? Your husband was just dumbfounded, that's all."

"No, it was more than that for Lisle. Sometimes . . . I wonder if Lisle wants me to step aside not because of the danger but what he sees as an affront to him."

My mother leans back. "You think Lisle is jealous?"

"'Jealous' may be overstating it, but it's something close. Not so long ago, *The Amsterdam News* always mentioned Dr. and Mrs. Lisle Carter at some society affair or opening night performance. But since I've been on Dewey's team, the newspapers refer to us as Dr. Lisle Carter and his wife, Eunice Carter, the attorney. And now, there are articles in *The New York Times* just about me, and reporters from *The Amsterdam News* call our home to get a quote from me."

My mother nods slowly. "And that's why Lisle wants you to step aside."

"That, and the ribbing he's taking from his friends. More than once, he's mentioned that the men at the Forum have a laugh at his expense over what I'm doing. Men's work, they call it."

My mother waves her hand in the air. "That's how menfolk are. They wouldn't know what to do with themselves if they couldn't razz each other."

"Perhaps, but it bothers Lisle, and I think he longs for a time when I was simply his wife and Junior's mother."

"Well, there's nothing wrong with that. Because being a wife and mother is God's highest calling for a colored woman."

"That was never enough for you," I snap. "That calling never kept you home with Alphaeus and me. How many times did you go away, leaving us behind to do the work you loved?"

My words cut sharper than I intend, but being away from my parents is perhaps the most indelible memory of my childhood. The first time was when I was eight years old and my father decided that after the violence and destruction of the Atlanta riot—which came within blocks of our home—living in the South was no longer safe. So he and my mother packed up my four-year-old brother and me and shipped us to Brooklyn, New York. Alphaeus and I lived with friends of my parents, people who were strangers to us.

Those scary days marked the first in a long chain of separations, when, even though my parents always came back—sometimes after two, three months—my brother and I often felt abandoned.

My mother says, "I did what I had to do. Because some of us are called to be wives, mothers . . . and more. I believe you have a calling to do more, too. But I have to tell you, sugar, that calling always carries a cost."

"I love my husband, Mama, and I don't want to pay that cost. But I've spent my whole life as someone's daughter, someone's wife, someone's mother. And while I'm proud of all of that, for the first time I'm doing something that is meaningful and for me." I rise and glance down at her. "I won't allow this to slip away. Not for anything. And not for anyone."

CHAPTER FIVE

POLLY

New York, New York
April 5, 1935

DAY IS GIVING way to dusk by the time I instruct the cabbie to let me out a block away from the Majestic. I sigh in relief at the sight of my apartment building. The prospect of sinking into a hot bath, washing away the grime of jail, and changing clothes after a day and a half in the same garb almost makes me feel like crying. And I never cry. Not anymore anyway.

Magistrate Anna M. Kross heard my case at the very end of the day, after court had supposedly closed. She was hoping to evade the journalists who would undoubtedly descend upon the 57th Street Courthouse like locusts when they heard Polly Adler, the "Jewish Jezebel" herself, had been arrested and was up for bail. But I could have told the magistrate that her efforts would be for naught. Every time I've been swept up in a raid or identified at an event, the reporters somehow find out and swarm, and my bail hearing was no exception; leaks abound in every jail and police station. So it looked like a Hollywood premiere in the hallway leading to Magistrate Kross' courtroom; that many reporters had lined up for a snapshot of me or a quote. And maybe that was what led to the judge's unusually foul mood and stringent bail, as she set it at two thousand five hundred dollars instead of the typical five hundred. I hope my girls will get off easier than me tomorrow, when they are hauled before her.

Scanning West 75th Street for any sign of a tail or a cop—and finding none—I walk toward my building, careful to skirt around the trilby-topped businessmen and housewives pushing prams. The Majestic's facade is subtle but elegant, designed to inspire confidence and a sense of respectability in its tenants. But if its walls could talk, I'd be in a heap of trouble.

As I pass by the uniformed porter who has already opened the heavy brass door for me, we are careful not to make eye contact. When I step into the marble-tiled lobby, the same is true for the concierge, who gives me the slightest of nods that only I would recognize. These men need plausible deniability if the cops ever find my house and come sniffing around, asking if they've seen me. And I need these men.

Instead of heading to the elevator bank or mounting the sweeping staircase to the second-floor landing, I step behind the stairs. There, amidst the lacquered wood and metallic Art Deco wall decor, is a panel that's not a panel. It is a secret door.

After checking behind me to ensure the coast is clear, I knock three times in a distinctive pattern. The wall panel opens up to reveal a hidden set of steps. There, barrel-chested, brawny-armed Jerry stands. He's ever trusty, ever present, ever ready to protect me.

"You all right, Miss Adler? After last night in the Big House, I mean," Jerry says, his face the picture of concern.

"It was a rough one, Jerry. But you know me, I'm hard-boiled."

"That you are, Miss Adler. That you are." His cheeks suddenly flush, and he stares down at the floor. "A-And I'm sorry that I couldn't stop the fuzz. I should've been with you at the Algonquin—"

I interrupt him with a wave of my hand. It's painful to watch the big man stammer, and anyway, I know it's not his fault. Jerry has been with me for nearly ten years, ever since I poached him from his bouncer job at the Stork Club. He's saved me and my girls from trouble more times than I can count, and I know he would've fended off the cops at the Algonquin if he could. But I cannot allow him to tag along to every tryst I arrange for the girls. My clients would never agree.

Jerry nods in thanks and gestures toward the staircase behind him. "Need any help getting upstairs, Miss Adler?"

I playfully slap his arm. "Help? Me? You know better than that."

He chuckles, and I trudge up the stairs, my heels silent as they land on the plush Oriental rug I selected. The luxurious experience of my house is meant to begin with the very first step.

Reaching the landing, I run my eyes over the expansive formal parlor, designed to resemble the library of an exclusive English private club. The plush patterned rug under an upholstered sofa with chairs arranged around the fireplace. Leather-bound volumes on built-in shelves, with one innocuous but all-important book hiding in plain sight.

Crossing the room, I slide out a toffee-colored tome, and the shelving unit pops open, revealing my second secret door. Opening it wide, I step within—into an entirely different world.

A gilded bar dominates the room, but it is hardly the most astonishing decor element. Faux limestone blocks line the walls, and an enormous replica sphinx and King Tut's sarcophagus, complete with artificial gems and precious metals, loom over the bar. The Broadway set designer I hired for the job knew her stuff, making my guests feel transported to ancient Egypt. Or so they tell me. It's one of the things that makes "Polly's" feel more like the most exclusive club in the city than a brothel.

The red velvet gambling room is just off the bar to the left, where fierce rounds of mahjong and poker take place on specially designed tables. A dramatic staircase leading up to the girls' ornately decorated rooms takes center stage in the middle of the King Tut bar. It serves as a reminder of what else is on offer, delights that are available but never required.

I hope I never have to move house again. Every time I get raided—or even get word that I might be—I've got to decamp to another location. I can't even count the number of times I've been through that rigamarole as I worked my way up from a dingy one-bedroom walk-up to this palace. Shaking my head, I tabulate the cost of breaking down and moving my house and then finding a new place. Not to mention that I'll never find a building as perfect for my clandestine activities as the Majestic.

Behind the bar, I reach for a drink. Not hooch—although it is tempting—but coffee, even though it's yesterday's stale brew. I've got to have my wits about me while I parse out this arrest situation. Was I identified entering the Algonquin with my girls? It's been known to happen, especially because my face is well-known to hotel managers across town, and not all of them approve of my trade. Or was there an insider with a hand in it, someone who knew Dutch had been in a suite with us? From my interactions with the cops during the past day and a half, the latter seems unlikely; no one has asked a single question about Dutch, Coll, or any gangster. True, the appearance of Assistant District Attorney Carter was unusual—and this Dewey team's crackdown on crime has everyone nervous, even though the word on the street is that prostitution is outside its mandate.

Coffee in hand, I plop down on one of the barstools. Just then I hear a soft padding from the staircase that leads to the girls' rooms. Who the hell is that? All my girls are still in the slammer, and I'm guessing my trusty right-hand woman and housekeeper, the Lion, is still at the friend's place she scampered to. That's her usual pattern when the heat is on. And she wouldn't be coming from upstairs in any case. She and I each have our own rooms on this floor, not too far from the kitchen.

I slide my hand over the bar and remove the gun I keep hidden underneath. I aim toward the staircase until I hear a screech.

"Miss Adler! It's only me, Mabel!"

One of my steadiest girls—one who's been with me for years, through at least seven houses—is descending the stairs. Her auburn hair is tousled, and her dressing gown has slipped off one shoulder. She's crouched down, ducking behind the bend in the banister and clutching on to it for dear life.

"Sorry, Mabel! You just startled me, that's all. And after the arrest and the slammer, well—"

"What happened? I got here at my usual eleven o'clock, and the place was deserted," she says, a little unsteady on her feet as she continues down. "Jerry said you guys got picked up at the Algonquin?"

I'd forgotten all about Mabel. She's a Columbia student—about to finish her master's degree, in fact—and only works one night a week. My other girls live here with me. Mabel arrives late and stays overnight on her evening with me, handling the wee-hour stragglers for whichever of my girls she's covering, and I completely forgot it was her night. She may have stayed on even when she got the news of our arrest, because I think she concocts some elaborate lie for her parents and may not have been able to return home.

"Yeah, it was a real doozy."

"But you got out all right?"

"Yup, although Magistrate Kross set a humdinger of a bail."

"How much?"

"Two thousand five hundred smackers. I can afford it, but I'd rather not spend hard-earned cash on that."

Mabel lets out a low whistle. "What about the other girls?"

"I am hoping they'll be out tomorrow morning. The magistrate has them next on the docket."

We settle down on the barstools, and Mabel asks, "How did they find you and the girls?"

"Isn't that the million-dollar question?"

Mabel stiffens and asks, "You don't think it was an inside job, do you?"

I know what she's really asking is whether I suspect her. And I don't. Mabel is nearly done with her time here, and getting her hands dirtier than absolutely necessary isn't her style. She's too smart for that. What about one of my two maids? They knew we were headed to the Algonquin. I'm good to my girls and my maids—much more generous and protective than any other madam—so I don't think spitefulness motivated any of them. But what if one was getting secretly swacked on opium or had a kid sister who needed an operation? Would they have ratted me out for the cash, even if it meant a stint in jail for themselves? Or could it be one of the other high-end madams, jealous of my prominence and wanting to steal my clients? All possible, but the most likely scenario is that an Algonquin Hotel employee spotted me.

Certainly, the Lion is the essence of trustworthiness, and I would never, ever consider that she would turn on me. My tiny, feisty, devoted housekeeper has been with me for years. She and I first became acquainted while she was working in the ladies' room of a restaurant I frequented. One evening, I discovered the colored attendant—usually the essence of efficient courtesy—crying in a stall. Her daughter had been in a terrible fire in South Carolina, and she didn't have the funds to go to her. I gave her everything I had on me and made excuses about her whereabouts to her boss, offering up a free night with one of my girls to hold her position. The forty dollars turned out to be enough for her train ticket. I had no expectation of seeing the money or her again, but one day, she turned up with the money on my doorstep and offered up her services. How she discovered the location of my house is anyone's guess. She wouldn't take no for an answer, so I refused her cash but took her in. Her steadfast presence is now such a part of the Polly's experience that my clients call her "Richard the Lion-Hearted," or the Lion for short. I wish she was here right now, as no one can calm me like the Lion when I'm feeling overwhelmed by this life.

"I doubt it. My best guess is dumb luck on the cops' part, emphasis on *dumb*. Probably a tip-off from some hotel pen pusher," I answer, finishing my coffee. I slide off the barstool and head toward my private suite, where I'll finally scrub off the stink of the jail and the courthouse.

But before I reach the door, I turn back and say, "One thing I do know, though. We'll have to keep our eyes out for Assistant District Attorney Eunice Carter."

CHAPTER SIX

EUNICE

New York, New York
April 25, 1935

THE CLANGING BELL of a passing trolley sounds as I hasten up the stairs of the Chambers Street IRT. I'm running late thanks to Lisle grumbling about the new brand of coffee, Junior spilling half his bowl of Cream of Wheat down the front of his trousers, and my mother needing warmed liniment rubbed onto her knees.

Then there's my ongoing quarrel with Lisle. He's imagining a menace where there isn't one. But not even the memory of Lisle's cross words this morning can dim my mood as I think of my day ahead and the case I'm quietly constructing.

I reach 233 Broadway, a cathedral-style, fifty-seven-floor building that, until a few years ago, claimed the title of the tallest in the world. The lobby is crowded as usual, as there are hundreds of companies housed in the Woolworth Building. I glance around the perimeter and spot five men covering the seven different entrances. Like the officers stationed throughout the premises, these men are built like prizefighters, with pistols on their hips. The one closest to the elevator locks eyes with me, and I nod as I pass.

Once on the fourteenth floor, I make my way to my office, which is tucked away at the very end of the hallway. As I settle behind my desk, laughter drifts in from the room beside mine, the space reserved for the rotating cast of sixty or so officers assigned to our protection. They gather there between shifts to shoot the breeze.

Unlocking my desk drawer, I pull out three files and set aside the bulging one labeled *Complaints*. In addition to the calls and visits I've received from dozens and dozens of New Yorkers, hundreds of letters have poured into this office. The overwhelming number of grievances are about brothels popping up, tucked between brownstones and apartment buildings. Prostitution is raging throughout the city. After what I saw in Women's Court, this is no surprise to me.

I turn my attention to the two slimmer folders labeled *Arraignments* and *Bail Records*. I asked Lisa to gather these for me for the last thirty days. I'm not certain what I'm looking for, but I begin jotting down the names and addresses of the girls arrested for prostitution. I'm searching for a pattern, perhaps in the addresses of the girls represented by Rachlin and the girls who are not.

But after a few minutes, a different pattern starts to emerge. I shift my focus—to the names of the bail bondsmen on the cases represented by Rachlin:

First sheet: Jesse Jacobs

Next sheet: Donald Jacobs

Then: Max Jacobs

Jesse Jacobs appears a few more times, followed by Max Jacobs again.

Then, there's a shift:

Morrison Jacobowitz

Shirley Klingsberg

Harry Klingsberg

Leo Klingsberg

Rose Klingsberg

And tucked between each of these names, every few pages, is Jesse Jacobs.

I recognize the name Jesse Jacobs as the bail bondsman for many of the girls from my days in Women's Court. But who are these other people with names that riff off of "Jacobs"? And the others—who are the Klingsbergs? Is this all one family? Two? Is this a family business?

Or something else?

I scan the pages once again. Fifty-two arraignment sheets and only these eight names appear. Is it possible that only a few bail bondsmen handle these types of cases? But then, there's the handwriting. Either all eight of these people had the same penmanship teacher . . . or the same person signed each page.

If there is only one "Jacobs" acting as bail bondsman for all these girls—which is strange but permissible—why would he be using different names? He would if he was trying to hide his identity. But why? And of course, forgery on any legal document is against the law.

This is all very suspicious.

A light tap on my door pulls me from the folders. "Mrs. Carter, here are the daily dockets." Lisa LaFrance, a fellow Smith graduate whom I personally recommended to Mr. Dewey, enters. She's been assigned to assist me and several other assistant district attorneys.

"Thank you," I say, taking the stapled stack of papers from her. The top sheet draws my attention.

Defendant: Adler, Polly

Charge: Pandering

It's been three weeks since our very brief encounter, where Polly told me nothing. But today, I might learn something from her silence.

I HEAR THE chatter and laughter before I step into the small, dim courtroom. Women's Court is always unruly compared to the solemn criminal courthouse two miles away. Today, the air is thick with heat and chaos, and every seat is packed with spectators and reporters. Along the walls, photographers stand with bulky cameras, jostling for space.

Squeezing onto the hard wooden bench at the back, I scan the room. It is never this crowded. Is everyone here to see Polly Adler?

Then I freeze.

At the prosecution table are District Attorney William Dodge and Assistant District Attorney Maurice Wahl. Why is the New York County district attorney here? Women's Court is usually reserved for junior prosecutors, not the elected district attorney.

Dodge, with his wire-rimmed glasses perched low on his nose, sits hunched next to Wahl, whispering and sharing notes. After a few moments, both rise, cross the room, and shake hands with the young defense attorney. The three men seem more like friends than adversaries.

At the defense table, a silver-haired lawyer I've never seen sits next to a blond young lady with her head bowed and hands folded, the picture of demureness. Behind her, three other girls perch the same way. All appear to be in their early twenties and are dressed in modest, floral, belted day dresses. I'm guessing they are defendants.

There are several cases on today's docket with the same arrest date and officer as Polly's. Are these all Polly's girls? If so, where is Polly? I'd expect her to be seated beside them, the protective mother hen I've heard her to be.

My eyes drift back to Dodge, Wahl, and the defense attorney.

When Dodge laughs and slaps the defense attorney on the back, the reason for his presence becomes clear. He's not here to prosecute; he's here to put on a show and silence his critics—the ones who demanded that Thomas Dewey be appointed special prosecutor because Dodge, who owes his election to Tammany Hall, the city's powerful Democratic machine, is more politician than prosecutor. And in their eyes, that makes him unfit for the job.

That's why the press is here. Dodge notified them, so they can watch him make an example of the city's most notorious madam. Polly and her girls aren't getting off.

From behind his high bench, the magistrate, Judge Steven Moore, a gray-faced man in his sixties with bushy brows and weathered skin, raps his gavel to bring the unruly courtroom to order. The morning has just begun, yet he looks both weary and bored—the usual expression among magistrates in this court.

I remove my leather-bound notepad and fountain pen from my briefcase. But before I can jot down the first word, Dodge stands and says, "Your Honor, if it pleases the court, the prosecution and the defense have reached a resolution in this matter of *The People of the State of New York versus Virginia Woodward, Katherine Jacoby, Angelica Evans, and Rosalie Luca.*"

I glance up, puzzled. Dodge and Wahl must have just reached a deal with the defense; otherwise, this would have been taken off today's docket.

"What's the agreement?" the magistrate asks, his eyes wary.

"For a plea of guilty, the defendants will all receive a suspended sentence of ninety days."

A suspended sentence? What happened to the spectacle? The trial? This isn't showing New Yorkers that Dodge is cracking down on crime.

After muttering a few words, the judge instructs all the girls to rise. "Are you in agreement with this sentence?"

The girls nod and in unison say, "Yes, Your Honor."

The judge accepts the agreement, and, relieved, the girls hurry from the courtroom. It has happened so quickly, but before I can grasp it all, the bailiff calls out, "The People of the State of New York versus Polly Adler!"

The murmurs return, louder now. Heads turn, everyone eager for a glimpse of the infamous madam. But the door doesn't open. The attorneys on both sides exchange glances. Would she dare miss her court appearance?

Just as the magistrate lifts his gavel, Polly saunters in, the epitome of style in her fur stole (despite the spring weather) and heels that defy gravity. With her shoulders squared and her chin high, she struts into the court with confidence. Like a woman about to sit on her throne.

What moxie.

Then, at the sight of Dodge, Polly falters. Her eyes narrow. He smirks. I scoot to the edge of my seat.

The courtroom quiets as Polly slides into her seat. She motions to a dark-haired young man, no older than eighteen, who sits on a seat behind her. She whispers a few words to him, and at first, he seems startled. But then he darts from the courtroom.

Just as Dodge stands, Polly curls forward, clutching her stomach.

"Your Honor," her attorney says. "May we have a few moments? My client isn't feeling well."

"What's wrong with her?" the magistrate asks.

"Your Honor," Polly says, her voice quivering, "it's something I ate. I'm sure my stomach will settle and I'll be fine if I can have a quick break."

"Give her some water," the magistrate says with a scowl. "You have one hour, but I'd be happier with fifteen minutes."

The noise swells again, and Dodge breaks into a grin so wide, the corners of his lips nearly touch his ears. Initially, I suspected that Dodge was here for a show, to send all the girls to jail. But he's here today for only one reason—to take down Polly Adler.

CHAPTER SEVEN

POLLY

New York, New York
April 25, 1935

THIRTY DAYS, I think as the bars slam behind me with a decisive clank. I can do thirty days in the House of D, as my girls call the Women's House of Detention on Greenwich Avenue in downtown Manhattan. I've endured far, far worse.

"Don't think you'll get any special treatment here because you're Polly Adler," the guard yells over her shoulder, the sound of her jam-packed key ring clanging along with her footsteps.

"No, ma'am," I reply. My volume is quieter than its usual boom, but loud enough for the guard to hear. I can't risk her thinking I'm disrespectful with a voice too soft or too boisterous.

"You better get used to mingling with lowlifes like yourself instead of hobnobbing with the rich and famous," she calls back, her words receding into the distance.

"Yes, ma'am," I reply. She's gone so far down the corridor that I doubt she can hear me. But I'm not taking any chances or leaving any doors open for retaliation.

My infamy may well work against me in here, it seems. Worse even than I'd envisioned. I hadn't kidded myself that it'd be pleasant in the slammer. True, I won't be scrounging for food, as I had to do when my cousin kicked me out at seventeen—out on my own, after I'd been in America for not quite five years and I was in dire straits—and I had to hunt for work that wasn't exactly forthcoming. Yeah, there will be three squares, but by all accounts, the House of D fare is near-poisonous. No, I won't have to spend my nights hustling for clients for the house and scanning for danger and protecting the girls and pretending like everything is all right. Acting as if my deepest desire isn't to leave this life behind me. But still, the life of a madam is better than being locked up.

Or is it? Time will tell.

The cell couldn't be more than five feet by eight feet, and a bunk bed and toilet are squeezed between its narrow walls. Tiny, I think, even for me. There's barely enough room to turn around, and my cellmate isn't even in here yet. Where is she, anyway? I should just be thankful for a few minutes alone in this overcrowded, dangerous place.

Just then, I hear whimpering from the cell next door. Peering through the bars, I can't crane my neck enough to get a look at her. The poor thing sounds pathetic. I'm guessing she's not one of the tougher types—the pickpockets and drunks and hookers and career criminals—who have called the House of D home. I wonder if she's one of the "wayward" girls, those "wrong" women who can be arrested and detained indefinitely for disobeying their parents, dressing like men, or liking other girls. How silly that sort of judgment is. I've had had a front-row seat to all sorts of sexual predilections over the years, and an attraction to another woman is hardly the worst thing I've seen. This latter group of inmates is forced to wear prison garb that's got a *D*—for degenerate—stitched on the front.

I stare down at my own drab prison uniform. This worn, scratchy, dun-colored dress is the only one assigned to me for the foreseeable future; *I better keep it clean.* I wonder whether the guards will emblazon it with a letter of their own—maybe *M* for madam or *S* for sinner? This horrible prison uniform isn't the worst thing I have to wear, though. I had to relinquish my heels in exchange for flat-soled work shoes, and I feel diminished without the added height.

Looming over everything is my astonishment that the usual tactics didn't keep me out of the slammer altogether. With every other arrest, I was able to count on a cocktail of pleading innocent, lawyering skills, well-placed bribes, and the press's fascination with me to keep me out of the Big House. Today I had to take extreme measures to land only a thirty-day sentence, the sort of measures I had promised myself I would never take.

But why? Why was the judge so determined to wield that gavel harshly on me and me alone? Why was the high-ranking Dodge handling my trial himself? Is it just the heightened crackdown on crime citywide? The rivalry between Dodge and Dewey to prove which one is the toughest on crime? These are the questions plaguing me. Just when I'd felt certain my arrest was simply an unlucky roundup, I got caught up in some political machinations between government lawyers, most like.

At least my girls got off easy.

Lowering myself onto the rock-hard lower bunk bed, I review the trial day. My girls went before the judge first, and I was so dang nervous I couldn't watch. So I slipped out of the courtroom—leaving the sea of reporters behind with their cameras and notepads—and hid in the bail bond office across the street from the courthouse. I nodded to Jack McDonough, the bail bondsman who runs the place—we are well acquainted—and paced the space. I'd planted my trusty, young, innocent-looking runner in the courtroom to give me regular updates, and I just prayed the judge went easy on the girls.

I wasn't alone in the bail bond shop. A few odd-looking fellows were on and off the pay phone and treading around as well. At first, I chalked their presence up to having family members in various states of distress across the street; they didn't look like the disgusting pimps who usually hung out here. But then, one of the fellows approached me. "Polly Adler?"

I didn't reply. Did the scruffy-looking redhead know me from the newspaper coverage of this arrest, or perhaps others? There had been a particularly unflattering but very clear picture of me stepping out of a police wagon on the front page of a newspaper when the police brought me to the station after the raid. Mercifully, my father, Moshe Adler—who emigrated alone to America from Russia several years ago and lives in Chicago with my brother Berl, now Ben—would never see that photo, since it was a local New York rag. For now, my family can continue to believe that I manage a corset factory. *Not* a bordello. A shiver passes through me at the thought of them finding out about my work.

"It's admirable, the way you support your girls. Very few madams do that," the redhead said.

My hackles were raised. What was this man's game? Was he a reporter? A detective trying to trap me into admitting I'm a madam? I said nothing and walked away from him.

But that didn't stop his yapping. "You could sidestep a lot of this trouble if you joined our group. We call it our little Combination. For just ten dollars per girl a week, I can promise you bail money if your girls get arrested. And none of our girls have ever been convicted. We've got that sorted with our lawyer and inside connections. It's the best money you'll ever spend."

I kept my lips sealed shut. What was this hooligan talking about with this Combination nonsense? A consolidated group for prostitutes? Some pimp trying to gather streetwalkers and organize their tricks, I could see, although it roiled; there's very little I loathe more than pimps, those exploiters of women without care for their safety or well-being. Men who never put themselves on the line. Men who drug women to make them pliable. But a Combination that included high-end brothels like mine? That makes no sense. The exclusivity, hand-selected girls, and coddled environment of my house are what make it a success, singular even among the more rarified of bordellos. Lumping my house in with prostitutes of all sorts would undermine everything. And I've got my own connections; I don't need this lowlife to barter and bribe on my behalf.

Fortunately, in that moment, my runner raced in. Breathless and sweating, he informed me that the girls had gotten suspended sentences in exchange for pleading guilty, and I'd been summoned.

When I walked over to the courthouse and entered the packed room, my head was held high. Given the judge's treatment of the girls, I expected the same leniency as quid pro quo for pleading guilty on pandering charges. But from the moment I spotted District Attorney Dodge and Assistant District Attorney Wahl, I knew I was in trouble. From the terrible smiles on their faces, the question wasn't going to be whether I'd get jail time, but how much; we all knew the charge could lead to years in jail. And I could never, ever plead innocent and subject myself to a full trial, where the names of my rich and powerful clients would become public. I'd never make it out of jail alive.

Only one path was open to me.

As I settled into my chair at the defense table, I signaled to my runner and whispered in his ear. This poor sod—who'd never so much as flinched at any of my other directives—pulled away and stared at me. All I could do was nod and push him in the direction of the door.

I then made a big show of clutching my stomach. I pled illness to my attorney and then the judge to buy myself some leeway for my runner to finish his task. I didn't expect that the judge would grant me more than an hour—or two, if I really hammed it up—and he didn't. But that was enough time.

When the slam of the gavel sounded on the judge's bench and he announced thirty days and five hundred dollars, I knew the secret deal had been struck. I'd received the lowest possible sentence for the charges, and Dodge and Wahl were shocked and furious. They'd expected I'd rot behind bars.

As I held out my hands for the handcuffs, I felt a pit form in my gut. Not because I was being carted off to the cooler, but because of the price I'd have to pay for the brevity of my time there. Yet without my own fancy footwork, I'd be in the House of D for God knows how long. Three years, four?

The courthouse guards kept the press and the onlookers and the protestors at bay as I made my way down the aisle toward the courtroom exit. Only then did I see her, in a row in the back of the courtroom. Assistant District Attorney Carter, who I now know for certain is part of Dewey's special team. As the cops led me out of the courtroom, my hands cuffed behind me, we locked eyes. And I didn't break my gaze until I'd been dragged out of the courthouse.

The clang of a billy club on the steel bars brings me back to the terrible present. It's the same sour-faced guard who led me to my cell. "There's someone here to see you. A lawyer."

Why would my lawyer be here so soon after the sentencing hearing? Is there a problem? I'm torn between hope that—maybe, just maybe—my sentence was reduced further and terror that the judge extended the sentence to three years. Even though I know the judge technically has no mechanism for reopening the sentencing once the hearing is concluded, stranger things have happened in my world. And I know the power of bribery; it's a necessary tool in my work.

Dangling her crowded key ring in front of my face—a taunting reminder of my current powerlessness—the guard opens my door, if the metal gate can be called that. Cuffing my hands behind my back—unnecessarily, I think—she beckons me down the same hallway I just came through not even an hour ago.

Once we're through two more sets of steel gates, the guard settles me in a stark meeting room. Pea-green walls and bolted-down tables and chairs constitute the decor. I wait for my attorney to enter the room and put my nerves at rest. Either way, I can handle it; I just need to know how long I'll be in this god-awful joint.

But when the door opens, I see that I've been misled. Assistant District Attorney Eunice Carter stands before me.

I jump up. I feel impossibly small, and I'm forced to stare up at the woman. "No way am I talking to you."

I rush to the door and start banging on it. "Let me out of here!"

I want—no, I need—everyone in this prison to hear me protest this meeting. And when the guard doesn't arrive, I only get louder.

"Miss Adler," Assistant District Attorney Carter says at a normal volume. When I don't reply, her voice grows louder. "Miss Adler, I only want a minute of your time!"

I will not turn in her direction. And I will not stop my hammering for even a second. But, without looking in her direction, I do reply. "Are you a fool? One minute is one minute too long. This prison has eyes and ears that report directly to some unsavory characters, and I cannot be seen talking to you—especially not willingly. I'll be dead within a day, and who knows? You might be, too. Or someone in your family. You got a husband, kids? Then you need to get out of here. Because they'll get all of you. That's what happens to snitches and the people who work with them."

CHAPTER EIGHT

EUNICE

New York, New York
April 26, 1935

I DON'T REALIZE I'm trembling until my mother links her arm around mine. "Put it in God's hands," she whispers.

Mr. Walker, the elevator operator, yanks back the gate, and my mother and I cross the marble-floored lobby. The doorman tips his cap before he swings open the dark-stained door. "Good afternoon, Mrs. Hunton, Mrs. Carter."

We thank him, then step into the golden afternoon. My mother takes a deep breath. "I needed this fresh air."

"Let me know if you want me to slow down," I say as we begin our stroll.

"I'll be fine. In a few minutes, the sun will begin to work its medicine." After just moments, my mother says, "Okay, sugar. First you and Lisle didn't exchange a word over breakfast, and now you're home in the middle of the day to pick up your son from school. What's going on?"

How can I tell my mother that I haven't had a calm breath since I spoke with Polly Adler yesterday? After that conversation, my only aim was to speak to Lisle. But even though I'd left Polly and dashed straight home, we weren't able to talk until the early hours of this morning, when Lisle had finally sauntered in from the Harlem Forum.

"Mama, it's getting worse with Lisle." As we amble along Edgecombe, I recount what began as a conversation and ended in a confrontation.

THE MOMENT HE came from the bathroom and into our bedroom this morning, I said, "Lisle, I've been thinking. You may be right . . . the streets may not be safe after Coll's murder." His face brightened until I continued. "We have to protect Junior, and I think we should send him to Barbados. To your mother."

"What? That's not what I was talking about."

"I know, but you made me really think about this. There *will be* more violence, and I will be worried about our son every moment of the day. We'll send him away just until we get a conviction."

"That is not the only way for our son to be safe, Eunice."

I SIGH. "AND the argument kept on from there, Mama."

"He told you to leave your job again."

"Of course. But he finally agreed to sending Junior away because I told him if we didn't and something happened to our son . . ." I leave my words there just as I did with Lisle.

"Oh!" my mother says.

"I wouldn't blame him, Mama. Not completely. But at least he did agree to sending Junior to Barbados."

We're silent again, and I think about Polly. I don't tell my mother, just as I didn't tell Lisle, about what Polly said yesterday and how her words had troubled my sleep all night.

"So that's why you're home early. To tell Junior."

"Yes." Squeezing her arm tighter, I add, "And I'm grateful you agreed to walk with me. Because I'll need your steady hand to do this."

She nods. "This is right. For you. For Lisle. For Junior."

For the next few minutes, we take in the springtime rhythm of Harlem. Through an open window, the breeze carries the soulful sweetness of the lone saxophone playing "In a Sentimental Mood," the notes drifting down like a ribbon from the sky. Well-dressed ladies carrying bags and hatboxes from Blumstein's sweep past us as children, still too young for school, skip and hop up and down the block under the watchful eyes of their mothers. This is the season I cherish most, when this neighborhood stirs awake from its winter slumber and the streets come alive with the music and magic that belong to Harlem alone.

But today, the promise of spring weighs heavy on me. This is Junior's favorite time of the year, too, and sending him away means we will miss so much: my taking him to the spring opening of the children's plays at the Lafayette Theatre, his afternoons flying kites with his father in Colonial Park, and Lisle and me cheering as he and his friends play a spirited game of stickball. It's just so heartbreaking, but safety comes before all else.

Just as we arrive at the school, the bell rings. A moment later, a flurry of kids spills through the doors, their faces glowing with end-of-the-school-day joy. I search for Junior in the mass of little boys, all in navy, black, or brown knickers, white shirts, and matching sweaters.

"Junior!" My mother spots him first and waves.

His face brightens with surprise. But then his glance shifts to me and his smile wilts. He moves toward us, his steps heavy with worry, as if seeing me at his school when I am normally at work is a sign of trouble ahead.

As my mother pulls him into a hug, he turns to me and asks, "Is something wrong?"

"Nothing's wrong," I say, adding as much cheer to my voice as the swollen stone in my throat will allow.

When I don't say anything else, my mother jumps in. "I wanted to go for a walk, and we walked so far we landed right here at your school. Now we can go home together."

"I was going to walk with Eric, Chris, and Herman," he says, pointing to his friends.

"Why don't you come with your grandmother and me?" I say. "You'll see them tomorrow."

"Okay," he says, his reluctance apparent. He waves to his friends, who dart off in the opposite direction. It takes him a moment to fall into stride beside me.

Putting my arm around my son's shoulders, I ask, "Did you have a good day in school?"

He gives me a small shrug. "Yes, ma'am."

I wait. When he offers nothing more, I ask, "What did you study today?"

Again, he hunches his shoulders. "We practiced our penmanship and multiplication tables. I got one hundred on my spelling words," he says.

"That's wonderful," my mother and I say together. I add, "But I'm not surprised. You've always been such a bright boy."

Then we go quiet. The steady putter of automobiles blends with the laughter and shouts from the schoolchildren, their glee rising like a chorus. I know Junior is disappointed about not walking home with his friends. But what I'm about to say will make that fade fast from his mind.

Finally, I say, "Son, your father and I are going to send you on a little trip."

He glances up at me, and I hope the sun shields my eyes. I don't want him to see my sorrow.

"A trip to where?" His words are edged with caution.

"To Barbados. We want you to spend a little time with your other grandmother."

He looks at Mama, then turns back to me. "All right," he says, his tone still uncertain. "For the summer?"

I glance at my mother, and she gives me the smallest nod of assurance. "No, son. You're leaving in a few days."

"What?" Junior stops. "Mama, no. I have school."

"You'll go to school there."

"I don't want to." His voice rises. "I don't want to go to Barbados. I want to stay here with my friends."

"I know, sweetheart. But sometimes we have to do things we don't want to do. This is for the best."

"Why?" he snaps, his tone sharper than I've ever heard. "Is it because you're going back to school?" His voice trembles. "Last time you sent me away it was because you were in law school."

His words astound me; I thought he'd enjoyed those few months with Lisle's brother during a particularly difficult time for me during my final year. "I only sent you away because I wanted you to be well cared for while I studied for my exams. I knew your aunt and uncle would give you their full attention."

"So why do I have to go now?"

"Because sometimes parents have to make difficult decisions for their children. You're going to have to trust me, sweetheart."

He presses his lips together as if sealing his feelings. When I crouch down and meet his eyes, my heart twists. "You're going to have a wonderful time. Your grandmother will be so happy to see you. And remember how close her house is to the beach? The ocean is practically in her backyard. You'll be swimming every day."

"I don't want to go swimming. I want to go to school. Right here. With my teachers and my friends."

"You'll be in a fine school in Barbados. You'll make new friends, and you'll be in classes with some of your cousins. Doesn't that sound like fun?"

"No!" The word bursts from him. "You just don't want me. You don't want me here with you and Daddy." Junior spins away, darting between a cluster of boys and girls walking in front of us.

I rise to go after him, but before I can take a single step, my mother grips my arm. "Let him be."

"I have to explain."

She shakes her head. "Some things are not meant to be explained to a child. I know." She looks at me pointedly. "In a few minutes, you can go home and talk to him. For now, let's sit down here." She gestures toward a nearby wrought-iron bench in front of the park.

As we sit, my son's words whisper to me in the breeze: *You just don't want me.* "I think Junior hates me," I say at last. The tears in my eyes have seeped into my voice.

"He doesn't hate you," Mama says softly. After a beat, she asks, "Did you hate me when I had to leave you and your brother?"

I remain silent. Because there were so many times when our parents left Alphaeus and me under the guardianship of their friends, I don't know which occasion she means. In this moment, I remember back to 1918 when my mother, serving as a representative of the YMCA, boarded a ship bound for France to support and care for the colored troops headed into war. At least by then I was in my first year at college. So it was Alphaeus who suffered most from her absence that time. Mama snatched him away from New York and shipped him to her friends in Philadelphia. All the other times, my brother and I were together, the source of each other's strength.

Never before had he been left to bear the burden of abandonment alone.

"You haven't answered my question," my mother says.

It takes a moment for me to come back to the present. I glance at her, then slowly look away.

She sighs. "All children hate their parents at some point. And then they grow up and realize their parents did the best they could."

I stare at my hands, having a sudden urge to hug my son. "I just want Junior to be safe, and someone said something yesterday that made me concerned. . . ."

My mother tilts her head, waiting for me to say more. When I don't elaborate, she says, "Do what you have to do to protect Junior. Family is most important."

I twist on the bench and face my mother. "Mama, maybe you should stay with Alphaeus for a while."

She waves her hand as if my words are foolishness. "Because of Dutch Schultz? You think I'm afraid of him and his goons?" She clicks her tongue. "Sugar, I've stared into the beady eyes of the Ku Klux Klan. All of them are little men, just cowards behind those hoods and guns. If I didn't back down from men who carried torches and hatred, I sure as hell am not backing down now."

My mother speaks the truth—another banner in her long line of accomplishments. She's crossed the country as a crusader, setting up NAACP field offices in towns where it's dangerous for a Negro to live, let alone speak, protest, and organize. Yet she sauntered into Southern cities and did just that, even after letters were sent warning her to stay out of Birmingham, Atlanta, Memphis . . . the list goes on. Mama persevered, traveling alone without fear, but always with God's favor. And she's never faltered. In pulpits and meeting halls, she stood before colored folks and urged them to rise and claim every right this country has promised.

"If these old knees worked like they used to, I'd be out there gangbusting those thugs right alongside you. Don't you know by now that I'm fearless?"

"Oh, I know that. I got my courage to face anything from you."

"No, that courage came from your father. That fire in your belly—that drive to rise higher than what the world expects of you—that came from me."

"My ambition." My drive, something that has been a source of pride, now feels like a millstone. I want to rise to the pride I hear in her voice and claim every triumph as my own. But the truth is, many of my achievements have been because of grace given to me in my mother's name.

It was my mother's friendship with Mary White Ovington—the suffragist I've long called the mother of the NAACP—who opened the doors of Smith College for me and paid for it, too. Even the short time I spent writing happened because my mother had reached out to her friend Charles Johnson, the editor of *Opportunity.*

So I say, "You're right, Mama. I got my ambition from watching you out there fighting to make a difference. I hated being away from you, but I always knew the work you did was important."

"And now that's what you're doing."

I nod. "But it's ripping at the seams of my family. I want this more than anything, but . . . I don't want to sacrifice my marriage. I don't want my son to feel abandoned."

"If God put the desire in you to do it, He will give you the protection and everything else you need to get through it."

"I wish God would have a little chat with my husband." A brittle chuckle slips through my lips.

"Lisle knows who you are. He just has to remember that he fell in love with Eunice Roberta Hunton, the Smith College graduate, who was reaching for the stars long before he asked for your hand in marriage.

"He's forgotten it was your ambition that drew him to you. Now, with other men whispering in his ear, he thinks he wants a wife like the ones they go home to. But you were never that woman. He'll remember that soon. And Junior will grow up to understand all of this, too." She pauses for a long moment before she adds, "Just like you came to understand your father and me—even if it did take you many years."

"I hope you're right, Mama."

My mother straightens my smart forward hat, which has slipped askew. And then she folds me into her arms. "Oh, I am, sugar. I'm your mother, I'm always right."

CHAPTER NINE

POLLY

New York, New York
September 12, 1935

"Hey, Walter, is it true that the Ziegfeld Follies producers are poaching some of Polly's girls for their revival?"

A familiar voice calls out across the bar. I don't need to see his face to know that it's Jock Whitney, one of the wealthiest men in America as well as an investor in Broadway shows and film. He's practically a fixture at the King Tut bar, which is back in full swing twenty-four hours a day since I returned from prison. Just in the nick of time, too, as my savings were running low and it was getting tougher and tougher to support the Lion and the girls, not to mention my family here and in Russia. So many people depend on me.

My guests erupt in laughter, which is good for business. This nugget of gossip has been circulating around town for the past week, and even though everyone knows it to be a joke, how better to poke fun at Walter Winchell? Syndicated gossip columnist, popular radio show host, and grade A snoop, Walter knows everyone and everything that happens in New York City and beyond. He is also one of my best customers. He'd put up quite a fuss if I ever lost one of my girls to Broadway; he's that attached to each and every one. But given that he holds a grudge and he's known to put an enemy on his "Drop Dead List" for the slightest infraction, this is the furthest anyone will go in teasing him. Walter Winchell can make or break a star, a show, a movie, even a political movement, so the ribbing only goes so far. Even for Jock Whitney.

I put a hand on Walter's arm and answer for him. Making my guests happy is one of my gifts. The happier they are, the more they spend.

"The Ziegfeld Follies is beneath my girls! You gents should know that!" I call back to Jock, setting him up for the retort. This way, both of the men are appeased.

"The only thing I like to see beneath your girls is me!" Jock calls back, as I knew he would. This delights the gaggle of fellow Yalie businessmen surrounding him. One of the men gives him a hearty slap on the back. These men are so predictable.

I force out a laugh at Jock's anticipated response. Playing along is expected of me, and in fact, this sort of accommodating camaraderie is one of the things that make Polly's stand apart. While I am welcoming and hospitable to all my guests, I make it a point to tailor my behavior to my clients' personalities and, of course, their needs and desires. Glancing over at the packed table to my right, where the creative crowd is gathered with one of my only female guests, Dorothy Parker, I think how I'd never set up one of these sorts of jokes for them. Too crass. This group of famous, brilliant writers, actors, and critics—a rotating cast of characters, but which generally included Dorothy, Robert Benchley, George Kaufman, and Harold Ross—started coming here years ago after long liquid lunches in the Algonquin Hotel, and Polly's operates almost as their second home.

It is then I hear one of Jock's friends use a falsetto and say, "Ze Ziegfeld Folliez iz beneath my girlz!"

Riotous laughter ensues at my expense, and when Jock catches my eyes, I make sure to laugh along at this mockery of my accent. My first schoolteacher in America taught me to smile along with those who poke fun, as it defuses the bullies. Not that the technique always works, and I've faced my fair share of taunting. But I don't find these men's ridicule funny, and I won't forget. It doesn't seem to matter how extensive my vocabulary or how eloquent I am—despite not speaking a word of English when I arrived in America at twelve years old—these types of men will always see me as a lowly, dumb immigrant. And a Jewish one at that. Never mind that I was the brightest student ever to come out of my region in Russia, so much so that I won one of the few spots reserved for Jews at a renowned high school in nearby Pinsk—and not to mention I was the only girl *ever* to receive a spot. I swallow the insult, though, and count myself lucky that my short jail stint this past spring hasn't turned the blue bloods against my house. If anything, the notoriety has added to my cachet.

I motion for Walter to join me at the bar, where I offer him a comped cocktail. Prohibition may be over and speakeasies along with it, but the craze for cocktails continues. Everyone likes a free drink, even millionaires like Jock Whitney. And Walter.

The spaces are abuzz with chatter and booze and the clack of mahjong tiles and the gentle strum of the cello from the jazz trio and the quiet flirtatious murmurings of one of my girls. All in order, exactly as I like it. It's been this merry and calm since I got out of jail in May, and I'd like to keep it that way.

"Thanks, Polls," Walter says. "Those Yalies get under my skin sometimes."

"Don't I know it," I mutter quietly, "between you and me, of course."

Strange though it may be, I know I can rely on Walter's discretion here. Though he trades in other people's secrets, I know too many of his for him to trade in mine. Not to mention, we have an unspoken kinship. We both hail from immigrant Russian Jewish stock—him through his parents and me directly—making us outsiders in our respective realms. It's a background he openly claims and defends; he's one of the few journalists speaking out against the Nazis' treatment of European Jews.

That sort of treatment of Jewish people—forcing us into certain jobs and specific communities and dictating every aspect of our segregated existence—precipitated my father Moshe's initial plans to move my family from our tiny Russian town of Yanow to America. That and the always-present pogroms, which only rose in intensity and frequency in the years before the Great War.

But my father's scheme involved sending me ahead of everyone else, and so, on a frigid December day, twelve-year-old Pearl, as I was then known, was trundled off on a thousand-mile train and hiking trek to the German port city of Bremen, where I boarded the third-class deck of a steamship for a two-week voyage to *Di Goldene Medine*, the Golden Land. Alone. I brought with me only a potato sack for luggage and strict instructions to send every cent home once I settled with acquaintances in Massachusetts, so my family could follow in my wake. But no one came except my brother Ben, who was sent to Chicago. Not until my father took the money I'd sent and sailed here alone a few years ago, leaving behind my mother, Gittel, and three younger brothers I've never even seen—with no fixed plan to bring them here even though I've pled and sent money to both my father and mother for their journey here. I often think that, if my father had ensured that the whole family immigrated to America earlier, when I was young and so desperately needed their help, I might not have had to enter this life.

Walter chuckles, bringing me back to the moment, and then replies, "I think you know you can trust me on that point, Polly."

"I do," I reply, accepting a drink from Marv, my bartender for over a decade. By all appearances, it's an effervescent champagne—my clients like to see me joining them in the fun—but in truth, it's watered-down. I need to keep my mind sharp and my guard up. On any given night, I won't have a stiff drink until my last client has gone upstairs. And that could be well into the morning.

Virginia descends the dramatic curving staircase that leads from the King Tut bar to the girls' rooms. Her platinum-blond hair catches the light as it bounces, and the shimmery fabric of her peignoir and silky slip dress set—technically bedtime attire but could easily serve as racy nightclub garb—sparkles as it sweeps. I motion for her, and the men part as she crosses the room toward me. As I tilt my head in Walter's direction, Virginia slips her arm through his and whispers into his ear. He is in need of her ministrations.

Suddenly the room grows quiet. Jock Whitney and his crew have stopped their banter, and the creative folks have ceased their intellectual repartee and witty barbs. Even the constant click-clack of the mahjong tiles has paused, and the players are frozen. Only the whisk of a steel brush on the drum and the low strum of the cello continues as the band plays, and even that is half-hearted.

Everyone's eyes are on the secret entrance to the King Tut bar, which sits directly behind me.

My heart sinks. I silently say the *Hashkiveinu* prayer for comfort and safety, one my mother often recited but that I haven't muttered, even to myself, since my childhood. Because there is bad, and then there is evil. Something I've managed to avoid for nearly six months, since I struck a bargain to keep my jail time low.

But now I'm guessing that my debt has come due, and it's being called in.

I turn, painting a smile on my lips, and for once, I am upset to be right in my guess. There, stepping through the secret door into the bar, is Dutch Schultz.

CHAPTER TEN

EUNICE

New York, New York
September 12, 1935

"We're listening, Mrs. Washington." I say the words I've repeated dozens and dozens of times to dozens and dozens of New Yorkers. "I wanted to follow up on the letter you sent."

"Bless you, Mrs. Carter. I've called the police more times than I can count; my sons have helped me write letters to *The Amsterdam News* and *The Crisis*. But when I heard Mr. Dewey on the radio urging all of us to speak up, I prayed someone would finally listen to me."

With the mention of her sons, I have to swallow a sob. It's been five months since we put Junior aboard the steamship bound for Barbados. Only the knowledge that he's safe two thousand miles away has helped me to bear the ache of missing him and the tension that has settled like a pall between Lisle and me.

Turning my attention back to Mrs. Washington, I say, "Please tell me more about this." I hold up her letter.

Her voice is heavy with frustration. "I've got the beautiful Hotel Olga on one side and a whorehouse on the other."

"How do you know it's a whorehouse?" I keep my tone neutral.

I believe her, but I always press for details from the residents, making no assumptions.

"Oh, I know a whorehouse when I see one. First, it's the girls, going in and out of that brownstone every day. But the way I know what's going on—it's the men. They're in and out, all hours; it never stops. They don't need a wooden door; they need a revolving one for all of those johns." She pauses and looks at me pointedly. "They're called johns, you know," she says, as if she's teaching me a lesson.

I nod and bite back my smile.

"Most of them look like family men. Probably got a wife and a house filled with kids, too." Mrs. Washington *tsks*. "They ought to be ashamed. The whole lot of them."

"Can you give me the exact address, please?"

As I write it down, I think I recognize the address. Is it from my review of the report conducted by the Committee of Fourteen or from another interview? I pick up the folder marked *Brothels* and scan the notes I took yesterday. I compare this with the address provided by Mr. Lewis, an eighty-one-year-old man who's lived in Harlem for the past thirty years, and I see it's the same street.

Over the past months, I've watched brothels multiply like pigeons in Central Park—with every letter, every interview, I add a new one to my list. I've also taken note how each new house seems to inch closer to the next. They're crowding in, practically stacked one atop the other. I can't make sense of this. How can they compete? The madams aren't fools; they know this.

Unless . . . the madams aren't rivals. Could they have formed some sort of an alliance? I smile at the thought. In the midst of this corruption, at least that would make the women more than just pawns in a man's game.

I lean in closer to Mrs. Washington. "You said you've called the police?"

"Over and over. They used to come out and shut that place down. But now? In the last two or three months, the police don't show up. They treat me like *I'm* the nuisance."

I frown. Could this really be a madam alliance? A single brothel here, another there . . . Yes, the madams might be able to pay a few cops to keep their doors open. But with so many houses packed so tightly together and operating without disruption, this is something else entirely. This is coordination. Something that's structured, organized . . . and protected.

"All right, Mrs. Washington, I will personally look into this for you."

"Thank you, Mrs. Carter"—she reaches across the meeting room table and squeezes my hand—"for doing what no one else has had the decency to do: listen to me."

"You're welcome. I think we're done for today. I'll walk you out, but first, let me just drop these files on my desk."

Mrs. Washington is right at my heels when she follows me into my office. She pauses, taking in the modest furnishings. Then her gaze pauses on the wall. Her chin juts, and her lips spread into the proudest smile at my Smith and Fordham degrees. For a colored woman, having this display of my credentials isn't vanity, it's a necessity.

"Mrs. Carter," Mrs. Washington says, her tone reverent, "when the girl at the front desk told me I'd be speaking with you, I was beside myself. Wait till I tell my sons. My oldest son read in *The Amsterdam News* that you were the first colored woman to get a law degree from Fordham."

"Yes, ma'am."

"He was so happy to tell me something I didn't know. And I gave it right back to him. I told him that you were Addie Hunton's daughter," she says, her chin held high.

My smile dims just a little, but I thank Mrs. Washington as I escort her to the door. Just as we exchange farewells, the corridor on the other side of the suite fills with laughter. Several of the assistant district attorneys stroll past me. They look like an assembly line—striding two by two, all white, all males, all dressed in white shirts, striped ties, and dark double-breasted suits.

My eyes narrow as I watch them leave another meeting I wasn't privy to. Only Murray glances my way and gives me a nod of apology. In the beginning, I often felt like an afterthought, but at least I was invited to participate in the team meetings. However, recently, it appears as if I'm not a thought at all.

"Mrs. Carter?"

I glance up and across the space. "Chief," I say, using Dewey's nickname as all the assistant district attorneys do.

"Do you have a moment?"

"Of course."

The chief's office is only slightly larger than ours, but with the walnut executive desk and the burgundy leather chesterfield chairs, it's imposing and grand. He directs me to one of the chairs as he settles across from me. "Our schedules have been so hectic, but I want you to know how grateful I am that you're on our team. You're a valuable member, and you've proven me to be a discerning judge of talent."

This isn't the conversation I expected. Instead of explaining why I'm excluded from meetings, it feels as if he's extending an apology swathed inside a compliment. Still I say, "Thank you, Chief."

"The work you did on the Salvatore Marrone case was the reason we won," he says, referring to a kidnapping and assault case this office prosecuted very early on. I'd researched and built the legal framework that allowed us to bring the strongest charges—and win the conviction. "And every week, I review your reports on the interviews you're conducting."

"Between the telephone calls, letters, and interviews, I've been in contact with more than one hundred people."

He steeples his fingers, tapping the tips together, a gesture I've come to recognize as meditative. "Mrs. Carter, I imagine the work you're doing may feel tedious, but I assure you—your work is important. The most critical evidence can be found in the smallest details."

"That seems to be proving true." Now I must weigh my words. So much of the work I'm doing goes beyond my assignment. And even with what I've amassed, it's still an unassembled jigsaw. I would prefer to speak with Dewey once I have more, but this is an unusual meeting between just the chief and me. Perhaps he can provide advice on shaping what I've discovered so far. "From my interviews, I've compiled a list of brothels. A pattern seems to be emerging. A pattern of collusion and protection—"

"Mrs. Carter"—the chief holds up his hand—"I'm certain you are aware that I will not be going after Schultz for prostitution."

Of course, I've heard the chief—and other men—dismiss prostitution as barely a crime. *Prostitution is a moral sin,* Dewey had declared about a year ago in a radio interview. But that was before he became the special prosecutor determined to rid the city of all organized crime.

"I understand how you feel, but I'm threading together evidence that reveals a coordinated operation. I may not have a direct link between the Mob and prostitution yet—"

"Mrs. Carter," he interrupts with a light chuckle, "I didn't bring together twenty of the top legal minds in this country to muck around in vice cases. Not only is that beneath this office, but New Yorkers want true reform. They've waited long enough."

"From the people I've spoken to, cleaning up prostitution would be a welcome change." I pause for a moment, then choose to press on. "And certainly, the Committee of Fourteen believed it important enough to spend thirty years investigating and documenting their findings." A flicker of surprise crosses his face, and I continue. "Because of what I'd been hearing in the interviews and seeing in the Women's Court, I decided it would be worth digging through the trove of data the committee compiled. I've read the transcripts of interviews with the girls and the madams, and I noticed links between police corruption and brothel locations. Links that still exist today. The only difference is, prostitution feels much bigger now, much more structured."

"What you've gathered, Mrs. Carter, may be impressive. But I'm not hearing evidence that prostitution is a Mob-operated enterprise," he says. "And organized crime is among the most profitable enterprises in this country; those men aren't chasing pennies from prostitution."

"Pennies or dollars, if it's a racket, it's a crime. I can lay the foundation for not only a prosecutable offense but a winnable one." I resist adding, *Just like I did with the Salvatore Marrone case.*

He rests his forearms on his desk. "My goal is to restore the rule of law."

His words— or rather, what he doesn't say—stun me. Is he implying that prostitution isn't against the law? Would Dewey be so flippant if he'd seen the battered, broken girls who stumbled into Women's Court, trembling before the judge, terrified of the pimps waiting outside? Would he think this way if he'd met an eighteen-year-old who'd been forced to smoke opium and was now hollow eyed, strung out, twitching for her next fix, and willing to do anything to get it?

It seems the girls don't matter to Dewey. But they matter to me.

Dewey says, "This investigation has one purpose—to bring down the Mob and Schultz. I've prosecuted him before, and I know his racketeering schemes, with everything from gambling, bootlegging, burglary, and extortion to even infiltrating unions and shaking down restaurant owners. Those are our targets. I will not betray this city's trust by wasting resources to chase a minor offense such as prostitution."

And herein lies his problem.

This isn't Dewey's first go-round with Schultz. As a United States attorney, Dewey vowed to put Schultz behind bars, and back then, tax evasion was his case. But Schultz beat those charges. Twice. And now Dewey wants to take down Schultz on something undeniably big.

My voice is steady when I say, "If that is your position, then how is what I'm doing—listening to New Yorkers' complaints—helping this team in the prosecution? It seems my work is for nothing."

As I watch him formulate a reply, I wonder . . . did Dewey only hire me to prove he was progressive? So that he could tell the press he'd hired a woman, and a Negro at that?

The press has always been suspicious of my appointment. Not the Negro press; in the pages of those newspapers, my inclusion on the team was heralded. But the white press framed my appointment as a political favor, a reward after I'd been asked to run in what the Republicans surely knew would be a losing race for State Assembly. Following my resounding defeat, the white press cast my appointment as nothing more than a consolation prize from the Republican Party. It was a symbolic gesture of goodwill, and I, merely a token.

Finally, Dewey says, "That's not true, Mrs. Carter. Your work is important because evidence can be found anywhere. I once uncovered a bootlegger's entire operation by combing through telephone records and connecting the calls. You might interview someone who overheard a conversation in the back of a nightclub or standing near a telephone booth. And then, just like that, we'll have what we need." He stands, my signal this meeting is over. "I wouldn't have given you that assignment if I didn't believe the work was crucial."

When I remain seated, he gives me a small nod.

"Mrs. Carter, I accepted this appointment to deliver to the people of New York the justice they've been denied for too long."

Dewey is being disingenuous if he claims altruism as his primary motive. Anyone who knows this thirty-three-year-old Wall Street lawyer from Owosso, Michigan, knows of his political aspirations: first City Hall, then the governor's mansion, and perhaps the White House.

But I only say, "I admire your dedication, Chief."

He is relieved when I finally rise. "Please continue to send your reports. I'm eager to see what you uncover—about anything except vice."

CHAPTER ELEVEN

POLLY

New York, New York
October 10, 1935

A SHARD OF broken crystal catches the early-morning sunlight streaming through the windows of the King Tut bar. It casts a rainbow on the wall opposite, and I shake my head. How can something so beautiful actually be a harbinger of doom?

I pick up the jagged shard and add it to the growing pile of shattered liquor bottles, crystal flutes, and wineglasses. They aren't the only evidence of last night's destruction; toppled chairs, tossed mahjong tiles, and strewn playing cards are everywhere. I cannot count the amount of dough I've spent on cleanup from Dutch's men's carousing or the number of times their bills for drinks and girls have gone unpaid. The only thing I've been able to prevent so far is damage to my girls. But being known as Dutch's place has its upside. For the most part, the cops don't threaten me when the girls and I are out and about. And as long as *his* cops are on duty, I'm protected from the wild packs of unorganized criminals who've been plaguing other brothels.

The Lion will manage all this cleanup when she rises for the day in a few hours' time. But the Lion's worried glances and quiet *tsk*ing—born from fierce loyalty, but no less annoying for their source—are more than I can bear this morning. She's so much more than a housekeeper; sometimes, she's more like a guardian angel. When you have no choice but to deal with the Devil, however, an angel can be awfully annoying.

Not to mention that Dutch will come stumbling down those steps any minute now, and I've got to be ready. Even though his goons are the wrecking ball that blew through the King Tut bar and gambling room last night, it won't do to have him trip on a book or cut himself on a jagged piece of glass.

I cannot imagine what might happen next. And I never want to find out.

I hear footsteps and brace myself. Which version of Dutch will I be facing this morning? Would the amenable Arthur Simon Flegenheimer, son of German Jewish immigrants, appear in my bar? The one who rescued me from three years in the slammer when I made a secret deal with him? Or will I be dealing with Dutch Schultz, as Arthur is now known, and his brutality? A violence that's only increased as he's become obsessed with Dewey's ongoing investigation into him.

Why has Dewey gotten under Dutch's skin this time when Dutch has conquered the much more fearsome enemies of the Mafia's Five Families and the Irish Mob? Not to mention, he's shaken off Dewey's earlier efforts to get him for tax evasion. I can't spend too much time in Dutch's warped mind trying to figure that out, because no matter the reason, bringing down Dewey has become Dutch's primary obsession.

The powerful thud of his boots grows louder. Dutch likes a steaming cup of coffee waiting for him when he emerges from one of the girls' rooms in the morning. And it behooves me to have it ready.

Just as he enters the bar, I place the oversized mug of coffee at his favorite spot. He ambles past me and thunks down on the chair. He draws deeply on his coffee, then pauses.

Lifting his mug in the air, he says, "I think I need some hair of the dog this morning, Polly."

"'Course, Dutch. Should've thought about that myself." I scamper behind the bar to grab his bottle of whiskey—the good stuff I keep just for him—and I pour a generous splash in his coffee.

A wry half grin appears on his face, and I guess I'm dealing with Arthur this morning. "Care to join me?" he asks.

I don't, in truth. I'd like this mercurial tornado to leave my house, and then I want nothing more than to crawl into bed until dinnertime. As is my habit. But it will not happen, as my house has become his de facto office these days; he's even begun to take meetings in my bathtub. And I could never, ever say such a thing. It would earn me the sort of slap or punch I've seen Dutch dole out more than once. And anyway, this is the deal I struck when I asked for his help in my sentencing.

"I'd be honored." Settling the bottle of whiskey in the center of the table, I pour myself a cup of coffee.

I usually don't sit across from Dutch in the cold light of day, which lays bare the crisscross of scars on his face and hands as well as the crooked nose. Trying hard not to think about the thieving and bootlegging and gambling and murdering that yielded this disfigurement, I aim for lighter topics. "Hope that Virginia was good for what ails you?"

Virginia is one of my most popular girls, certainly with Walter. With her pale blond hair and icy blue eyes, she cultivates the air of a society matron, even though she actually hails from the Bronx, where her drunk of a mother raised her alone on beatings and sparse food. My patrons seem to enjoy the "chase" she provides, as well as the "class." If only they knew.

"Nothing is good for what ails me except bringing Dewey down," he says, then chugs his spiked coffee. If only I had a dollar for every time he's said this.

I rush to pour him another coffee and whiskey. If I'm very, very lucky, the liquor will compound that already in his system, and tiredness will overtake him. Maybe even until nighttime, when the distractions of the girls and the cards will lighten his mood. But I don't count my chickens, because Dutch only ever seems to need four hours of sleep a night.

I try to change the subject. "Ever think of giving up the life? Retiring to a Florida beach and taking in the sun, a fruity cocktail in hand?"

Dutch laughs. The first authentic, deep laughter I've ever heard from him. "Polly, that's the best joke I've heard in a long time."

I'm perplexed. "What do you mean?"

"Once you're tagged a criminal, you're tagged for life. There's no getting out." He stares at me with eyes that almost look sad. "I thought you knew that?"

I'm quiet for a long minute while I take it in. Before I return to myself and wrangle command of the conversation, Dutch blurts out, "I've got to get rid of Dewey."

I try to buoy him up and away from the darkness I can see nipping at his heels. "It seems to me that you've already given him a good beating. Throwing off those tax evasion charges was like a dozen eggs on his face. Eggs he can't wash off."

When he slams the mug down on the table, I have to keep

myself from jumping. What's next? Will he slug me as a way to slake his anger?

His hand comes toward me, but instead of a punch or slap I feel a pat on my arm. A gentle pat.

"You've hit the nail on the head, Polly. A good beating. That's exactly what Dewey needs to put him off my scent."

CHAPTER TWELVE

EUNICE

New York, New York
October 10, 1935

I HAVE SAT in Women's Court watching an endless number of cases over these last weeks, and yet, it is still difficult to ignore the noise and chaos. Only when the bailiff enters, followed by the magistrate, does a modicum of order settle over the courtroom.

The bailiff calls out, *"The People of the State of New York versus Ginger Sanders."*

We rise, and this affords me a better look at Assistant District Attorney Kessler, who has been the prosecutor of these cases for the last month. Across at the defense table, a young woman wearing a Peter Pan–collared floral day dress—whom I presume is the defendant—and her defense attorney, Max Rachlin, rise.

For weeks, I've watched thirty-year-old Max Rachlin, with his slicked-back hair and pencil-thin mustache, perform in the courtroom. Always dressed in custom-tailored three-piece suits and shoes polished to a mirror shine, Rachlin resembles a headliner at the Paramount more than he does a defense attorney. He's especially given to theatrics—the way his voice rises to a crescendo, then crashes to a whisper when he's questioning a police officer about something as simple as what time an arrest was made.

In the row behind the defense table sits the disbarred Abe Karp. He is the opposite of the flamboyant Rachlin in stature and style—shorter, heavier, and he buys his suits off the rack. He's not performative, he's calculating.

Kessler delivers his opening statement—practically identical to what he says in every prostitution case—and then the magistrate asks him, "Are you prepared to call your witnesses?"

"The prosecution calls Officer Walter Harrison."

The uniformed officer lumbers to the stand. As the bailiff swears him in, beads of sweat cling to his brow. After going through the formalities, Kessler gets to the crux of his questioning. "I'd like to discuss the circumstances of the arrest of Miss Ginger Sanders on the evening of August eighteenth. Do you recall the events that led to Miss Sanders' arrest?"

The officer shifts his glance from Kessler to the defense side of the room.

"Officer Harrison, do you need me to repeat the question?"

"Uh, no. But to be honest, I'm not sure I remember," he says.

Kessler's eyes narrow as he picks up a folder from the prosecution table. "What do you mean you don't remember? The police report you filed that night was very detailed."

Officer Harrison shakes his head.

Kessler continues. "According to your report, you arrested Miss Sanders at a gathering at the Crystal Room on 142nd Street after you raided the establishment."

Quickly, I scribble down the name to compare it to my list of brothels.

"Well, now I'm not sure," Harrison mutters.

"Not sure of what, Officer Harrison?" Kessler asks, his voice laced with the frustration I've often heard from him.

The police officer's gaze drops to the report in Kessler's hands. His silence drags on. "I'm . . . I'm not certain of the arrest circumstances because there was a lot going on that night."

Kessler reads aloud from the report, and when that doesn't elicit any refreshed recollections from the officer, he asks, "If you can't recall the specifics, what do you recall in general, Officer?"

Officer Harrison glances at Karp, and then his voice rises. "I don't recall much. In fact, it's possible Miss Sanders may have been mistaken for one of the other girls I brought in that night."

Kessler turns to the magistrate. "Your Honor"—his tone is measured now—"if Officer Harrison cannot remember the events of that evening, I have his original statement regarding the arrest of Miss Sanders. I believe Officer Harrison was telling the truth the night of the arrest in his report, and now I respectfully ask the court to disregard his contradictory testimony today and accept his earlier statement as a recorded recollection."

As Kessler hands the magistrate the statement, Officer Harrison glances at Karp, and my eyes dart back and forth between the two. The magistrate studies the report, and I inhale, feeling equal parts hope and dread.

The judge raises his gaze from the paper. "Request denied. Do you have any other questions for this witness?"

Kessler shakes his head, and my shoulders sag along with his. "No, Your Honor," he says.

"You may step down," the magistrate says to Officer Harrison. As the officer leaves the stand, the magistrate asks Kessler, "Do you have any other witnesses?"

"No, Your Honor." Kessler sits down, dejected.

Rachlin rushes to stand. "Your Honor, I move to dismiss. There is not enough evidence to support a conviction against Miss Sanders."

The magistrate looks toward Kessler for a response, but he just shakes his head. With one rap of the gavel, the magistrate says, "The case against Ginger Sanders is dismissed."

The young woman spins around. Even though she has just scored a victory, her eyes are blazing. She fixes her gaze on Karp. "The Combination may have gotten me off, but it bungled this from the start," she hisses just loud enough for me to hear. "I pay ten dollars a week to have a bond issued so that I never have to step foot inside the slammer. I don't pay to spend two days in the clink. I'll handle this with Red Sadie, too."

She stomps down the aisle. Hurriedly, I scribble: *Red Sadie, ten dollars a week*, and *the Combination*. Then, next to that, I add: *Case dismissed.*

For the rest of the morning, I sit through trial after trial. I take notes, collecting the names and arrest locations. There are no surprises. The pattern continues: All of the girls represented by Max Rachlin are set free. At a quarter to noon, the magistrate releases the court for the lunch break, but I won't be returning. After all of these weeks of being here, I've seen enough.

I rise from my row and slip with the crowd into the corridor. The hallway is more jam-packed than the courtroom. Clerks, defendants, attorneys all spill from the doorways, everyone eager to make the most of the hour-long break. Just before I reach the front door, I'm bumped from behind. "Oh," I exclaim, and spin around.

"Pardon me, miss." I glance down at the young colored boy, no more than nine or ten, in a white shirt and dark wool pants hitched up by suspenders. The brim of his flat cap hides his eyes. "I have a message for you."

"For me?" Confusion is the only reason why I take the folded paper from his hand. Before I can say another word, he scurries away, disappearing into the crowd. Stepping aside, I unfold the paper and read the one line scribbled in the center:

How is your son in Barbados?

"MAMA!" I SHOUT the moment I enter the apartment.

"Gracious, Eunice." My mother rushes into the foyer. "What's going on?"

I collapse in her arms, and as she leads me to the sofa, I choke out the details about the note and how I dashed to the office after receiving it. "The chief took charge without delay," I explain. "We sent two telegrams—one to Lisle's mother and the other to the Barbados authorities. But, Mama, I can't stop worrying. What have I done?" I cry.

"You've done what you're supposed to do. You've loved your son, and you've protected him."

"But what if the telegrams don't reach them in time? What if one of Schultz's hoodlums has already gotten to Junior?" I am devastated at that thought.

"You don't know that's the Mob's plan. They are probably just trying to scare you."

"But surely they've been watching me and—"

The shrill of the ringing telephone is as jarring as a scream at midnight. I rush to the hallway and hold the telephone receiver with both hands to keep it steady in my grasp.

"Mrs. Carter, this is Thomas Dewey." His words come quickly, succinctly. "The authorities in Barbados have received our communication, and we've heard back. Your son is fine."

"Oh, thank God," I exclaim, wanting to drop to my knees right then.

He continues. "Two officers will be assigned to watch over your family. One will accompany your son to and from school."

I imagine Junior's eyes, wide with curiosity and questions, when an officer escorts him to class. Will he be frightened? Confused? Or will he puff out his chest, just a little, fancying himself a boy on an important mission? I hope it's the latter.

"Thank you," I say, not able to recall when my heart has been filled with more gratitude.

"We're taking every precaution, but you should know this is a common tactic used by the Mob. You're the third assistant DA to receive such a note. And while we have no indication that they're acting on their threats, we won't take any chances."

"Oh, I didn't know," I say, surprised I haven't heard so much as a rumble or a rumor about this in the office.

"And truth be told, my wife has received more than her share of telephone calls. We've changed our telephone number and kept it quiet. It's important that this doesn't leak. The Mob feeds on fear, and we don't want to give them any satisfaction. So I'm making the same request of you."

"Of course," I say. "I've only spoken with my mother and left a message for my husband."

"All right. I'll see you in the morning."

"Yes, I'll see you tomorrow." I thank him and hang up, prepared to tell my mother the details of Dewey's call. But when I turn, she's standing right behind me, a smile blooming across her face. How can she smile in the midst of this storm?

She says, "I'm glad to hear you're going back to work."

I stagger into the parlor. "Maybe I shouldn't. Maybe Lisle is right. Perhaps it's time to quit."

My mother shakes her head, her conviction apparent. "You don't believe that."

I shrug. "The only thing I believe is that if I were not part of the special prosecutor's team, my son wouldn't need a police escort to school. He was supposed to be safe in Barbados."

"And he is. Once again, you've made certain of that."

It doesn't feel like enough. "I just wish . . ."

"Don't start questioning your purpose now. You've been chosen for a time such as this. To be the first colored woman in your position. That's a heavy burden to carry, but you were chosen because God knew you could bear it with grace and, most importantly, without faltering."

"It's terribly hard. To have this purpose outside of my home, and to watch my son struggle beneath the weight of not being with me."

"He'll be fine," she says with certainty. "Just like you and your brother were. You're not sending Junior away for the rest of his life, and there are far worse things than spending a few months in Barbados. That's not a punishment." She steps closer, placing both hands on my shoulders. "Listen to me, sugar, if there's one thing I know from my own life, it's that you can't be a good mother, or wife for that matter, if you're not walking the path God set for you."

The front door slams against the wall as Lisle rushes in. "What happened?"

I melt into his embrace. It's been weeks since he's held me with such tenderness.

He leans back, and his eyes search mine until I show him the note. Lisle reads it, then glances up. He's silent for a moment, as if the words have stolen his breath away. Quickly, I tell him about the telegrams that have been sent and how officers are already at his mother's home.

There is a flicker in his eye—an alarm. "*That's* the plan?" he says incredulously. "That is not enough. There is only one thing that will truly protect our son."

So many times, Lisle has made this demand of me. And I have never wavered—until this moment. He sees my hesitation and moves in. As he takes my hands, his voice is softer now, wrapped in that Bajan lilt that has done more than just enthrall me; it's always made me feel safe. "Sweetheart, there is only one way."

I part my lips to agree, but my mother moves faster than the speed of my voice. She steps between us, breaking our grasp. Facing my husband, Mama says, "You're right. There is only one way to make sure Junior is safe. I'm going to Barbados."

CHAPTER THIRTEEN

EUNICE

New York, New York
October 23, 1935

THE SAVOY BALLROOM shimmers like a spray of pink diamonds beneath the chandeliers. More than fifty tables, each draped in gold cloth and adorned with crystal candelabras, stretch across the massive ballroom that comfortably accommodates the five hundred gala guests who've each paid five dollars for this fundraiser for the Harlem Commission.

Although the dinner plates have long been cleared, not a soul has moved. Chick Webb and his orchestra have every guest spellbound—bodies swaying, fingers snapping—everyone except for Lisle and me.

I cast a quick glance at my husband. Throughout our marriage, a single look between us would stir a smile, or one of us would reach a hand across the space, closing the divide between us. Tonight, Lisle stares straight ahead, his bourbon in one hand, a cigarette in the other, and his gaze fixed on the bandstand. The lights are dim, but he knows I'm looking at him. Yet his eyes neither shift nor soften.

Since I received that note two weeks ago, Lisle has been cold with fury. Once I told him that I would not resign, he has uttered not a single word beyond "Good morning," "Good night," and "Have you seen my silver cuff links?"

I can only wonder how long his punishing silence will go on.

As the orchestra plays, I glance around our table. Walter White, the executive secretary of the NAACP and my childhood friend from Atlanta, sits with his wife, Gladys, nestled against him. Beside them, Roy Wilkins, the editor of *The Crisis* magazine, lifts his wife Aminda's hand to his lips. Jessie Fauset Harris, once my literary mentor and now a dear friend, sits tucked beneath her husband Herbert's arm.

When my eyes settle on my closest friend, Regina, she, too, is leaning into her husband, William Andrews, the assemblyman from Harlem. Only Lisle and I sit as if there is more than just distance between us.

Regina's eyes flick between Lisle and me, and her smile fades. She gives me a small shrug, her way of silently asking, *What's wrong?*

I shake my head and look toward the stage. When the music ends, applause fills the room, and Regina and I rise. Our husbands follow suit. I half expected Lisle to remain seated and stone-faced, continuing to pretend like I didn't exist. But I should have known. Whatever our rift, public decorum is paramount.

Our husbands escort us to the stage. Then, as they return to their seats, the guests quiet.

I begin, "On behalf of the Harlem Commission, thank you for being here tonight. The riots this past March marked one of Harlem's darkest hours, when businesses were ravaged, many of our neighbors were severely injured, and our overall sense of safety was torn apart. I never imagined I'd witness such devastation again. I was only seven years old back in 1906, when Atlanta erupted into utter chaos.

"My family fled Atlanta after that. And while the circumstances are different here, the destruction, the pain, the suffering is the same. But I don't want anyone to flee from Harlem. I want our neighbors to know that together, we will rise again."

The audience erupts in applause, and then Regina begins. "At the heart of the unrest is the harsh truth that white-owned businesses want our money but will never hire a Negro. Our charge is to pursue real and lasting solutions to the discrimination that runs rampant through Harlem.

"We are pleased to announce that Mayor La Guardia, along with the commission, will be meeting with white businesses to confront these discriminatory policies." We have to pause for the standing ovation. "And while we do that work, the commission is equally committed to supporting the residents of Harlem. Your generosity this evening will assist the colored-owned businesses that suffered damages and provide relief to families burdened with medical expenses. So we are grateful for every donation. And please continue to enjoy the evening. Thank—"

I give Regina's arm a gentle squeeze. "Before we leave the stage, we want to thank our husbands, Dr. Lisle Carter and Assemblyman William Andrews." I turn my gaze to Lisle, and this time, his eyes are steady on me. "Thank you for standing beside us, for understanding the long hours we work, and for supporting our dreams."

William offers a wide smile. Lisle only takes a long sip of his drink.

As Regina and I step off the stage, the band bursts into "Stompin' at the Savoy," and shouts rise across the ballroom. Men in black silk-lapel dinner jackets grab their wives and dates, equally as elegant in backless gowns, and make a mad rush to the dance floor. Couples kick and glide, twirl and leap, throwing themselves into the wild rhythm of the Lindy Hop.

"Shall we give it a try?" William asks Regina when we return to the table.

"Absolutely not." She laughs. "We have to work in the morning, and I don't want to end up rubbing liniment on either of us." They chuckle, and Regina glances at me. "There are a few final points Eunice and I have to review. Pardon us." She grabs my hand and guides me away.

Lifting the hems of our gowns, we slip into an empty parlor across the hall. With a sigh, I sink into a chair.

Regina stands, arms crossed. "So what's going on?"

My first instinct is to brush it off. But Regina is my closest friend, and for the past eleven years, we've carried each other's secrets and sorrows.

It was at Jessie Fauset Harris' book launch for her first novel, *There Is Confusion*, where we were drawn together over our shared love of literature. That was the time when I was truly considering writing as a career.

While I've drifted away from writing, Regina has stayed true to her love, first working as a library clerk at the 135th Street library, and then by penning scripts, her best being *Climbing Jacob's Ladder*, a haunting piece about a man lynched outside of a church while congregants prayed inside.

We have taken pride in each other's accomplishments, but we've shared grief, too. The deaths of our fathers and the toll of the racism in our careers bind us.

But it is the anguish in my friend's eyes now that undoes me. "What's going on, Eunice?" She pulls a chair close and sits.

When she places her hand over mine, my composure shatters. I hold her hand as I close my eyes, and I take my friend back two weeks, to the day the boy left me standing stunned and silent in the lobby of Women's Court. By the time I walk Regina through the plan to keep Junior safe and Lisle's fury over it, her eyes are glassed with disbelief and grief as if I've told her too much, too fast.

"Oh my heavens!" Regina says when I finish. "You must have been so scared. I wish you had telephoned me."

"I couldn't. And I probably shouldn't have even told you now. But what's most important is that Junior and my mother are safe in Barbados. While those seven days on the steamship had to be hard, my mother sent a telegram just yesterday. She's heartened that her rheumatism hasn't flared up as much in the warmer weather." I shake my head. "But Lisle has turned away from me, and I don't know how to mend things. For all the pride I take in my work, my husband carries an equal measure of disdain."

"You know, Eunice," Regina begins, her voice soft and gentle, "maybe it's not your job or Junior being away that Lisle resents. Maybe it's the time and attention you're giving to everyone except him."

I pause, letting her words settle in the quiet for a moment. My thoughts drift back to the days before I joined Dewey's team. When I was still in private practice and my work in Women's Court allowed me to always be home before five. Lisle and I spent almost every evening together, inseparable as we swept through Harlem attending intimate salons at the home of Mr. and Mrs. James Weldon Johnson and elegant dinners hosted by Mr. and Mrs. W. E. B. Du Bois. At every opening performance at the Lafayette Theatre and lively amateur night at the Apollo, we were there, together.

I nearly leap from my seat and wrap my arms around my friend. "I should have talked to you sooner."

Minutes later, Lisle and I have taken our leave from the gala, and now we stand beneath the Savoy's marquee, its bright lights winking in rhythm to the Savoy swing I still hear pulsing from inside. I break our silence as we wait for the attendant to bring our car around. "I hope you enjoyed tonight."

"I did," he says, without giving me a single glance.

Our car arrives, and I slide into the front seat of our Ford Model 48. As Lisle pulls away from the curb, I say, "I don't like this distance between us, and I want to find a way to get back to who we've always been together. Maybe we can get away this weekend." Lisle doesn't react, but I continue. "You've wanted to visit Martha's Vineyard. It may be a bit chilly this time of the year, but I'm certain it's still lovely."

A faint smile curls his lips. "That would be nice."

When he reaches for my hand, I sigh. "I'll start making plans tomorrow. If you can get away, maybe we can extend it beyond this weekend."

"I can get away," he says. "But can you?"

"There is nothing more important to me than you," I say, already thinking about what I will tell the chief. Given the gravity of what we've endured, I'm sure he will understand that I need a few days with my family.

Those are the words Lisle needed to hear. After we park our car in the garage, he takes my hand. As we stroll along Edgecombe Avenue, he slips his arm around my waist. The street is nearly deserted, and the streetlamps cast long shadows that move as we do, with the hush of midnight wrapping around us. I feel so buoyant with hope as we stroll together. This is the start of a new beginning.

We step into the lobby, and Mr. Meeks, our night shift doorman, greets us, then says, "Mrs. Carter, a telegram was delivered to you just about an hour ago."

I frown as he hands the envelope to me. "Mama just sent a telegram yesterday," I say, my heart already hammering. And then I begin to read. "Dear God," I whisper, and press my hand against my chest, my eyes still riveted to the telegram.

"What is it?" Lisle asks as he almost snatches the paper from my hands. He scans the message. His jaw tightens. His tone is cold and brittle when he says, "I won't mark Martha's Vineyard on my calendar."

CHAPTER FOURTEEN

POLLY

New York, New York
October 23, 1935

It's nearly midnight, and Dutch and his crew haven't made an appearance. There's a chance they may not show up at all. While they've stormed the place as late as three o'clock in the morning, it is decidedly not the norm. They've usually taken the run of my house long before then.

How I wish I hadn't made that damn deal with Dutch. The toll it takes on the house, the girls, the Lion, and me to have him and his men here so frequently is too much. The three years in prison I would've received without Dutch's help sometimes seems a small price to pay to have the control of my house back. The worry about what would happen to the Lion and my girls during that long absence—since my money would have run out during the first year of my imprisonment—is the only thing that gives me pause, even now. Never mind what would happen to my family here and abroad without my financial support.

I entered this life with a vow to run a different kind of house—one where the girls would be safe; where the clients would be entertained, and not only by the girls; and where I called the shots. A house unlike any other, from what I saw—more of an upscale club than a brothel. The deal with Dutch threatens that.

"Polly?" the Lion whispers in my ear. Although the Lion sees all and knows all, she very rarely emerges from her post in the corner of the room. Unless she must. Something serious is up.

"Excuse me," I say, turning away from Donald Ogden Stewart. The writer is on his usual rant about Hollywood politics—who gets what project and why, all that nonsense—and just wants a sympathetic ear. Hopefully the other man standing with us, Robert Benchley, will provide that. If not, I'll get one of my girls on it.

"What is it?" I ask the Lion quietly.

"A kid is at the door downstairs. He doesn't want to come up but wants to tell you something."

"Can't he just tell Jerry to tell me whatever it is?" While the chatter and the booze and cards all seemed to be percolating along smoothly, I know better. Three of the four girls are about to turn over clients, and the gents awaiting their turns are getting anxious. That anxiousness can lead to kerfuffles. Or worse.

"He said it's for your ears alone," she persists.

I make as invisible an exit as possible. Opening the secret bookshelf door as surreptitiously as I know how, then quietly closing it behind me, I pass through the parlor and down the stairs to where Jerry stands guard. A raggedy-looking kid who couldn't be more than fourteen years old stands at the bottom, gazing up at me expectantly, his eyes hard. I know this type of kid; I was this type of kid. Young, scrappy, unprotected.

"Dutch, Abe, Otto, and Lulu were at the Palace Chop House," he blurts out, then pauses for a breath.

"Alrighty," I answer warily to this unsolicited update about Dutch and his companions' whereabouts. Dutch can usually be found in the company of his accountant, Otto Berman; his lieutenant, Abe

Landau; and always, his bodyguard, Bernard Rosenkrantz, who goes by Lulu for reasons I've been too scared to ask. And they can often be found at the Newark restaurant and saloon called the Palace Chop House. It's always a relief when they decide to spend the entire night there.

"That's one of their usual haunts. I'm not sure why that's so newsworthy I had to be dragged out of my place of business," I say.

The kid's mouth opens, then closes. When I don't get an immediate explanation, I swivel away from him and start walking back up the stairs.

"Wait, wait, Miss Adler."

Without turning around, I ask, "What is it, kid?"

"Dutch has been shot."

Pivoting back to face him, I screech, "What?"

"Yeah, yeah." Now he's talking so fast that he's practically stammering. "Some gunmen stormed the Chop House. Dutch was in the gents' near the bar, and they went inside and shot him first. Then the shooters went into the dining room, where they mowed down the other three."

I clutch the banister, simultaneously shocked and elated. I don't really wish Arthur Simon Flegenheimer dead, but in many ways, he passed a long time ago. Arthur died when his father walked out on him and his mom, leaving Arthur to become Dutch and support his family by whatever means necessary, a story Dutch disclosed to me one late and drunken night. A story that I can relate to. But the violent, obsessive Dutch he's become—well, his death is a very different matter. His death is a sigh of relief.

"I didn't think Dutch could die. He's got more lives than a cat," I say.

"Oh, you misunderstand me, Miss Adler. All four of the guys have been shot, but they somehow kept their wits and returned fire.

They're headed to the hospital by ambulance now, although truth be told, Abe doesn't look so good. Hit right in the neck, and you know how that goes."

I do. This isn't the first shoot-out I've been privy to—or experienced firsthand.

"What about Dutch?" I ask the million-dollar question.

"Hit in the belly, blood everywhere. Needs surgery, or so the ambulance guys said. All four are headed to the New York Polyclinic."

"He sent you here to tell me this?" I ask, and as I say the words, they sound odd. I'm not Dutch's mother or wife or fellow mobster or rabbi or priest or friend, if he has any of those. I'm just a madam who's beholden to him. Why would I deserve special notification of his fate?

"He asked me to make the rounds to all his loyal contacts. He wants your ears to the ground—so he can find out exactly who ordered the hit. So he can start making plans."

"Alrighty, kid. I'll put out some feelers in the morning," I reply, motioning for Jerry to give the kid a tip.

"I don't think you understand, Miss Adler. You've got to start asking around now. No one is sure Dutch will survive until morning, so he wants to get his revenge."

CHAPTER FIFTEEN

EUNICE

New York, New York

October 24, 1935

"DUTCH SCHULTZ IS not dead."

The chief's words hang in the air, thick and heavy like cheap cigar smoke. The nineteen other assistant district attorneys exhale. Is it dread or is it relief? Schultz is the centerpiece of each and every one of their cases, after all.

Dewey has clearly had a rough night. His eyes are rimmed with red, and the skin beneath his lids sags from his exhaustion. He's always immaculate, but today, his necktie is askew, as if he hasn't had the time or the inclination to adjust it properly.

"Several men have been stationed at New York Polyclinic since Schultz was rushed in last night. He's in bad shape—multiple gunshot wounds. He's lost a lot of blood, and he needs surgery. Basically, he's clinging to life."

"Is he conscious?" Murray asks.

"Can we get a deathbed confession?" another pipes in.

"Awake, yes, but talking to us, no," the chief says. "The doctors have advised me anything Schultz says at this point can't be trusted because of his medicine. We'll just bide our time until after his surgery, and we'll see what comes of this."

The room erupts with opinions and questions. Dewey raises his hand, and as if he's wielded a gavel, the room quiets again. But before he can say anything else, I speak up. "What does this mean for the case?"

Every assistant district attorney turns toward me before their glances return to Dewey. It's the question everyone wants to ask.

Dewey is silent as he presses his fingertips together. Then he says, "Mobsters like Schultz make deals with the Devil. I have no doubt Schultz has more life in him yet. We'll proceed with the case against him."

He stands, ending the meeting. The rest of us follow, and the men gather in clusters of two and three, engaging in hushed conversations. I slip out unnoticed and hasten to my office.

Beneath the chief's calm, there was an edge. He's worried, and I understand why. If Schultz dies, a good part of the cases he's had the other nineteen assistant district attorneys investigating will evaporate. I have no doubt Dewey already had a stockpile of evidence against Schultz from his prior efforts at prosecuting him: informants, backroom chatter, perhaps even a few witnesses who, with a little more persuasion, would be ready to flip. And since he became special prosecutor, Dewey has had his assistant district attorneys collecting evidence in every racket where Schultz is rumored to have a hand. The way the case is being constructed, all roads are meant to lead to Schultz.

So . . . if Schultz dies, the crux of Dewey's investigations crumbles. Simple truth—cut off the head, and the body will die.

The Mob will reorganize, of course, but it will take time for a new kingpin to emerge. There will be a vicious struggle for power, not without bloodshed. And more crucially for Dewey—not without time passing. With the city watching and waiting, Schultz's death will change everything.

But it might open a door for me.

Because the case I've been quietly investigating doesn't necessarily involve Schultz. It isn't designed to lead to Schultz specifically; it will lead to *whoever* is in charge, Schultz or not.

I unlock my desk drawer and pull out the folders I've been compiling from my observations in Women's Court and my review of the records. Inside are pages listing each case: the girls' names, arresting officers, the bail bondsmen of record, the defense attorney, and the outcome.

Opening one folder, I scan the pages. Across dozens of cases, the arresting officers vary, but the bondsmen don't. Only one of eight names appears—all bearing one of the three surnames: Jacobs, Jacobowitz, Klingsberg. And in every case the defense attorney is Max Rachlin, who managed to either win a suspended sentence or have the case dismissed for every girl.

Even with just a quick glance, there is an unmistakable pattern.

Next, I review the file marked *Resident Complaints*. The overwhelming concern among residents is the spread of prostitution. Brothels popping up on every block, and for these houses to not only continue but thrive, some sort of orchestration must be afoot. Among the madams? With the cooperation of the police? Certainly, it seems, the police are cooperating with *someone*.

Finally, I think of Ginger Sanders' mutterings in court: *The Combination may have gotten me off, but it bungled this from the start. . . . I pay ten dollars a week to have a bond issued so that I never have to step foot inside the slammer. I don't pay to spend two days in the clink. I'll handle this with Red Sadie, too.*

There are still so many questions, but on one point, I have no doubt—what I've compiled is indicative of a racket. And if I had to say who's behind it, with every finger I have, I'd point to the Mob. I just don't believe that the Mob would stand by and allow prostitution to thrive like this. No one, not Schultz or anyone else, would give free rein to Jacobs, Rachlin, and Karp to work their courtroom racket with prostitutes without giving their nod to it all.

So is the Mob the Combination?

"Eunice." I glance up, and Murray stands in my doorway. "The chief wants to speak with us again."

Grabbing my notepad, I follow Murray, but when we enter the meeting room, no one is sitting. The men line the perimeter, their faces stiff. Every eye is on the chief. His countenance delivers the news before he's spoken a word.

"Schultz is dead," he finally announces. "That deal with the Devil didn't stand, and he succumbed to his injuries."

We stay silent, all of us in shock.

"There's more." His tone is so grim, my stomach clenches. "According to our sources, Schultz was assassinated by his own . . . by Murder, Inc."

I inhale. Murder, Inc. is the nickname of a Mob hit squad, the private enforcement arm of the National Crime Syndicate, the confederation of several Mob families. Its members have only one job: to carry out murder at the direction of the bosses. The FBI reported that Murder, Inc. has racked up close to five hundred murders in the past ten years alone, and not once did they leave a trail solid enough to prosecute.

Dewey's voice brings me back. "We've heard that Schultz was murdered because he put out a hit on me." There is a collective gasp, and more than one of the men mutters a curse. "Apparently, he thought if I was dead, the investigation would end."

"Oh dear Lord," I whisper, astonished by how composed the

chief remains. And then it strikes me, and I blurt out, "But the Mob killed him first because they knew killing you would only draw more attention to them."

The chief's gaze lands on me. "Exactly. We have some unlikely protectors out there who understand that harm to me will only hasten justice for them."

I nod slowly, suddenly filled with strange relief. Does this mean we are all somehow safer? Perhaps this news will ease some of the strain that still remains between Lisle and me.

"But they're not the good guys, and we must keep on," Dewey says, sounding more resolute than he did this morning. "We will have to refocus our case, of course. Those evidentiary chains that have been constructed leading only to Schultz will have to be reconfigured. I'll be meeting with each of you in the upcoming days to assess how your investigations will have to change to proceed."

Every investigation will have to change except for mine, I think.

There is no reason for me to change anything. I already have Dewey's winning case.

CHAPTER SIXTEEN

POLLY

New York, New York
October 24, 1935

In the end, I didn't need to pursue the task Dutch laid out for me—to find out who tried to kill him—because he wasn't around to enforce its fulfillment. In typical Dutch fashion, he lashed out at doctors at the hospital while awaiting surgery, and then handed three thousand dollars to an intern to keep watch over him, to make sure no one else tried to slaughter him. Even as he received last rites from a Catholic priest—covering all the religious bases before he went under the knife—he seemed indomitable. But even Dutch Schultz couldn't survive a Mob hit, and he died of his wounds within twenty-four hours of the shooting.

Not that it would have been hard to do what Dutch asked and validate the rumors that drift into my house through my maids and guards and girls and even delivery boys. The word on the street is clear as day: Dutch practically pulled the trigger on himself. He'd asked Murder, Inc., the hit squad for the vast group of mobsters called the National Crime Syndicate, to assassinate Dewey, and when the National Crime Syndicate vetoed the proposal as bringing too much heat, Dutch stormed out of the meeting, railing that he'd murder Dewey anyway. And Dutch, who'd always operated as an independent mobster outside the National Crime Syndicate, was just enough of a loose cannon to make them worry. By insisting on Dewey's murder and making plans to undertake it against the National Crime Syndicate's ruling, Dutch left his fellow mafiosi with no choice but to kill him.

Who ordered the actual deed? No one is saying the name out loud, but we all know only one person has the power to bring down Dutch Schultz. Only the creator of the National Crime Syndicate itself, which oversees New York City's Five Families as well as the bosses of Chicago, Buffalo, Philadelphia, and Detroit crime families and all the vice they orchestrate, would have the moxie to order a hit on a mobster of Dutch's stature: Lucky Luciano.

I've never met the man himself, but I've sent him girls, and I've heard stories. Fantastical tales have been wafting through my King Tut bar and across the mahjong and poker tables about Lucky's rung-by-rung climb from Sicilian-born kid hoodlum to Mafia hit man to regional capo to boss. Not satisfied with this astonishing ascent, Lucky did something no other mobster had been able to do before—unite the crime factions under one governing whole. Even though he eschewed the traditional title of *capo di tutti capi*, he does assume the role of boss of all bosses over every facet of Mafia life, from the narcotics trade to theft to loan sharking to bookmaking to extortion to gambling to union exploitation, you name it. Only prostitution has been spared, as far as I know, notwithstanding that peculiar ask by the goon at the bail bondsman. But I wonder. Will Dutch's death have any impact on that? Will Lucky become interested in running prostitution, now that Dutch is out of the picture? Not that Dutch seemed to exercise any interest or control over the "skirt trade," as he liked to call it. He simply liked "skirts" and my house, which would have been reason enough for Lucky to steer clear. No one liked dealing with the volatile Dutch unless they absolutely had to.

Who knows the answer? For now, all I care about is that my house is spared Lucky's gaze. I hope I'm too far down on the crime ladder to merit his attention. I've never craved anonymity—bad for business, except around the cops and my family, who are oblivious to my line of work—but I long for it now. Complete obscurity would be nice, or, at the very least, the sort of somewhat benign neglect Dutch treated me with—until I made the mistake of inviting him into an unholy alliance to lessen my jail sentence.

Time will tell, I think. Until then, I'm determined to celebrate being out from under Dutch's thumb.

I lift my crystal brandy snifter to the window of the little parlor off my bedroom, encouraging the wan afternoon light to stream through it. There isn't enough sun to cast rainbows on the opposite wall today, but still, I allow myself to feel relief and even contentment for a long moment. Soon enough, the cacophony of my girls' rising and the maids' cleaning and the chef's cooking will overtake the place as we ready for the night; while I do operate a twenty-four-hours-a-day joint to cover the bills, that just means a girl can always be available, not that the glitz and glamour of Polly's is constantly on display. To gift myself a few more minutes in this cocoon, I rise and put a Duke Ellington record on my gramophone, turning it up pretty loud and allowing the growl of the trombone and Duke's own piano playing to wash over me.

Clinking the air in a toast to myself, I then draw deeply of the amber liquid and sink back into the soft, apple-green upholstery of my favorite chair. The brandy heats me from within, soothing my jangling mind and worries. It is the only tall, stiff drink I'll allow myself until the last client of the night leaves. How I wish I could sit here all night.

And then I hear a knock.

"Miss Adler," the Lion's voice calls to me through the closed door. She sounds shaky, even meek, which is a far cry from her usual demeanor of quiet firmness and frankness with me. The Lion may have a certain reserve about her person, but she's never docile. As many a client has learned the hard way.

Then something occurs to me. Why is the Lion calling me Miss Adler? She only ever refers to me as Polly unless clients are here. And there shouldn't be anyone here other than me, her, the girls, Jerry, and the maids.

Could the cops be here?

I leap up and rush toward the door. "Yes," I call out, flinging the door open. "What is it?"

There the Lion stands, a gleaming knife to her throat and a copper-headed man behind her. Her eyes meet mine, and her gaze is surprisingly steady and unafraid. I know she's been in far worse pickles than this—as have I—but the terror that something might happen to the stalwart Lion immobilizes me momentarily.

I cannot allow fear to overtake me. Shaking it off as I have over and over in my life, I step toward them, with my hand outstretched in a gesture of appeasement but my ears searching for Jerry. Keeping my voice steady and my tone placating, I say, "There's no need for violence, sir. I'm certain we can get whatever you need without all that fuss. Liquor? Girls? Money?"

The knife remains in place, and the man—somehow familiar, I think—doesn't flinch. He doesn't even move, except to chuckle. This is no random break-in, and this man is no amateur criminal here for a quick buck. How do I know this redheaded goon? Have I seen him around with one of the other, lower-level gangsters? No, I think, redheads aren't common among the dark-haired Italian mobster ranks—even those gangs that include the smattering of Jewish and Irish men—and so I'd remember him from that.

I steal a quick glance behind him to suss out the state of the house. Broken glass lies on the floor alongside several books torn from shelves. Where is Jerry? He'd normally put an end to this onslaught before it even began. But when I see the big lug face down with his hands tied behind him and a behemoth looming over him, I know we are in trouble.

"What do you want?" I ask.

"Well," he says with a sickening smile, "we came for one purpose, but on our way here, we remembered another."

"And what's that?"

"Rumor is that Dutch commissioned a safe just a couple months before his death, specifically to hold his assets in case he ended up in jail. Seven million dollars in cash and bonds stored in that strongbox, by all accounts. That got Johnny and me thinking"—he turns back for a split second toward the giant guarding Jerry—"what if Dutch hid that safe here? I heard he spent a lot of time here before he got what he deserved. We thought we'd take a gander while we conducted our other business."

"I don't know anything about a safe." I speak the truth. Dutch never mentioned a safe, and I would have noticed if he brought in a strongbox large enough to hold that kind of loot into my house.

"It ain't out here, Murph," the giant Johnny calls out.

"Take a poke around this room," Murph says, and Johnny enters my sanctuary. He opens every drawer and door in the parlor, then storms into the connecting bedroom, where he throws perfume bottles and toiletries and clothing all over the place.

"Nothing," he pronounces.

"Then it must be upstairs. In the girls' bedrooms," Murph calls back. He nudges the Lion and says, "We'll search up there next."

I think about my girls up there. If they heard all the racket, maybe they were smart and snuck down the back staircase from their rooms to the servants' access. But what if, like me, they were playing music? Or what if they're still knocked out from the booze or draughts some of them take to get their sleep?

I can't have these monsters springing on them. And I can imagine what this "search" Murph referred to might then entail. I can't let them go up to the bedrooms alone. Or with the Lion. I've got to protect them all as best I can.

I take a few steps forward and attempt to wedge myself between the Lion and this Murph. "Take me instead of my friend here. I'll go upstairs with you to search the bedrooms."

"No," the Lion whispers, but barely moves her mouth. She can't risk a slip of Murph's knife.

"You'd put yourself in harm's way for this . . . this servant." He spits out the word. I know he wants to use a much more venomous term—one that begins with an *n*—and I'm surprised he holds back. It's a good thing he does. I never, ever allow anyone to demean the Lion for the color of her skin or anything else.

"I'd do much more than that for her."

"If the famous Polly Adler wants to feel the tip of my knife, she is welcome to it," he says, pushing the Lion aside and grabbing me instead. "Lead the way."

With the blade firmly lodged against my throat, Murph shoves me ahead of him. Gingerly, I walk across the path of destruction these two hoodlums have wreaked upon my bar, ever cognizant of the knife. A stumble or a trip could cause the switchblade to pierce my neck, whether or not Murph means it. I tread with care through the room and mount the first stair.

Slowly, I climb to the second step. Murph follows so closely that I can feel his hot, quick breath on my neck. The sensation makes me shiver, and I almost prefer the knife to his panting. Can I turn this situation around?

I want to know the real reason these men are here. This treasure hunt for Dutch's safe—which seems the stuff of fiction—is a secondary concern only. That much is clear. But who sent Murph and Johnny, and what does that person want?

"You mentioned that Dutch's rumored strongbox isn't the reason you came here," I say, keeping my stare fixed ahead on the next step I must climb with care.

"Yeah. What of it?"

"I'm just curious why you came to Polly's."

"You should be more concerned about your health," he says with a stomach-churning chortle.

"I am worried about that, Murph." I keep my voice small. This is a man who relishes his power, however limited it may be. However violently it may manifest itself. "But I am also curious."

That chuckle returns, and he says, "I'm surprised you haven't guessed."

"Guessed what?" I ask.

"Why I'm here. Don't you remember me?" He sounds genuinely surprised. Even a little hurt.

"Remember you from where?"

"From the bail bond office."

I suddenly feel sick. Because I do remember this man now. And I know why he's here; he doesn't need to explain. But he wants to make his purpose abundantly clear.

"I'm here to make certain you and your girls join our Combination."

CHAPTER SEVENTEEN

EUNICE

New York, New York
November 1, 1935

"Are you ready?" Murray asks me, just as I'm about to knock on Dewey's door.

I nod, grateful to have Murray beside me. He's the only one who's known from the outset that I was investigating the prostitution racket. And while he's never questioned me about the specifics, he's supported my decision to consider a different angle.

It's because of our friendship that I took my case to him. After I presented all the information I'd gathered, Murray had challenged me, pushing back on several of my points, often echoing some of Dewey's arguments. But finally, he was convinced by my arguments, and he agreed not only to help me present the case to Dewey, but to help persuade him as well.

The chief invites us into his office. "How is your son, Mrs. Carter?"

"He's fine. I received another telegram from my mother last night. All is well."

"And it will stay that way," Dewey says, directing Murray and me to the chairs.

As soon as we're seated, I begin, "With Schultz's death, there is much to reconsider."

Dewey interjects, "There is, but our goal remains the same."

"I agree. And"—I take a deep breath—"I believe I've identified a racket that will allow us to not only indict but secure convictions against the Mob despite Dutch's death. And it centers on prostitution."

The chief's sigh cuts through the air like a switchblade. Still, I launch into my presentation as if he's asked me to proceed, spreading the papers across his desk.

I begin with what first drew my attention—the string of dismissed prostitution cases with the cabal of lawyers and bail bondsmen with the laughable aliases. Then I chart the spread of the brothels, noting how they are often in clusters, operating just feet from each other.

Slowly, the chief unfolds his arms and leans forward as I share my suspicions about the police collusion in this scheme and Ginger Sanders' statement in court about the Combination.

"I believe that the Combination is the name of the organization behind this racket. Based on what I've uncovered so far, I suspect there could be upward of a thousand girls involved. The Mob would never permit any profitable vice to flourish like this without their approval, especially not one on this scale."

The chief leans back in his chair, his eyes on the papers, and he begins to nod. Not emphatically, but he's nodding nonetheless. I glance at Murray, and he gives me a small smile.

After a moment, Dewey says, "It appears there might be something here." He holds up a finger. "Heavy emphasis on the 'might.'" He turns his glance to Murray. "Murray?"

It is easy enough to overlook this deferential treatment of Murray over me, since I asked Murray to join me for this very purpose. I have a single objective: to advance my theory. If the chief needs to hear the opinion of a man to support me, so be it. For today.

Murray says, "Like you, I was skeptical, Chief. But Mrs. Carter has made a case for the necessity of gathering more information."

"I agree. This does warrant a closer look. Now, whether this rises to the level of Mob-boss control rather than some penny-ante racket run by small-time hoods remains to be seen. But you have convinced me, Mrs. Carter, there is something afoot with prostitution in this city. Now you have to come up with solid evidence to link the Mob to all of this."

The chief turns back to Murray. "So what do you recommend? How should we proceed?"

Murray says, "What about starting with the girls?"

I shake my head, not mentioning my two failed attempts to speak with Polly Adler. "It's difficult to get access to them. And contacting the girls puts them in danger."

Murray says, "I would say talk to one of the girls who's been arrested and is still in custody—"

"None of the girls I need ever end up in jail for any appreciable period of time. The whole point of Karp's scheme is to get them in and out and off lickety-split. But I do have an idea for how we can get some firsthand knowledge of the inner workings." The chief and Murray both turn to me. "Chief, I want authorization for a wiretap."

Murray leans back, and Dewey's eyebrows shoot up so high they nearly touch his hairline. Their astonishment is no surprise.

Wiretapping is a fraught legal tactic, even though seven years ago, the Supreme Court upheld a conviction won based on evidence garnered through wiretapping. Roy Olmstead was found guilty of bootlegging after his telephone calls had been tapped. He took his case all the way to the top court, claiming that his right to privacy had been violated. Although the Supreme Court upheld that conviction, their five-four decision left many of us doubtful that wiretapping will remain lawful.

But for now, tapping is acceptable evidence.

As the idea of such a bold move settles in, I say, "If we wiretap the right people—starting with the corrupt attorneys and the bondsmen—we will get more information, more names, and may find out where the bodies are buried, so to speak."

Dewey gives me a hard stare. "You do realize what you're asking?" His reluctance sounds like it's rooted deep.

"I do. I know wiretapping is not without risk. We could be challenged in court, and God forbid, if the press gets hold of it, we know public sentiment is against what they see as nothing more than snooping, and we could be discredited. But if we succeed, this could give us the evidence we need to crack all of this wide open."

He sighs, but then says, "All right. Reach out to Justice McCook for a subpoena."

This time, it's my eyebrows that lift in surprise and satisfaction. Justice Philip McCook is a New York Supreme Court justice who's been appointed by Governor Lehman to be the judicial guide for this special prosecution. This directive from Dewey—for *me* to contact the judge—is high praise.

It's a battle to rein in my smile. "I'll contact Judge McCook at once."

As Murray and I stand, the chief says, "This is good work, Mrs. Carter."

"Thank you, Chief."

Now my smile comes easily. But it doesn't last when the chief adds, "One thing, though. As you continue your work on this, remain diligent. The Mob may have called off the hit on me, but the closer we get, the more desperate they'll become. At any point, one of them may decide Schultz was right after all."

CHAPTER EIGHTEEN

POLLY

New York, New York
November 1, 1935

"I REALLY WISH you'd stay at the house tonight," the Lion says. Her voice is quiet, but no less firm for its low volume.

"No one should bother the place since the girls are out at the Waldorf for a private party, and I've put the word out about that. I don't expect *they* will come around if the girls are gone," I say, hoping to placate her, if indeed her worry is that the lowlifes in league with Murph and Johnny—who have visited my house three times now to "make clear" to us that we will be joining the Combination—might overtake the place when she's alone. "And anyway, Jerry is on guard, and he hired a second man to help him. Just in case."

"That's really kept them away so far," she snorts, and I know she's right. I believed I had lost control of my house and my girls when I made my deal with Dutch. But I'd been wrong. I hadn't fully appreciated that with Dutch around, I still retained all decision-making about my girls, the clients, and the management of the gambling and bar. Tolerating the constant presence and occasional outbursts of Dutch and his men had been the biggest sacrifice. I could still protect my girls, which is always my foremost concern. But now that power is under urgent, imminent threat by this so-called Combination.

"Well, Jerry has kept the violence to a minimum. If not the destruction," I admit. My house has been torn up several times before—more often than not by Dutch and his men—but this experience with these new thugs has shaken me. The way these upstart gangsters, low men on some other mobster's totem pole, saunter into my house as if they own the joint—destroying my property and taunting my girls in the name of "fun"—signals an unpleasant change afoot. Their boss is making a move to consolidate and control the brothels, mine among them.

"You misunderstand me. I'm not worried about what will happen *here* while you're out. I'm worried about what message you're sending while *you* are out," she says, her tone more insistent now. This is an oddity for the Lion, who is always watchful and protective and free speaking but never strident. "This task you've set for yourself tonight is not just a fool's errand. It's also a sign of weakness when you need to be telegraphing strength."

Her hands are on her hips now. She is serious about squashing this impulse of mine to see if we can get out of this business before the Combination—whatever that really is, whoever is in charge of it—takes over. Tonight, I'm going to test Dutch's bold, terribly disheartening proclamation that once you're tagged as a criminal, you're tagged forever. I want to try to get myself, the Lion, and my girls out. I want to give Mabel, Virginia, Kit, Angelica, Rosalie, and the Lion the sort of protection and fresh start I was never, ever granted myself.

"Listen," I say to the Lion with a clasp of her hand, "I know you mean well. No one is more loyal or well-intentioned than you. But the weight of this house and our well-being doesn't rest on your shoulders. It rests on mine."

"Polly Adler, as I live and breathe!" a voice calls out, and I pivot away from the coat check, where I've handed over my coat.

Burly arms encircle me with such force, I nearly topple over onto the floor in the foyer of Lou Richman's Dizzy Club on 52nd Street. "Harold! I didn't know you'd be this happy to see me!" I call back.

Standing on my tippy-toes, I glance up at the six-foot-tall, silver-haired Harold Montague, who spent an inordinate amount of time at my house when he and his wife briefly separated. A New York gadabout who knows everyone who's anyone, Harold is the sort of person who'd be in the loop on business opportunities I might be able to join.

"I don't think I've seen you since, since—"

He doesn't want to say prison, so I fill in the blank for him. "Since the House of Detention?" I ask with a swagger, tossing my fur stole over my shoulder.

Giving me a smile that more closely resembles a grimace, he says, "I didn't know if you'd feel comfortable talking about it."

I playfully slap his arm as the maître d' leads us to our table for two. "Please, a stint in the clink only adds to my cachet!"

"Especially since you kept your clients' names quiet, instead of trading on them like so many other madams would do," he says.

We order drinks, take in the scatty jazz, make some small talk, and then I can wait no longer. "So, what did your friend say?"

I'd rung Harold earlier in the day to make my business inquiries. He mentioned that he'd just lunched with a friend who was opening a factory in New Jersey and looking for someone to take charge. The friend would grant the right person—even a woman—twenty-five percent interest to do the job, as long as they could invest a small amount of money in the factory as a show of good faith. Harold had asserted that if I could run the city's most famous brothel, I could easily run a factory—and he put me forward for the role. How full circle it would be for me—the girl who'd been kicked out of her own factory job at seventeen because the supervisor raped and impregnated her—to run a factory myself, I think. I'd finally have a job I could be proud of when writing to my parents or when they came to visit—*if* they ever came. Instead of the lies I usually tell them about managing a corset factory.

"Well." Harold quaffs his drink and signals to the waitress for another. Then he shoots me an apologetic smile. "You see, Polly, my friend is worried that a partnership with Polly Adler might hurt his credit and his Dun and Bradstreet rating."

"I should've known better," I snap at him, although it's hardly his fault. It was a pipe dream. I reach out and touch his arm. "I'm sorry, Harold. You were just trying to be a pal and connect me with your friend. It seems I'm stuck with myself and my past. I guess I'll just go back to the whorehouse, where I belong."

"No, no, Polly, don't be that way about it." He places his hand over mine. "I'm sure something will surface. I'll keep my ear to the ground for you."

"You're a swell guy, Harold. You know that?" I say with as much lightness as I can muster. Never mind that I feel as heavy as a baby grand.

I chitter-chat with him as long as I can stand it, then push myself to standing. Claiming "duties at the house," I wave off his protests to stay longer and weave through the tightly packed tables toward the foyer. I know that if I stay here and make small talk any longer, emotions might bubble to the surface, and I can't risk showing how much his words upset me.

Queuing at the coat check, I spot club owner Lou Richman

chatting with the maître d'. Scuttling in his direction, I call out, "Lou? Is that you?"

"Polly?" he calls back, leaning toward me and bussing me on each cheek in the European manner, leaving a slight slick of his ubiquitous hair oil on my cheek. "What a pleasant surprise! You should have told me you were coming. I'd have rolled out the red carpet."

"Very kind of you, Lou, but not necessary. I was meeting a friend, and he took care of the reservation."

"If there is anything else you need, you know I'm here for you, Polly."

I appreciate the offer. Lou and I have had a symbiotic relationship over the years, where we've fed each other clients, albeit of a very different sort. But now I wonder, Is there something he could actually do?

"You know, Lou, there might be something you can help me with."

He steps closer to me, not wanting the little crowd in the foyer to overhear us. Given my profession, he probably assumes our conversation may not be appropriate for all ears. And usually he'd be right.

"Anything, Polly. I think you know that by now."

"Late one evening at my King Tut bar, you said that you found my ability to handle people so impressive that you'd like me to partner with you. In a legit business. I'm curious as to whether you meant it."

Tilting his head, his expression goes soft and apologetic. "Oh, Polly. I wish that was possible. But with your notoriety and the recent prison stay, there might be too much heat. Especially with this whole Dewey crackdown. I don't think the police would ever leave us alone and—"

I cut him off. Listening to two rejections in the span of an hour is more than I can bear. Painting on a smile like so much lipstick, I force my tone to sound bright. "Just a fantasy, Lou! And I broker in fantasies, don't I? Nothing for you to apologize for. I should know when a fantasy hits up against reality."

Turning away from him, I approach the now-available coat-check girl—undoubtedly a wannabe showgirl—and hand her my ticket. I cannot get out of here fast enough. The Lion was right: I've got to keep up a show of strength so word doesn't spread that Polly Adler is weak and desperate to get out of the brothel business. As I watch the girl paw through the racks of coats, I think that no one would even hire me to work in a coat check or cigarette concession. I'd never pass the new legislation that requires all coat check and cigarette concessionaires be fingerprinted; my criminal past would be clear.

As I wait for the Broadway hopeful to find my coat, I hear a familiar female voice in my ear, saying my name. I turn to face the woman, a statuesque, six-foot-tall blond beauty. Even if we weren't already acquainted, I might have guessed she's the infamous burlesque dancer–turned-madam Diamond Lil. The diamonds in her ears and clothes and hair and even implanted in her teeth are the giveaway. If I didn't know that she was actually born to a Montana cattleman—and that everything about her is a fiction—then her height and her periodic encroachment on my territory might irritate me more.

Trying to keep my voice bright, I say, "Evening, Lil."

I brace myself for some nasty remark about my prison term from my rival Lil. To my surprise, her usually wry, sometimes combative expression changes, and she takes another step toward me.

She whispers, "Have you been approached about this 'Combination' yet?"

So I'm not the only one, I think. Who is running this Combination, and what's their endgame? And why are the highest of high-end brothels, like mine and the one Diamond Lil runs, being targeted? It simply doesn't make sense, even from a business perspective.

But I hesitate before I reply. How should I answer? I don't trust Diamond Lil as far as I can throw her. Yet I need to know what she knows, and I won't get anything out of her unless I give a little.

I take a leap, but only a small one. "I have."

"Me, too." She pauses, undoubtedly weighing her next move as carefully as I did. "Were you approached by a redheaded gentleman?"

"If you could call his visit to my house an approach," I reply. "And if he qualifies as a gentleman."

Lil chuckles in response, saying, "He sure knows how to make an entrance and charm a gal."

"That he does," I say. Knowing it's my turn to offer a bit more, I add, "Have you seen him or any of his friends since he delivered his invitation?"

"Yes, have you?"

"Yes, which leaves me a bit on edge on when he may pop in again. And with who."

"Same."

"Do we know who else the redhead might be working with?"

Her face grows more serious, and the pause before her answer gets longer and longer. Lil's back must be against the wall, or she'd never take the next step toward trusting me. "I've heard a rumor from a friend. That the Combination is being formed by Lucky Luciano. The whole thing is his idea, part of his plan to oversee every racket in the city."

Any hope I harbored that Murph is a minor gangster trying to gather and control the city's prostitutes disappears. If this endeavor has been orchestrated and blessed by the kingpin himself, I don't stand a chance at staying independent. Or getting out. In that moment, I realize that Dutch was right: I will never be allowed to leave this life.

I lean against the wall and close my eyes, absorbing Lil's words. When I open them again, she's gone. As I knew she'd be. There may come a time when we must unite against a common enemy—one that threatens to undo all we've built—but that time is not now.

In the meantime, I have only one choice, and it won't involve fleeing the madam life. Since it seems I can't live my reputation down, I'll have to live up to it.

CHAPTER NINETEEN

EUNICE

New York, New York
November 10, 1935

"Born Salvatore Luciano," the chief says as he stands in front of the meeting room, composed and impeccable. "But better known as Charles 'Lucky' Luciano. He is the new target of our investigations."

The name sends a ripple through the room. We're familiar with Lucky.

Still, Dewey gives us a profile. "He's thirty-seven years old, born in Italy, but he's been living in New York since he was nine. This city is where he's made his money, everything from drug peddling to the most savage of murders.

"Luciano is the one who called for Schultz's last meal to become a massacre. It was a bloody scene. The murderers opened fire and didn't stop until their clips were empty. It was overkill. Luciano was sending a message.

"This man is no ordinary tommy-gun-wielding hoodlum. While Schultz used brawn, Luciano uses his brain, and that makes him not only far more dangerous but more elusive. He knows how to keep his hands clean. To this point, he's built an organization so layered that he's untouchable . . . or so he thinks." The chief pauses and glances at me. "We are now seeking to imprison one of the most cold-blooded criminals alive. And understand that while he is more thoughtful and calculating than Dutch Schultz, Luciano won't hesitate to have anyone gunned down. Any questions?" With no response, Dewey continues. "The first order of business is to see if your rackets have been taken over by Lucky; in those instances, your investigations might be salvageable. Even if we have to start over in some areas, we will win this. We will use subpoenas and warrants . . ."

In my mind, I add, *And wiretaps.*

When Dewey glances at me again and gives me a curt nod, it's almost as if he's reading my mind. I understand why he didn't mention the wiretaps—the fewer people who know about this, the better. I agree with Dewey's caution. For the sake of what I'm building, this cannot leak.

"We will fight this war with every legal weapon at our disposal. And one last thing. While we are certain Luciano ordered the hit on Schultz, we're not chasing justice for a dead man. Our focus remains on bringing the Mob down for extortion, gambling, drugs . . . and the other, typical rackets."

Dewey dismisses us, and Murray and I fall into stride. His voice drops to a whisper. "Now that we have a target, those wiretaps could become our lifeline to Luciano, if he's the one in charge. Have you listened to any?"

"Not yet. I begin right after lunch," I say. "The monitoring room was only ready this morning. We're using the storage closet at the end of the hallway. Dewey had the room gutted and sealed tight. And yesterday, he handpicked Lisa LaFrance and another secretary to cover shifts to record the live conversations when I'm not in there."

"This is some operation because of you," Murray says, sounding impressed. "Let's hope we get something from those taps. But I'm still convinced it all comes back to the girls. Have you spoken to anyone else?"

"Not yet."

"Even with all the evidence you're gathering and the wiretaps, if we can get one woman to talk, I believe that will be the key," Murray pushes.

That was exactly what I hoped when I visited Polly Adler all those months ago. But she showed me just how thick and unbreakable the walls around this world are.

Twilight has long gone, but Lenox Avenue is still pulsing with the rhythm of Harlem when I step out of the subway. I pull the mink collar of my coat higher against my neck and bow my head as I push through the wind gusts on 145th Street. As I move, my mind wanders to the scratchy voices that I strained to hear through the wiretaps all afternoon.

I was thrilled, at first, when I sat in front of that switchboard with the bulky earphones clamped tight over my head. But it didn't take long for frustration to set in. I'd expected the voices caught in telephone calls to be crisp. But instead, Jesse Jacobs' and Abe Karp's conversations drifted in and out, most of the time foggy and garbled as if they were mumbling from the bottom of the ocean.

And I hadn't expected all of the other sounds—the hiss of the static, and voices from other lines tangling with theirs. Sometimes they spoke so low, I half wanted to pick up the telephone, ring them directly, and tell them to repeat themselves—and this time, speak louder. I chuckle as I reach St. Nicholas Avenue. Wouldn't that have been a laugh?

When I round the corner, the sounds of the city—the bark of the street vendors and the blaring car horns—are swallowed by the hush of my Sugar Hill neighborhood. The sudden quiet prickles my nerves. My gaze sweeps to the left, then the right, skimming the shadows that darken the stoops and alleyways. I shiver, but I push it aside. Surely I'm only feeling a little unnerved because of my day, first learning that Luciano is our new target, and then the hours I spent on the wiretaps.

Still, I quicken my steps, hurrying to get to the warmth—and safety—of my own front door. I should have taken a taxicab home. Not that any would have stopped for me downtown. Not for a colored lady, and not at this hour. But if I'd had the sense to plan ahead, I could have called Edward Johnson and his colored jitney service, the one Lisle and I often rely on when New York cabs won't bother to slow down for folks like us.

I exhale when I see the soft glow from the light of my building's entrance, but then a tall white man steps from the lobby. It's not unusual to see white folks in this neighborhood. A few even still live in the building.

But the man is wearing dark glasses that I can see from yards away. A white man in dark glasses at night. My gut squeezes, and every warning rushes me at once—Schultz, Luciano, and the note slipped to me by the shoeshine boy.

I wrap my fingers tightly around my briefcase handle. This will be my weapon. My eyes do not leave the man as he strolls closer. When we are inches apart, he touches the brim of his fedora and gives me a polite smile before he continues on his way.

My shoulders loosen just enough for me to breathe. Surely that wasn't one of Luciano's hired thugs—or was it? I couldn't ever recall a white man tipping his hat at me.

"Stop it, Eunice," I murmur as I step into the lobby.

I glance to the left, where Mr. Meeks is speaking to two gentlemen. "Good evening, Mrs. Carter," the doorman shouts out. "I apologize for the door—"

I wave his words away, then cross the lobby to the elevator, where I greet the elevator operator. It is not until the gate rattles shut that I feel complete relief. I draw in a steadying breath and chide myself. It is good to stay vigilant, but I cannot flinch at every shadow or stranger. This is New York City, for heaven's sake.

As the chamber rises, my mind shifts to what I might face with Lisle tonight. Once again, I'm guessing I'll spend the evening alone. Since I backed out on Martha's Vineyard, Lisle has found reasons to remain in his office long past normal hours. He claims he's had late clients, but I imagine him at the Harlem Forum letting bourbon drown out the silence that has settled between us. If I weren't a teetotaler, I'd have grabbed Regina and ducked into the nearest local bar to toss back a few Bee's Knees myself. I'm a gangbuster by day, but the real battle is in my home at night. The divide between Lisle and me is widening, and I am at a loss as to how to change our course.

Mr. Walker bids me a good night when I exit the elevator. But just steps away from my front door, I pause. A postal box sits at my doorstep. Why didn't Mr. Meeks hold this for me downstairs?

Then I glimpse the return address: 233 Broadway. What in blazes is this? I just left the office, and Lisa, my secretary, didn't mention posting a parcel to my home.

With a sigh, I slip into my apartment and flick on the foyer light. Perhaps there is something that Dewey or Murray wanted me to read and they forgot to mention it.

I rest the box on the dining room table, then find a paring knife and slice through the box's string.

I lift the box's flaps—and freeze. Inside sits a white doll, its cloth face smeared with black ink. The eyes have been gouged out and the mouth sealed with gray tape.

The rush of my blood pounds in my ears. This was delivered right to my doorstep. But by whom? In an instant, I see the white man in front of my building. Was it him? How did he get to my door? And if he could reach my door, what would stop him from breaking into my apartment?

"Eunice."

I scream and spin, gripping the knife in my hand, ready to strike. But just as I raise my arm to plunge forward, I see it is only my husband. "Lisle"—I can barely get his name out—"what are you doing here?"

"I'm sorry. I didn't mean to startle you."

"No," I say, placing the knife on the table. "I didn't know you were home."

"I wanted to come home early tonight because I don't like what's happening between us."

His words are like a balm, untangling the knot in my chest. But then Lisle glances past me, and I shift, trying to hide the box from his view. "What's that?"

"Just . . . some papers . . . I brought home . . . from the office," I stammer as I fold the flaps shut. Lisle can never see what's inside this box.

"Oh," he says, "I was hoping we could have dinner tonight . . . and talk."

"Really?" His words steady me even more. "I'd like that, Lisle. I can have dinner ready in about an hour."

Once again, he glances over my shoulder. "You brought work home."

"This can wait." Looking straight into his eyes, I add, "I'd much rather have dinner with you."

"Good." His grin spreads wide as he steps closer. "But I don't want you fussing in the kitchen. Let's go out to the Hotel Theresa for dinner."

"I'd love that. Can you give me a few minutes to freshen up?" I say, briefly turning away from him and grabbing the box.

The box is between us when he presses a quick kiss to my lips. "Take all the time you need, sweetheart. I'll be right here when you're ready."

CHAPTER TWENTY

POLLY

New York, New York
January 12, 1936

I've known Lucky by reputation for years, of course. Even though I've never been formally introduced. You can't run in the sort of circles I do and not know the infamous boss of all bosses, or even spot him across the room in a nightclub from time to time. And I could claim a sort of tangential relationship with him, in that when he's wanted to impress and entertain out-of-town guests, he has requested a couple of my girls to visit the gents' hotel rooms. But that's a far sight from knowing the man. As now I do. Quite unluckily.

I study Lucky as he holds court at the King Tut bar. His silvery-gray pin-striped suit is handmade from the finest wool, tailored to perfection, and his distinctive oxfords can only have been made by the famed British shoemaker John Lobb, whose one-hundred-and-ninety-step process entails the creation of exact replicas of clients' feet, called lasts. When Lucky arrived earlier, I helped him slip off his cashmere overcoat and detected the scent of a Clive Christian cologne, one of the priciest and most exclusive British fragrances out there. With one sidelong glance and one inhale, an observer might mistake Lucky for an English gentleman, and I guess that's the point. But an assessment of his demeanor and a long gander at his face would change all that.

He has an air of quiet, almost polite menace, which I find much more terrifying than Dutch's obvious seething. I never know where I stand with Lucky. Neither his unsettling bearing nor his hard-as-nails gaze, however, instills as much fear in me as his scar.

A simple scar wouldn't faze me. I see all sorts of defacement in here, and my girls get up close and personal glimpses, of course. Sometimes, we laugh about it at the kitchen table before we turn in for the day. But Lucky's disfigurement is of an entirely different nature. The angry, red, raised mark runs from one ear to another and connects across his neck. If the rumors are correct, rival mobsters slit his throat from ear to ear when he tried to encroach on their territory and left him for dead. No one, and I mean no one, lives through that sort of slashing. The fact that he survived an unsurvivable wound—leaving him with that grisly scar, a droopy eye, and a fierce notoriety—launched his nickname, "Lucky." And it telegraphs his indomitable character.

Lucky nods in my direction, a signal that I should scamper over. It simply won't do to keep the *capo di tutti capi* waiting, particularly in front of his guests. He doesn't make a habit out of appearing at my house; he certainly doesn't make it his office, as Dutch did. Instead, he pops in when he has a special client or celebrity visitor that he wants to influence, not that he needs to do much swaying given his role as Mob boss. The rest of the time, Lucky leaves his thugs to mind "the shop," as they've taken to calling my place, and wreak all sorts of damage.

All this, I can tolerate. What I cannot bear are the Combination practices Lucky has recently instituted elsewhere. How I'm going to handle the gossiped-about consolidation when it comes my way, I haven't quite figured out.

"This is *the* Polly Adler," Lucky says to the man standing opposite him before I can even offer them another drink or one of the special Cuban cigars I've set aside.

Lucky then gestures to me as if I were a well-dressed mannequin at Bergdorf's wearing a pricey fur he's about to purchase. Again, this I can take, if it keeps the peace. If it gives my girls and my house a modicum of protection.

"I am indeed," I say, waiting to be introduced. But Lucky doesn't bother to share the other fellow's name with me, another well-dressed gangster, by the looks of him. And the man doesn't bother to greet me; he just stares me up and down.

I stand stock-still, awaiting my next instruction. The man returns his gaze to Lucky, disgust flashing on his face.

"She's got the best girls in town? This woman? She's hardly a looker."

Lucky chortles. "She don't need to be a looker to offer up lookers to us gents."

My stomach roils at these insults, delivered as if I am not standing right in front of them. These days, I've grown used to entertaining the crème de la crème—American blue bloods, stars of the stage, famous singers, noted writers, even the odd British aristocrat—and I've become used to their slights. But they're never quite so crass, and this stings.

Endure it I must, so I keep my expression even and my smile in place. This placid expression is what Lucky sees when he turns to me and says, "Anyway, Polly is the best madam in the city."

Is this meant to smooth over his guest's comments? Or Lucky's own? I doubt it. I'm just another cog in his grand machine of consolidating crime and vice.

The man puts his drink down on the bar, crosses his arms, and announces, "Then I'd like to have the very best girl. Bring her to me."

Giving them my broadest smile and coyest glance, I trot out the usual patter. “All my girls are the very best. Which one you’d prefer is a matter of taste. And we cater to all tastes.”

“I like a girl who’s game for anything.” The man actually licks his lips as he says this, a vile gesture that my usual clients would never make. Then he has the audacity to rub his hands together expectantly. I do not want to give any of my girls over to this man.

Hoping that a delay might temper his appetite, I say, “I’d be happy to introduce you to a few of them. They’re currently busy but should be available quite soon.”

This is a lie. Virginia happens to be free, awaiting her standing ten-o’clock-Friday-night client, who will not arrive for nearly another hour.

Lucky’s face whips toward me, and he reaches for my upper arm. Squeezing it so tightly it nearly takes my breath away, he seethes, “I’m sure you can rustle up your very best girl for my friend right now.”

He releases my arm, and I stumble backward. “Of c-course,” I stammer, then right myself and weave through the room toward the staircase.

The Lion meets me there, and we walk up together. “Heat’s turning up, is it?” she mutters, having seen the exchange between me and Lucky.

“Yup,” I answer, keeping my lips tight in case Lucky is watching.

“Matter of time, from what we’ve heard,” she replies. Since Dutch died, the gossip about Lucky’s actions as the head of the Combination has grown and become fearsome. Streetwalkers have been rounded up and reallocated all over the city, and smaller whorehouses have folded as their girls are combined into newly formed, midsized brothels, all under the command of Lucky and his central bookers, who dole out assignments to the girls on a day-by-day, hour-by-hour, and, in some cases, minute-by-minute basis. Only bigger, more exclusive houses like mine and Diamond Lil's have escaped this consolidation. So far.

We push open Virginia's door, stepping inside her apple-green-and-peach-colored bedchamber and closing the door behind us. The blond-haired beauty is lounging on the bed, smoking, and reading a celebrity magazine, all without smudging her crimson lipstick. "You two look a fright," she says with a giggle.

"Lucky's here—" the Lion starts.

"He's always here these days," Virginia interrupts with a roll of her eyes.

How can she be so flippant? We would only be in here if we were worried, and she knows that. "He wants you to meet with some man he's got with him. Someone he wants to impress," I say, hoping to instill some urgency in Virginia.

"I can handle that," she says with a shrug, grinding out her cigarette in the crystal ashtray on her nightstand.

"This is Lucky Luciano we are talking about," the Lion says, not bothering to mask her irritation at Virginia's lightness.

The lanky blonde pushes herself to standing. Her frothy white robe swirls around her ankles as she towers over us. "Ladies, if I could handle Dutch Schultz's loathsome men, I can handle Lucky's guest."

Swinging open her door with a dramatic slam, Virginia pauses on the landing overlooking King Tut's bar. Waiting until every eye in the room is upon her, she slowly sashays down the stairs. The Lion and I remain on the top step, taking in the scene and holding our collective breath. Virginia has got to be able to pull this off.

A path opens for her amidst the crowd as she saunters toward the bar. Sidling up to Lucky, Virginia holds out a cigarette for his guest to light. The threesome chat for a minute while the Lion and

I watch. And then Virginia's body becomes erect as the scene grows tense.

I hurry down the stairs. Signaling to my barman to pour two champagnes lickety-split, I approach Virginia, Lucky, and the man. "I see you gents have met Virginia," I say, keeping my tone merry and offering them the drinks.

"She is a beaut," the man says, never taking his eyes off her.

"I am glad you find Virginia pleasing," I reply.

Lucky says, "In fact, he finds her so pleasing that he'd like to install her at his local brothel."

"It's no Polly's, but it's close to my business in New Jersey," he says almost apologetically to Virginia. Then to Lucky, he says with a leer, "It may be a bit too close to the wife for comfort, but that way, I can see this whore whenever I like."

I give Virginia a sidelong glance, and her eyes are wild. Just then, I feel her hand on my hand, secretly pleading for this to stop. "My apologies, sir, but Virginia lives and works here. She has for years. But you are welcome to see her here whenever you like. I'll make certain she is always free for you. I'll even send her to you whenever you wish."

Lucky slams the crystal champagne flute down on the bar so hard that the stem breaks and golden liquid spills everywhere. "Virginia is my whore, not yours, Polly. And I will say where she lives and works from now on."

Lucky reaches for Virginia's arm and begins tugging her toward the secret bookshelf door, the man right behind them. Virginia resists, twisting and turning back toward me. All the rage simmering beneath my surface—rage over my loss of power, rage over my inability to protect my girls, rage over being forced into this life because my family sent me to this country at twelve when I was innocent and vulnerable—bursts forth. I race toward Lucky and yell, "She will stay here."

Lucky freezes, his left hand still on Virginia's arm. He pivots toward me and, with his right hand, punches me in the face.

And then everything goes black.

CHAPTER TWENTY-ONE

EUNICE

New York, New York
January 12, 1936

"I HOPE THAT smile on your face is because you're thinking of me," Lisle says as he climbs into bed, wearing the black silk pajamas I gave him for Christmas.

"Always," I say. "I'm always thinking of you."

He joins me, leaning against the headboard, and takes my hand. "We had a good day." This has become our nightly ritual. An assessment of our time together.

Indeed, today has been wonderful, beginning with services at the Abyssinian Baptist Church, before we joined Regina and William at Tillie's Chicken Shack, where our husbands debated whether the menu mainstay—chicken and waffles—belonged on the same plate. But it was when Lisle and I returned home that we shared our most precious moments, lounging in the parlor, leafing through *The New York Times*, *The Amsterdam News*, and *The New Yorker*.

"I'm guessing your workload will get heavier now that the holidays are over." He speaks as if he's stating a fact, but it feels like a question—will our life return to what it was before?

It is true that the investigation—at least my part—has slowed because of the calendar. The brothels have been quieter through Christmas. Even the wiretaps have yielded little more than attorneys, bondsmen, and bookers chatting about their conquests.

I weigh my words before I say, "It will be busy again, but I don't want that to change anything with us."

"I know you don't."

"I promise to put us first."

He hesitates before he softly says, "Please don't make promises you can't keep." His voice has an edge I haven't heard in weeks. But he lightens up when he adds, "Let's just say this has been a fine holiday." He draws me to him. "All that was missing was—"

"Our son." I complete his sentence. "I wish we could have visited Barbados."

"I know. But three weeks away wasn't possible for either of us right now. And . . . from his letters and the telegrams from your mother, I can tell he's happy." There is a quiet acknowledgment in his tone. "It seems it was right for your mother to go to Barbados."

This is as near to an *I stand corrected* as I'm ever likely to hear from Lisle. I hug him, and he kisses my forehead, then clicks off the bedside lamp. I sink into his arms. As I close my eyes, my thoughts drift across these weeks that have felt like a promise kept. It's been this way since that night Lisle and I had dinner at the Hotel Theresa.

I now have the connection I so dearly wanted and Lisle and I so badly needed. But this peace would have never come to us if Lisle had known about the doll.

When I informed Dewey, who's been facing threats of his own, about the doll, he wasn't terribly concerned but did insist that I take precautionary measures, like traveling to and from work by car instead of opening myself up to the greater danger of public transport.

However, the weight of my regret has taken root within me. I hate that I can only have this contentment with my husband if he doesn't know my truth.

Just as I drift off, the shrill sound of the telephone startles us from sleep. Lisle leaps from the bed, and I grab my housecoat, scurrying behind him into the front hall. There is never any good news behind a call at midnight. I silently pray, *Please, Lord. Let my son and my mother be safe.*

I hold my breath and bow my head as Lisle answers, and then, silence. Until he hands the telephone receiver to me.

I press the telephone to my ear. "I'm sorry to disturb you, Mrs. Carter, but this is Officer Calcagnini from the 30th Precinct. We've got a girl here who says she wants to speak with you."

"With me?" I ask, lowering myself to the chair.

"She asked to speak to the district attorney, but I knew Dodge wouldn't come down here. Not at this hour. And anyway, none of these streetwalkers have ever asked to speak to the DA, Mrs. Carter."

"Did she say anything else besides wanting to speak with someone?"

"Only that she has something to say. But she looks like she needs help badly, and I didn't want to just lock her up. Not with the way she came in here. So I thought of you."

Officer Arthur Bernard Calcagnini was one of the first men I met when I began volunteering in the Women's Court and the only one who made me feel welcomed. My first day there, his brows had arched high when he realized I was an attorney. But before I left court that day, he caught up to me in the hallway just to say, "My granddaughter wants to be a lady lawyer someday."

"We picked her up running down 37th Street," he continues, "like hell was on her heels. But if you think I should just put her in a cell—"

"No, Officer, it's fine." Something made Officer Calcagnini call me. I trust his instincts—and I trust mine. I've needed to speak to one of the girls. This one is a streetwalker, not one of the girls working in a brothel, protected by a madam like Polly or Red Sadie. So it's doubtful she will know anything about the workings of the racket. But maybe the Combination extends to streetwalkers, too.

"I'll be right there. Thank you for calling me."

I hang up and turn, nearly bumping into Lisle. That quickly, I forgot my husband. "Where are you going?"

"There's someone at the police station," I say. "She could be an important witness."

His narrowed eyes and pinched brow tell me everything. But all he says is "I'll drive you," and he turns away.

I am grateful that this didn't become another variation of our same quarrel. But still, I know that with that telephone call, our peace has come undone.

I ENTER THE interrogation room and see the girl sitting alone at the small wooden table. She holds a cigarette, but it's unlit. Her hand is trembling so much, I doubt she could smoke it anyway.

The sight of her is shocking . . . one eye is swollen purple and blue; her lip is split and crusted with dried blood. From the scrapes on her face and arms to the cut above her right eye, this looks less like a beating and more like someone was trying to finish her off. How did she even get away?

Finally, she glances up, and her glassy eyes narrow at the sight of me. I see the question in her eyes: *What is this colored woman doing here when I asked for the district attorney?*

But she looks familiar to me. Perhaps I've seen her in Women's Court.

I slide into a chair across from her. "I'm Assistant District Attorney Eunice Carter." Her eyes flicker with disbelief. "What's your name?"

Pulling out a dinged-up lighter from the pocket of her torn robe, she attempts to light her cigarette, her hand trembling like a leaf in a breeze. "Virginia," she says as the cigarette tip finally catches and begins to smolder.

Officer Calcagnini said she was picked up on the street, but Virginia's appearance says otherwise. She is dressed in what was, probably only hours ago, a very elegant (and expensive) fur-trimmed sheer robe over a barely there nightie. Her slippers are dainty, made for the bedroom, certainly not designed to take a single step on the sidewalk.

Even bruised and beaten, the blue-eyed Marlene Dietrich look-alike is stunning. And even now, her blond hair falls in cascading waves around her shoulders.

Her regal bearing. Her delicate nightclothes. What was she doing on the streets?

"Virginia, do you need to see a doctor?"

She shakes her head as she inhales deeply.

"I understand you wanted to speak with someone from the district attorney's office?"

She nods.

"I'm here."

She studies me, her cigarette smoke curling between us. "I've never seen a colored lawyer before." When I meet her gaze but say nothing, she continues. "But then, no one's ever hit me before either." She gingerly touches her face.

"Who did this to you?"

"I was just supposed to entertain a man," she says, sidestepping my question. "He wanted to impress one of his friends." Her trembling fades as she stubs out her cigarette hard. Now her voice is steel. "I won't let him or anyone else treat me this way!"

"Who?" My voice is low, not wanting to rattle her.

Virginia sits taller, juts her chin. "I won't ever let Lucky—"

Lucky!

Before she can continue, we turn at the hard rap on the door.

Officer Calcagnini steps into the room. "Her attorney is here to post her bail."

Virginia draws her brows together and panic flares in her eyes. "I didn't call anyone," she whispers to me.

I turn to the officer. "Why would her attorney be here? She hasn't seen a judge or been charged. There is no bail."

He shrugs. "I told him all of that, but he's demanding to see his client."

"Who?" Virginia's voice hitches. "Who's asking to see me?"

"Abe Karp. He's with another lawyer, but Karp is doing all the talking."

Virginia shrieks. Her chair screeches across the floor as she shoves herself away from the table—and from me. She scrambles to the corner and huddles there, drawing her knees to her chest.

"Virginia," I whisper as I motion for the officer to leave us alone.

Her eyes glisten with fear. "Please. You can't send me out there. He's not my lawyer. He's only here because—" She stops, gasping for air.

I step closer. "Because what, Virginia? He's only here because . . ."

"Because someone sent him. Please, Mrs. Carter. He's only here because someone sent him to kill me!"

CHAPTER TWENTY-TWO

POLLY

New York, New York
January 13, 1936

I AM BACK in the factory in Brooklyn. My hands hold a piece of machinery over two parts of a soldier's shirt, ready to stitch the arm and body together. My fingers appear so youthful that I'm taken aback for a long moment. Then I return to myself and the factory, remembering there is work to do. Even though I just turned seventeen, I've been promoted to this machinery position, placing me in charge of the girls who were sewing the shirt uniform sections by hand. I am proud; after all, I came to this country all alone from Russia only five years ago, without a word of English. But sometimes, I wonder. Is this the sort of success for which my father sent me to America? After all, I send back home every penny I can, but no one else has come aside from Ben, who I've never seen, as he was sent to Chicago. Would my father truly believe this factory work and the pittance I'm able to ship to my family is worth the sacrifice he forced upon me—giving up my hard-won academic scholarship to the Gymnazia at Pinsk? An education that could have me well on the way to an actual profession, like teaching, by now?

Finishing up the last shirt in my pile, I stare down the row, wondering when the others will have pieces ready for me. Woman after woman, girl after girl, all bend low over their work areas, squinting to use needle and thread in the low light of this grubby factory. The more shirts we make, the more money we make. And I, for one, will be in dire need of more money soon.

I glance over at my friend Sidonia, who heads up another machine and another row of girls and women and is my main ally here at the factory. We smile at each other, and Sidonia gives me a playful shimmy. A nod to our Sunday afternoons spent in the dance halls with all the other young people. An activity I haven't felt up to for several weeks.

"You wanted to talk to me? Come to my office now," a low, deep voice says quietly. I do not need to glance up from my machine to know who stands beside me. It is the new foreman, Frank, the one with the dark swoop of hair and piercing blue eyes I used to find attractive. The one who was the focus of my daydreams. Until six Saturdays ago.

My heart pounds and my palms sweat as I follow him, every eye upon us. Earlier today, I asked to speak with him privately, but now I regret it. I'd felt certain that he wouldn't act here as he had that Saturday, but seeing him up close, I'm not so sure. I become even less positive when he closes the door behind us, and I am faced with this man—this monster—alone.

My fingers instinctively flutter to my cheek and then my eye, where the bruises he gave me have barely healed. Six weeks ago, I accepted his invitation to Coney Island, walking on air that this man I fancied might actually fancy me back. Heedlessly, I'd followed him to an empty cottage near Coney Island where he'd "left a few things." When I resisted him, his fists came out.

Frank faces me, his hands on his hips. Staring me up and down with now-reptilian eyes, he says, "Came back for a little more of what I gave you?"

He hasn't moved toward me, but I feel the menace coming off him as if he stood an inch away.

"No," I say, backing away. But then I stop. "I came to demand you do your duty."

"What the hell are you talking about?"

"You got me pregnant," I answer, trying everything in my power to stand firm and keep my voice from wavering. What I must say next is odious to me, but what other choice do I have? My distant and cold cousin Lena, with whom I now live—after moving to New York from Massachusetts a few years back—has made it plain she does not condone unwed mothers and would toss me out of the apartment I share with her and her family if she knew my situation. She doesn't like me as it is. "Now you have to marry me."

"You? You think I'd marry you?" Frank starts laughing, a horrible, raspy sound. "Anyway, there are probably a dozen guys who could have knocked you up. A Yiddish whore like you."

I hold back the tears. "You were the first and the only. It is your duty."

The laughter stops, and his smile vanishes. He takes one long step toward me, and I can feel his hot breath on my face. Just as I did that terrible Saturday night. "I will never, ever marry you. In fact, I won't keep you on as an employee. We don't employ unmarried pregnant girls at this factory."

In one rough movement, he spins me around and takes a hold of my shirt collar from the back. Slamming his office door open, he pushes me down past the rows of girls and women and marches me off the factory floor. The squeal of chair legs on cement sounds out as my fellow factory workers scramble to follow us. To watch this awful spectacle.

We reach the main factory door, then the heavy metal gates through which I've passed for the past year. Holding me with one hand and opening the gate with the other, Frank pushes me outside—and toward the rough sidewalk.

A stifled cry sounds out from a girl standing behind him, and a grumbling begins to build. "Pearl." I hear Sidonia call out my real name—not the name I call myself in the dance halls or in the factory—as I fall to my knees.

Frank turns away from me to them. "Any one of you that steps through these gates to help Polly here will suffer her same fate. A shove to the ground and a firing. Do you understand me?"

As I push myself to standing, brushing pebbles off my bloodied knees, I watch as the girls and women file back into the factory. Sidonia shoots me a pitying look—she knows what Frank did to me—but scurries back inside. Jobs are scarce, and these women and girls support not only themselves but their families. And now there is a terrible stain upon me, one they will not want to spread to themselves. Even as word about my condition spreads throughout our area.

Alone, I limp away from the factory, toward an uncertain future.

GASPING, I LUNGE forward in my bed. I am suddenly, terribly awake, although the painful tentacles of the familiar dream still have a hold on me. My head throbs, and when I reach up to touch my face, I feel something wet around my swollen nose. When I remove my hand, my fingers are sticky with metallic-smelling blood. Lucky's first punch landed square on my nose. He must have also struck me in the eye and on the forehead before I hit the ground, because my temple throbs and I cannot fully open my left eye.

My bedroom door opens, and the Lion tiptoes in, a cloth in one hand and a basin in the other. She settles the items on my nightstand and sits on the edge of my bed. Dipping the cloth into the water, she wrings it out and dabs it around my nose. "He got you good, Polly."

"Don't I know it," I answer, clutching my temple. Even the slight increase in illumination from the hallway light makes my head pulse in excruciating pain. "I feel worse than a night up drinking with Dutch."

"Lucky ain't no Dutch."

"So I've learned."

"The hard way," she mutters, unnecessarily, I think.

"Is Virginia back?" Never mind my head, I need to know she's okay.

"Not yet."

"Any word from her?"

"No," the Lion says. "And I've got my network listening."

The Lion has a fierce clan of women like her. Women on the fringes who've been welcomed in by someone else on the fringes. They keep tabs on each other and all of us.

"I've got to make sure she's okay." I try to sit up, but it's too painful.

"We can't let him take our girls," the Lion says. She is the closest to crying I've ever seen her—except that one fateful time. "Can't let him corral every girl in the city into one big group and dole them out through bookers to different brothels or men every night. That's not right."

With the Lion's words, the dream returns, along with the terror and anger and sorrow and shame I felt when Frank tossed me out of the factory. Emotions that have followed me ever since, fueling my future. I will never allow my girls to experience that. I will never permit my girls to be treated in the dismissive, subhuman manner

I endured. I didn't choose to be in this business—my father's decision to ship me off to America and Frank's rape and my cousin Lena's eviction and the rumors about my pregnancy and a back-alley abortion took care of that. But I did choose to run my house differently. And I have no intention of letting anyone—even Lucky Luciano—take that away from me.

CHAPTER TWENTY-THREE

EUNICE

New York, New York
January 14, 1936

Abe Karp's and Jesse Jacobs' laughter crackles through the earphones, yanking me from my thoughts. I'm not sure how much I've missed. Too much. I cannot allow my mind to drift this way. These wiretaps are too valuable to squander. Still, I toss the earphones onto the table. I need a moment, just to steady myself.

It's difficult to focus when my thoughts keep rushing back to Virginia. Her last moments in the police station have haunted me for the past two nights.

Virginia had shaken with fear when I'd taken her hand and helped her to stand. But when I grabbed my coat from the back of the chair and draped it across her shoulders, she looked at me, puzzled. I reached for my pocketbook, pulled out all the cash I had, and folded the three dollars into Virginia's hand.

Then I summoned Officer Calcagnini back into the room. "We have no grounds to hold Virginia. Please release her through the back door."

For a moment, the officer studied me; then he nodded like I knew he would.

"Thank you," she whispered, and in a flash, the officer and Virginia were gone.

My steps carried the weight of my fear for Virginia as I paced. When Officer Calcagnini returned, I followed him down the corridor, stopping short of entering the waiting area.

From the shadows, I watched the policeman talk to Karp.

"I'm sorry," Officer Calcagnini said. "There's no one back there named Virginia."

"What are you talking about?" Karp growled in a tone I'd often heard him use on the wiretaps. "You said she was here."

"I thought you were talking about someone else." The officer stayed steadfast. "I checked the list of girls brought in tonight. No Virginia here."

Karp glared at the cop, then barged toward the corridor where I'd hidden. I pressed my back against the wall, shrinking into the shadows as Officer Calcagnini blocked Karp.

Karp shouted, "I'm going back there to check for myself."

"I can't let you do that." The policeman stared down Karp until the attorney backed away.

Only when Karp exited the station did I breathe.

Ever since, I've been troubled with questions about what happened. How had Karp known that Virginia was there? Had they somehow followed her from where the cops picked her up? Or were the eyes of the Mob in that police station—although I'm confident Officer Calcagnini isn't part of any conspiracy. And the question that torments me: Did Virginia get away? Is she safe now?

I'd hoped that maybe Karp would have mentioned Virginia on the wiretaps, but nothing has come through about her.

I sigh. If only I'd had just five more minutes with Virginia. She'd been so close to revealing something vital, I'm certain of that: *I won't ever let Lucky*—but then the knock on the door finished what she'd started to say. I had to let her go, even if it meant losing a promising piece of evidence.

Still, she'd said the name Lucky. It had to be Lucky Luciano. And this would be our first connection to him and the prostitution racket. But Virginia's statement is not enough, and I cannot share what she said with anyone without revealing what I did.

I try to push the memory aside. I cannot dwell on that missed opportunity, not when new leads are unfolding before me.

Shifting the earphones back into place, I will myself to focus. I hear the hiss of air, then the voice I've come to recognize as Abe Karp, especially after hearing him at the precinct. "Pete's got those girls running double shifts now. They're working harder than factory hands."

The two men explode with laughter as though Karp's words were the cleverest ever spoken.

"Pete brings in the numbers." The other man, Jesse Jacobs, wheezes, sounding like he's choking on his chuckles. "You gotta hand it to him; he flips those girls faster than a cook down at Schrafft's flips flapjacks. If he brings them in before noon, they're on their backs before sundown."

"That's what keeps the cash rolling in," Karp snorts. "I don't care if he works them till they drop dead in the gutter. There're plenty more where those whores come from."

This time, their laughter sounds vicious, and my stomach twists. I have to force my pencil to keep moving, to write down all that I've heard.

From these wiretaps, I've learned that Pete is Pete Harris, a booker and a central figure to the operation. Apparently, Harris and the other bookers manage this racket like a finely tuned enterprise—organizing, coordinating, and dispatching the girls between the brothels with precision. This finding has given me more than a glimpse into this corner of the business—it's brought me one step closer to Luciano.

Pete Harris is more than just a top booker. According to Murray, Harris is rumored to be an associate of Luciano's. Of course, rumors don't stand up as evidence in court, but a wiretapped conversation linking Harris and Luciano will.

"I was with one last night, a real looker with a big mouth," Karp says, dragging my mind back to their filth. "Had to slap her around a couple of times. Told her she was being paid to keep her legs open and her mouth shut."

The disgust rises like bile in my throat. This is the difficult part—hearing men speak about these girls as if they're nothing more than meat to be chewed up, then spit out. Every day since I started listening to these tapes, I remind myself that this is the path to justice.

When I return to the conversation, Karp and Jacobs have drifted from their crass talk to the bolts of their business. They discuss upcoming cases, arrange bonds, and sort through the stories they've given the girls in case any of them have to testify.

This is another thing I've come to understand from the wiretaps. The few times I've heard any of the girls represented by Rachlin testify in their defense, they all had a variation of the same story when asked why they were caught up in a raid.

"I don't know," they all said, and then would add another line: "I'm a student," "I'm a tourist," "I'm a model." And of course, none of them admitted to keeping company in a brothel: "I was at a party," "I was having dinner with my boyfriend," "I wasn't there. I don't know what you're talking about."

Finally, the wiretap line goes silent, and I exhale. Even though I have to trudge through the trash of their conversations, a chain is forming. From the wiretaps, I can tie Karp, Jacobs, and Harris—an attorney, bondsman, and booker—together in a corrupt scheme to organize the girls' prostitution activities. This would yield a charge of pandering—if we were so inclined—and bribery of the cops and the courts. In addition, I have Pete Harris' name mentioned enough times to justify another wiretap for him.

I want to listen to every man tied up in this racket. Eventually this will answer the question: Is this just a handful of bottom-feeders like Karp and Jacobs—which is what Dewey believes? Or is it what I believe in my gut—that this leads straight to the man at the top?

I gather my notes, and just as I prepare to turn off the machine, a scratch of static from the earphones catches my attention. Sliding the earphones back on, I hear Jacobs' voice first:

"Hey, I damn near forgot to ask you. Did you hear what Carmen pulled in court yesterday?" He laughs again. "I heard she asked for her ten dollars back for this week."

"I was there, and it wasn't funny." Karp's voice snaps like a whip.

"Ah, come on. If I was shelling out ten bucks a week for guaranteed bail and a suspended sentence, I'd be mad, too, after two nights in the can."

"Haven't you heard what happened to Viola when she shot her mouth off like that in court?" Karp continues, his voice lower, sharper. "Tommy the Bull handled her. . . ."

Quickly, I scratch: *Carmen . . . ten dollars/week . . . guaranteed bail . . . suspended sentences . . . Viola . . . Tommy the Bull.*

Karp says, "All of those girls know. Any one of them so much as whispers about the Combination, they'll have a date with the bottom of the Hudson."

My back stiffens, and I wait. What did Carmen say about the Combination? More silence, this time as heavy as a shroud. And neither man speaks again. Slowly, I remove the earphones.

The Combination. Words I was waiting to hear from these men.

But now my thoughts are with the girl named Viola . . . and

Tommy the Bull. What did he do to her? I close my eyes because I'm afraid to know—but I do. This is another name that's been mentioned before. Thomas Pennochio, once a bootlegger, now muscle at the top of the Mob's ranks. He could be another link in this chain getting us closer to Lucky Luciano.

I rise and collect my papers. But before I take a step, I bow my head and say a little prayer for Ginger and this girl who was mentioned today, Carmen. I hope neither met the same fate as Viola.

And then I take another moment and whisper a prayer for Virginia, too.

CHAPTER TWENTY-FOUR

POLLY

New York, New York
January 15, 1936

Billboards for Camel cigarettes promising to pick up your energy and others for Coca-Cola pledging ice-cold sunshine capture my eye with their riotous color. Buses and trolleys and automobiles compete with these advertisements for my attention with their incessant honking and rumbling and clanging. But, like the other passersby on the corner of 42nd Street and Fifth Avenue, I pay them no mind. I have a fixed goal—to find Virginia. Five days have passed since Lucky dragged her out my door, and we have neither seen nor heard from her. Not a call, not a note, not a rumor. Virginia seems to have vanished into thin air.

As I head west on 42nd Street, the brisk winter wind picks up, and the already down-at-heel neighborhood grows decidedly seedy. Just like I remember. In the weeks after I was thrown out of my cousin's apartment, I lived in a squalid, windowless basement room on this very street. After the long, fruitless days hoofing it through the city hunting for work, I'd spend the long terrifying nights in 42nd Street's dingy coffee shops, where I could stretch the hours with a single nickel cup of coffee and a single nickel doughnut.

Until I was down to my last nickel, anyway. It was then, in one of those coffee shops, I ran into Abe, a friend of a friend of Sidonia's.

Abe threw me a lifeline of sorts by introducing me to Joan Smith, a tall, icy blond, sapphire-eyed beauty with a penchant for opium and a desperate need for companionship. She, in turn, introduced me to the life of a kept woman. I moved into her nine-room apartment on Riverside Drive, rented for her by some Wall Street fellow, and became a sort of mascot for her and her circle, always ready with a joke and quick to pour drinks. I worried about my future; what if Joan tired of me? But then one of Joan's set, a bootlegger named Tony, asked if I'd keep an apartment on the Upper West Side where he and his friends could bring girls from time to time. And my career as a madam was born. Not before turning a few tricks myself, and not by choice. Those tricks made me determined to become a madam no longer under anyone's control—and different from the abusive and heartless madams, johns, and pimps I'd encountered.

I reach the alley that I passed countless times back in my destitute days, always averting my eyes from the activities taking place there. *How green I was,* I think, *and how priggish.* Today is different. I stride into the surprisingly empty alleyway, push on the nondescript door cut into the brick exterior of the building on the left, and enter the Elk Hotel.

No doorman or front desk receptionist greets me at this establishment, and I would never expect one. Only a brute of a man with a revolver tucked into his pants awaits me. This is a hot sheet hotel, where "guests" procured by a group of streetwalkers pay by the hour. Or, in some cases, by the half hour.

"Ginny here?" I ask the thug guarding the door.

"Who's asking?" he croaks.

"Polly."

"Polly what?"

"She'll know which Polly."

He shoots me a murderous look and ducks behind a curtain. One grumbled conversation later, a woman with unnaturally red hair pushes aside the tattered mauve fabric and steps out. "Well, well, well, I never thought I'd see *the* Polly Adler in my neck of the woods." Her tone is not kind or welcoming. It is acidic.

"Good evening to you, too, Ginny." Ginny and I go way back, to the days when I was running that very first Upper West Side apartment and she was one of Tony's girls. Now we are two very different sorts of madams in two very different worlds, and she is bitter and resentful.

"What the hell do you want, Polly?"

"One of my girls is missing. A pretty blonde who goes by Virginia?"

Ginny bursts into laughter. "And you think she'd land here?" She gestures around the dark, wretched entry of the hotel and gives me a mock curtsy before crossing her arms over her chest protectively. "Never seen some blond whore named Virginia. And if I had, I wouldn't let her in here if she told me she was one of yours, no matter if she begged. Now, get the hell out. I've got too much trouble breathing down my neck with the damnable Combination to tolerate your shenanigans. Or to worry about one lost girl."

It takes everything I have not to cry at another failed attempt to find Virginia. I've been reaching out to every brothel owner and pimp in New York and New Jersey I've ever heard of to see if Lucky farmed her out to one of them, but they all claim ignorance. As my search has gone on, I've decided that if I can't find out anything about Virginia from the people I encounter, I might at least find out more about this Combination. Information might help me protect my house and my girls from this new racket, even if it's too late for Virginia. So I'm learning about how this nefarious Combination is working—the way the bookers, lawyers, cops, bondsmen, and mobsters operate. I need to know what I'm up against. And it's worse than I imagined.

I take a leap and try to question Ginny. "So the Combination has got you in its grips, too?"

A single one of Ginny's drawn-in eyebrows rises. She's never liked me, a disdain that's grown in proportion to my success, but do I see some softening in her loathing and wariness?

"What of it?" she asks.

"I've just heard a lot of stories about this Combination getting into everyone's business as I've been out searching for my girl." I answer with this open-ended reply. I'll take whatever crumbs Ginny wants to dole out.

Her arms uncross, and she places her hands on her hips. Then she asks, "You see many johns in the alley? Run into many of my girls in the street out front?"

I shake my head slowly. The traditional territory of the Elk Hotel—the street, the alley, and the hotel itself—did seem oddly barren.

"That's because today my girls have all been moved to the docks to service some big cargo ship that's just come in. No warning, no explanation, just a bus pulling up to the hotel and three men with tommy guns ordering my girls inside. Who knows if I'll ever see them again?"

At this, I *definitely* see emotion around Ginny's typically steely eyes. Although most of her girls—many of them strung out or at the rock bottom of their so-called careers—rotate through her place like a revolving door, she still cares for them, in her way. No matter how hardened this life has made her.

But she would never, ever want me to see her as soft. Her arms cross in front of her chest again, and she blurts out, "How am I supposed to make any money if all my whores are taken from me at the drop of a hat? I won't see a penny from my girls' work down at the dock, and God knows what shape they'll be in after servicing a boatload of sailors. This Combination will ruin us all."

"Any news?" I ask Mabel, tromping up the secret staircase to my house at the Majestic. She stands in the parlor, shaking off the cold and hanging her coat up on the rack. I do the same as I anxiously await her answer. Maybe she's had better luck than me.

"Nothing," she says, unfurling a soft, pale blue scarf from around her neck. Its stitching is uneven, and I wonder if it's handmade. Alone among my girls, Mabel not only has contact with her family but lives with them. Most prostitutes end up with me because they have no one. Or because their own families are far, far worse than the life I'm offering. Even still, I don't let just any girl into my house out of pity. My interview process is the strictest in the business; my girls must be clean from drugs and disease, smart and well-spoken, good-looking, savvy and experienced about this life, and most of all, must feel like my house could be their home.

"You went to her mother's house?" I ask. Virginia has been estranged from her mother for some years, but Mabel heard Virginia complain about her often enough that she figured out where Virginia's mom lived in the Bronx. And she volunteered to take the trek.

Mabel nods, stamping her feet to bring back feeling and warmth. The evening is bitterly cold, and all I can think about is Virginia being dragged into the brisk wind and frigid temperatures five nights ago in lingerie and bedroom slippers.

"Her mother wasn't exactly what you'd call coherent, but from what I could glean, she hadn't heard from Virginia in years."

Sighing, I fall into one of the upholstered chairs in front of the parlor fire. Mabel plops down in the one opposite. Although I can hear the socializing and drinking and gambling happening behind the bookshelf, the sound is mercifully low, and I'm able to block it out. Worries about Virginia have beset me for the past five days, and I'm finding it almost impossible to interact normally with my guests; thank goodness the Lion has stepped in. Not that the King Tut bar is populated with a full complement of my usual guests. Since Lucky's outburst, several of my regulars have grown fearful of the mercurial man and stayed away, only to be replaced by more and more of the Mob boss's sidekicks.

I reach for the decanter on the side table and pour myself a stiff brandy. Downing it in one, I lament, "Where could she possibly be?"

Mabel, not typically much of a drinker, leans toward me, grabs a glass, and holds it out for me to fill with brandy. "I hate to even say this—I mean, I hate to even think it—but could that man Lucky brought here have taken her home? Could he be keeping her there as a prisoner?"

"I thought I heard him say something about a wife, although I've seen everything in this business," I say, turning the exchange over and over in my mind, as I have countless times since that night. "Even if that's true, what would prevent her from phoning us from his house? Or his business?"

Mabel says nothing and neither do I; the answer is too terrible. Virginia could be held captive—by that man, by Lucky, by any number of his goons. Or worse. She might not have phoned because she cannot—because she's been killed. I feel sick.

"I can't just sit here and allow Lucky to take Virginia without doing something about it. Who knows who he might take next. And where he might take them," I say. "I've got to act."

I haven't told Mabel what I've learned in talking to madams from brothels high and brothels low, lower even than the Elk Hotel—and even the pimps I forced myself to contact. Lucky is indeed consolidating the prostitutes in New York City; he's working toward creating a single pool of thousands of girls organized by a few central bookers. By the time he's done, no girl will have a house or a protector, not even mine. Lucky hasn't made a move to ship off any more of my girls, but I am wary. It feels like only a matter of time before Kit, Angelica, Mabel, and Rosalie are marched out the door toward destinations unknown. And I'm fearful that if I press him about Virginia, he might respond by rounding them up pronto.

"What can you do, Polly? He's Lucky Luciano," Mabel says, sipping her brandy as delicately as a schoolgirl taking her first drink.

I pause for a long moment, processing her words. Mabel is both right and wrong, and an idea surfaces. It's risky. But the possibility galvanizes me.

"Well, I may not have much power when it comes to Lucky Luciano, but there are two things I can do. The first thing"—I rise from my chair, reaching for the blue scarf that Mabel dropped on the coffee table—"is to get you out of here, Mabel. You are almost done with your education, and you can do without the money you make here for the next few months. If you're too hard up to pay your tuition, I'll give you the money to finish up at Columbia. It's too risky for you to remain, and I'd never forgive myself if something happened to you, too. This work isn't your life, unlike some of the other girls."

I wrap the nubby wool scarf around her. This beautiful, brilliant young woman has been with me for nearly four years, operating in this business on her own terms so that she can secure the degrees to become a teacher. She will have the future that was stolen away from me. How could I let Lucky get his hooks into her?

Mabel starts crying, gentle weeping, which quickly escalates until her whole body quakes. Her wracking sobs shock me. After all, she's a girl who's shown nothing but perfect reserve all these years, even when I pulled a gun on her that night I came back from jail. I pat her back gently and wonder what's been hidden beneath her calm facade all this time.

I allow Mabel's tears to subside before I reach for and then slip on her coat. While I'm buttoning up the front, she sniffles and asks, "What's the second thing?"

"Excuse me?" I ask, not sure what she means.

"You said there were two things you could do."

"Ah," I reply, then, with false bravado, add, "that's for me to know and you to never, ever find out."

This brings a half smile to Mabel's lips. She doesn't resist as I gently guide her toward the steps. I wait until I hear her descend and say her farewells to Jerry. Then I head toward the little desk in the corner of the parlor.

As I settle into the ornate mahogany chair that sits before the rolltop desk, I wonder if anyone has ever used this piece of furniture. When I hired a Broadway set designer to decorate this place, I asked her to furnish and adorn the parlor in the manner of an exclusive English club library. Elegant and the opposite of a brothel, I'd told her; I wanted the decor to disarm any police officer who wormed his way in here. The morning that movers carried this dainty desk up these stairs from the Majestic lobby, I demurred, "What on earth am I going to do with a desk in a bordello?" To which she responded, "Isn't that the point?"

Rolling back the carved top, I find the clicking sound strangely satisfying. Beneath the domed surface, I am delighted to find rows of shallow drawers, some of which hold heavy, gold-edged paper for letters, matching envelopes, and even a few fountain pens. Who would have thought my decorator's attention to detail would have gone this far?

I slide out a piece of paper and select a blue enamel fountain pen. How do I phrase so delicate a request? An inquiry I never, ever thought I'd be making? One that could get me in a heap of hot water—or worse—should anyone in my world find out?

A phrase comes to me, a snippet of a Robert Frost poem that I overheard one of the creative folks say to another late one night: *The best way out is always through.* I cannot remember if they were lauding or ridiculing Frost, but the line struck me.

Inhaling deeply, I place the sharp tip of the pen on the surface of the paper.

"Dear Mrs. Carter . . ."

CHAPTER TWENTY-FIVE

EUNICE

New York, New York
January 16, 1936

Dear Mrs. Carter:

I need to speak with you about an important matter. Please meet me tomorrow, Thursday, at the Chock full o'Nuts at Penn Station at noon. This is urgent. Please do not share this with anyone and please come alone.

Miss Polly Adler

I slip the letter back into the envelope in which it was delivered. Peering out of the jitney's window as it rumbles down Lenox Avenue, I am as perplexed—and as hopeful—now as I was when I first opened Polly's note nearly a day ago.

"You sure are quiet, Mrs. Carter." Edward Johnson, the proprietor of Harlem Jitney Line, draws me from my thoughts. He glances at me in the rearview mirror of his Buick.

"I'm sorry, Mr. Johnson. I was just reviewing some matters for work."

"I beg your pardon for interrupting," he says, his slow Southern drawl showing plainly that he hails from the red clay hills of Mississippi. "But I sure was glad to get your call. Harlem's own lady lawyer ought not be climbing on and off the subway every day."

"I've been driving lately."

"Oh! Well now, you ought not be driving yourself around the city either," he says, kindly scolding me. "A lady of your standing ought to be escorted every time she steps out of her house, whether for work or for pleasure."

I nod. Mr. Johnson has no idea he may never have spoken truer words.

"We're all mighty proud of you in Harlem. The colored lady lawyer taking down all the crooks."

I chuckle. "I'm not doing it alone, Mr. Johnson."

"Well, we know you're doing your share of the work and then some. Yes indeed. Anytime you and Mr. Carter need a ride, just ring me. You know my outfit has four men, four cars now."

"Congratulations," I say, just as Mr. Johnson eases the Buick to the curb on the corner of 34th Street and Broadway in front of the Hotel McAlpin.

We make arrangements for him to return in an hour. Then, the moment my shoe strikes the pavement, I'm swept into the chaotic rhythm of the city. Despite the biting thirty-degree chill, the sidewalk is bustling with the lunchtime throng.

I navigate through the crush of the crowd to the wide glass door of Chock full o'Nuts. Although I've been to this coffee shop before, I draw a deep breath, then brace myself before I step over the threshold—my constant habit, no matter the establishment. When I enter and see the colored and white patrons inside, I exhale.

The sharp scent of fresh-brewed coffee mingles with the chatter and the clatter, and it all warms me. My eyes circle the diner. The booths and tables are packed with patrons. There are a few stools at the counter, but I'm certain Polly wouldn't want us to be sitting in plain sight that way.

In the far corner, partially obscured by the swinging kitchen doors, I spot a narrow booth. It isn't ideal for the average customer, but it is perfect for *this* meeting—away from prying eyes and ears.

I slide into the seat facing the entrance. Crumbs dot the tabletop, but just as I settle, a young, weary-looking waitress approaches. It's not even noon, yet the lines in her face bear the weight of a day that has already been too long.

Still, she offers me a tired smile. "What'll it be, hon?" she asks, wiping the surface down with a gray cloth that appears to add more grime than it removes.

I pause. Polly asked for a meeting; I didn't expect to share a meal with her, although I wouldn't mind a cup of coffee at least.

"I'm waiting for . . . a friend," I say. "We'll order when she arrives."

"All right, hon," she murmurs, and shuffles to another table.

I glance around the diner. This isn't the most elegant of eateries, but it is a perfect place to blend in with the city's working folk.

Again, I take out Polly's note from my satchel. It's still uncanny to me. The very moment this letter arrived, Murray and I were discussing this exact matter.

"I've been telling you to speak to the girls, but, Eunice, I've been thinking . . . what about the madams? You should speak to one of them."

"If the girls won't talk to me, what makes you think a madam will? They're under the same threats, if not worse."

He shrugged. "And maybe that's the point. If Luciano's behind this prostitution racket, the madams may be more desperate than the girls to see him fall."

I took notice of Murray's words—*if* Luciano is behind this. I'm gathering names, I'm assembling wiretaps, and every day my evidence inches closer to Luciano. Yet Dewey still clings to the hope that *they* will pin Luciano for something else. Something the men of this city will see as more worthy of prosecution than prostitution.

"Excuse me, Mrs. Carter?" I glanced up at my secretary. "This was just delivered for you. The boy said it was urgent."

"Thank you, Miss LaFrance." I noticed the perfect cursive on the outer envelope before I opened it and quickly scanned the three lines.

"Something wrong?" Murray asked when I didn't raise my eyes from the letter.

"No, no." I tucked the letter back inside. "I'll think about what you said, Murray. Perhaps there is a way."

Long after Murray left, I sat, turning Polly's letter over and over. Murray's insistence that I find a madam to speak to, and then, as if on cue, a letter arrives from Polly Adler—is this Providence?

THE BELL ABOVE the front door jingles, and my gaze shoots to the entrance. It only takes a moment to recognize Polly, even if today she's dressed rather plainly, bundled in an oversized wool coat. This is one of the few times I've seen her—in person or in a photograph—without a mink stole. Her overcoat and fedora are a far cry from the glamorous ensemble she wore to court.

Her fedora dips low, casting a shadow over her face and masking her expression for a moment. When she glances up, her eyes meet mine. And I wonder: Will Polly Adler be the definitive fracture in the foundation that has kept this racket standing?

CHAPTER TWENTY-SIX

POLLY

New York, New York
January 16, 1936

I STEP UNDER the familiar dark blue and white Chock full o'Nuts sign and into the pleasingly shabby and perfectly full coffee shop. Situated in no-man's-land on 34th Street near Penn Station, this Chock full o'Nuts outpost is so far from either of our workplaces that we shouldn't encounter anyone we know here. Only Penn Station travelers might be considered "regulars" in this busy establishment, making it easier for us to go unnoticed. Perhaps most importantly, Chock full o'Nuts is one of the few spots in the city where a white woman and a colored woman can both be served.

I pull my fedora low on my forehead as I gaze around the room, looking for Mrs. Carter. Instead of a disguise, which might have made it more likely that I'd stand out than blend in, I dressed more dowdily than is my norm. No fur today, despite the cold, and I feel naked without the luxurious items for which I saved and saved. Only a heavy wool overcoat, a gray scarf up to my neck, and the fedora; no beret or cloche hat that leaves my features exposed. I want to be an invisible traveler, just an ordinary, forgettable woman on her way to somewhere else.

I scan the room first for cops waiting to set me up and, seeing none, for Mrs. Carter. I nearly despair of locating her when I finally spot the prim-looking colored woman in an undesirable booth in the far rear. Why on earth is she sitting there? The two of us at a booth will stick out like two sore thumbs. We don't need any extra eyes upon us, especially ones that might recognize us.

I wait a long moment as I gaze in her direction—willing her to notice me. Our eyes finally meet, and then I pointedly glance at the counter. It is packed with dark-suited businessmen going to and from the office, as well as travelers of all shapes and sizes, laden down with bags and suitcases. There is nowhere more perfect for us to hide in plain sight.

Two empty stools sit at the very end of the counter to the right, and I slowly walk toward them. I take the one next to a gray-haired woman, leaving the stool closest to the wall free for Mrs. Carter. Then I hold up my coffee cup for the waitress to fill. After she pours the steaming, fragrant liquid into my cup, I keep my eyes fixed on the menu laid out on the counter, as if I'm considering the date nut bread with cream cheese. I pay no attention to Mrs. Carter as she settles on the stool next to me and orders a coffee of her own.

Even though I arranged the meeting, I wait for her to speak first. I don't want to relinquish any advantage that initial silence might bring. What I might learn.

"Thank you for reaching out, Miss Adler. Although, I confess to being surprised. I certainly never thought I'd be hearing from you. Not after our last encounter," she says quietly and primly, taking a sip of her coffee while she, too, studies the menu.

"Do you mean at the jail or the courthouse? I saw you at my trial," I say, my voice also quiet but sharper than I'd intended. *Dang it,* I think, *don't alienate her.*

"I meant the jail. Where you made clear that you had no intention of sharing any information with me whatsoever," she replies, continuing to drink her coffee calmly. I admire her unruffled demeanor; she's impervious to my tone and the strangeness of this meeting. But then, she'd need to be self-possessed to work as a colored woman lawyer in the district attorney's office.

I take another sip of my coffee. Two can play at unflappability. "You know better than most that situations can change."

"Indeed, Miss Adler," she says, taking the next turn at silence.

"And I think we can both acknowledge that the larger situation in the city has altered. After all, a certain loss has taken place." I continue, hinting at the death of Dutch and the fact I might have inside Mob knowledge about the latest developments.

Mrs. Carter leans toward me ever so slightly. A tiny motion that wouldn't register to any other patrons sitting at the counter. She's inviting me in. "I'm wondering how this recent change and loss have affected you—and your business."

I hesitate. How to reveal just enough to have her understand the gravity of the situation under Lucky, and not so much to be considered a snitch in my world? I remember those words of Robert Frost again.

"The change created uncertainty in my area of business. And whether by coincidence or design, a very lucky fellow has taken advantage of that uncertainty," I say.

"I see. And that lucky fellow has stepped into your industry and is making alterations that are less than pleasing?" she asks, settling her cup carefully in its saucer. She attempts nonchalance in her tone, but she can't hide her excitement at what I might know about Lucky and his involvement in the prostitution business. We both know how enormous this development could be to her.

"Yes, he's consolidating the structure and centralizing the way employees are deployed. And that works in tandem with a group of lawyers and bondsmen who keep those employees from being . . . detained," I answer, closing my menu as if I've finally settled on my order.

"And this is having a negative impact on your business?"

"Not just on my own business. But the consolidation and centralization is harming everyone who works in my industry here in New York." I pause. I want to make certain she understands that this isn't simply about Lucky's interference or the bottom line. "The most troubling impact—the one that prompted me to write you and meet you here today—is the inability to protect my employees in this new structure."

She scooches a little closer. "They are being placed in harm's way with the new structure?"

"The employees are being moved from establishment to establishment at a moment's notice, oftentimes to very unsavory places, and, in some cases, disappearing altogether."

I hear the softest intake of breath. "Disappearing?" Mrs. Carter asks, as if she can't quite believe it. This surprises me, as I heard she worked in the Women's Court. When there, wouldn't she have encountered all sorts of violence done to women? From abused wives, to drugged-up streetwalkers at the mercy of their pimps, to desperate petty criminals, any of whom might be covered in wounds and bruises. In that realm, women vanish all the time.

I nod, and an image of Virginia on that terrible night flashes through my mind. Tears threaten to well up, and I push them back. I must stay on task here.

"Mrs. Carter, would I be right in assuming that you have a professional interest in my business?" I venture.

Keeping her gaze straight ahead, Mrs. Carter murmurs, "You

would be correct in supposing I have a professional interest in your work. Perhaps not your business specifically but the industry as a whole."

"Would I also be right in assuming that you find what I'm telling you about the recent changes to that business deplorable?" I tiptoe a little closer toward my real request.

"I do indeed."

The elderly woman sitting to my left rises and departs, probably for a train. Mrs. Carter and I freeze. The empty stool poses a threat. Anyone might settle there—a nosy businessman, a bored housewife traveling to visit family, or even someone from Mrs. Carter's office stopping in for a bite before heading home on the train. Either way, neither one of us exhales until a portly letter carrier, his navy cap emblazoned in brass with his post office number, plops down on it.

As I sigh in relief, I give the room a quick scan. It is then that I see him. A uniformed officer is chatting with the hostess. Not just any cop, but a cop I know.

"We need to leave right now," I hiss at Mrs. Carter.

"What do you mean?"

"Don't look now, but there's a policeman near the front door."

"That doesn't mean we have to run out of here," she hisses right back. "We're just two ladies waiting for our trains."

"I know him."

"From prison?"

"From greasing his palm more times than I can count so he'd leave my house alone."

A sharp intake of breath from Mrs. Carter, and I know she understands. "We'd have to walk right past him to leave," she protests.

"Get up and walk toward the ladies' room," I whisper. "You'll see a service door between the toilet and the kitchen. Slide out and wait for me in the back alley."

"How on earth do you know about that?"

"In my line of work, I've always got to know where the nearest exit is."

I watch as Mrs. Carter puts coins for her coffee on the counter and walks in the direction of the ladies' room, as if she has all the time in the world. *She's good,* I cannot help but think. Once she nears the service exit, I rise and follow her lead.

By the time I step into the back alley heaped high with garbage bins and strewn with refuse, I can't help but laugh. If you would've told me that I'd be shimmying out the back of a Chock full o'Nuts to willingly meet a prosecutor in an alley, I would have bet one thousand dollars at my mahjong table on no. I see a small smile on Mrs. Carter's face, and I think now is as good a time as any.

"Mrs. Carter, I have a proposition for you."

PART II

CHAPTER TWENTY-SEVEN

EUNICE

New York, New York
January 22, 1936

I SPREAD THE transcripts of the new wiretaps that we've captured over the past few days across my desk. It's a treasure trove, all courtesy of Polly Adler.

I learned more from Polly than I dared hope. In that alley, with my back pressed against the brick wall, she filled in several blanks. I scribbled down every name she whispered, every role she mapped out. As I made notes, I prayed these were the men who would form a strong chain of evidence reaching to the top. I didn't even notice I was shivering until my fingertips went numb, the chill completely forgotten in the urgency of what Polly was giving to me.

We hadn't lingered long. After just a few minutes, Polly said, "That should be good enough to do whatever you need to do. With what I've given you, you could wiretap a slew of gangsters and raid every brothel in the city if you need to." That was her farewell, and she walked away.

Back in the office, I pored over my notes before taking the information to Dewey, giving him the names from Polly, some that we'd heard before. But it was the name of Dave Betillo that made Dewey sit upright in his chair.

According to street chatter and police investigations, Betillo had once served as Al Capone's bodyguard and was now a killer for Luciano. Although he had never been charged with more than pick-pocketing and attempted grand larceny, the FBI had linked Betillo to several murders. However, there was never enough evidence to charge him with and convict him of those crimes.

"Did your source say there was a direct link between Betillo and Luciano?" Dewey had asked.

"Not exactly, but my source knows what we're after."

The chief nodded as he flipped through my notes. "Where did you get this information, Mrs. Carter?"

"My source has to remain anonymous. I gave my word."

"And you trust this source?"

"Yes, this person has every reason to want us to succeed with this investigation."

With a nod, Dewey said, "Reach out to Judge McCook for more wiretaps."

Now, AS I sift through these folders thick with transcripts, I am astonished by the scope of what we've gathered. Each file bears a name; I begin with the ones Polly gave me:

Thomas Pennochio, or Tommy the Bull. A name we heard on the taps before. An enforcer, a muscleman who roughs up the girls who get out of line.

Ralph Liguori and Jack Ellerstein, both bookers, although Liguori is also a strong-arm who handles the madams if they don't co-operate.

Pete Harris, the top booker, whose role is already well-documented in the conversations between Abe Karp and Jesse Jacobs.

Then there are files from the names gathered from the wiretaps:

Meyer Berkman, a bondsman whose name surfaced on the wiretap of the other bondsman, Jesse Jacobs.

Benny Spiller, who runs Luciano's loan shark racket.

And Dave Betillo, the final name Polly gave me.

It didn't take long to tie Betillo to the day-to-day workings of this racket. We heard him barking orders at bookers, coordinating cash collections, and handling any problems with the madams. He ran it all like grease on glass—it was smooth, it was slick, it was efficient.

The door to the monitoring room swings open and Murray barges in, brandishing a newspaper. He only stepped away to get us coffee, but he thrusts the *New York Evening Journal* at me.

"You'd better read this," he says, his voice pulled tight like a wire. "The chief was on his way to your office, but then he got a call. He gave this to me."

My eyes land on the bold headline first: *Dewey and His Twenty Against the Underworld Poised to Strike—Arrests Imminent.* My jaw clamps down as I continue reading. Everything we've worked on is here—the ten-dollar payments from the girls to the bookers to Karp and the bondsmen; how Karp makes sure the girls don't spend a night behind bars; how the girls are moved around by the bookers. The article continues, quoting Dewey as saying an arrest for the head Mob man in charge is coming.

To this point, every newspaper report has stated that the investigation's focus is on racketeering of all sorts. No one has printed a word about prostitution. But this is so thorough, I could have written it myself.

"You know Dewey didn't say any of this. There's a leak in the office." I'm so angry, the edge in my tone could slice through steel.

"That's what the chief said."

"Who is it?"

Murray shrugs. "You know how leaks are. It could be any one of the attorneys, investigators, accountants, secretaries, or clerks. And there are cops coming in and out of here all hours of the day and night. This place has more foot traffic than Grand Central."

Dewey did all he could to secure this place—locked files, closed windows. Even now, Murray and I are sitting behind a sealed door. But it's impossible to put a lock on loose lips, and stopping leaks is beyond reason and reach.

"This changes everything," I mutter, scanning the article once again. "Our whole case is laid out here."

"It's not all that we have," Murray says, finally handing me my coffee.

"Is the chief in his office?" When Murray nods, I slide my chair back. "Let's go talk to him."

The chief waves us into his office as if he was expecting Murray and me. "Everything we've learned is here." I hold up the newspaper. "All that's missing are the wiretaps, the Combination, and the identity of this 'head Mob man in charge' that you mentioned," I say wryly.

"That I allegedly mentioned." Dewey chuckles, very accustomed to being misquoted in the press.

"At least they don't know it's Luciano we're circling. I'd like to keep that out of the press because we don't have a direct evidentiary connection to him yet," I admit.

"Actually, Mrs. Carter, we may be closer than you think. Luciano may have just shown his hand." The chief continues. "I just got a telephone call—Luciano's on the run."

Murray and I gasp.

"Seems this newspaper article cut too close to the truth. He left New York a few hours ago, and from what the men tailing him have said, it doesn't look like he's taking a short trip."

"It's an admission of guilt," I say.

"I believe so," Dewey says, and a flicker of satisfaction stirs inside me. Is the chief finally beginning to agree with me? He adds, "Not that we can use it as a confession in court."

"Is he fleeing the country?" Murray asks.

"It doesn't look like it. He's on a train. We don't know his destination yet, but we will. In the meantime, with a little more evidence, we may be able to compel his return wherever he lands." The chief glances between Murray and me, inviting us to share a plan.

"I have an idea, Chief." Without even glancing at Murray, I lay out a strategy that's been taking shape in my mind ever since Polly mentioned it offhandedly in the alley that day. "It's the testimony from the girls and the madams that we need, right? There's a way to force their cooperation. What if we raided every single brothel on my list—there are eighty—all at once? One surprise hit across the city. Same night, same hour—we round up the girls and madams in one sweep."

"Interesting," Dewey says, but I don't hear confidence in his voice.

Still, I continue. "But the night *before*, we lock up the bookers, the bondsmen, and the attorneys. So the night of the raids, when the girls and madams make their usual calls to get out, no one answers. They'll be sitting in those cells with no protection. I think after a few days under arrest without any chance of paying for bail, they'll be ready to talk." I pause and look at Dewey. "That's how we'll finally get their statements; that's how we'll finally crack this case."

Dewey stares at me silently for a long moment. "Raiding eighty brothels? At one time? I don't believe anything like this has ever been attempted. Certainly not on this scale."

"That's precisely why it will work," I say.

The corners of his lips twitch into a slow smile. "You're absolutely right, Mrs. Carter. It's bold, it's brilliant, it's damn good. Let's do it."

CHAPTER TWENTY-EIGHT

POLLY

New York, New York
January 31, 1936

It's business as usual at Polly's. It has been for the past two weeks, ever since I met with Mrs. Carter. It must be.

At least, that's what I repeat to myself over and over, night after night. Whenever one of Lucky's men swills a drink at the bar next to Robert Benchley or Donald Ogden Stewart, illustrious regulars who've become accustomed to standing side by side with notorious gangsters. Whenever one of my girls retires to her apple-green-and-peach bedroom at dawn's light, safe from being swept into the Combination for just one more day. Whenever I pass Virginia's empty room, which I refuse to fill with another girl. Whenever my stomach roils and my heart pounds at Lucky's crew. And I tell myself to act the part again tonight, no matter how much I loathe the sight of these men.

I will have my revenge. But pretending that all is swell is a crucial piece of moving that forward.

Paint on some fresh lipstick along with your smile, I think as I catch a glimpse of myself in the mirror over the bar, a dour expression on my face. *Cast no suspicion upon yourself,* I admonish myself. *Or neither you nor your girls will ever be safe again.*

"You bastard!" a voice cries out, and two men spring back from the bar.

The slur brings me back to the moment. I can't see who did the yelling, but the two guests who've retreated from the kerfuffle at the bar are visible. They are two of my creative regulars, just back after a few weeks' absence. I suppose they decided Polly's is safe enough, mobsters or not. Not that anyone would dare discuss it. We all pretend that it's normal to have America's most wanted man and his goons among us, but I see the wariness in my regulars' eyes and their jumpiness every time they hear a loud noise. Like now.

I crane my neck to see who's responsible for the outburst and to assess whether I need to call Jerry up from downstairs. But I cannot see over the men—or the lone woman, Dorothy Parker—and I curse my short stature for the millionth time.

Stepping back from the bar, I hear someone yell back, "No, you're the bastard!"

The two name-callers come into view, and I realize that the insults aren't coming from Lucky's thugs, who showed up tonight as usual even though I've seen newspaper reports that Lucky has fled town thanks to the heat of Dewey's investigation. No, it's two of Lucky's out-of-town friends who have stopped in to play some poker—Jack McGurn, a rumored hit man; and Bugsy Siegel, a racketeer who recently moved out West to launch some big project. But the two men aren't about to launch into fisticuffs. In fact, they're laughing.

"No way you won that game without cheating, Bugsy," Jack calls out, a smile still curling on his lips.

"What are you talking about? My opening hand was a pair of

aces. There's no better chance of winning than starting a round with two aces," Bugsy replies with a self-satisfied grin, much to my relief. Unlike my regulars, the moods of Lucky's people can turn on a dime, bringing violence along with the change in temperament. The vigilance it takes to preserve a modicum of peace is exhausting. Especially now.

But hopefully not for long.

Walking over to the table of writers and artists, I apologize and signal for the bartender to deliver a complimentary drink of their choice for their troubles. Walter Winchell materializes, and I order him his favorite drink as well. He always knows when and where to get free liquor.

Unlike some of the literary folks, Walter has never taken a temporary respite from my house. He knows that even mobsters can be good for the gossip business, and so he's continued to patronize me throughout Dutch's and now Lucky's tenure. Plus, he can never go too long without visiting my girls.

"Still no Virginia?" Walter asks as he slugs back the dregs of his drink to accept the free one. "I'd love some time with her tonight."

I have been dreading this question. Among all my guests, Walter knows my girls best. Not just their names, but their routines, their specialties, even their backgrounds. Or at least what they present to him as their "backgrounds." Of course, he's noticed that Virginia's been absent.

"Still not back from visiting family." I trot out the lie that the Lion and I have concocted, trying to keep my voice steady along with my gaze as I lie. It hurts me to think about her out there. Or worse.

"Must be some family emergency," he comments.

Walter doesn't challenge me overtly, but he raises a single eyebrow quizzically, and I know he doesn't believe me. Has he heard rumors from people who were here the night Lucky took Virginia? Has he heard some scuttlebutt about this "Combination" that's spreading across the city like wildfire? Or—my stomach lurches at the thought—does he know something about Virginia's whereabouts?

I want to ask him, but I can't. I must keep up appearances. So I nod, as I don't trust myself to discuss Virginia any further.

"You'll let me know when she's back?" he asks.

"I promise," I say, thinking how delighted I'd be to share that news with Walter. Tears threaten to well up in my eyes at the thought of the still-missing Virginia, for whom I continue to search. These days, the hunt is quieter, as I'm trying to pretend I'm the same old Polly I was before Lucky infiltrated my house and stole Virginia away. And I'm trying not to draw attention to myself in light of Mrs. Carter's impending plan. But before Walter can ask any more questions, the bartender mercifully arrives with his drink.

The rest of my guests have turned and are staring at something in the gambling room. Following their gaze, I see that Jack and Bugsy are carrying one of my velvet chaise lounges across the room. And they are directing two of their lackeys to move a poker table into the bar area.

What on earth is going on? Do they think they are interior decorators? Or is something more nefarious afoot? I weigh whether it's worth it—or safe—to intervene. After all, they aren't hurting my girls or me, so what difference does it really make?

But then, just as quickly as these shenanigans begin, they stop; the men become distracted by the notion of playing mahjong instead. I hold my breath for a long moment, waiting for the jazz trio and the gambling and the chatter to recommence. Only when the usual sounds fill the space do I exhale. Yet none of this return to the usual order displaces my hidden anger at Lucky. Because he may not be here tonight, but his presence looms nonetheless.

The Lion catches my eye and glances toward the bookshelf. This well-practiced gesture is a signal for me to check in with Jerry downstairs. Usually this means that someone has asked for me, someone that Jerry—and even the Lion sometimes—has already vetted. Could this be the message I've been waiting for? The signal from Mrs. Carter that the plan is underway?

I cannot take a chance that my exit will be noticed and that Lucky's goons will trail me. Kit has recently returned to the bar, and once I get her attention, I crook my head toward the most problematic of Lucky's thugs. She sidles up to Bugsy and Jack and offers them a glass of champagne. As she busies them, I back away toward the bookshelves, as unobtrusively as possible.

Sliding the critical book off the shelf and waiting for the all-important click of the door, I take one look back toward the bar. Bugsy and Jack are fully engrossed in a lascivious exchange with Kit.

I almost turn back. I almost chicken out. Almost.

Then I remember the night Lucky stole Virginia. And I resolve to proceed. Whatever the cost.

CHAPTER TWENTY-NINE

EUNICE

New York, New York
February 1, 1936

As I STEER through the deserted streets of Harlem, I wonder if this is what it was like for my mother. Stealing into a Southern town under the cover of night, never certain what dangers lurked in the shadows. Was she ever afraid? Did she ever wish to turn back?

One thing my mother never had to endure on those Southern nights was the brutal bite of a New York winter. The Arctic freeze that has gripped the East Coast has turned the city into a treacherous icebox. All day, radio announcers have droned on about the deathly danger of being outdoors. But nothing has prepared me for the way my Ford skids across the pavement.

I gasp as I come within inches of sideswiping a parked car. But I grip the wheel and steer forward. My heart is hammering, and I murmur a prayer. One block later, I nudge my car to the curb, and I thank Jesus again before I cut off the engine.

I never should have attempted such foolishness. And if Lisle had been home, he would have chained the front door rather than allowing me to venture into what he would call utter madness. But

Lisle is in Nashville, Tennessee, giving the keynote address at the National Association of Colored Dentists. It is no coincidence that I chose this night for the raids.

My driving may have been reckless, but my timing is impeccable. I glance at my wristwatch—the raids will begin in less than ten minutes. Over 160 officers have been assigned to this sweep across the city. To maintain secrecy, no one will be riding with their usual partner. In fact, they won't know the details of their mission until they arrive at their destinations and open envelopes at precisely eight fifty-five. Then they'll spring into action.

The wind howls, rattling the car, and I double-check the doors. Both are locked, although truly, I have no fear of Luciano's men lurking tonight. This cold isn't fit for any man—it'd freeze the sin right off a sinner.

But the cold became a consideration today—was it too dangerous to conduct a raid in subzero temperatures? I was the one to convince Dewey that we had no choice but to proceed. We had too many in custody from our roundup last night—Dave Betillo, Thomas Pennochio, Jesse Jacobs, and Pete Harris, among others—and we'd lose the element of surprise and our leverage over the women if we delayed.

Through the windshield, I glance up at the brownstone. From the moment I conceived of this plan, I wanted to be present for the strike on this Harlem brownstone. It's the place about which I've received the most resident complaints, and it holds a brothel run by one of the city's most notorious madams.

Most of all, this is where Deputy Chief Inspector David McAuliffe, the senior officer overseeing this most ambitious police operation in the city's history, will be.

I hear the rumble of a car engine, and I glance through the

rearview mirror. Headlights approach—a patrol car followed by a paddy wagon. The patrol car comes to a stop in front of me, and inside, McAuliffe sits in the passenger seat.

I steel myself, ready to make my move. McAuliffe opens his car door, and I open mine. Police spill from the paddy wagon, their boots crushing the ice on the pavement. No one notices me—until suddenly McAuliffe does.

"Mrs. Carter!" he hisses into the frigid air. His voice is thick with rage. "I told you earlier that we do not allow civilians to be present for official police missions."

"In this case, I am not a civilian, Inspector McAuliffe."

"I don't care what you are!" His face flushes with the same indignation he had this afternoon when I told him I would be here for this raid. Then he pauses and clears his throat. "We do not allow civilians *or prosecutors* or anyone who doesn't wear a badge on-site. It's for your safety."

"I'm not concerned about my safety."

"That's another reason we don't ride with civilians—you don't grasp the danger. These policemen have enough to worry about, keeping an eye on their own backs."

"Inspector McAuliffe"—I hold up my gloved hands—"I will stay out of your way. I just need to be here."

"Why?" His question drips with exasperation—and frustration.

It is impossible to list the many reasons I need to be present: If anything goes wrong, I'll be blamed. Corruption festers within the police department, and I won't let it poison my plan. I want to serve as my own witness. This is the raid I organized, and I also arranged for the press coverage.

To McAuliffe, I say only, "As we prepare the cases for court, I must understand how these raids were conducted."

He studies me, but officers are already dashing up the dozen steps leading to the entry of the three-story brownstone. He has no more time to argue. "Stay right here with them," he warns in a growl, and jabs his finger, pointing behind me to two men lugging heavy cameras. The press has arrived.

I stand on the icy sidewalk looking up, hoping I'll have a view of something through the parlor windows. But only a shimmer of light peeks through the heavy velvet drapes.

Then, *crash!* The front door is kicked open and smashes against the wall.

"This is a raid. Put your hands up!" the officers shout.

Shrieks, screams, and curses spill from the brothel alongside Bing Crosby's croon of romance—the words of "It's Easy to Remember" floating like silk through the mayhem. I want to rush up the brownstone's steps and witness it all. But I stand steadfast. If any of Luciano's men are inside, this will turn into more than a raid.

Within a minute, I have a ringside seat. I, along with the neighbors who peek from every window on both sides of this brownstone, watch as men in open shirts and unzipped trousers—a couple in only their underwear—scurry down the fire escape, then scatter like rats up and down Seventh Avenue.

When the girls emerge, each escorted by an officer, the night blazes with camera flashes. Women in glittery gowns, their necklaces sparkling like the constellations above, file out next to others clad in nothing more than silk negligees and fur-trimmed slippers. I shiver. Suddenly the union suit and thermal stockings that I wear beneath three layers of clothing offer me no protection from the cold as I watch these poor girls. Perhaps I should have given orders for the girls to dress before stepping out in this weather.

I say to the passing officers, "Get them into the paddy wagon quickly."

The air swells with the stench of perfume and cigarettes, just as a woman shouts, "You never showed me your warrant!" She is so hysterical, two officers have to wrangle her toward the paddy wagon. "This is a respectable house, you flatfoot bastard!" Her scarlet-painted lips curl in brazen defiance, and her curses explode in the nighttime air.

This is one of the things I wanted to witness. Red Sadie—the former prostitute who rose above her circumstances and now has a reputation that looms large in the city. She's the opposite of what I imagined. She's short, stout, and rather ordinary. Except for her steely green eyes, which are as sharp as her tongue and burn with fire as red-hot as her hair.

As Red Sadie wiggles in the officers' grasp, the cameras click, and the flashes light up the street like high noon.

The newspaper headlines . . . the photographs of Red Sadie . . . the pictures of the girls being dragged away—all of this will crash through the city in the morning like a thunderclap.

Exactly as I planned.

I RIDE THE elevator to the thirteenth floor. The level beneath our offices has been empty for months, but tonight, it will be the epicenter of our operation. This is where the girls will be processed and questioned until they're transferred to the Women's House of Detention tomorrow.

It was my idea to bring the women here. The sheer number of the arrests would have made it impossible to process them all at the Women's Court or even at the prison. I wanted every step—from the arrests to the arraignments—to be under my observation.

When I exit the elevator, it feels strange to see the office humming with quiet chatter. Yesterday, all the assistant district attorneys on Dewey's team were told—without explanation—that today they would work through the night. It wasn't until the raids began that the men learned of this operation. Now they are all here to help process the girls, while Dewey is up in his office, continuing to coordinate the police operations.

The paddy wagons will arrive any minute, so I have little time to weave through the offices. But as I cross the space, I slow down as the men, who for the past year have given me little more than a glance, pause to smile and offer the occasional "Good job, Mrs. Carter."

I nod my gratitude at their compliments before I check the office set aside for Justice McCook to arraign the girls. Just as I reach the freight elevators, the doors open. Cops and girls file out, filling the air with the cloying sweetness of perfume; nearly all the girls are white, with the exception of a few colored and Spanish-looking girls. I greet them all, almost as if they're guests, offering coffee to warm them, before the other attorneys guide them to the offices where they'll be confined.

"Why are we here?" many ask as their eyes dart around the bare offices with nothing more than desks and metal folding chairs.

The girls are accustomed to raids and arrests, but not like this.

"I'll be speaking with each of you," I tell them. "Please give me a few minutes to begin."

The chatter grows louder and angrier. About an hour later, Justice McCook settles into his designated space to arraign the girls and set bail. The other attorneys and I start processing the arrested girls—taking their names, addresses, and occupations. I'm not surprised to hear the responses to the question of their employment:

"I'm a model."

"I'm a housewife."

"I'm a student studying opera."

I note their responses without comment.

I lead the first girl, Daisy Wilson, into Judge McCook's "chamber." Even though he's crammed behind a small desk in an office that, until last year, housed an insurance company, the heavyset, barrel-chested justice still wears his black robe with the stiff white collar. I imagine that in his sixteen years on the New York Supreme Court, he never pictured a scene such as this—arraigning prostitutes inside the Woolworth Building.

His jowled face is stern when he asks Daisy her name. And then the justice says, "You have been charged with compulsory prostitution. How do you plead?"

"Not guilty," Daisy proclaims. There is a bit of amusement in her tone as she tightens her mink stole around her bare shoulders.

The justice nods. "Bail is set at ten thousand dollars."

Her smirk fades fast. "Ten. Thousand. Dollars?" She blinks, her merriment gone. "My bail is supposed to be three hundred dollars."

"Your bail is whatever I say it is, Miss Wilson," he says gruffly before he cracks his gavel down hard on the desk.

I lead Daisy to the office for her interview. She sits on the edge of the chair, her expression a clash of incredulity and confusion. "I've never had bail set so high."

"These are serious charges, Miss Wilson."

"No more serious than usual," she replies, flicking her bangs from her eyes.

"Oh?" I feign surprise. "You've been arrested before? I thought you were an art student."

Her lips press into a thin line, and she glances away.

"I have a few questions, Miss Wilson. You work with Red Sadie, correct?"

"I told you, I'm an art student," she snaps.

"At Red Sadie's, how much of your earnings do you retain?"

She says nothing.

"Are you aware of how the clients are procured and managed there?" More silence. "Besides Red Sadie, is there anyone else who oversees the management of that establishment?" She refuses to reply. "Are you from New York, or were you brought here by someone?"

Daisy remains silent through my next six questions. I end by telling her the truth, a statement that all the girls will hear. "Miss Wilson, while this is serious, we're not here to prosecute you or any of the women. We want your testimony to convict the men at the top."

"I'm not going to tell you anything about any of them." She shakes her head, shedding the art student pretense.

"Then we'll have no choice but to proceed with the charges against you. You'll be sent to prison to await your trial."

Her shoulders sag beneath the weight of my words. "It's been rough, Mrs. Carter," she whispers. "This life . . . working with the Combination . . ."

I inhale. "The Combination? What can you tell me about that? Who's the head of the Combination?"

She gives me a long stare. "Do you have any idea what will happen to me if I say anything?" With slow deliberation, she lifts her finger to her throat and drags it across her skin. She holds her finger there for a beat before she folds her arms and sits back.

"Thank you, Miss Wilson" is all I can say before I leave her alone.

I suspect Daisy is telling herself not to be concerned. Yes, the raid, this building, and the bail are all surprises. She may even suspect that she'll have to spend one night in jail. But three nights—and beyond—in a cell will certainly change her perspective.

We repeat the process, girl after girl. But no one offers us anything more than their rehearsed lies. Their unrelenting fear is the Mob's greatest weapon. The girls believe losing their freedom is a far better fate than losing their lives.

The madams are even more obstinate. We have quite a few in custody: Jenny the Factory, Silver-Tongued Elsie, Fat Rae, even Max the Barber—the one male madam among them—and, of course, Red Sadie. We receive no cooperation from any of them.

By midnight, my voice is only a rasp. By three in the morning, it's my sanity that's fraying. Exhaustion has overtaken me, and I am edging toward delirium. The new morning sun's first rays peek through the venetian blinds when I process the last of over one hundred girls and I take the elevator up to my office. We instructed the cops to search the brothels for paperwork and diaries, and now all of that is stacked atop my desk.

But I am so bushed, I don't even have the strength to drive home. Just as I consider resting my head on my desk, Murray knocks on my door.

His eyes are as bloodshot as mine, but he grins as he collapses into the chair. "We did it." He sounds hoarse.

"Now we wait for them to turn from prostitutes to state witnesses."

He brushes his fingers through his hair. "Did you hear we had another leak?"

"No! What happened?"

"The cops went out to the eighty brothels you gave them but only raided forty-one. Seems like the others were tipped off."

I bounce back in my chair. "So we only got half?"

Murray nods. "But we got enough. We missed a few, like Florence Brown, Diamond Lil, and Polly Adler, but we have plenty of girls and madams down there."

I freeze at Murray's words—*We missed a few . . . Polly Adler.*

I am no leaker, but I made sure Polly would be missed. She gave me what I needed, and I made sure she and her girls were safe from the raid. That was our deal.

And now, after last night, Polly Adler and I can return to pretending we never met.

CHAPTER THIRTY

POLLY

Honolulu, Hawaii
March 5, 1936

Largest Vice Raid Ever.

Bosses Nabbed in New York Raids.

Dewey Smashes Vice Ring.

These are the sort of headlines that have been following me for the past month. I couldn't have missed them if I tried. And believe me, for over a month, I've tried. I know so much about the raids at this point, I feel I was there. Even though I did everything I could to avoid them.

I've been trying to outrun them ever since Mrs. Carter unleashed her forces through New York City's five boroughs. In point of fact, I have been running from the very moment that the messenger stopped by my house to alert me that the raids were about to begin. Mrs. Carter kept to the bargain we'd struck in that alleyway behind the Chock full o'Nuts. I'd given her the names of the bookers and fixers I'd heard about when I was searching for Virginia so she could wiretap them. That way, she'd finally have the right kind of evidence to conduct a large-scale raid. She promised me that I'd get a heads-up so I could get out of New York if indeed she ever did a sweep based on the evidence I provided. Tit for tat, so to speak. If you don't mind pardoning the pun.

Leaving town was and is a tightrope. Although I knew something was coming, I kept my house humming along even on the night of the raids, up until the very last second. No one could suspect I knew what was what. So I kept the booze flowing and the cards flying and the mahjong tiles clicking and the jazz strumming until I got word—and the Lion, the girls, Jerry, and I slipped out the back. The Lion, of course, knew what might be happening—I'd trust her with my life—but the girls were in the dark until we walked out the door. Anyone would understand why, in my line of work, I hightailed it out of the city in the wake of the raids, but I do wonder if my ability to evade them altogether raises any eyebrows.

While the Lion, Jerry, and the girls holed up with friends in the city and its outskirts on my dime—I've got to protect and support them until my return—I've been slipping away ever since, traveling farther and farther west. Taking a train by myself in the dead of night and wearing the same drab outfit I sported at the Chock full o'Nuts, I first headed to Chicago.

Steering clear of the Lexington Hotel, which contains a brothel frequented by mobsters, I stayed at the more conservative Drake Hotel. There, I hosted dinner for my brother Ben and my father, who has lived with him in an apartment since he arrived in America alone several years ago. Holding my father at arm's length in Chicago has been instrumental in keeping him in the dark about my life.

"So how's the corset factory?" my father asked during an awkward silence in our meal of delicious seafood at the Drake's famed restaurant, the Cape Cod Room. He usually didn't bother asking about my fictional job, but I had run out of questions about my father's position at a shoemaker's and Ben's work as a bartender. After fits and starts in a variety of industries, Ben had landed in a role that suited him, much to my relief. I knew how easily the siren song of crime could lure a person in otherwise, as it had in his youth.

"Busy as usual," I answered, keeping it short because I actually knew nothing about running a corset factory other than what I'd learned on the factory line as a young woman. In fact, I'd chosen a *corset* factory because I figured my family wouldn't probe too hard about a job involving women's undergarments.

"Paychecks still coming in, though, right?" My father asked the question most important to him as Ben averted his eyes. I knew Ben appreciated the financial support I gave him and my father, but I also knew it was embarrassing for him to have to rely on me.

I took a long look at my father's pomaded hair and three-piece suit—modern finery he could never afford in Yanow—for which my money paid. And in that moment, I knew that he saw me only as a source of moolah. Just as he always had.

"You're wearing some of those paychecks, aren't you?" I retorted, unable to keep the mounting anger from my voice.

"You wouldn't want your father to look a pauper, would you? You wouldn't want that," he said, half joking. But I could see that he was miffed at being called out.

"What do *I want*? I want my father to use the money I give him to help my mother and younger brothers immigrate here." I scolded him because I knew my mother would never come until he summoned her. In fact, I'd grown so frustrated with his reluctance that recently I'd sent her money and instructions on the process, which she refused, informing me that her wife's duty meant that she had to await my father's directives. What I didn't admit to my father, however, was that I felt some relief at his delay; I didn't know how long I could cling to the ruse of managing a corset factory while staring into my mother's eyes.

"Do you know how hard it is to get people out of Yanow? You know it sits right near the Poland–Soviet Union border." He sounded both defensive and angry, although he had no right to either.

"I've been giving you money for the *whole* family's journey here since before Russia became the Soviet Union."

He could say nothing to that. We stared at one another until a waiter arrived tableside and inquired about our dessert order. "I think we are done here," I said, pushing my chair out and standing as Ben shot me an apologetic glance. Then I added, "Put the bill on my room."

Unwilling to spend a minute longer in the city my father inhabited, I hightailed it to California. I found the Golden State not so welcoming; folks I'd known well enough in New York and hosted at my house plenty pretended not to know me at the nightclubs I popped into, bending to the pressure to maintain a public facade of morality against the backdrop of the news about the New York raids. So I took a ship to Hawaii, the luxurious SS *Malolo*. I'm not sure anyone is looking for me in these exotic isles, but I figure neither cop nor Mob can catch me if I never land.

I STROLL ACROSS the swanky lobby of the Royal Hawaiian Hotel toward the restaurant for my first morning coffee. Dubbed the "Pink Palace of the Pacific" when it opened nine years ago, this pink, Spanish-Moorish, beachfront confection—one of the very first on Waikiki Beach—has quickly become *the* destination in Hawaii. I figure I deserve to pass my exile in temporary style, even as I understand that the bills here, in Chicago, in Yanow, and in New York are adding up.

As I pass the newsstand, I do my level best to avert my gaze. I need a break from those fraught headlines. But a particular phrase catches my eye: *White Slaves Kept for Questioning as Key Witnesses.*

I stop dead in my tracks at the phrase "white slaves," not because I haven't heard it before but because I know it's referring to the girls. It started out as a description of white Europeans captured by African nations, but it's now commonly used in newspapers to refer to prostitutes. I reach for the paper. Scanning past the headline to the article, I read: *Early-morning raids weeks ago at houses of ill repute have turned into long jail stays for the white slaves swept up by cops. Authorities hope that infamous prostitutes and their madams bearing names like Jenny the Factory, Gas-House Lil, Red Sadie, Frisco Jean, and Silver-Tongued Elsie will find their tongues loosened the longer they sit behind bars. All this despite the fact that District Attorney Thomas Dewey has professed that he's only interested in 'organized forms' of vice, not the individuals who perpetrate it. Dewey's team continues to build its case with ongoing interrogations of the prostitutes behind bars.*

I feel sick. My goal in meeting Mrs. Carter and guiding her toward bookers, fixers, and bail bondsmen who'd provide fruitful wiretap testimony was to bring down Lucky and his Combination, to stop his expansion. Not to subject girls to weeks of grilling, interrogations that would make them only more susceptible to threats by the mobsters. Cutthroat madams like Red Sadie don't deserve protection, but her girls do. I didn't expect that a raid would yield weeks upon weeks of jail time for the girls. I'd just blindly hoped that the madams would spill all the goods right from the start, freeing up the girls from prison stints.

But if I'm really being honest, did I allow myself to think through my plan? Even as I ask myself the question, I know now—and I knew then—that there's no way to bring Lucky down without bringing down some girls in the process. I didn't want to think about the impact the raid would have on the girls, beyond ensuring the safety of my own. And this goes against my goal to do better by the girls in this business.

After all, when I examine my own life, the most glimmering moments are those of me and the Lion and the girls sitting around the kitchen table, coffees in our hands, and laughing about the long night before we turn in for our daytime sleep. They are my strange, illicit family—more precious than my own flesh and blood—and the only shining thing about my existence. But perhaps I should care about *all* the girls, not just my own. After all, for every girl I've brought into the safety of my house, there are ten girls who meet the qualifications and need shelter from the storm on the streets, girls I didn't protect from awful fates. Am I kidding myself that I provide even fleeting golden moments to my girls—and that I'm entitled to experience golden moments—when the whole business is nasty and dirty?

"No free reads, lady," the newsman barks, and grabs the paper out of my hands.

I reach into my handbag and hand the guy a nickel. He gifts me a toothless smile as he hands the newspaper back. I return to the article, and, distracted, I walk away from the newsstand and right into Robert Benchley.

"Well, aren't you a sight for sore eyes!" Robert exclaims.

I almost burst into tears at the hearty welcome. As I've traveled west, I've faced nothing but disregard from those I counted as friends back in New York, particularly on the heels of the headlines. The women have looked down their noses at me, and the men have given me sidelong glances when their wives and dates turn away. I know what they think of me. Exploiter of women. Dealing in the unspeakable and unsavory and immoral. But what they don't want to admit is that the exploitation and the unsavoriness was in place long, long before the "Jewish Jezebel" came on the scene, and that it was men who dreamed it all up. And if they knew the truth—that I was forced into this life like every other girl, and that I'm a rarity among madams in only taking seasoned girls who understand this work, and in giving them a protected house with security, weekly medical checkups, healthy meals, and even weekly beauty appointments—would that change their minds? I doubt it.

Forcing myself into my usual jaunty, sardonic persona, I retort, "What's an old codger like you doing in a swell place like the Royal Hawaiian Hotel?"

He snorts in laughter, then links his arm through mine. "I've been hunting high and low for a companion that can keep up with me, and I do believe I've finally found someone up to the task. Fancy a drink?"

"Robert, it's not even noon." He laughs, and I go on. "Well, noon, schmoon. A drink would be just the thing to get the sour taste out of my mouth, the one that's been with me since I left New York."

We march into the largely empty hotel bar and take a seat before the bartender. "You've got to try this drink they make at the House Without A Key," Robert says, referencing the well-known lounge at the nearby Halekulani Hotel.

"What's it called?" I ask, lighting a cigarette.

"The Halekulani, of course," he says.

"Should've guessed," I reply, and listen to Robert list the ingredients for the Royal Hawaiian bartender.

When we have the two colorful drinks in hand, we clink glasses and sip. "Delicious," I declare, and we chat amiably about the Honolulu nightlife. Downing one Halekulani and then another and another, all on empty stomachs.

For the first time in weeks, I feel a bit like my old self, and a bit tipsy, if I'm honest. And then Robert says, "You know we have to talk about them. The raids."

I signal the bartender for a fourth Halekulani for us both. The last thing on earth I want to talk about is the raids; I am sick to death of thinking about them and fearful of a misstep discussing them with someone else. But I nod, because if I seem reluctant to chat about the most-discussed topic in my world, I will appear very, very suspicious.

"Damn awful business," I say.

"It is. So many terrific gals behind bars," he says, finishing his drink. "How did you manage to get out in the nick of time?"

This is the sort of question I've been dreading. But for which I've prepared.

"Dumb luck. I'd sent one of my runners out for supplies, and he got word from a house that got raided before mine. My girls and I packed up lickety-split and got the heck out of Dodge." I recite my practiced excuse.

"Thank heavens." Robert sighs.

"I'm not sure the heavens are responsible, but I'll take what I can get," I say, then, reminding him that the long arm of the law hasn't always bypassed me, add, "I mean, I just got out of jail a few months ago. I can't imagine what my sentence would be if I'd been caught. I thought I'd get as far away as I could."

"Your escape is cause for celebration," Robert pronounces, lifting his glass to mine for another clink. And then he swills his new drink back in one.

"I'm grateful." As I sip, I wonder whether I passed muster with my lie and my tone.

"No one is happier than me that you are safe," Robert adds. "Except perhaps Walter Winchell." We both laugh at the thought of Walter being deprived of "Polly's girls" for too long.

But Robert isn't done. "Polly, people back in New York get why you left—and they're damned grateful you got out. But they're wondering . . ." He trails off.

My stomach lurches, and my heart starts to race. What do people know? What are they wondering about? Has there been scuttlebutt that I am a snitch?

"About what?" I ask, trying to keep the cigarette between my fingers from shaking.

"About why you're staying away. I mean, New York City isn't the same without Polly's. We need you back," he says, and I breathe a sigh of relief that Robert's primary curiosity is whether Polly's will be up and running again.

"Soon, I hope. Just want to make sure the heat has died down before I open up shop again."

"You know, Polly," he says, his words beginning to slur. He is two drinks ahead of me, after all, and I've been accused of having a hollow leg. "I've often thought that your life story would make a terrific book."

I burst into laughter. "My life? A book? That's rich."

"I'm serious," he says, and even though he's drunk, he's earnest. "It has all the hallmarks of the greatest Horatio Alger rags-to-riches stories."

"Come on," I say with a smile and a playful slap on his arm. "Discretion is key in my line of work. Telling my story would mean sharing my secrets, and I'm pretty sure that could get me in a heap of trouble. Not to mention, can you imagine me writing a book?"

"Well, if you ever change your mind, I'd be happy to help," he says, staring at the bottom of yet another empty glass. How on earth is he gulping down all these Halekulanis and still standing? "I am known for my scribbling, after all."

"I'll keep that in mind."

"Bartender," Robert suddenly calls out across the bar, which has gotten a bit more crowded in the time we've been here. A group of five other bar patrons take notice of his state, but I'm not worried. Despite the fact that the Royal Hawaiian is the poshest new hotel, this morning's bar clientele appears a little rough around the edges. Not so much their attire, but a certain hardness in their expressions that I've come to recognize in my profession. So I'm unconcerned that Robert's morning inebriation will ruffle their feathers.

When Robert doesn't get an immediate reaction, he yells out again, "Bartender, don't you know who you've got sitting at your bar? You can't keep *the* Polly Adler—the world's most famous madam—waiting for a drink!"

I want to disappear. The very last thing I want in this faraway outpost is to have attention drawn to my identity. I came here to flee all the notoriety. But I suppose, no matter how far I travel, I can never flee myself.

CHAPTER THIRTY-ONE

EUNICE

New York, New York
March 12, 1936

"It's been a month," the chief begins. "We've made the arrests, garnered the press, have potential witnesses sitting in jail . . . and yet, we have no firm connection to a major mobster."

He glances at each one of the assistant district attorneys, as we are, once again, gathered in the meeting room.

"Those girls are sticking to their stories," one of my colleagues says, frustration evident in his tone. "All of them are models or students or tourists. They have nothing to do with the prostitution racket. And the Combination? They've never heard of it."

Others chime in:

"The girls I've spoken with can't remember who they work for, can't recall the brothel locations, and they have no knowledge of anyone above the madams."

"Most of the girls refuse to speak to me at all."

Even Murray adds, "I've done more than a dozen interviews, and not one of the girls has opened up."

I understand their challenges. If I were one of the girls, I would stay silent, too. The district attorneys haven't treated the girls with any more respect than the men who exploit them. They've questioned the girls in the most insolent manner—with sharp words, cutting tones, and threatening scowls. Some of the men have made the women sit across the room, or they've worn gloves as if, just by answering questions, the girls might infect them with some vile disease.

"I've been able to gather more information from my interviews," I say, and watch as every eye turns to me. "Several girls have named Tommy the Bull, Ralph Liguori—the bruisers, as they call them—and known Mob associates. And when I ask the girls who those men work for, they've all said the same thing—*the Boss*."

"That's it?" One of the assistant district attorneys scoffs. *"The Boss."*

I'm tempted to retort that I've obtained more information than he has, but I only say, "None of the girls know the Boss' name, although one did say Liguori was one of the Boss' top lieutenants, and others have pointed to Dave Betillo."

"This isn't news," the assistant district attorney pipes in again. "We all know who the Boss is, but unless we can get one of these girls to say it's Luciano, we won't have anything more than we had a month ago."

"The point is the girls *are* talking to me. Every time I interview them, I gain a little more. I'm on the right track." Turning to the chief, I say, "The girls trust me." I pause, letting the unspoken words—*and they don't trust any of you*—linger. "I just need a little more time."

"Perhaps we need to reconsider our strategy," Murray says. "Mrs. Carter has the girls' trust; she should handle the interviews."

The room hums until the chief raises his hand. "All right. Mrs. Carter, you're in charge of the ladies moving forward." To the men, he says, "That will leave more time for you to handle the bookers like Pete Harris and the bondsmen. And, of course, your own investigations separate and apart from prostitution," he finishes.

Dewey has kept most of the assistant district attorneys on their initial assignments, holding fast to the hope that it will be some extortion racket or its like that will bring down Luciano.

"None of the bookers or bondsmen have talked either," one of the men says.

Murray says, "Actually, Pete Harris has asked to speak to an assistant district attorney. But we're letting him sit on ice for a little bit more. They've been behind bars for so long now, I expect that if Harris talks, others will follow."

"This could be big," another assistant district attorney says. "Harris has to know more than any of those girls."

Dewey says, "Proceed and keep me posted."

We all rise, but the chief stops me. "Mrs. Carter, a word in private."

I stiffen but sink back into my seat. Dread curls around me. I'm certain the chief wants to express his disappointment that we haven't gotten better results from the biggest raid in the city's history.

But once the room clears, Dewey says, "I'm worried that Luciano isn't at the top of the Combination."

His words jolt me. This isn't an admonishment; it's worse.

"Chief," I begin cautiously, "the girls have all spoken about the Combination and a boss, one man being at the top."

He raises his hand. "I'm not questioning the existence of the Combination or that prostitution is an organized operation. You've convinced me there, Mrs. Carter. What I'm questioning is whether *Luciano* is the 'one man.' No one has mentioned Luciano or implicated him in any way."

"The girls are just starting to talk. And soon we may have the opportunity to unlock Pete Harris. Once we have him, others will follow. We'll get the link to Luciano."

Dewey sighs. "All of the men we have—Thomas Pennochio, Ralph Liguori, Dave Betillo—they are all extortionists, loan sharks, murderers. Any one, or all of them together, could be running the Combination."

"We know Luciano insulates himself with layers of men. But that doesn't change the fact that he's at the top," I say. "Even if one of his underlings is handling day-to-day operations, not one of them would dare run a racket of this scale without his direct approval."

Dewey's disdain for a case based on prostitution never wavers. But today, I wonder if his skepticism is tied to the fact that Luciano has returned to New York. After fleeing the city on the heels of the *New York Evening Journal* article, he returned, checking into the Barbizon Plaza Hotel under his usual alias of Charlie Ross. Luciano has been gallivanting through the city, dining at the finest restaurants, throwing lavish parties at the swankiest nightclubs, and parading around with an entourage of menacing men and glamorous women. It feels brazen, as if he's taunting Dewey, saying that the law doesn't apply to him.

A month ago, he looked guilty. Now he seems anything but.

"We'll get the evidence, Chief." I rise. "We'll get what we need to stop Lucky Luciano."

As I settle back at my desk, I feel a suffocating frustration with Dewey's hesitation and the women. For the past month, I've spent so many hours inside the New York House of Detention, speaking to the girls and madams, that the prison guards not only know my name, but they know I prefer the chair next to the radiator in the visitors' room.

Every day, their words stay and resonate with me:

Daisy Wilson: "I thought I was coming to New York to be a seamstress, but by the time I figured it out, it was too late."

Helen Martin: "Lil Davie tells me where to go. He keeps me moving from house to house, and I hate it!"

Frances Cooper: "I once caught a glimpse of the Boss when I heard Tommy the Bull say he was waiting outside. But by the time I got to the window, I only saw a shadowy figure slipping into the back of a black Packard."

Nearly every girl ended their interviews with some variation: "I can't say anything more, Mrs. Carter. If I do, the police will find me folded inside some suitcase tucked behind an alley dumpster."

I won't get to Luciano through the girls. The madams are my path. Two—Jenny the Factory and Fat Rae—have spoken to me but have shared little. Two—Mildred Balitzer and Nancy Presser—are addicts. While the physical withdrawal has passed, I'm certain after the years of dependency on heroin, the psychological effects still linger. And finally, there's Red Sadie.

No matter how many requests I've made, Red Sadie won't even acknowledge that I exist. Her silence is as unyielding as the iron bars that confine her . . . and it speaks louder than anything she could say.

She has information.

But how can I make her talk? She believes that she can outlast us, that all she has to do is endure this confinement and eventually she'll walk free.

I must break her resolve. And then, an idea comes to me.

CHAPTER THIRTY-TWO

POLLY

Honolulu, Hawaii
March 12, 1936

Tap, tap, tap.

The repetitive sound becomes part of my dreamscape. I am back on the SS *Neckar*, traversing the dangerous Atlantic waters from Bremen, Germany, to New York, and I hear the final rap of the sailor as he locks the door to steerage. I recoil. For the next two weeks, I'll be locked in the dark, dank basement of this ship, shoulder to shoulder with hundreds of other immigrants in bunk beds stacked four high. Scrabbling for food and space and safety. A twelve-year-old alone on this ship. Alone in the world.

Tap, tap, tap. The noise grows louder and more insistent. The sailor's rapping transforms into the thudding of a branch on a window of a Coney Island cottage, blown by a strong, late-autumn wind. This scraping and banging is the terrible background sound of the assault on me by Frank the foreman.

I lurch forward, dragged from two of the most excruciating moments of my past into the present, only to realize that the tapping is a knock on my hotel room door. I folded the sound into my nightmares, transforming it wildly and terribly. I've worked hard to put my history behind me, and I refuse to let it hook me back now.

But who the hell is at my door?

Ever since Robert Benchley blew in and out of here like a Hawaiian hurricane this past week, I've been hounded. Initially by letters and telegrams from the Lion on behalf of her and the girls—who need me to pay my Majestic rent, their own board and temporary housing, and the myriad daily expenses I always cover for them—and my father, who wants money for a new business venture. All on no income. This has left me unable to lay hands on enough cash to keep up on my hotel bill, about which the hotel manager has been reminding me.

Then I was hounded by the gaggle of shady gentlemen who were at the bar that fateful morning with Robert. As I'd suspected, they were petty criminals who fancied themselves big shots, since the real gangsters haven't hit Hawaii yet. Upon learning my identity, they cobbled together some grand scheme about how I could open an upscale brothel on the island with their support. It doesn't seem to matter where I go at the Royal Hawaiian—pool, beach, lobby, restaurant, bar—one of them is there with another layer to their proposition: "What if we opened a house near the Royal Hawaiian to get top-notch clientele?"; "What if we made a shell-shaped front door to the bordello?"; "What if we installed a glass-sided pool for the girls to perform as mermaids?" I wave them off like gnats, but like gnats, they are annoying and persistent. I hope to hell that neither the local, small-time thugs nor the Royal Hawaiian Hotel accounting staff are behind that door.

"Miss Adler! Are you there?" a young female voice asks.

Ripping off the eye mask I always sleep in, even now when I keep to normal nighttime hours, I grab my robe and call out, "Who's asking?"

"I have a telegram here for you. It's marked urgent."

A telegram? Who would be reaching out to me here? Only the Lion knows where I am, and I just heard from her when she forwarded me bills and my father's letter asking for money. I'm not exactly hiding, but I'm not exactly broadcasting my whereabouts either. Instead, I've allowed myself to exist in a haze of sun, ocean breezes, swaying trees, and cocktails, forgetting—for a time—about the madam life I led in New York with all its dangers. Except when the local lowlifes nag at me, and the bills. Hawaii will intoxicate you if you let it, and I've given it full berth. I know it can't last forever. If nothing else, I'll be down to my last nickel soon enough. I should leave the Royal Hawaiian to save on cash, but I can't quite tear myself away.

Opening the door warily, I'm greeted by a wide-eyed young woman, lovely with dark eyes and shining black hair enhanced by the pink Royal Hawaiian uniform. With an eager smile, she hands me a sealed envelope bearing the Royal Hawaiian logo.

She pivots and walks back toward the staircase to the lobby. "Hold on, miss," I call to her.

Wanting to give her a generous tip, I slide a dollar out of my handbag. Curiosity overtakes me, and before the door closes, I open the envelope—forgetting to hand her the tip. Staring up at me on a Western Union telegram slip is a most unexpected message:

NEED INFO ON SALLY KAPLAN, AKA RED SADIE.
TO FORCE TESTIMONY.
COULD USE YOUR HELP HERE
EC

"EC" can only refer to Eunice Carter. I step away from the open door and fall into the desk chair. All the way from New York City,

Eunice Carter is reaching out to me again? How did she even find out where I am? I'd thought that, once I gave her the information she needed for her wiretaps and she secured her targets, our arrangement would come to an end. She'd have the key to unlock the web of relationships entangling Lucky with the Combination of bookers, madams, johns, and girls that he's created, and enough evidence to nail the boss of all bosses. From the newspaper articles highlighting the fact that Mrs. Carter still has girls and madams in prison for questioning, I have guessed that they aren't exactly spilling secrets. I had figured, however, she'd gather enough eventually. Sooner rather than later, I hoped.

But I was wrong. It seems that Dutch's pronouncement—that once you've committed yourself to one kind of life, you're committed forever—applies not just to criminals. It goes for snitches, too.

My instinct is to toss the telegram into the wastebasket. To keep silent and put this chapter behind me. But then I remind myself why I took the hazardous step of reaching out to Mrs. Carter in the first place: to put an end to the Mob's Combination, to restore whatever modicum of control and dignity is possible to a horribly undignified profession. If I refuse to help Mrs. Carter, will her case unravel, leaving streetwalkers and high-end brothel girls exposed to the exploitation of the Combination? Leaving my own girls without a safe path forward? And leaving me without the ability to run a house and meet my many financial obligations?

"Ma'am?" the young woman asks.

Her question brings me back to myself. The poor thing has been standing in the doorway while this battle plays out in my mind.

"Sorry, miss," I apologize, handing her the dollar I fished out of my handbag.

With her shiny black hair and winsome, grateful smile, the girl puts me in mind of Annie. The exquisite Midwesterner worked in my house for three years, until she returned home, having purchased a small farm for herself and her family with her earnings. How can I deprive girls like Annie of the only chance they might have to change their paths? Even if it means telling the prosecutor what I know about Red Sadie, a fellow madam?

Sadie *is* despicable. When the Combination started to take hold, Sadie was first in line to offer up her girls; at least, that's the rumor. She gathered them up on a silver platter for the Mob, making them available on any given night to fifteen different brothels via the bookers. Kit, who'd been friendly with one of Sadie's girls, shocked us with stories of girls used to living and servicing regular clients in Sadie's upmarket brothel being forced into two-dollar houses in Hell's Kitchen, where they were required to service fifteen men a night. Fifteen rough men, at that.

Suddenly I remember a conversation I overheard at my own bar. About a week before the raid, Dave Miller and Jimmy Frederico were deep in their cups, leaning against the King Tut bar. In actuality, I'd say the bar was keeping them upright. They weren't tremendously intelligible, but I'm certain I heard them talking about working with Sadie on the placement of her girls. I was too busy at the time worrying about my own hide and those of my girls to think much about it, but it seems I filed it away for this precise moment.

This tidbit would be crucial for Mrs. Carter, because Dave Miller and Jimmy Frederico are two of Lucky's top aides. Could this prompt the sort of direct link between the Combination and Lucky that the Dewey Commission is looking for? It's a step beyond the kind of link she currently has, I'm guessing, if she's reaching out to me here.

I call down the hallway to the young woman, who's waiting for the elevator. "Miss, would you be willing to do me a favor?"

"Of course, ma'am. That's my job."

I start scribbling on the hotel stationery, then glance up at her. "If I give you the details of a telegram I'd like to have sent, would you be able to orchestrate sending it personally?"

"Yes, ma'am."

"And not share anything about this with anyone, even your boss?"

"The Royal Hawaiian prides itself on providing discretion for our guests, ma'am."

I almost snort. Only about a hundred times, I've overheard the staff chatting about this guest or that one in very public spaces. But one thing I've learned over the years is that discretion can be bought.

I finish the text of the telegram: TELL HER YOU KNOW SHE WORKED WITH MILLER AND FREDERICO TO PLACE GIRLS. Then I copy down Mrs. Carter's information and pull a fifty-dollar bill from my wallet. This is likely more than the young lady makes in a month.

Handing her both, I say, "Please make sure this telegram gets directly to Mrs. Eunice Carter, following these instructions. And that no one at the hotel is the wiser. If you do your job well, another fifty will come your way."

Her eyes widen at this prospect, and then she scurries off. Undoubtedly the girl wants to get the telegram sent and report back before I change my mind. I close the door behind her and lean up against it, feeling the pull of my financial obligations and Mrs. Carter's requests alongside the push of the pesky local hooligans. It seems my time in the tropics is up.

CHAPTER THIRTY-THREE

EUNICE

New York, New York
March 27, 1936

"WHAT IS THIS?" Red Sadie barks as her eyes dart between me and the guard. "You said my lawyer was here."

The guard steps back and shuts the heavy metal door of the visitation room with a thud. Just as I instructed.

"You were told *a* lawyer was here for you. I am a lawyer. I'm Assistant District Attorney Eunice Carter."

Her lips curl into a sneer. "I know who you are. You were there gloating at the raid, and you've been nagging to meet with me ever since. You think I'm gonna talk to you?" She swings around and pounds on the door, each rap jarringly rapid, like a jackhammer.

"Miss Kaplan," I say, my voice cutting through her noise, "you'll want to hear what I have to say."

"I don't." Her banging grows louder, but I asked the guard to remain in the corridor and not react until I stood before the observation panel.

"You don't have to say a word. But if you value your freedom, you'll listen."

Her fist freezes in midair, and she faces me. "Your lawyer talk doesn't scare me. I've faced worse than you."

I meet her glare. "I'm not here to scare you. I'm here to tell you the truth. The fifty days you've spent here are about to feel like no time at all."

"Oh yeah?" she scoffs.

"Yes. Because now you're facing fifteen years."

My words strike her square in her gut, and Red Sadie's face drains of color. I slide onto the chair next to the radiator. She hesitates, then slowly lowers herself into the seat across from me. "Fifteen years?" she repeats, her bravado fading fast.

"Yes, because I've decided to move forward with your prosecution. I hadn't wanted to pursue any of the girls or madams, but your silence leaves me with no choice."

At another time, Red Sadie would have dismissed me with a laugh. But with an exorbitant ten-thousand-dollar bond and fifty days without contact from anyone besides the prison matrons, doubt must be whispering in her ear.

I say, "We're being pressured to show results from the raid."

"So you want to send me to prison for your own gain?" She jabs her finger on the table. "No one's ever gotten fifteen years for this."

"No one has ever received a ten-thousand-dollar bond, either, but these are different times, Miss Kaplan. We need a high-profile conviction, and prosecuting you will give us the headlines we need."

Her eyes narrow with disdain. "This is my life, and you're talking about headlines. Just so you can make a name for yourself."

"That's not what I'm doing," I say. "This is my duty. But if it furthers my career, that's a bonus."

Red Sadie folds her arms. "So this is only about winning for you, huh?"

"Winning is what we do in the prosecutor's office," I say as I stand and pick up my coat and briefcase. "And since we know all about how you worked directly with Miller and Frederico to place girls, I feel good about our odds of winning your case."

She was already pale, but with these words, now she looks almost ashen.

I pivot, but before I get to the door, in a softer voice, Red Sadie asks, "How many are you threatening with fifteen years?"

I don't turn around to face her. "I can't discuss other cases, but I can say that while you've stayed silent, others have been talking."

"Talking and walking. But how long will they be living?"

Red Sadie, like the other women, is terrified of the men behind the Combination. I want to tell her she will be protected. But in this moment, I have to remain the impassive, unshakable face of the law.

"I'll be in touch," I say without looking at her, and knock on the door to signal the guard.

The officer slides the observation panel open, and then, as he unlocks the door, Red Sadie asks quietly, "If I talk . . . do I receive the same deal as the others? And protection?"

"I didn't say anyone has a deal."

Her chuckle is bitter and knowing. "There's always a deal for a snitch."

Once outside, I wonder if I should have stayed longer, pressed her harder. Or will it serve us better to let her sit with the fear of being behind bars until 1951?

I make my way to the entry hall. But just as I wrap my coat around my shoulders, the guard calls out, "Mrs. Carter? The prisoner said she's not finished talking to you."

My eyebrows rise. I handled it perfectly.

When I return to the visitation room, Red Sadie launches in before I even sit down. "I need to know what I'm going to get for putting my life on the line."

"We won't move forward with your prosecution," I say. "You'll be free."

She chokes out a bitter laugh. "Free? To do what? Do you know what they do to girls who talk? I'm sure you've heard the stories. Of girls hanging on clotheslines like laundry on rooftops. Of bodies floating face down in the Hudson. What kind of freedom is that?"

"I can make sure you're safe. I can arrange protection."

"Protection?" Her eyebrows arch. "By who exactly? The cops? They're the ones who've been protecting me from you. There's no one out there I can trust."

"You can trust me. And I'll make sure you have proper protection. Even a new identity."

Her laugh is hollow. "Trust the woman who has one foot on my neck and the other halfway up the courthouse steps?"

"You can trust the woman who wants to prosecute the men you fear." I allow those words to simmer.

She is quiet for so long, I wonder if she's changed her mind. Finally, she continues in a whisper. "What do you want to know?"

I don't waste any time launching into my prepared questions: "Your brothel was one of the most successful in the Combination. Tell me about that operation."

For the next twenty minutes, Red Sadie recounts the rise and success of her brothel under her management. Then she details the changes that came when the Combination swept in.

"I didn't have a choice," she says. "The Combination promised protection, no competition, and that none of my girls would ever see the inside of a jail. All I had to do was turn over control of the girls' schedules to the bookers and hand over a hefty part of my profits. I only went along because I didn't want to find myself dangling from some rooftop."

She continues with her confection that she was only a victim. Because of Polly, I know that Red Sadie was not only a willing participant, but she was one of the first to sidle up to the Combination.

Then she lays bare how far up the corruption ran: "Everyone's palms are getting greased—from the beat cops to the precinct captains, and even some of the local political ward leaders. Girls turning tricks? That's a moneymaking machine for half of this damn city.

"And it's not enough that the girls are tossed around like rag dolls and treated like stray dogs. They're forced to take drugs, to keep them docile. The Combination sells that stuff right out of my place. It didn't matter that I didn't want none of that," Red Sadie says, waving her hands. "But if I were to say a word . . ." Her voice fades.

"Have you ever been personally threatened?"

"I'm threatened every day. Just by their presence. They come into my house and do what they want. Every time they look at me, I wonder if today's the day they'll break my neck."

Her words make my heart stop, and I want to take a moment to collect myself. But I must remain steadfast. I ask her about the men: Tommy the Bull, Ralph Liguori, Dave Betillo.

Then I turn to the first name Polly gave me. "What about Dave Miller? What's his role?"

"Miller is the money man. He collects the payments and gives the money to the Boss."

My pulse quickens. If Miller handles the money, he has to be one of Luciano's most trusted men.

"And Jimmy Frederico?"

That name makes her recoil. "He's a killer," she says with a slight quiver in her voice. "The others might rough us up, but Frederico handles the ones who end up dead. I've never seen him do it, but he laughs about it in front of all of us. And why wouldn't he? He knows he's untouchable. He's one of the Boss' top men."

I inhale. "And who's the Boss?"

She stiffens. "You know."

"You need to tell me."

She purses her lips, crosses her arms, and shakes her head.

"Miss Kaplan?"

Her eyes are glassy with tears. "Once I say his name, it won't be safe for you or me." Her fear is no longer a mere shadow between us; it's palpable.

"Please. It's the only way we can stop this."

Finally, she utters the words. "The Boss is Lucky Luciano."

As I STEP from the elevator to the jail parking garage, I'm thrilled. But I'm already thinking ahead—who might strengthen Red Sadie's account? I need someone to corroborate what she told me today, because I question whether, as a madam, she alone will be believed by a jury of twelve men.

My mind brims with questions as I reach my car, and then I freeze at the sight. On the driver's side, red paint is splattered across the door and hood. No message. No symbols. Just paint. It's so vivid that for a moment, I think it's blood.

A chill crawls up my spine as I recall Red Sadie's words—*Once I say his name, it won't be safe for you or me.*

Quickly, I scan the garage, and then, slowly, carefully, I glance through the car's windows. No one's crouched in the back seat, so I slide in and lock the doors. It takes a few seconds for me to catch my breath. How did this happen here? In the parking garage of the Women's House of Detention?

In just moments, my elation has curdled into dread. Paint alone cannot be a message, can it? The Mob isn't known for subtlety. This is probably vandalism. Some kids, out to get a kick. In the parking garage of a city jail.

I crank up the engine and ease out of the garage, scanning every vehicle I pass. At red lights, I check the mirrors and grip the steering wheel—not to drive but to keep myself from shaking.

Thank God it is only a ten-minute ride from the Women's House of Detention to our offices. But when I roll into this garage, I don't feel any relief. The first man at the entry nods in recognition, but I eye him warily. I do the same with the man on the second floor. I can no longer assume the men in place to guard us will protect us. Anyone, everyone could be on Luciano's payroll.

It isn't until I shut the door to my office that I allow myself to breathe. My thoughts churn. Less than an hour ago, I felt such triumph. We finally have a path to Luciano. But the closer we get, the more dangerous this becomes.

I need to speak to Dewey. Quickly.

But when I rush to his door and knock, I say only, "Chief, we have what we need."

Although I'm tempted, I cannot say anything about the damage to my car. Fear travels fast, and this news will silence every possible witness, completely slowing down this investigation. So I focus on Red Sadie and recount my exchange with her. I give the chief all the details she gave to me: two hundred brothels, two thousand girls, operations spread across all five boroughs. And the name at the top—Lucky Luciano.

"This is just the beginning, Chief. Red Sadie is the first to speak Luciano's name aloud; I'll use that as leverage for others."

"Well done, Mrs. Carter." Dewey nods, then rises to his feet. "Who will you get to substantiate her testimony?"

I balance his praise with his question, the same one that's been running through my mind. "We have several other madams in custody. First, I'll speak to Mildred Balitzer."

"Balitzer? Isn't she a junkie?"

"Yes, but she's been clean since she's been inside. My gut tells me that she could know a lot. She's been on both sides, as a prostitute and a madam. And if she isn't cooperative, there's Nancy Presser."

"Another junkie." Dewey shakes his head slowly.

"And . . ." I hesitate but then tell the chief about another addict. "Cokey Flo is in custody, too. We missed her in the raids because she was in treatment, but we picked her up a few days ago for pandering."

"What an array of witnesses—madams and junkies who are madams. Not exactly ideal. I wish we had someone else."

I nod, but I stay silent. From the beginning, my instincts pointed to Polly Adler, who—given her elevated position among madams—may have been the only one deemed credible. But she'll only operate on her terms. Only in ways that will protect her. So I have to settle for the information Polly has given to me and the madams we have in custody.

"Mr. Dewey, I have a note for you." Miss Rosse, Dewey's secretary, steps inside and hands him a piece of paper.

He studies the message in his hands and doesn't speak until she's left the room. "Luciano has fled the city again. The men tailing him believe he may have been tipped off. And if that's true, he knows how close we're getting."

My mind leaps to my car . . . and to Red Sadie! I know the Mob has eyes and ears everywhere, but I left her less than an hour ago. No, Luciano's fleeing couldn't be connected to my meeting—could it?

"If he knows we're closing in, he won't just run, he'll vanish," he says, his eyes still on that note.

"And he could go anywhere," I say.

"If he makes it back to Sicily, extradition will be nearly impossible." Finally, the chief glances up. "We don't have any more time, Mrs. Carter. We're going to indict Lucky Luciano for a prostitution racket."

CHAPTER THIRTY-FOUR

POLLY

New York, New York
March 27, 1936

"How much will you give me for them?" I ask, stroking my fur stoles in farewell. I experienced one of my proudest moments when I'd finally saved enough to buy these beauties, the ultimate sign of success in my book. I adored strutting through the streets of New York with one of them draped over my shoulders, like some Fifth Avenue matron. The thought of parting with them now hurts.

The man winces at my blunt ask. "That's not how we do things here at Rhodes."

I know this is no Stuyvesant Curiosity Shop, where any old thing is bartered and pawned in the hopes of buying it back one day. A place where towers of flimsy rings and ropes of cheap chains hang in the storefront windows and carousels of five-dollar shotguns spin on the street outside. This elegantly turned-out establishment is a secret pawnshop for the well-to-do, not that they'd ever use so crass a word for it. I overheard two of my grande dames discussing it one night while deep in their cups as *the* place where wealthy ladies off-load unfashionable jewels or jewels given to them by unfashionable men to acquire some secret "pin money" for themselves.

I haven't got all day for the niceties; I have an appointment to keep. But the bills are coming in, so I've got to playact at nice. Even while it breaks my heart to sell the treasures for which I saved and saved, I need the money.

"Pardon me for my bluntness, sir," I say, lowering my eyes in a semblance of humility. "I'm rushing to meet my mother at the hospital for an urgent procedure, and I've got to have cash on hand just in case. As my bank has decided to take an unexpected holiday, this is my only recourse." I seize upon a hot topic of the day as my excuse; President Roosevelt has been working to create consistency in banking—to help avoid panics of the sort we had a few years back—but banks are still known to declare the odd day off unexpectedly.

"Ah, I see," he says, nodding as if he believes me. He's used to the stories women tell for parting with their valuable possessions, and that seems to be part of the requisite exchange here. "That is what Rhodes is for. To assist you in a time of need."

"I am very grateful," I reply, keeping my gaze low. I can perform with the best of them. It's part of my job description.

He stretches out his hands over the sparkling display case, brimming with miner's-cut diamonds and gleaming pearls. "May I see the items? If you are ready, that is."

I nod, unable to hide the regret and unwilling to try. Unwrapping the stole from my neck and shoulders, I give it one last stroke before passing it to him, along with the second one draped over my arm. As I do, I say a silent word of thanks that I never found the time to have the crimson silk lining of the furs personalized. Because how much would I really get for fur stoles embroidered with the infamous name of the "Jewish Jezebel"?

Back in my new apartment in 65 Central Park West, my low mood at the loss of my furs is compounded by the state of the place. As I glance around at the familiar King Tut bar, English country house decor, and mahjong and poker tables from my vantage point on the sofa with a stiff drink in hand, everything looks diminished in the bright light of day. The gilt overlay on the faux Egyptian sarcophagus is flaking off, and the elaborate mahjong tiles are chipping. Even the leather chairs, rolltop desk, and intricately carved table that had seemed so elegant now feel overdone and out of place. This one-floor apartment, while spacious, doesn't have the multiple stories, grand staircase, secret entrance, and elegance of the Majestic flat. But it suits my changed purpose, I remind myself. And it's much, much cheaper.

The Lion and my three remaining girls have been installed here with me. For now, I run no trade from this house, and I hold no soirees, so I don't need Jerry regularly; it broke my heart to let him go, as well as the two maids. It's not safe to fully set up shop, so I cannot justify the expense. I keep the glitzier items around to keep up appearances and remind us of who we are, but I must remain squeaky-clean while the Dewey investigation continues and—hopefully—a trial looms. Not to mention, if I ran my usual business, I'd open myself up to the firm hand of the Combination, if they're still operating as they did before the raids. To offset my expenses and to keep some income flowing, I send the girls out to clients at hotels from time to time, but mostly we lie low and live on my ever-dwindling savings. On those quiet nights when we gather in the kitchen, it feels empty without Mabel and Virginia. The absence of Virginia, in fact, haunts me, and I continue to keep my ear to the ground as to her whereabouts. But with so many girls off the streets these days—many locked up in Mrs. Carter's prison—it feels a fool's errand.

The only saving grace has been that Lucky has hightailed it out of his swanky hotel suite to destinations unknown as Mrs. Carter's noose gets tighter around his neck. I feel more comfortable in New York thinking that he's not here, that the next time he'll traverse the city streets will be in cuffs. It's a ways until we reach that milestone, yet *I* don't have unlimited time. I find myself in a pickle. I can't make enough money to keep my operation going and my girls afloat long-term unless I run my house, but I can't run my house until Lucky is behind bars and the Combination shut down. So I've got to help get Mrs. Carter's show on the road, which, of course, risks everything. Assisting her feels like slowly digging my own grave; sooner or later, I will get caught snitching. The whole situation gives me a pit in my stomach, but I've got no choice other than to plunge back in.

I rise from the sofa and head to the foyer. Slipping into my navy wool coat, I reach for the belt to tie it around me. I feel hands on my shoulders. Looking back, I see the Lion's warm brown eyes studying me.

"Be careful out there," she cautions. She alone knows where I'm headed. I can trust no one else.

"It's a sunny spring day. Perfect for a stroll," I say with a small smile, downplaying today's task.

"Let's hope it stays sunny," the Lion replies, ever the pessimist. Ever the protector.

"It will," I reassure her.

Then I remember. Before I open the door, I hand her an envelope with a Rhodes logo from my purse, so full it practically won't seal. "This is for the bills. And something to squirrel away for a rainy day," I say.

With an apologetic look on her face—she knows how hard it was for me to part with my furs—the Lion slides the envelope into the big pocket on the front of her apron. Then, with a wry grin, she says, "I thought you just told me it was going to stay sunny."

HEADING DOWN TO the lobby from my sixth-floor apartment, I give the doorman a discreet nod as I pass through the front doors. It simply won't do to acknowledge each other publicly. I'm too notorious for congeniality.

The green awning shades me from the blinding spring sunlight as I step out onto Central Park West. Squinting, I proceed onto the corner of Central Park West and 66th Street, and as I wait for the streetlight to change, I glance back at my new apartment building. The structure has none of the glitz and glamour of famed architect Emery Roth's other, more dramatic dwellings, like the San Remo, the El Dorado, or the Beresford. But the sixteen-story tan brick and terra-cotta building does have a certain Neo-Renaissance charm and, most importantly, solidity. The qualities I now need in droves.

I enter the park and walk north on the path closest to Central Park West. Strolling, as if I have nowhere to be and not a care in the world, I linger once the path nears the lake. A mother and her young son stand hand in hand by the water's edge, chatting companionably. An unexpected tear wells up in my eye at this maternal scene, although I'm not sure why.

My wristwatch shows that the hour is near eleven o'clock. I only have three blocks until I reach my destination near 75th Street—the Ladies Pavilion.

Approaching Hernshead, the rocky outcropping along the lake's western shore, I spot the pavilion tucked away. The fanciful structure, with its stone floor, slate roof, and intricate wrought-iron sides, was designed first as a shelter for those waiting for carriages and then as a shady respite for the strolling ladies. But I know this meeting place was not chosen for its views of the lake or its protection from the sun or wind. It was selected for its seclusion. That, and the fact that no man would be caught dead here at the "Ladies Pavilion." Or, at the very least, would stick out.

A lone figure sits on one of two pavilion benches, gazing out at the water. I can't see the finer details from this distance, but I don't need them to know that it's Mrs. Carter. The perfectly erect posture, the prim folding of hands on her lap, and the tucking of crossed feet underneath her give her away. As I walk closer to her, the starched white collar on her dark suit and the two-toned oxford pumps confirm her identity. I cannot decide if she looks like a consummate professional or a church lady.

I do not speak as I walk into the rectangular pavilion, maybe ten feet wide and sixteen feet long. I do not even look her way. Instead, I settle onto the bench on the opposite side of the gazebo and stare out at the lake. As she is doing.

"Thank you for the information on Sadie," Mrs. Carter says, loud enough for me to hear, but no one else. Not that there's another soul in eyeshot.

"Did it help?" I reply, matching her volume.

"Yes, she confirmed that Miller and Frederico were involved in the Combination."

"And you have evidence for who they work for?" I ask about Lucky without saying his name.

"Yes, Sadie was especially helpful on that front, thanks to you. And the wiretaps and statements from the bookers, girls, and madams we brought in from the raids have filled in some gaps, even though they haven't yet named the name I need."

I think how precise and formal she is in her speech. Never a "yeah," always a "yes," unlike most of the people I encounter every day. Does Mrs. Carter think less of me for my accent—the one mocked by the blue bloods who used to frequent my house at the Majestic—never mind how elevated my vocabulary?

"You're getting closer," I say, knowing that there's a "but" in there somewhere. Or we wouldn't be here.

"We are," she says. Then she hesitates before continuing. "But it's still not enough. We need more witnesses to name the Boss."

"So I figured," I reply, fishing a cigarette from my handbag and turning away from the wind to light it. "Or you wouldn't have arranged this meeting."

"We're homing in on Mildred Balitzer," she says.

An image of the bottle-blond prostitute-turned-madam flashes in my mind. She might've been beautiful once, but the ravages of heroin have left her with only the occasional flash of prettiness. All her money—what little her "husband," Pete Harris, didn't wrestle away from her—ended up in a syringe and then in her arm.

Drawing deeply on my cigarette, I lean back into my seat. Never, ever taking my gaze off the lake. "You've got her behind bars?"

"We do."

"Is she functioning without shooting up?"

Mrs. Carter grows quiet. "After a spell."

"I bet that was a doozy of a spell. She's got to be one of the most voracious consumers of Cadillac I know."

"It wasn't pretty. She's recovered, so we're going to focus on her now. Her lips haven't loosened yet, but I think she might have some promising tidbits to offer."

"Even though she's been locked up for weeks? With no end in sight? And no drugs in her veins?" I ask, incredulous that all that time behind bars hasn't combined with her hunger for heroin to force a confession. I would've guessed she'd be trading secrets left and right for her next hit.

"Even still. Although we haven't really pushed, given her state. Until now."

"I'm surprised you haven't used her husband as leverage to get her talking yet. I know you've got him in custody."

"Her husband?"

Is it possible that Mrs. Carter and her cronies don't know that Pete Harris is Mildred's so-called husband?

"Pete Harris."

"Pete Harris is Mildred Balitzer's husband?" She sounds shocked, and I wish I could see her face. I figured Mrs. Carter was unflappable.

Mrs. Carter stands up abruptly, and I caution her, "Don't blow your wig. Sit down."

Lowering herself back onto her bench, she turns her eyes back to the lake. "Mildred Balitzer and Pete Harris are married?"

"After a fashion. I can't say that I've ever met a witness from their wedding, if you know what I mean. What I can tell you is that Pete is dizzy with the dame. Mad as a hatter for her. No one can figure why."

"So if I've got Mildred . . ."

"And you've also got Pete . . ." I let her finish the sentence.

"Then I've got leverage."

"With both of them, I'd guess."

"This opens up several promising avenues," she says slowly. Mostly to herself.

"I should hope so," I say. Lighting a new cigarette from the butt of the prior one, I inhale deeply. "I guess my work here is done."

"Not yet," Mrs. Carter says, her tone turning hard. "We need to know everything you know about Pete Harris' work as a booker—

including his contacts—and Mildred's work as a madam. And the intersection of their work together. In addition, I'll need to know their contacts in the Combination, the addresses of the places they lived, worked, and supplied girls, the names of the girls—"

"I'm no professor of the Harris-Balitzer empire," I interrupt her with a snort. "If you can call the dealings of a booker and a junkie madam an empire."

"But that doesn't exempt you from sharing what you do know," she says. "You need to keep helping me until we bring down Luciano."

Her words infuriate me; I did not build this life from nothing by following other people's edicts and rules. I want to resist, but I know she's right. What would happen to my girls and the Lion if I didn't continue? The case against Lucky might not proceed—not quickly anyway—and we'd all fall prey to the Combination in one way or another. How would my family here in America and in Yanow fare without my support?

Even still, I find myself asking, "Don't you have enough to build your case with the information I've already given you? Especially after today?"

"I don't think either of us can rest until Luciano is behind bars, do you?" The strength of her gaze and her tone is impressive. She's given up all pretense of not talking to me. "We're about to indict him and hopefully extradite him back to New York, Miss Adler. But we need every scrap of evidence to make the charges stick."

We meet each other's eyes, and I know we are going to have to stand together to fight the Mob. Until the deed is done.

CHAPTER THIRTY-FIVE

EUNICE

New York, New York
April 1, 1936

As I STEP out of my building, Mr. Johnson tips his cap the way he has every day for the past week. "Good morning," he says, holding open the rear door of his Buick.

I nod in return, then settle into the back seat of the car.

"We're heading to Crown and Glory this morning?" He slides behind the wheel.

"Yes, but would you mind stopping by the library first? Mrs. Andrews will be joining me."

"Sure thing." He eases the car from the curb. "And congratulations, Mrs. Carter," he says, glancing at me through the rearview mirror. "All of us here in Harlem are so proud of you."

"Thank you."

The fresh morning air steals through the cracked window, and I take in the scent of fresh bread wafting from the bakery, the giggles of schoolchildren skipping along with book straps slung over their shoulders, and the cries of the newsboys shouting out this morning's headlines:

"Big boss nabbed! Luciano arrested!" And then, on the next corner, *"Dewey's men get Lucky!"*

With the announcement of the indictment, this is a historic milestone for New York and a moment that ought to swell me with pride. Yet it is difficult to feel any sense of triumph when the paint on our car wasn't just vandalism—it may have been the final blow to my marriage.

If there had been any way to conceal that incident from Lisle, I would have once again kept the truth from my husband. But unlike the doll, it was impossible to hide the car. So on the evening Dewey decided to indict Luciano, I hurried home to speak to Lisle.

My intention was to tell him as soon as he walked through the door. But he'd come home with a bouquet of tulips and a trail of kisses, part of a steady effort he'd been making these past weeks to mend the rift between us. How could I have ruined that moment? So I waited until after dinner, although the quiet, candlelit meal hadn't prepared either of us for what I had to say.

THE SCENT OF the roasted chicken still lingered in the air, even though the dishes had long been put away. As Lisle relaxed in the parlor, puffing on a cigar and reading the evening edition of *The New York Times*, I stood at the window looking out at Colonial Park. Even in the shadows of the night, the first signs of spring were evident—buds blooming and the faintest tint of green on the trees. But I felt none of spring's promise; instead, I was laden with the weight of what I had to say and the fear of what my words might do.

Finally, I spoke. "Lisle, while I was at the House of Detention this morning, someone splattered our car with paint. Across the driver's door and the hood."

"Paint?" His brows pinched together.

"Yes. Red paint so dark, at first I thought it was blood." Then I added quickly, "But it could have been a kids' prank."

Deliberately, he folded the newspaper and placed it aside. "Please, Eunice. Don't stand there and feed me what you don't believe."

"I don't know what to believe. But what I know is that this will be over soon. We're indicting Luciano. We're coming to the end, and all of these threats will go away."

"Is that what you think? Don't you know that an indictment will put you in more danger? Shackles won't stop him, prison won't stop him. He will intimidate witnesses, and he will certainly try to strike fear into all of you. We are not any closer to this ending. An indictment is just a new beginning."

I shook my head, but I had no new words to convince him. "I don't want this to become an argument, Lisle. I just wanted you to know what was going on."

"Fighting with you is the last thing I want to do. But damn it, Eunice, first the letter about Junior and now this. What will be next?" His voice was so soft when he asked, "You?"

"No, because I'm being so careful."

"And yet, today . . . someone smeared bloodred paint on our car."

"It was the car and not me."

"Not you. Not yet."

My breath caught; his words sounded like a prophecy.

When I stayed silent, he shook his head. "You won't have to worry about us having this conversation again. I'm finished with it. But God help us, if something happens to you, I will go to my grave never forgiving Luciano." His voice was barely a whisper when he added, "And what scares me even more—I will never forgive you either."

Even now, the echo of his words stings. Tears burn my eyes as I reach inside my pocketbook and draw out the note I found on our bed the next day when I came home from work:

Eunice: I'm going away for a few days to clear my head. I've hired Mr. Johnson to drive you wherever you need to go. And I'll be praying every moment for your well-being.

I've read this letter so many times, the paper is tattered at the edges. And still, I don't understand. Lisle has never gone away leaving me with just a note. He did send a telegram saying he'd "arrived" safely, but there was no mention of where he was or how long he would be gone.

My thoughts scatter as the car lurches to a stop in front of the library. Before Mr. Johnson can get out of the car, the library's door flies open, and Regina bounds down the steps.

"Good heavens," I say as she bounces into the back seat. "You didn't even give Mr. Johnson time to properly open the door for you."

She's radiant, her smile a mile wide, and suddenly I feel a bit of joy. She says, "I didn't want to miss one minute with you. Not today. And not with Mr. Johnson driving us around in style." She pauses to greet him properly as he pulls the car into traffic on 135th Street. "We're so fancy today. Did Lisle hire the car to help you celebrate?"

Thank goodness she doesn't wait for my response. Instead, she reaches into her satchel and starts piling newspapers onto her lap.

"Gracious me! Are you opening a newsstand?"

She laughs as she fans the newspapers out like a deck of cards. "Josh if you must, but this is a banner day. Literally. Look at these headlines." Regina reads with reverence: *"Dewey Seizes Vice Leader in Arkansas . . . Luciano Arrested in Hot Springs as Dewey Rounds*

Out His Case . . . Luciano on His Way Under Guard . . . Dewey Proposes Three-Hundred-and-Fifty-Thousand-Dollar Bond . . . Salvatore Luciano Arrested and Extradited to New York to Face Dewey."

She sighs. "Eunice, this is monumental. I'm so very proud of you."

"I think you've made up a few of your own headlines." I manage a half smile. "Not one of those newspapers mentions me. It's all about Dewey."

She flicks her hand, dismissing my modesty. "Behind every successful prosecutor is a woman toiling away so the man can be given all the credit." Regina taps the papers. "They may not say it in the newspapers, Eunice, but I'd wager a dollar that you're the one who pinned Luciano to the wall. You're the only woman on the team, so you worked harder. Once again, you're the Queen of Harlem!" she exclaims. "Lisle must be bursting with pride."

I turn my gaze to the window. The joy Regina carried into the car fizzles, the air now flat.

"Are you all right?" Regina covers my hand with hers as we approach the salon.

"I'm fine," I say, although I don't meet her eyes.

As we slip out of the car, Mr. Johnson assures me, "I'll be here when you're ready to go."

Regina and I step into Crown & Glory, one of Harlem's most celebrated beauty salons. America Pinkston, the proprietor, has designed this space to dazzle: the black tufted velvet chairs, the gleaming white lacquered tables, the rows of round-bulbed lights circling every mirror, and the black-and-white checkerboard flooring, shining as if it has just been waxed. Overhead, the black metal chandeliers add to the glamour.

"Miss Eunice," America calls from her station. She was one of the first to earn her certificate as a hair culturist from Madam CJ Walker's Lelia College of Beauty Culture.

America excuses herself from her client and sweeps me into a warm embrace. "I was so glad you called for you and Miss Regina." She greets Regina with a hug, too.

I say, "I appreciate you fitting us in."

"Everybody has been coming in to get gussied up for the Apollo tonight." She gestures toward the chairs lined against the wall. "Please make yourselves comfortable. I won't be too long." She winks as she adds, "I wouldn't dream of keeping the woman who's putting Lucky Luciano behind bars waiting."

I manage a light chuckle and follow Regina to a pair of chairs, tucked away far from the buzz of the dryers. Regina hardly waits for us to settle before she says, "So, is there anything new you can share that's not in the newspapers?"

I glance around the salon. Women in chairs are chatting with the stylists. Others, sitting beneath the hood dryers, are flipping through the latest issues of *The Crisis* or *The Messenger*. No one is paying attention to Regina and me.

Still, when I turn to my friend, I whisper, "Nothing about the case, but so much has happened with me."

"Something else? Besides the note about Junior?"

I nod, and then it all spills out. I tell Regina everything: the doll, the paint on the car, and the real reason why Mr. Johnson is now behind the wheel. I tell her about the fragile peace Lisle and I had for months and how it shattered.

I pull Lisle's note from my pocketbook and hand it to my friend.

"Lord, you've been carrying all of this," she says softly when she finishes reading. "I wish you had told me."

"I've just been so busy, trying to keep my head down and stay focused." I blink, damming every emotion inside me. "But it's come to this—he said he'd be gone for a few days, but I don't know."

"Oh, he'll be home," she says with a conviction that surprises me. "He told my husband he'd see him at the Apollo. And he loves you, Eunice. That's why he's so beside himself." She sighs and shakes her head, and I see the weight of unspoken words in her eyes.

I tilt my head. "What?"

She hesitates for a moment. "Please don't take this the wrong way, but I don't understand. You're risking everything—your marriage, your son's peace, and maybe even his safety. And while I'm so proud of you, I can't make sense of why you want this job so badly. Maybe it is time to do what Lisle wants. When the Mob is getting this close, maybe it's time to quit."

Her words astonish me. "You, of all people, know the importance of my work and—"

"I don't want to hear what you've practiced for the press," she interrupts, leaning in closer to me. "I'm asking you woman to woman, friend to friend. You have a husband who loves you and a son who needs you. Yet you seem so willing to put it at risk. What's driving you to do this?"

I sit with her question for a moment. "I can't give it up. I don't know how to walk away," I say, quietly. And then I ask, "Have I ever told you about my grandfather?"

She squints as if she's trying to recall, then shakes her head.

"I'm surprised, because Stanton Hunton, my father's father, is my hero. He died before I was born, but with my father's stories, it was like my grandfather was alive in our home.

"My grandfather was enslaved, but he refused to accept those shackles. He escaped, only to be hunted down and dragged back. But being captured didn't keep him in chains. Because he was never going to give up on being free. So he escaped again and was dragged back. And then he escaped again. Three times, until he was given what he desired most. He was given his freedom; he was manumitted.

"What I learned from my grandfather's life is never to give up on what you really believe. But what I've learned from my life is that shackles aren't always made of iron. I've felt bound for so long—not by chains that I could see, but by all of my failures."

"You failed? At what?"

I give her a faint smile. "Only a friend would say that. But if you were being honest, you know, I was like a ship adrift. Yes, everyone said I was smart and educated, but I was floundering. It took me six years to decide to go to law school. And even when I finished, I didn't know if I was going to return to social work, or try writing again, or do something else entirely. I never felt free to sit and ask myself what it was that I really wanted to do. Because I was living for the blessing of my mother, the approval of my husband, and the favor of the Harlem society ladies who expected so much from me simply because I was Addie Hunton's daughter and Dr. Lisle Carter's wife."

"But you're one of the most successful people I know."

"Maybe by your standards, but not by mine. Not until now. This is the first time I've attained something without giving thought to what Lisle would say or my mother would think. I interviewed for the prosecution team without telling anyone. I walked into that interview feeling free. I was confident and determined because it was my decision and it was for me.

"And once I was selected, I blazed my own trail. Even when I felt pushed aside, I did the work and got results. I did all of that—not as a Hunton, not as Lisle's wife. I did it as Eunice Roberta. And even with all the challenges that come with being a colored woman on that team, I can live with it because I'm free."

"I've only ever thought of freedom in one way."

"I'm not saying that what I'm talking about is equivalent to the emancipation that my grandfather and the other slaves received. But I know my grandfather and the others fought to break the chains of slavery so that every one of us could live up to our God-given potential.

"I'm thirty-six years old, and for the first time, I feel like I'm not bound by any chains. Yes, there are still forces that seek to keep me in my place. But I'm a colored woman on the most important prosecution team in the country." My voice falters. "And yet, I can't even celebrate, because while finding myself, I'm losing my husband. God knows this isn't what I want, but shouldn't Lisle and Junior have the best of me?"

She nods.

"I can only give them that once I believe that I *am* the best version of myself. I'm just now beginning to believe that."

"Wow." Regina sits for a while, taking it in. Her eyes glisten as her fingers close around mine. "I've always looked up to you, Eunice, but in just these few minutes, you've given me a lifetime of lessons. You've stopped dimming your light to please others, and now you're shining like God intended. You're right: There's no greater freedom than that. And I hope one day to be as brave as you, so I can be free, too."

As THE APOLLO Theater fills up, I fight to hold myself together. What made me think I could attend this performance alone? Everything reminds me that Lisle isn't here—from the people who stopped me as I entered the theater to the empty aisle seat beside me.

I need to leave. But as I have that thought, Regina leans in close to me. "It's going to be fine," she whispers, as if she read my mind.

I nod, and when she turns back to her conversation with her

husband and Adam Clayton Powell Jr. and his wife, Belle, I shrink into my seat.

The theater lights begin to dim, and for the first time since I arrived, I'm relieved. I can hide in the darkness. And then . . . Lisle slips into the empty seat next to me.

I stare at him, astounded. "What . . ."

He presses his forefinger against my lips before he gives me a small kiss. "Let's just enjoy the show."

From the wings of the stage, the tuxedoed announcer says, "Ladies and gentlemen, Mr. Duke Ellington," and the ovation erupts. As the dapper Duke strides onto the stage in his charcoal-gray three-piece suit, almost everyone in the two thousand seats in the Apollo Theater rises. The Duke hasn't struck a single note, but the walls of the Apollo quiver with admiration and reverence for him.

He gives the audience a gracious wave, and the cheers break out. Women are swooning—the Duke has already cast his spell on every lady in the theater.

I've always admired Duke Ellington, and I've had my moments of swooning, but right now, I just want to take my husband by the arm, go home, and set our marriage right.

But then Lisle intertwines his fingers with mine, and I settle with the rest of the audience as Duke bows before his fifteen-piece orchestra. It's only because Lisle keeps holding me that I can be still.

For the next hour, Duke and his orchestra blow the roof off the Apollo with his hits: "Harlem Speaks," "Mood Indigo," and of course, "In a Sentimental Mood." Finally, he rises from the piano and comes to the center of the stage.

"Before we perform our last number, I want to thank everyone for joining us this evening. You know, I may have been born in Washington, DC, but Harlem is where I belong."

With our applause, we welcome him home.

"If you will allow me a few minutes of personal privilege, there are a few Harlem dignitaries I'd like to recognize. Of course, Reverend Adam Clayton Powell Jr. and his lovely wife, Belle. And Assemblyman William T. Anderson and his lovely wife, Regina."

Duke Ellington continues, calling out Walter White and Roy Wilkins and his favorite writer, Langston Hughes.

Then he says, "And a name we all know from her bid for assemblyman and for her tireless work with the special prosecutor's office. Mrs. Lisle Carter."

Me?

I am taken aback.

Lisle grins as he offers me his hand to help me stand—and I wonder if my husband knows his gesture means as much to me as Duke Ellington calling my name.

But once I rise, my legs feel like jelly. It is Duke Ellington, after all, acknowledging me. The theater is loud with thundering applause, and I turn, waving to everyone.

I am walking on air. Duke Ellington knows my name, and my husband is home. And I will see to it that Lisle and I stand firm, even as I fight to keep my own light burning.

CHAPTER THIRTY-SIX

POLLY

New York, New York
April 22, 1936

THE PHONE RINGS as I'm applying a final swipe of lipstick in front of the hallway mirror. I'm considering whether I should try a different shade than my signature crimson when the Lion appears in the entry hall. I hope it's nothing urgent; Mrs. Carter awaits in Central Park.

"The call is for you," she says, her tone wary.

"Usually is," I answer, then turn away from the mirror toward her. A strange expression has overtaken her face. "You've got quite the look on your mug. It's not the fuzz, is it?" My stomach lurches. "Is it about Virginia?"

I've tried to leave no stone unturned in my search for her, but in this world, some stones are very well hidden. So I'm always worrying that I've somehow missed her.

"No," she says slowly, then pauses as if she can't quite believe what she must say next. "The caller says she's your mother."

"My mother?" I ask, gobsmacked. I haven't heard my mother's voice for nearly twenty-five years. Not since I was packed off on the first leg of that terrible journey from Yanow to America. Letters, yes, those I've received, and even the occasional telegram. But telephones aren't exactly in abundance in Yanow. "Are you sure?"

"Am I sure it's your mother? No. Am I certain she described herself as your mother? Yes. I asked twice because her accent is very thick," the Lion says, and I don't doubt it. If it's indeed Mama, I'm surprised she knows English at all. Although heaven knows, she's had years enough to practice.

"My God," I cry out, and feel a brief squeeze from the Lion's comforting hand on my arm. She's the only person in the world who knows my *full* story. As well as my mixed feelings—frustration and relief—over my mother's ongoing decision to stay in Yanow.

I race toward the phone. Sitting down at the little desk in the parlor where it perches, I pick up the receiver with a shaking hand and say, *"Mamele?"*

The word slips out; I don't recall ever using the diminutive, affectionate form of the word "mother" with her before. The line is quiet for a long moment, and I wonder if the Lion got it all wrong.

Then I hear the familiar sound of my mother's voice. *"Iz dos meyn Perle?"*

Suddenly I'm twelve again. I'm Pearl, the young Jewish girl living in a small, segregated Russian town where people have dressed and acted and lived the same way for hundreds of years. A bright, ambitious girl who wants a different sort of existence and believes she's found it with a scholarship to the Pinsk Gymnazia. A girl who had her anticipated future and her familiar present torn away from her when she was sent to America. A girl who missed—and misses—her mother. I start to cry.

"Mama! It's Pearl! Where are you that you can call me?" I ask her in my now-rusty Yiddish. She's never had access to a telephone in Yanow before.

Laughter resonates through the receiver, and I can hardly believe it. My mother isn't known for her delight. She must have good news. Perhaps my father has finally summoned her, after my endless needling. But why wouldn't my brother or father have informed me that my mother was finally, *finally* coming here?

"I am in Brooklyn, Pearl, staying with old friends from Yanow."

"Brooklyn?!" I squeal. "You've already made the journey?"

"Yes, with your three younger brothers. I wanted to surprise you."

"You've done more than surprise me—you've shocked me," I cry out, but my reaction is far more knotty than mere shock. A queasiness settles in my stomach alongside the excitement at finally seeing my mother after all these years. With Mama so close, will she find out who I really am? I decide not to think about this terrible prospect now, but to revel in her arrival.

I am going to lay eyes on my mother. Imagine.

"Can you come to where we are staying? Now?" my mother asks.

"Of course, Mama. I cannot wait."

MY STEP FEELS curiously heavy and light as I traverse the intersection from my apartment to Central Park. The thought of my mother nearby is unfathomable after so long, and I want to rush to her side. I couldn't tell her that a meeting with an assistant district attorney investigating the Mob would delay my departure by an hour or more. That would only be the beginning of an inquiry that might lead to the truth.

The iron gate to the park swings shut behind me as I step inside, and I jump. The clang so closely resembles the slam of a prison cell door that, for a second, I'm transported back to that horrible month in the House of D. Then the chirps of blue jays and warblers and the sight of vivid green buds on the cherry trees—stunning harbingers of spring—brings me back to myself, but not completely.

I stride toward the agreed-upon meeting place near the beds of riotous red, yellow, and white tulips that line the rambling pathways in Shakespeare Garden. From the looks of it, we won't be alone here on this sunny spring day—mothers with prams and pairs of women weave in and out of the walkways, pausing for sniffs of blooms here and there—and I feel exposed, as though anyone's eyes might land and linger on us. But I haven't been able to dissuade Mrs. Carter from her view that the public space acts as a camouflage for our meetings.

Sauntering in the direction of Mrs. Carter, I approach a bed of purple flowers directly behind her and lean forward to study them.

"You're late. I've been twiddling my thumbs for thirty minutes, no doubt drawing attention to myself the whole time," she says, as angry as I've ever heard her. "I was just about to leave."

I stand up and reply, always peering in the opposite direction. "My mother called me as I was about to step out the door."

"Your mother? If I stopped what I was doing every time my mother wanted to talk to me, I'd never leave my apartment or get any work done. She's never had an opinion she didn't share."

"I hadn't heard my mother's voice for twenty-five years."

Mrs. Carter doesn't turn toward me, but she does stop moving. She half whispers, "Twenty-five years?"

"Yes. Not since I left Russia by myself at twelve."

"My goodness, I'm sorry for my harshness about you being late," she murmurs. "That must've been hard."

"There were times I didn't think I'd survive it. I certainly never thought I'd see my mother again."

"Was the call to tell you she's on her way?"

"The call was to inform me that she's arrived. And that she's waiting for me in Brooklyn."

"Oh my," she says, her voice heavy with emotion. "I've been

separated from my child since the investigation began. I cannot imagine being parted as long as you and your mother have been."

"It's difficult, isn't it?" I glance in her direction for a brief second, just as she does the same. Our eyes meet, and I see her eyes brim with tears. My own eyes well up, at her loss and my own.

"More challenging with every passing day," she says. "Let's get down to business and get you out of here fast. Back with your mother."

A BRISK TWENTY minutes later, I hustle out of the park, reversing my path. Our time together may have been short, but Mrs. Carter's list of questions was anything but. Today, she poked and prodded on the topics of a bunch of Red Sadie's girls, Lucky Luciano's girlfriend, and syndicate enforcer Ralph Liguori and his girlfriend, Nancy Presser. She's trying to make an airtight case, and I'm only too happy to provide answers. But I'll have to do some investigating of my own to get them.

Crossing Central Park West, I walk down the empty sidewalk toward my apartment building; I want to fetch several items to bring my mother. An odd sensation passes through me, as if I'm being watched, but I chalk it up to the fact of Lucky's extradition to New York. Never mind that he entered the city in shackles and sits behind heavily guarded prison bars. I feel his presence and know that vice and violence can be conducted from a jail just as easily as the streets. I'm sure he has eyes on his empire from the slammer. Maybe even me. *Stop,* I tell myself, *Lucky has got bigger fish to fry than Polly Adler.*

Just then I hear the squeal of tires, the sound of a car cruising at top speed. I scan the vicinity. No vehicles are peeling down Central Park West, and when I don't hear the noise again, I disregard it. Just another joyrider.

I'm at the corner of 65th Street and Central Park West when I hear the shriek of tires again. I look up quickly and see a huge black sedan—the size of a battleship—barreling down the road. Until it comes to a screaming halt a quarter of a block away from me.

I freeze. Should I run? Race into my house, grab my bag of necessities—the hidden cash, fake identification card, and some jewels I always keep on hand—and flee? But where could I go that Lucky Luciano wouldn't find me? Anyway, wouldn't taking off telegraph guilt to him? And what punishment would he exact upon the Lion and the girls? And I risk never seeing my mother again. Just when she's so close.

Instead, I pivot toward the sedan, staring at it head-on. Hand on hip, cigarette between my lips, I face the vehicle and whoever is inside. I hope I appear more confident than I feel.

An interminable pause ensues before someone finally opens the car door. Out steps a man I've never seen at the King Tut bar before but who has been pointed out to me at several speakeasies and nightclubs over the years. Rumor has it that this minor gangster has recently been promoted, undoubtedly because the ranks of Lucky's usual men have been depleted. Beggars can't be choosers, I guess, especially when most of your best men are in jail.

Without a word, the thug in a charcoal-gray suit gestures for me to walk toward the car. That urge toward flight returns, but I know I could never outrun a gun. And I'm fairly certain that there is one trained on me right now. A bullet could sail down 65th Street and kill me on the spot, and these men would make sure that no one on the street ever saw them do it. I would simply disappear. That is one of their specialties.

Without a choice, I walk in his direction. Not fast, not slow. More of a guarded stroll. I never look away from him; that would signal weakness or nerves. A woman without secrets or guilt has no reason to be hesitant or fearful. Especially a woman like me, who's seen it all.

Coming within ten feet of the man, I stop. I know better than to speak first. What if I make the wrong guess as to why he's here? Or use the wrong tone, inciting the worst? After all, he could be using this unorthodox approach to book one of my girls, and I could ruin an innocent encounter by babbling on about Mrs. Carter simply being an old friend. I almost laugh at the preposterousness of this wishful thinking.

The gangster doesn't say a word. He only points toward the interior of the car and stands back to give me space to enter. Sliding across the black leather back seat, I nearly bump into another person on my right. The interior is so dark I can't see him at first, particularly since my eyes don't immediately adjust from the bright spring day. When my vision does adapt, I realize the man's face isn't familiar. But the expensive cut of his suit, its wool and cashmere fabric, and the swanky silk tie are known to me. They signify power.

Who is this man?

The gangster settles onto the back seat to my left. I am sandwiched between the men so tightly that I couldn't move if I tried. The car is silent except for the driver closing the passenger door. Even when the driver returns to the front seat, we sit immobile, no one uttering a word. What are we waiting for?

Another long black sedan, nearly identical to this one, crawls down the street and pulls in front of us. The man to my right turns around and glances through the back window. I follow his stare. There behind us is a third automobile, just like the first two. Only when we assemble into a caravan do we begin to proceed.

It is then that I understand, and it is then that the hysteria begins to set in. My hands begin to tremble, so I slip them under the handbag on my lap. My eyes well up with tears as I think of the girls and the Lion back at my house—and my mother in Brooklyn—but I force them wide and refuse to blink, so the tears dry.

There can only be one reason I'm here in the back seat of this sedan between these mobsters: Lucky knows that I've been feeding damning information to the Dewey Commission. And he's sent his goons for me. My time is up.

CHAPTER THIRTY-SEVEN

POLLY

New York, New York
April 22, 1936

I DON'T RESIST. I don't twist and turn against the pressure of my captors' bodies. I don't lunge across one or the other for the car door when we stop at a traffic light. In fact, my fiercest desire at this moment isn't freedom. It's for time enough to say goodbye.

I long to embrace the Lion and tell her how much her friendship and loyalty have meant to me, how she gave me the unconditional love that my father never did. And I do wish I could see my mother's face one last time; it seems terribly unfair to miss that when she's finally nearby. I long to give a farewell embrace to Kit, Angelica, and Rosalie, my current girls, and to all my girls lost. To Virginia. They are the sisters—or, in some ways, the children—that I never had and will never bear.

But then a thought strikes me, one that sucks the wind out of me like a punch. Do the girls feel the same way about me? Do they blame me for what goes on behind their closed doors, something I try not to think about? The tawdry games they have to play and the risky surrender of their bodies night after night. Because when I do allow myself to venture to those dark places, I have to acknowledge that I'm no hero. That the protection I offer them is only surface deep and that the biggest sacrifice is borne by the girls themselves. That the house I offer them is no home, and that in fact, it's the minimal atonement I can offer for benefiting from their submission to this terrible vice. No, the girls probably don't think of me as family the same way I think about them. Maybe, it sickens me to think, they perceive me just as I perceived my own father.

The sedan takes a sharp right turn, and the mounting danger supplants my sadness over my girls. Glancing out the window, I try to keep track of the twists and cuts the caravan makes down a series of increasingly dark streets, but I soon lose all sense of direction. Even though I attempt to catch the names of the street signs as we zoom past, I can't even say for certain that we are still in Manhattan.

After three-quarters of an hour, our vehicle slows, and we pass into a tunnel. A tunnel to where, I have no idea. The passageway narrows and becomes almost pitch-black. Finally, I see a glimmer of light in the distance. As it grows brighter and brighter, I realize that we have driven into a vast, underground garage, where a line of black sedans, almost identical to this one, are parked.

The man to my left turns to me with a smile. I can't tell if it's meant to reassure or terrify. Either way, my fear mounts as he reaches for my arm to help me out of the vehicle.

I scan the cavernous space, my senses alert to danger. The man leads me through the maze of vehicles, with the other man close behind, until we reach a staircase. We climb three flights, and I begin to tremble, thinking that they're planning to toss me off the top of this building. I know more than one streetwalker or john who died that way. Instead, at the fourth-floor landing, the first man stops and opens a door.

Inside is a standard office layout, a real plain vanilla work area with offices and secretarial stations. I'm relieved that it's not the roof of the building—or some god-awful torture chamber—but I'm confused and still spooked. Why in the hell have a pair of mobsters brought me to what looks like an accountant's office?

Weaving through rows of desks, we slow as we approach a set of ajar double doors. The man leading me pauses, peering inside what must be a conference room.

I watch as he nods to someone. Then he turns to me and speaks for the first time. "They're ready for you."

My mouth opens, and I'm about to ask, "Who is ready for me?" when I think better of it. Confidence and coolness have got to rule the day if there's a chance in hell I'm getting out of here in one piece.

I square my shoulders and muster up what little height I've got, and I step inside. The half smirk I've forced onto my lips vanishes.

There, sitting around a garden-variety conference table, are a dozen of the top mobsters in the country, racket men who may have never been assembled together before. From sightings at nightclubs and parties and shows, I recognize Joseph Bonanno, Tommy Gagliano, Joseph Profaci, and Frank Costello sitting on one side of the table. On the other, we've got Alfred Polizzi, Owney Madden, Joseph Aiuppa, and a few I don't recognize. It's a regular gangsters' heaven.

If there's a heaven, there's bound to be a hell. And I guess that's where I'm headed.

"Enjoy the ride?" Joseph Bonanno breaks the silence, a cigar dangling from his lips. This guy's nickname might be the comical Joe Bananas, but there is nothing funny about him.

"A regular gasser."

The words slip out before I can even think. If I had the presence of mind to craft my response before speaking aloud, I wouldn't have chosen anything that smacked of humor or disrespect.

But a couple of the men snort at my retort, and soon everyone is chuckling. Have I done all right here? One of the men I don't recognize says, "I don't think anyone has ever called our goon over there a gasser before. Eh, Bruno?" He nods in the direction of the man from the car, who stands inside the conference room. Bruno doesn't move a muscle.

"I'll cut to the chase, Miss Adler," Bonanno says. "We're behind the eight ball on this Lucky trial."

A couple of the men nod, and several grumble. I have a million questions, but I know better, and I've gathered myself enough to wait.

"It seems this blasted Dewey is locked onto the idea that Lucky combined every hooker and brothel in New York into one big organization, if you can believe it."

I can. Because it's the truth. But it'd be a death sentence to admit it, so I shake my head and scoff like everyone else. I almost laugh at the thought that, if these goons weren't so entrenched in the Mob life, they might consider having a run at Broadway. Their acting skills are that good.

Another one of the bosses chimes in. This time, it's Tommy Gagliano. "Now, they've hauled in dozens of girls and madams. Not to mention nearly every one of the bookers and fixers. And they're milking them like cows for information."

Again I *tsk*, just like everyone else. I'm still not sure what these bosses of bosses want from me. Unless they know about my meetings with Mrs. Carter. So far, I'm not sensing fury or retribution, but it's too early to be hopeful. I've seen men like these play terrible games with their victims.

"That's where you come in," Bonanno says, the ball back in his court. "Information."

I freeze. Is he suggesting that I've given the Dewey team information? The tone of this meeting suggests otherwise; that and the fact that I'm still alive. But I'm not sure what he's driving at.

"You know I'm no blabbermouth," I say quietly.

"Nobody would ever call you a snitch, Miss Adler."

Relief courses through my body at these words. I could sag to the ground at this reprieve.

Instead, I say, "I would hope not."

"Actually, talking to us is the opposite of snitching. It's helping family." Bonanno gives me a terrible smile.

I force myself to smile back. "What is it you'd like to know? I'd do anything to help family."

"Well," Gagliano says, taking another turn now, "our person on the inside, not on the Dewey trial team exactly but on the fringes, has told us that Mildred Balitzer is being considered as one of the prosecution witnesses."

I freeze as two thoughts seize my mind at once. First, Mrs. Carter is making hay of the information I gave her about Mildred. Second, as usual, the Mob has someone on the inside feeding them information. Nothing new there.

"Do you know Mildred?" Bonanno asks.

"I've heard the name."

"What's the scuttlebutt?"

"I may not be the best person to tell you. Mildred is a few rungs down on the madam ladder, if you know what I mean. We don't exactly travel in the same circles."

"We get it," Bonanno says after a glance at Gagliano. "But anything you know—anything we could use against her in court, to discredit her testimony against Lucky—would help us. And we know how to show our gratitude."

I nod, sifting through the reams of stories I've heard about the opium-addled Mildred. I've got to offer them something; it's not believable that I know nothing. But what could I tell them that would get me off the hook but still preserve the power of her testimony against Lucky? I mean, I could tell them about Mildred's well-known grudge against Lucky for some beef he had with an old lover of hers, but that wouldn't help Mrs. Carter's case. I decide to start with other details.

"She's an addict, you know?" I say. "Big-time."

"We've heard she likes the stuff," Gagliano says. "But lots of girls take junk from time to time."

"Lots of gents, too!" one of the men toward the end of the table calls out, to much guffawing.

"Yeah, this is no ordinary case," I say, trying not to sound too eager. "She started out as a two-dollar girl and worked her way up to madam of two-dollar houses. She could've been more successful, but she's hooked on the junk something awful. That's been her downfall."

"She got a drug of choice?" Bonanno asks.

"I think she'll take anything you give her, but I hear her favorite is heroin."

"Maybe we could slip her some behind bars—" Bonanno says, and Gagliano interrupts, "Make her unfit for the witness stand?"

"That's a good idea," I say enthusiastically.

Bonanno gives me an approving nod. "That's helpful stuff, Miss Adler. We could get her so drugged up she can't testify. You got anything else?"

"I'm guessing that you already know Pete Harris is her husband? Not that you'd find a marriage certificate filed in any courthouse."

"Yeah, that we've learned. 'Course, Pete is locked up, too."

"You do know the two are mad as hatters for each other, right?"

"He better not start talking," Gagliano seethes, "to protect his woman."

"Or vice versa," I suggest.

Bonanno, Gagliano, Profaci, and Costello then lean toward a man sitting at the end of the rectangular conference room table, and the five whisper to one another. With his full head of silvery hair, glasses, and conservatively cut pin-striped navy suit, he looks more like a lawyer than a gangster. He stands up and walks toward me, holding a single sheet of paper in my direction.

"Miss Adler, I am an attorney here to assist in this unjust persecution of Charles Luciano. I cannot tell you more than that without violating the attorney-client privilege, as I'm certain you understand. In fact, I think an argument could be made that everything said in this room today is covered by that privilege of confidentiality, if you catch my meaning."

I nod, even though I doubt that the attorney-client privilege applies here. And I'm worried about that paper in his hand.

The lawyer passes it to me, and I see it contains women's names. "Before you is a list of women in your line of work who are being considered as witnesses. At least that's what we've been given to understand. Are you familiar with anyone on that list? Even if you've only ever heard the nicknames set forth next to the full name?"

I study it. Pointing to the fourth and seventh names—a Bella and a Mary—I say, "I've heard the nicknames of these two before, but I've never met them. All I know is that they're higher-end girls. They might work for Diamond Lil?"

"That's something we can work with," Bonanno chimes in. "We could bring Lil in here, see what she can tell us about those two girls. Assuming she didn't get swept up in the raids—"

"Where have you heard the names Bella and Mary?" The attorney interrupts Bonanno's patter.

"At my house. At the bar. You know how men talk about their conquests when they've had a few. And they like to compare notes."

Knowing laughter ripples through the room. Once the men settle down, the lawyer continues. "Do you recall the nature of the conversation about these two girls?"

"I think it was something like 'Is Bella as good as Mary?' Then they compared the two girls to one of mine, discussing who was the best."

"Do you remember who had this conversation?"

"I don't. They were two regular gents standing at my King Tut bar with their backs to me, and I was on my way to break up a fight. The only reason I remember the exchange at all is that it involved an assessment of one of my girls. As a businesswoman, I've got to keep on top of my clients' observations."

"Pardon the pun," Profaci calls out, and the room breaks out in laughter again. I laugh along, of course. Even though I feel like throwing up.

"Was Diamond Lil brought in during the raid?" Bonanno asks Gagliano, and then they both turn toward the lawyer.

"No," he says, consulting a different folder. "As you suggested, we might want to bring Diamond Lil in, ask her about her girls. And that also begs one last question, Miss Adler. How is it that your house wasn't even touched? How is it that you managed to evade arrest when so many of your peers are behind bars? Diamond Lil excepted."

Keep it together, I tell myself. *This moment determines your future. Time to tell the tale you've practiced over and over.*

"I'd sent my runner out for bar supplies, and he ran into one of the guys he knows from another house. That house had just been raided, and he warned my runner. Fortunately for me and my girls, he returned to my house and informed us—instead of just saving his own skin."

His expression implacable, the lawyer says, "Indeed, Miss Adler. I would say that's very, very lucky." Then he adds, "Anything else you'd like to offer?"

I place my free hand on my hip and give these terrifying men the sort of smirk I'd give to any old john at my house. No matter what happens from here, I want them to think of me as the sassy Polly Adler of legend. I *need* them to think of me that way. Because a guilty Polly wouldn't be a sassy one.

So I say, "I wish I could invite all you gents over to my house and give you a taste of how a high-end bordello operates. But unfortunately, there's been too much heat to open up shop. So let's upend this trial fast and get the show back on the road. Then I can introduce you to all the glories of Polly Adler's house."

CHAPTER THIRTY-EIGHT

EUNICE

New York, New York
April 26, 1936

WHEN MILDRED BALITZER crosses her arms and fixes me with a glare, I'm reminded of Polly Adler and her moxie.

"I'm tired of you, Mrs. Carter," Mildred snaps.

I sigh. Red Sadie gave me the same look—as if I'm no better than the men who exploit them. Yet beyond putting Luciano behind bars, I want this case to give these ladies a chance to live free.

"Why do you have to keep asking me the same questions?" She pushes her chair back, but she doesn't rise. Of course she won't leave. Now that she knows that I know about her relationship with Pete Harris, she's desperate to get herself and Pete out of police custody. And she knows cooperating with me is her ticket to making that happen. I've come to understand Mildred's love for her *husband.* As Polly implied, this is also my greatest leverage with her.

"Forgive me," I say sincerely. "This will be the final time you have to answer these questions."

She wipes her teary eyes. She isn't crying; watery eyes are simply one of the symptoms of a recovering junkie. Her addiction has left other marks as well—irritability and agitation—although I'm certain those traits are just part of her nature, with or without drugs.

Even though she's only thirty, the years of drug use have aged her decades beyond. The toll is etched into the sallow ruddiness of her complexion and the thinning of her hair. Yet beneath the ravages of addiction and prostitution, traces of the striking woman remain. She very well could have been a model—as she so often claims, each time she's been arrested.

"I'm asking these questions again to ensure that you're consistent."

She nods.

"How do you know Lucky Luciano?"

"Through my business. And my husband is one of his bookers."

"Have you met Mr. Luciano personally?"

"A couple of times."

"Do you have personal knowledge of Mr. Luciano's connection with the prostitution ring?"

"Yeah."

"Do you have personal knowledge of Mr. Luciano being the leader of the prostitution ring?"

"Yeah, he's the man at the top."

"How do you know this?"

"Lots of ways. I've been friends with Lil Davie and—"

"Lil Davie?" I ask. I know who she's referencing, but she needs to practice naming him the way she will have to in court.

"Yeah, Davie Betillo. I've been friends with Davie Betillo and Tommy the . . ." She stops. "Tommy Pennochio. I've known them for years. We've been out a few times together and have run into Lucky. The first time, Davie introduced him to me as his boss."

"What did you believe that to mean?"

"It meant that Lucky was the man, the number one guy, the Boss."

"The boss of what?"

"The boss of this whole Combination thing. Davie was the manager of all the cathouses. If anything ever went wrong or I had a problem, I called Davie. So if he was saying Lucky was his boss, that meant that Lucky was in charge. Because no one was above Davie . . . except *the Boss*."

"Did you have any other occasion to believe that Mr. Luciano was involved in the prostitution ring?"

"Yeah, one day, about a year back, he was trying to make a deal with some guy. Offered to pay him forty dollars a week if he'd become a collector."

"A collector?" I ask, knowing what Mildred means, but again, preparing her for trial.

"Yeah, Lucky was gonna pay him to collect money from all the houses."

"Do you know the name of the man Mr. Luciano made the offer to?"

"Nah," she says.

I pause and fix my gaze on Mildred. This is the crux of her testimony. "Did you ever have occasion to speak to Mr. Luciano directly?"

"Yeah."

"And what were the circumstances of that conversation?"

"My husband, Pete Harris"—she glares at me—"got himself in deep, owing the Combination some money. I wanted my husband to get out of the business, and since I'd been friends with Lil Davie, I thought he would do me a good turn. But he didn't do nothing, so I decided to go straight to Lucky myself."

"Why did you want to speak to Mr. Luciano?"

"Because I told you, he was the Boss. So I went to Lucky." She sits up straighter. "I told him I wanted my husband out of the business."

"And what was Mr. Luciano's response?"

"He told me Pete wasn't going anywhere. Not until he made him square."

"Made him square?"

She huffs. I've told Mildred before that not everyone will understand her slang. "Not until he paid back every dime. He told me I knew how his rackets worked."

"His rackets?"

"Yeah. His operation. He told me Pete was one of his top bookers, and he would never let him leave his business."

"And what did you understand he meant by his 'business'?"

"He meant his prostitution business. Because that's the only business Pete was in."

Although I've heard this three times, it still thrills me. Mildred has been unwavering. If I can keep her away from the drugs—and keep her alive—she will be one of our key witnesses.

Mildred rubs her arms as if she's warding off a sudden chill. "When will I see my husband?"

"Once you're released from here and settled into your secure location, I'll see what I can do."

All the way from the House of Detention to my office, I sit in the back seat of Mr. Johnson's car, smiling. Another link to Luciano. Now we have two witnesses definitely linking him to the prostitution ring. Can I get three . . . ?

But the moment I enter the office, my smile crumbles. Eight prosecutors—no Murray among them—file out two by two from the chief's office.

What kind of meeting could they have had without me?

I march to the chief's office and stand at his open door. Dewey is at his desk making notes when I knock. He glances up, and I ask, "Chief, do you have a moment?"

He sits back in his chair and nods slowly. Only when I stride in do I realize I'm still wearing my coat and holding my briefcase. Placing the briefcase down, I say, "It seems I missed a meeting. I apologize. I had the final interview with Mildred Balitzer."

He shakes his head. "You didn't miss a meeting, Mrs. Carter. I only asked a few of the assistant district attorneys to join me." He breaks my gaze and stares down at his writing pad. "I just assigned the attorneys for the Luciano trial."

His words astound me. Everyone in the office has been waiting for those assignments. I had every confidence I'd be chosen. Not only because of my trial experience but because the entire case against Luciano is based on my work, my theory.

I cross my arms. "Are you saying I'm not going to be one of the trial attorneys?" I can barely keep my voice steady.

He lifts his eyes. "I had to put together the best team to win."

My voice quivers with anger when I ask, "And you don't think I'm one of the best?"

"That's not what I'm saying at all, Mrs. Carter. We certainly wouldn't be here without you."

"Then why am I not on the trial team?"

The chief sighs. "There was so much for me to consider beyond experience. Here in the office, we're a team, but in a courtroom, there's the judge and, most importantly, the jury."

"I realize that. I've been in a courtroom before. I'm one of the only prosecutors on this team who has."

"Yes." He nods. "That was one of the things that impressed me during your interview. But your cases before . . . well, they are certainly no match for what we'll be up against with Luciano."

"The cases I've represented are a better match than someone walking into the court without any experience at all."

I wait for him to explain what he means, but he remains silent. So now I fill in the blanks. He's saying the clients I've represented were colored or women, therefore a colored lawyer was accepted in *those* courtrooms. But in this one . . .

"Mrs. Carter, you've done so much good work on this case. I know you wouldn't want to do anything to jeopardize it."

"Of course not. But I don't understand how my presence at the prosecution table will jeopardize anything. Especially when I know this case best."

He gives me a hard stare, asking me not to force him. He doesn't want to say aloud that I cannot sit alongside him because I am a Negro.

"You will still have a prominent role, Mrs. Carter. Like you said, no one knows this case better than you. I've chosen four prosecutors to handle the actual trial, but I've assigned Mr. Ten Eyck to prepare the girls for trial and . . ."

Of all the assistant district attorneys, Dewey has chosen Barent Ten Eyck? The one who's been investigating racketeering *in the baking industry*? How can the chief believe Ten Eyck will be able to handle the women whom I've developed relationships with, whom I've managed to get talking? Hasn't this team learned whom the women trust?

Dewey goes on. "I'm sure Mr. Ten Eyck will need your assistance. And I'd like your help with the exhibits I plan to use during the prosecution's case. I want charts to lay out the evidence showing all the patterns you uncovered."

I don't speak. I cannot.

We stare at each other until Dewey says, "Is there anything else, Mrs. Carter?"

I shake my head and pick up my briefcase. "No, Chief, there's nothing else. I've certainly heard enough."

I'M STILL OFF-KILTER as Mr. Johnson eases the car to a stop before the colossal three-arched facade of Grand Central Station. My mind is spinning from my conversation with Dewey. "All right, Mrs. Carter. Is this where I should pick you up as well?"

"Yes. In about an hour," I say, slipping from the back seat. As I enter the terminal, with its towering arched windows letting in golden sunlight and the celestial mural painted high above, my thoughts scatter.

New Yorkers surge all around me, and the clamor in the terminal is constant. Heels clicking on the marble floor, the muffled roar of the steam engines pulsing from the platforms below, and porters wheeling carts piled high with luggage as they weave between men in business suits and women hurrying children along. And this is precisely why I chose this as a meeting place with Polly, since she's refused to meet in Central Park again. She was adamant about a new meeting locale, and I wonder if something happened after our last meeting.

I move past the newsstand, past the shoeshine parlor, and make my way to the opal clock perched atop the information booth at the center. Searching the crowd, I see no sign of Polly. I'm a bit early. She will certainly find me.

As I wait, I take in the space. Usually I'm swept up in the energy here, feeding off the travelers' frenzy, as thrilled as if I were traveling myself. But today I feel untethered. I have given up so much personally to be a part of this team fighting to clean up crime, making the city safer for New Yorkers. But this justice I seek for others feels beyond my reach when it comes to me.

Yes, I know America is steeped in discrimination and inequality. Just because of the color of my skin, I will not be served in certain restaurants, cannot enter certain nightclubs, cannot shop in certain stores, cannot even catch a picture show in some theaters. Still, with my law credentials and the work I've done on this case, how can Dewey refuse to make me one of the trial lawyers because I'm colored? Without the foundation I've laid, Dewey and the nineteen other assistant district attorneys would be in Hell's Kitchen helping Mr. Ten Eyck search for clues inside strawberry cupcakes.

Maybe I should give up. Perhaps that's best. Walking away would save my marriage and bring my son home. Yes, I've earned my place, but that is not enough. And I don't have the strength to wage two wars—one at home and one at work. If I can win only one fight, I choose my family.

I take a deep breath—my decision made.

"Mrs. Carter?"

I almost don't recognize her. Polly Adler stands just a few feet in front of me with her back turned. Today she's wearing just a light swagger coat, and I wonder, Where is her fur stole? I've scarcely seen her without it, even in warmer weather.

She takes a few steps forward. Her eyes are partially hidden by her tilt hat, but I can see her glancing at the departure board. And I follow.

Then I wait for her to speak.

For the final time.

CHAPTER THIRTY-NINE

POLLY

New York, New York
April 26, 1936

No more so-called clandestine tête-à-têtes in Central Park for me. I made that clear when I received Mrs. Carter's note and agreed to a meeting. Not after getting swept up by the Mob just as I stepped out of the park, even though I'd kept the details of my encounter with those mafiosi to a minimum, other than to tell her to keep Mildred protected so no one would slip her Cadillac. Knowing that I'm in those gangsters' sights makes it imperative we meet elsewhere; my nerves can't stand it otherwise. Particularly since those nerves are being taxed to the limit with regularity as I toggle between Brooklyn and my family, where I playact as the dutiful daughter who manages a corset factory, and Manhattan, where I arrange hotel assignations for my girls so I can stay afloat until I assume my full madam mantle again—all the while praying that never the twain lives shall meet.

All that apprehension is worth it, of course. All for that moment when I first saw my mother's face again. My hands shook as I knocked on that apartment door in Brooklyn where she was staying. When Mama herself opened that door—her brown hair now gray and her face lined with wrinkles of worry and time, but otherwise the same—I collapsed in a heap of tears and emotion. And so did she.

So the crowded anonymity of Grand Central Station it is for this meeting. I sidle up next to Mrs. Carter in front of the departure board. I study the changing train times and compare them against the timetable in my hand, as if I don't know which to trust. We are not alone. Throngs of travelers flank us, which is the point. Why would we draw any attention if we are just two middle-aged women on our way to somewhere else? Just like so many others here.

"This will be our last meeting, Miss Adler," Mrs. Carter says, her eyes fixed on the board as well. "So anything you've got to share, now is the moment. Speak now or forever hold your peace and all that."

With all the hullaballoo around us, I wonder if I heard her correctly. Surely she did not just agree to end these meetings. But I cannot look at her directly to suss out her expression.

"Are you pulling my leg?" I ask.

"No, I'm not," she says with a sigh.

I'm worried, if a little relieved, that this precarious chapter in my life has come to an end. Is there no need for more meetings because the case against Lucky is all set, or because it is falling apart? The trial *must* proceed soon and end with Lucky behind bars so I can get back to business and pay for my family to have their own apartment in Brooklyn with all the modern fixings and clothes. I don't want them to start suggesting they live with me. Mama has decided the whole family should settle in New York closer to me, since I'm the one with the "best job." If only she knew. But getting them settled will be expensive. And the fear of discovery has me scouring the newspapers every day to make sure some snapshot of me hasn't made the front page.

"What has changed?" I ask. "I thought the information I've been giving you has been helpful."

"You've done your best to deliver supportive information." I hear Mrs. Carter amidst the cacophony.

I freeze. Now I'm really concerned. "Is the case against Lucky too weak to proceed?"

"No," she replies.

"Then what's happening?"

"I'm not going to be part of the trial team."

I'm not sure what that has to do with anything. "But the case itself is strong enough to go ahead, right?"

"Yes. Just largely without me. Since I will not be one of the attorneys at the trial, I don't feel any obligation to gather more information from you."

Never mind the risk, I turn to look at Mrs. Carter. Fury courses through me, and I don't care who sees me talking to her at this moment. "You're abandoning your quest for the best evidence because you won't be at the trial table next to Dewey? So all you've ever cared about was your career?"

"No—"

I don't let her finish. "You don't care about the girls. About what will happen to them when the Mob makes every prostitute in this city—maybe even the country—part of one big organization under their control?" I try to keep my voice low, but I notice at least one person turning toward me at the words "Mob" and "prostitute."

Now she glares at me and seethes. "That is rich, Miss Adler. Coming from you."

"What the hell is that supposed to mean?"

"You are putting on quite the show—that you are concerned about each and every prostitute in this city. All you care about are *your* brothel and *your* girls and the money they bring in for *you*." She squares her shoulders, raising herself to her full height, and stares down at me. "You don't think I know that you've got your own personal experiences with Luciano that you could share with me? That you probably have more firsthand testimony that could bring Luciano down than any of the girls or madams or bookers that you've named for me? But no, you'd never tell me about those conversations or observations, because that would put *you* at risk. And Polly Adler would never risk her own hide. Even for the precious girls you pretend to care so much about."

I almost gasp at her statements. Not only because they're so offensive but because they're true. And that truth has begun to plague me, as I hear tales about what the girls and madams are suffering in the slammer and the way they're putting themselves in harm's way to provide testimony against the Combination. When in fact, I do have a wealth of personal information about Lucky; I could describe countless interactions and overheard conversations between Lucky and a slew of known gangsters at my Majestic house and set out his involvement in Virginia's disappearance. Not that I could ever admit that to the all-too-righteous Mrs. Carter—or anyone else for that matter—without writing a ticket for myself to the witness stand. And anyway, how did she know?

We face one another, no longer pretending we don't know each other. Our feelings are too heated for feigning. Up until this point, we've been working together toward a common goal, albeit reluctantly and awkwardly, and I've been too focused on getting Lucky behind bars and shutting down his wretched Combination as soon as possible to think about whether I like Mrs. Carter. She'd certainly evoked irritation and admiration at different points—and I appreciated her empathy about my long separation from my mother. But at the end of the day, she was a means to an end. Now I feel real anger, though.

"As if you aren't motivated by *yourself* and *your* own career." I am fuming. Then, instead of falling on my sword, I get on my high horse. "Anyway, how dare you condemn me? Your life has been easier than mine or my girls'. You had family who cared about you, and you got an education that gave you choices. You know hardly anything about me—or my girls! You have no right to judge me. I've done everything I can to protect my girls—even Virginia," I hiss. Guilt is mixed into my self-righteous anger, and Virginia's name pops out.

It's almost comical how quickly Mrs. Carter's expression changes from anger to surprise.

"Did you say Virginia?"

"Yeah," I answer warily, crossing my arms protectively across my chest, trying to pull myself together, caught off guard by the shift in Mrs. Carter. "What of it?"

"It's just that a prostitute with that name was arrested in January. She'd been found in a nasty part of town in an unusually elegant robe and nightgown. Not your typical streetwalker attire. And she was banged up."

Virginia! Is that even possible? "Was she all right? What happened to her?"

Mrs. Carter's gaze softens. "Do you know her? I thought she looked familiar."

It's all so surreal. I have the oddest sensation, like I'm floating up above, looking down on me and Mrs. Carter. Then, in a rush, I'm back in my own body, and tears come, unbidden and unfamiliar. My line of work doesn't allow for vulnerability, especially not sadness. "I do. She was one of my longtime girls. Then one night—"

I clear my throat, and I don't hesitate to tell one of my own Lucky stories for the very first time. "Lucky took her to meet with some gangster he wanted to impress. And I never saw her again. She must have escaped from Lucky or the other guy, running down the streets in her nightgown—and that's when the cops must have found her and brought her into the station. But I've never seen her again, and I've been looking for her ever since." More tears threaten, but I choke them back; I want to get this story right. "Up until that time, I'd always been in control of my house and my girls, and I had the ability to take good care of them, to run a different sort of house than all the other madams. But that control was taken away from me as the Combination came onto the scene, and I swore I would never let that happen to me or my girls ever again. That's why I reached out to you. To put an end to this evil Combination."

She nods, understanding more about what drove me to meet with her in the first place, even as my explanation reveals much about my personal knowledge of Lucky. To my surprise, she says nothing about my encounter with Lucky, even though it confirms her suspicion that I know more about him than I've let on. She doesn't press me for more.

Instead, she gives me a good long stare, as if she's making up her mind about me. Then she finally speaks. "I met with Virginia soon after her arrest. I'd just started to interview her when her lawyer appeared to post bail. An attorney whose name we both know—Abe Karp."

"What? She didn't have Abe Karp as her lawyer. My house wasn't officially part of the Combination that he covered. I didn't even really know much about it at that time, but I learned more as I went out in search of Virginia, talking to every madam, girl, pimp, and streetwalker I know. All of whom were getting strong-armed by the Combination."

Mrs. Carter nods. "Virginia told me that Abe Karp wasn't her lawyer. And that's why she became so panicked when the police officer announced Karp was there for her."

All the elements of Virginia's situation click. "Karp was there to threaten her. Lucky had sent him to the station to inform her that they knew where she was."

"Exactly. And that she better keep her mouth shut." She hesitates. I sense she wants to tell me more. But something is holding her back.

"What happened then? Did she meet with Karp? Did she end up going before the judge?" I blurt out, panic rising within me. "Do you know where she is now?"

Mrs. Carter looks at me—really looks at me—and makes a decision. "I let her go. Even though I knew she had information linked to Luciano that I could really use."

"What? You let her go?"

"Virginia was terrified. She told me that if I gave Karp access to her and he got her out on bail, she'd be killed. And I believed her." She takes a deep breath and makes a full confession of how she got Virginia out of there.

I'm shocked. I cannot believe that law-abiding Assistant District Attorney Eunice Carter released Virginia from jail—for the girl's own protection. And to the detriment of her own case. My perception of her has utterly changed.

"Thank you, Mrs. Carter, for doing that for Virginia. And I apologize. You are not who I believed you to be."

"And neither are you, Miss Adler. Now I understand why you came to me and how much you genuinely care about your girls. It isn't all about the money after all."

We stand in silence under the departure board, trying to compose ourselves as we pretend interest in the train schedule. I breathe deeply of this new understanding, and finally speak. "You know, Mrs. Carter, I am going to do something about getting you a spot on that trial team. I'll find a piece of evidence for you to exchange for a seat at that table."

She looks even more surprised than when I blurted out Virginia's name. "Why would you do that?"

"Who else will protect the girls? *All* the girls."

CHAPTER FORTY

POLLY

New York, New York
May 1, 1936

TWILIGHT CASTS A violet hue over my bedroom, darkening my private space. I consider rising from my comfortable upholstered chair and switching on a few lights, but instead I allow the shadows to wrap around me like a cloak. This darkness is the right place to assess the past few days, and wallow in my guilt. Guilt over asking others to put themselves on the line when I haven't done the same. Guilt over how my girls really feel about me and what we do. Guilt over the stories I tell myself about the sort of person I really am. Guilt over what I've done and how I've involved the people I profess to care about most. Guilt over lying to my mother and brother Ben and the three brothers that I just met, and even my father, about how I earn the living that is supporting them. The emotions overwhelm, and I'm not yet ready for the light.

I sip at my whiskey and ask myself the question I've considered more times than I can count over the past few days: Was it worth the risk to gather the necessary evidence from my girls and share it with Mrs. Carter? I believe the case could've plowed ahead on the evidence already assembled. After all, with my help, Mrs. Carter has established links from the girls to the madams; from the madams to the bookers like Jackie Ellerstein, Dave Miller, and Pete Harris; from the bookers to the strong-arm squad shaking down the bookers, which includes Jimmy Frederico and Little Abie Wahrman; from the shakedown squad to the Mob treasurer, Tommy the Bull; from Tommy the Bull to Combination day-to-day head of operations, Little Davie Betillo. But we both knew the link between Betillo and Lucky was weak, and mostly based on the testimony of madams, who won't exactly have stellar credibility in court. And that's where I came in to help the case and her.

Two days after I'd met with Mrs. Carter, Kit, the Lion, and I were spending the night sipping drinks and listening to jazz at the little kitchen table in my new digs. The door slammed as Angelica and Rosalie returned to my house after visiting guests at hotels, flush with cash and in a merry mood. When they plopped down at the table with us and asked for drinks, I knew my moment had come to do the sort of digging I'd been reluctant to do.

I poured tall flutes of champagne for each of us. Keeping the bottle close at hand, I refilled everyone's glasses as soon as they took a sip. Everyone's except mine, as I needed to keep my wits about me. I waited until the girls and the Lion downed a second bottle before asking my first question.

I sighed and said, "Wonder what's happening with that Dewey mess. You girls heard anything?"

The Lion shot me a startled look. Even tipsy, she was on high alert. She alone knew about my meetings with Mrs. Carter. And while she didn't like them, she understood their importance. Neither of us wanted to be under the Mob's thumb, and we were worried for the girls. Especially after Virginia. And she knows as well as I do how badly we need to reopen the house and make serious money again; my coffers border on empty. But I have never, ever involved my girls in my snitching, not in any way. Too risky for them and for me.

"Nah," Rosalie said, finishing off her champagne and holding her glass out for another refill. "Same old, same old."

I stood up and wandered over to the icebox, where a third bottle awaited. "How about you, Angelica?" I asked as I popped the top.

"You still talking about the Dewey case?"

"How much champagne have you had?" I chuckled. "Don't think anyone has changed the subject yet."

"Why are you curious?" she asked, a single eyebrow raised.

I had steered clear of discussions about the raids and the trial before. Once the girls, the Lion, and I reunited in New York, we resumed our living arrangement without a lot of conversation about why we no longer conducted business in my house. Angelica's reaction was a warning. She wasn't as liquored up as I might have hoped; maybe she'd even wondered about how we escaped the raids in the first place. I had to tread carefully.

"Want to make sure we're protected. Seems like the whole of our business is on trial—in one way or another," I explained.

Rosalie half snorted, half laughed. "Seems more like every person in our business is in the slammer, awaiting trial."

"Just don't want any of us to end up there, too," I said.

"You're keeping your nose out of trouble." Angelica gave me a sidelong glance. "Not seeing guests here, not hosting parties. What have you got to worry about?"

"Never know what some of the girls will say when they've been behind bars for weeks." I paused for a beat, letting the possibility sink in. "Or the madams who've got an axe to grind."

"I think it's a good sign that the cops haven't come knocking on the front door. They've had those girls in custody for months. Even the boozehounds and the junkies are clean now and are capable of talking if they want," Angelica proclaimed. "I think you're in the clear."

"I don't know about that," Rosalie said with another big gulp of champagne. "I heard Nancy Presser has just dried out. And you and I both know she's got stories to tell."

Kit piped up, "Excuse me! You can't drop a bomb like that and not tell us the scuttlebutt. What stories?"

Rosalie leaned toward us, a conspiratorial grin on her face. "Well, the rumor is Nancy Presser used to be one of Lucky's favorite girls—"

Goose bumps started to rise on my arms. But before Rosalie could continue, Kit interjected, "Boy, she's slid down the ladder since then. Doesn't she have that disgusting mobster Ralph Liguori as her pimp now? I heard he made her work at Jenny the Factory's two-dollar house."

"Snorting all that Cadillac will do that to you," Rosalie replied, then continued. "As I was saying, Nancy used to be one of Lucky's favorites. And I heard she and Lucky would meet at Keen's English Chop House near Madison Square Garden for a few drinks before they headed to either the Barbizon or the Waldorf, depending on where Lucky was staying."

"You're making me hungry for a chop right now," Kit squealed, but Rosalie was on a roll and couldn't be stopped.

"Lucky would hold court while he and Nancy drank at Keen's. Little Davie, Tommy the Bull, Little Abie, and Jimmy Frederico would join them some nights, and they'd talk about girls and houses right in front of Nancy. As if she wasn't one herself."

"What kind of stuff did they say?" I blurted without thinking. Damn it. It wouldn't do for me to appear too eager.

But my question didn't give Rosalie any pause—and even Angelica seemed interested now. "Nancy overheard discussions about the girls' prices being raised and putting the madams and bookers on low salaries. But what really got her goat were the instructions to trash the houses when they didn't fork over bond money and straighten out the girls who didn't play ball."

"That kind of talk doesn't surprise me from thugs like Tommy the Bull or Little Davie," I said.

"Funny thing is, it wasn't Tommy the Bull or Little Davie that said those things. It wasn't even Little Abie or Jimmy Frederico." Rosalie scooched even closer to us. "It was Lucky."

Had she just said what I thought she said?

This was the kind of direct, specific link between Lucky and his underlings that Mrs. Carter needed for the trial. It showed Lucky's active role in managing the prostitution business in New York City. I was giddy but couldn't show it at that moment. Lord knows I didn't mask it when I handed over this new information to Mrs. Carter and gave her specific ideas on how to elicit this testimony from Nancy Presser. In fact, she and I were both giddy right then.

As I THINK back on this from my cocoon of darkness, the guilt remains. But it is tinged with hope. Hope that we might just bring down the Boss yet. And the Combination along with him.

As I sink back into my upholstered chair with my whiskey in hand to contemplate this conundrum, I hear commotion outside my door. Are the girls fighting over which one gets to go to the swanky Pierre Hotel tonight for the booked assignation? Sighing in frustration, I put my whiskey on the end table and walk out into the brighter hallway.

The raised voices emanate from the foyer. As I progress toward the din, I pass all three girls in the living room listening to the radio and lounging in their housedresses; nothing fazes them. So they aren't part of whatever kerfuffle is brewing. The closer I get to the noise, the more it seems like the Lion is having firm words with someone at the door. I hate for her to be the front line for any drama, and it's moments like these that I really miss Jerry.

"What seems to be the trouble here?" I ask the Lion, who's half in and half out of the doorway.

Before the Lion can reply, a voice trails in from the hallway. "Pearl? Pearl, is that you?"

It is my mother's voice, in Yiddish. My mother. *Here.*

The dread I've felt since her arrival nearly two weeks ago bubbles forth. I cannot allow her to step inside this apartment. One glance at the girls, surrounded by the King Tut bar and the mahjong and poker tables, and she'll know who and what I am. Even if she does find out one day that I am New York City's most famous madam, I can never, ever allow her to *see* it. She will forever view me as Polly, not Pearl.

Placing my hands on the Lion's shoulders, I gently move her aside. She's only trying to protect me, as usual, even if the threat comes from my family. "I'll take it from here."

I enter the corridor, closing the door to my world behind me. How incongruous this elegant, restrained hallway, with its crystal wall sconces and tasteful damask wallpaper, seems compared to my tear-streaked mother with her old-fashioned headscarf and my father with his flushed face and crumpled hat in hand. My mother may wear the American clothes I bought for her, but they are ill fitting. Not in terms of tailoring, but in terms of suiting her character. At her essence, she is still a woman from rural Yanow.

Ignoring the clear signs of distress on my parents' faces, I offer a polite excuse for keeping them outside my apartment, as if they were social acquaintances popping by for a visit. It's the only way I know to compose myself—to pretend like this is a normal, everyday interaction. Even if just for a second.

"I'm sorry I can't invite you inside. The place is a wreck. If I'd have known you were coming, I would have arranged a cleaning."

"Is it true, Pearl?" My mother's voice is shaking.

"I don't know what you're referring to, Mama," I say, although I can hazard a good guess.

She waves a copy of the *Daily Mirror* in the air. "Is *this* true, Pearl? Or should I call you Polly?"

My heart pounds wildly. She knows.

I glance at the front page of the *Daily Mirror*. There, emblazoned under the headline *Why Isn't the Vice Queen in Jail?*, is an old picture of me exiting a paddy wagon, my facial features on full display. I suppose it doesn't matter that I missed this piece in my regular scan of the newspapers; they would've found out about me sooner or later.

"Probably not all of it, Mama," I reply, blurring the lines with my answer.

"How about the part calling you a whore?" she yells, and I'm thankful her words are in Yiddish.

"I'm not a whore, Mama. I run the most exclusive brothel in New York City. It's more like a club," I confess, torn between keeping my head high and throwing myself at her feet to ask forgiveness. "But I'm not running it anymore." This is technically true.

"So you hire out whores instead of whoring yourself out," my father hisses. "There is no difference. You should be ashamed of yourself, Pearl."

It is one thing for my mother to chastise me for this path and quite another for my father to do so. Rage supplants my guilt and shame. "You think *I* am the one who should bear the burden of this shame? Moshe Adler, *you* are the one who should feel regret and mortification. You are the one who sent your defenseless twelve-year-old daughter alone to America to make money for the family. A girl who didn't speak a word of English, cast out to live with strangers and labor in a garment factory. A girl who was raped and thrown out onto the street, without any means to support herself. Yet I still sent money home—whether to Mama in Yanow or to you in Chicago—in amounts that increased according to your demands. You are the one who gave Pearl no choice but to turn into Polly."

My mother drops the newspaper and places that hand over her mouth. Is she horrified at me? Or do I see a softening in her features—and her heart—at the truth of what I've endured? I yearn to be wrapped up in her arms, forgiven for my transgressions and loved regardless. But I know that it is a pipe dream.

"I will not stand here and listen to these insults from a whore," my father yells at me. "From this point forward, you are not my daughter, whether you call yourself Pearl or Polly. You will not see us again."

Mama's eyes are on me as Moshe—if I'm no longer his daughter, then he certainly isn't my father—tugs her away from me. As he begins marching toward the elevator with her in tow, she reaches out for my arm and gives me the gentlest, briefest squeeze. Perhaps there is still hope with her. But not today.

Sobs begin to overtake me. I open the door to my apartment, and there stand all four women, waiting for me. They do not need to understand Yiddish to comprehend what just transpired between me and my parents, it seems. My girls and the Lion, with their arms outstretched and their expressions mournful on my behalf. The sort of response I wish my mother had given me when she heard my full story.

I allow myself to be folded into their embrace, comforted by this strange reversal of our roles. Very quietly, Rosalie says, "We have all been where you are now, Polly. And *we* are here for you."

Kit adds, "What is it you always say, Polly? No one wakes up and dreams of becoming a whore? It's also true that no one wakes up admitting to the role they played in forcing us into this business. Not society, not the men we entertain, and not our families."

CHAPTER FORTY-ONE

EUNICE

New York, New York
May 2, 1936

I GLANCE AT my watch as I step off the elevator. It's just half past six. I rush to Dewey's office. "Miss Rosse, has Mr. Dewey returned?"

"Yes, Mrs. Carter. His train arrived a little late, but he's in his office now. I told him you'd been asking to speak with him. I will let you know when he's available."

"Thank you."

Back inside my office, I pull my notepad from my desk drawer. For all of these months, I was the one reaching out to Polly, pressing her for more and more. But when she contacted me just a few days ago, not only did she give me my ticket to my rightful place in the courtroom, but she gave me a lever that could tighten our case like a snare around Luciano's operation.

These notes from our meeting have been scorching my palms for the three days since Dewey has been away "meeting with people connected with the case."

Knowing that Dewey was returning tonight, I was prepared to sit in my office until midnight, if necessary. But just over two hours ago, I lifted the telephone receiver to hear Lisle's voice, an unexpected interruption.

"I hope I'm not disturbing you."

"Of course not, darling," I said, even as I glanced at the stack of charts piled on my desk. With the trial beginning less than two weeks from now, I could ill afford even a moment's pause.

"I wanted to give you some good news."

I set aside the chart I was working on. "Then you rang the right telephone number."

Lisle chuckled. "I was just informed that at the NAACP dinner this year, I'll receive the prestigious Carter G. Woodson Award for Civic Race Advancement."

Sitting back in my chair, I pressed my hand to my chest. "Oh, darling, I'm so very proud of you."

He only said "Thank you," but in those two words, I heard the swell of pride he carried for the work he'd done, especially leading the drive for a women's wing in Harlem Hospital.

I was bubbling over for my husband. "We must celebrate. I'll host a party on the night of the dinner."

He hesitated. "Wonderful. But I was hoping we could celebrate now."

My smile faltered, my excitement waning as swiftly as it had come. With all that was before me, how could I step away?

But Lisle had promised that it would be no more than a quick dinner. So I agreed, and even though my time was short, Mr. Johnson drove me uptown, where Lisle and I were welcomed at one of Harlem's fixtures, Frank's. Over pot roast for him and beef stew for me, Lisle shared his excitement, and I shone with pride for him. Truly, I could hardly wait to stand by his side as he received this recognition.

"Mrs. Carter." Miss Rosse pulls me from my reverie. "Mr. Dewey can see you now."

Grabbing my notepad, I make my way through the corridor. The office is humming as if it's noon and not seven in the evening. But my thoughts are on what feels like gold in my hands.

When I get to the chief's door, he gestures for me to enter.

"Welcome back, Chief."

"Thank you, Mrs. Carter." His voice is weighted with exhaustion as he sets papers on his desk aside. "I was just reviewing these charts you prepared. Excellent work. Good visuals always help the jury grasp important facts. The organizational chart will be especially helpful."

"I want to make sure you have everything you need for the trial."

"Everything *we* need, Mrs. Carter," he corrects. "I want to reiterate how important your work has been, even if you won't be in court."

I pause, then say, "I'm preparing a map now—every brothel across the boroughs under Luciano's control."

"That will be useful. And of course, if you think there is anything else—"

"There is," I cut in. "I have something that will make our case significantly stronger."

Dewey leans forward. By now he knows that if I have something, it's worth hearing. "What is it?"

With a deep breath, I draw up every bit of Hunton moxie within me. "Before I share this with you, Chief, I want something in return."

Dewey's eyes narrow, and he's quiet for what seems an interminable minute. But then the creases in his forehead smooth, his composure restored. "What is it?"

"I want to be on the trial team."

His eyebrows rise at my audacity. "I thought we discussed this."

"We did," I say. "And I understand your concern about my race.

But what I've contributed so far should far outweigh any apprehension."

"All right, Mrs. Carter. This isn't something I've wanted to discuss directly, but since you brought it up, I am concerned the press will seize on your presence in the courtroom and you will become the focus over the facts. It could distract from the case."

"The press has already made a spectacle of my race. There's little left for them to exploit. But even if every article puts me in the spotlight, it won't diminish the strength of our evidence. And this last piece"—I hold up my notepad—"could be the linchpin to the prosecution." When he doesn't respond, I say, "I'm not asking to argue before the judge and jury, I'm asking to be present at the trial. Behind the prosecution table where the lead trial attorneys sit would be fine. I've earned that much."

The muscle in his jaw twitches. Finally, he says, "What do you have?"

I hesitate. Part of me wants his agreement first. But I have more trust in him than he has in me, so I place the notepad on his desk. As he reads, I explain, "Nancy Presser, one of the madams we have in custody, was one of Luciano's favorite girls." Even though he's reading the notes, I continue. "I've spoken with Nancy, and she can connect Luciano to everything, from dictating what brothels were opened and closed to setting prices. And if any of the girls stepped out of line, the order to take care of them came from Luciano. She can give us everything we need."

Slowly, he nods. "And she's clean now?"

"Like Mildred Balitzer, she's been clean for almost two months. And her testimony will strengthen Mildred Balitzer's and Red Sadie's. With all three witnesses, I believe a jury will find Lucky Luciano guilty beyond a reasonable doubt."

Dewey sits back, steepling his fingers beneath his chin. The silence stretches, and my heart thuds. This is crucial evidence, direct links from the girls all the way to Luciano. But Dewey can still say no. He has every right to use this evidence and give me nothing in return.

"You'll be at the trial, Mrs. Carter," he finally says, his words landing like a gavel and carrying as much warmth. He slides the notepad back to me. "Type up these notes. I want her statement in hand as soon as possible."

"Yes, Chief." I slip out of his office. I don't know if he is impressed with my gumption or irritated by it. Maybe both. But once I'm back at my desk, I'm giddy—almost as giddy as I was when Polly gave me this information.

This is a victory that would never have happened without her.

Over these months, I've asked myself: Who is Polly Adler? Of course I have always placed the bulk of the blame on the men in the racket. But the madams, women like Polly, profited, too. She built power in a trade exploiting women. And yet, there is one truth that I've come to know—Polly Adler cares. Not just for her girls but for all the girls who've been exploited. She risks her life with every meeting we have. Even if she never sacrifices herself completely by offering her personal testimony in court.

So much of what we will present at trial was assembled by me but made possible because of Polly. It makes me smile to think that she and I built this case. History would probably have a laugh at this, too—the prosecutor and the madam, the unlikely pair behind the downfall of America's most notorious mobster. If all goes to plan.

But my smile fades as I remember that no one can ever know that Assistant District Attorney Eunice Carter and the notorious madam Polly Adler stood side by side against Lucky Luciano.

The prosecutor and the madam—strange and secret bedfellows, indeed!

PART III

CHAPTER FORTY-TWO

EUNICE

New York, New York
May 13, 1936

THE CHIEF WANTS to make a statement with our arrival at the New York County Supreme Court for the opening of *The People of the State of New York v. Charles Luciano, et al.* So just before eight o'clock in the morning, nearly a dozen of us pile into Packard Twelves to take the one-mile ride to 60 Centre Street.

When we round the corner from Chambers to Centre, I gasp. The sidewalk in front of the Supreme Court teems with people. Several hundred men and women, it seems, surround the entrance of this imposing templelike structure. Curious New Yorkers are pressed on one side, and on the other, reporters and men with flashing cameras jostle for position behind a line of cops.

I'm flabbergasted, although I shouldn't be. Since Luciano's arrest, this case has dominated the city's newspapers' headlines.

"Dewey said for us to speak to no one," Mr. Ten Eyck reminds us.

No one needs that reminder. We are all aware of the leaks. And aware of our public image. Me most of all.

I grab the box that holds the exhibits I've prepared and pause before exiting the car. Per the plan, the Packard with Dewey inside opens first. We knew he'd be met with reporters' flashes, but he's greeted with shouts and heckles as well.

"Give 'em hell, Dewey!"

"You can't take Lucky down!"

"Put Luciano behind bars!"

"You're just after headlines, Dewey!"

Unfazed, the chief and the prosecutors who rode with him press through the throng. Then, as they begin to ascend the steps, the second car empties before it's our turn.

"Clean up New York!" someone shouts the moment we step out of our car.

The camera light bulbs blind me, and I clutch the box and rush up the stairs leading to the colonnade and the massive front doors. There's a bit of a logjam, and as I look over the shoulders of the attorneys in front of me, I see the guards at the door questioning everyone.

"Shoot," I mutter. "I should have taken out my identification card." But I relax when I see lawyers are just giving their names to gain entry.

Finally, I reach the door, but a ruddy-faced cop blocks my path. "How did you get past the ropes?" he barks. "No spectators inside. Get back over there." He points to the swarm of onlookers.

"I am *not* a spectator, Officer. I'm Assistant District Attorney Eunice Carter."

"I don't care if your name is Jesus Christ. Step aside or you'll be arrested." His face darkens with his threat.

Over his shoulder, I see the other prosecutors moving farther into the lobby. I fumble for my identification card as I shout out, "Mr. Ten Eyck!" just as the cop shoves me back. I stumble, nearly losing my balance. But Mr. Ten Eyck turns at the sound of my voice. Standing on my toes, I clutch the box with one hand and wave frantically with the other. "Please, he won't let me in."

Mr. Ten Eyck's eyes widen in understanding, and he rushes back. "She's with us. One of Dewey's team."

The cop's eyebrows stretch high as he glances between me and Ten Eyck. He's still uncertain but steps aside without apology. I'm annoyed, but the moment I enter the lobby, it's forgotten as I hurry behind Mr. Ten Eyck, down the wide marble-wainscoted corridor to the end. When I step inside the courtroom, I pause. No matter how many times I've been in one of these courtrooms, I'm always struck by how majestic this space feels compared to the cramped and chaotic magistrate courts. Here, the sunlight streams through wide windows, highlighting leather-covered seats and polished wood paneling. Even the jury box is enclosed behind an ornate railing.

The courtroom is already bustling, jam-packed even though it is not even half past eight; the trial is not set to begin until ten. Scanning the crowd, I'm taken aback when I glance to the left. A dozen chairs are lined against the wall, and I recognize the co-defendants: Thomas Pennochio, Dave Betillo, Ralph Liguori, Jimmy Frederico, and Pete Harris are the most familiar to me. But I made a point to know the others: Abie Wahrman, Jackie Ellerstein, Dave Miller, Al Weiner, Jesse Jacobs, Benny Spiller, Meyer Berkman . . . all twelve of them, handcuffed and flanked by guards.

Not a one is behaving like a man who's been detained for weeks in prison, facing grievous charges and lengthy sentences. They are chewing the fat and laughing as if they are passing the morning in one of those exclusive invitation-only private clubs.

When my gaze shifts to the defense table, I finally see him. For the first time, I lay eyes on Lucky Luciano. The Boss. The man who's raking in millions annually with this racket alone.

Luciano sits casually, shooting the breeze with his attorneys, Francis W. H. Adams and George Morton Levy. He is immaculately dressed in one of the handmade suits he's known to wear: a navy jacket and pants, white shirt, and silk tie the exact shade of his suit. With his dark hair slicked back, he looks more like the chief executive of General Electric than a ruthless kingpin.

As Luciano talks to his lawyers, he casually takes in the room. Then his eyes stop roving. His gaze narrows. He's spotted me.

The chatter mutes, the laughter fades . . . time holds its breath. Even with his right eyelid drooping, his stare is piercing and unrelenting. His expression is so cold, so calculating, so cruel that the box I'm holding slips from my grasp and hits the floor with a thud.

Quickly, I bend to retrieve it. But when I rise, Luciano has turned away, now laughing at something one of his attorneys has said. I've already been dismissed from his mind. For now.

I am unnerved. The note, the doll, the paint on my car reel through my mind. For the past year, I've wondered if I've been in Luciano's sights. There is no question that I am now. And I will be. Every day.

Turning away, I place the carton on the floor and take my place in one of the seats behind the prosecution table with actual trial attorneys. I keep my eyes away from the defendants' side of the courtroom and focus on my notes.

As the minutes pass, the activity in the room begins to subside. The mood becomes subdued, and when the clock strikes ten, the bailiff calls the court to order. Justice McCook enters and takes his place behind the judge's bench.

The judge motions to the bailiff, undoubtedly to give him instructions for bringing in the jury. Selecting a jury was an arduous process, dragging on for weeks rather than the typical four or five days. The relentless press coverage had tainted the jury pool long before the first summonses were sent out. Finding twelve impartial men had proven nearly impossible.

The challenge wasn't bias—it was fear. Serving on a case against the country's most ruthless mobster was a harrowing notion for prospective jurors.

I had stayed behind in the office for this part of the trial, preparing the charts that we'd use in Dewey's opening argument and in witness examinations. But through Dewey's daily team briefings, I learned that more than a few juror candidates had paled in Lucky's presence; several refused to enter the courtroom when they realized Luciano was inside. When days passed, I began to wonder if we would ever find twelve men willing to pass judgment on a man like him. But we finally did.

The judge announces, "Bailiff, bring in the jury."

Before the bailiff even takes a step toward the side door, Dewey stands. I inhale. All of us on the prosecution team have been waiting for this moment:

"Your Honor, before the jury enters, I must apprise the court of a significant development regarding three of the defendants."

The courtroom begins to hum with whispers until Judge McCook strikes his gavel. "Order in the court," he commands. He turns to Dewey. "Continue, Counselor."

The chief says, "Your Honor, the defendants Dave Miller, Al Weiner, and Pete Harris wish to change their pleas. They will be entering pleas of guilty."

Because of the concern over leaks, only a few of us were privy to this news, and now the courtroom buzzes with hushed whispers of surprise.

Judge McCook hammers his gavel three times. "Silence!"

My gaze shifts to Luciano. He and his lawyers sit as seemingly relaxed as before. I am astonished. Surely the defense team and Luciano understand what this means.

Three out of four of Luciano's most trusted bookers have entered guilty pleas, and everyone in here knows what will follow. All three men will testify not only to the Mob's operation but to the fact that the Combination is led by Luciano. This is without precedent.

Ordinarily, an arrangement of this kind would have been announced well before the beginning of the trial. But this was Dewey's doing, a deliberate maneuver. First, to put the defense on its heels. And second, to create a sensation—for days, this will be the lead in every newspaper and on every broadcast.

Imagine that. The jury hasn't even been seated and the People have fired the opening shot. From the sound of the chatter that continues in the courtroom, it has landed like a thunderclap.

And what's to come will rattle the Luciano team even further.

CHAPTER FORTY-THREE

POLLY

New York, New York
May 20, 1936

I PACE THE parlor in a repetitive loop, listening intently to the radio. Every word, every tone, every nuance feels momentous. When the announcer changes the subject, I stride over and change the station until I find what I'm looking for. I'm on the hunt for any and all details about the trial of Lucky Luciano.

As the pull my family has on me loosens—I haven't heard a peep from them since my parents walked away from me—my tie to my girls and the Lion has only grown. Along with my desire to end the threat posed by Lucky and return to business as usual. I want to do the very best for the Lion and the girls, and all this waiting is driving me crazy. Meeting with Mrs. Carter and gathering up useful tidbits for her gave me purpose during this fallow time in my work, and I didn't realize how helpful those tasks were for a woman of action like myself until they were over. Now I find myself at loose ends, and I want to do *something* to shore up the case.

"You're going to wear a hole in the floor," the Lion calls out to me from the kitchen, where she's fixing us a pot of tea. I'd wanted a stiff drink for my nerves, but the Lion pointed out that the mantel clock had just chimed eleven o'clock in the morning. "We've got hours to go before we receive a real report on the trial, and you'll lose those famous wits that you're always trying to keep if you start drinking too early," the Lion declared. Normally the hour wouldn't stop me.

She's right, as usual. The runner I hired to gather information from courtroom staff and deliver it back to me will not arrive until later this afternoon. So tea it is.

As she steps into the parlor balancing a tray, I'm struck with the strongest sense of déjà vu. As if the Lion and I have lived this day before. Maybe even more than once. Then I quickly shake my head and shake off the feeling; it's only that we've been holed up in my house for days now, waiting for Lucky's trial to end, along with my fear that he won't be convicted and he'll be back on the streets, trying to control us. Or worse.

When she sees I haven't ceased my pacing, she says, "I see you're still at it."

"It's either that or set fire to the place with my cigarettes, right?" I retort, referencing one of the other complaints the Lion has been voicing lately. I keep a cigarette constantly in my mouth, lighting one from the other as soon as the snipe burns down.

"Something like that," she says, settling the tea set on the table between the wingback chairs and plopping down into one. "Sit down and take a sip. Calm yourself."

"I can't stop moving."

"What do you think will happen if you do?"

"I don't know," I say with an inhale. "Maybe we'll lose the trial."

The Lion snorts. "That's superstition. Plain and simple."

"I know, but I can't help but think—"

A familiar series of notes from the radio followed by an announcement interrupt me. "Breaking news in the case of Charles 'Lucky' Luciano."

I inch closer to the radio console, and the Lion leans forward in her seat. "As our listeners know, after a rousing opening statement, Special Prosecutor Thomas Dewey has treated the jury to two witnesses who are ladies of the evening. They gave consistent accounts of exactly how the prostitution business works, particularly the brothels that have been the subject of the alleged Mob-controlled Combination, as well as the role the infamous bookers play in arranging the schedules of the ladies of the evening at various houses of ill repute around town. Special Prosecutor Dewey then brought two of the bookers onto the witness stand, Mr. Al Weiner and Mr. Dave Miller, both of whom have now pled guilty and agreed to give evidence on behalf of the prosecution. Mr. Weiner and Mr. Miller further explained the inner workings of the world of vice. But the defense has been merciless on cross-examination of these witnesses, and a sentiment is brewing among reporters covering the trial. How credible are the prosecution's witnesses? After all, the women are both addicted to narcotics, and Mr. Weiner and Mr. Miller have been tainted by this business and the prosecution's promises of leniency in exchange for testimony."

The Lion and I glance at each other. What does this mean? Is all of Mrs. Carter's hard work for nothing—and all my risks and the girls' sacrifices meaningless, too—because the witnesses hail from the very business that's on trial? Who else but prostitutes and madams and bookers and fixers and their bosses can describe how the business operates and how the Mafia has infiltrated it? How can onlookers possibly expect squeaky-clean witnesses from a business that is the antithesis of squeaky-clean? And anyway, why does everyone assume that because we trade in vice, we can't speak the truth?

Anger supersedes worry—I'm fired up by the hypocrisy and judgment of men who are only too eager to engage in vice in secret but deride it in public. I leap up, ready to storm around instead of pace, when the radio announcer continues. "Rumor has it that Special Prosecutor Dewey is calling a promising witness. If the whispers are true, Miss Nancy Presser will be on the stand next. She may be more than just a prostitute; allegedly, she was once a favorite companion of Lucky Luciano. Perhaps she'll have more verifiable testimony to share than the tawdry witnesses that have preceded her."

When the announcer moves on to sports news—namely the debut of a hot new baseball player on the New York Yankees, Joe DiMaggio—I turn to face the Lion to get her take before I change the station again. What does she think about Nancy Presser being called next? I wonder. It seems awfully soon in the lineup, but perhaps the information I gave Mrs. Carter about Nancy bore fruit. Significant fruit, if Dewey is putting her on the witness stand this early. I wish I had a reason to reach out to Mrs. Carter for an update. I know my curiosity alone doesn't justify disturbing her during this busy time, but my future depends on the outcome of this trial. As do those of the girls and the Lion. Returning to business for the sake of my family's financial future doesn't factor into it anymore.

Unless I hear from Mama, of course. The thought of that final squeeze from her makes my stomach flutter with hope. But not too much. I'm nothing if not realistic about the hold Moshe has on her.

Only then do I notice Angelica standing in the doorframe to the parlor, and I jump a little at the sight of her. She rarely rises this early, and anyway, her expression is strange.

"You gave me a start. You're not usually up before noon," I mock scold her.

The Lion lifts a cup. "Care for some tea?"

Angelica doesn't reply, but she does walk toward us. She refuses the offer to sit in the empty leather wingback chair next to the Lion and shakes her head at the offer of tea.

Wrapping her flimsy nightgown around her, she turns toward me. "Did I hear Nancy Presser's name on the radio?"

My heart begins to race, but I try at nonchalance. "I think so."

"Why is she suddenly an important witness?" Her voice is sharp.

"How would I know?" I ask with a shrug. Then, as if the question is outlandish, I add, "It's not as if I'm on Dewey's team."

"Aren't you?" Her tone turns knifelike.

My heart thumps so loudly I worry that Angelica can hear it. What exactly does she suspect?

"What's that supposed to mean?" I try to sound offended instead of afraid.

"Weren't we just talking about Nancy Presser the other night? Didn't Rosalie tell you some stories about Nancy's experiences as Lucky's companion? And now isn't Nancy being called as an important witness?"

I'm at a loss for words. Then, realizing how crucial my reply is, I muster up some outrage. "I'm hardly the only one who knows that story about Nancy Presser and Lucky Luciano, Angelica. Do you think it's impossible that one of the other girls in the slammer shared it? Do you really think the prosecutors couldn't get it out of Nancy themselves? What exactly are you accusing me of? Conspiring with Thomas Dewey, the man who wants to get rid of women like us in New York City?"

Now it's Angelica's turn to grow silent. She blanches, in fact. Did she think I wouldn't address her insinuation head-on? Or when I laid out plainly the nature of her allegation—the top madam in New York City working hand in hand with the authorities to bring down Lucky—did it seem preposterous to her?

"No, Polly, that's not what I meant. I guess I'm just surprised by the coincidence." She races to explain herself, and her eyes are pleading. "And a little afraid. I'm just a cog in this big machine, and I'm worried about the future."

I hear deception in her tone. Truth coexists with lies in Angelica's words, and I will have to be careful around her. After all, if Lucky manages to evade jail and takes over prostitution in New York City again, Angelica's suspicions could resurface and be whispered in all the wrong ears.

But there is something else in her statements, something that could prove very helpful to Dewey and his team, something that might ensure Lucky is locked behind bars for a long, long time. Mrs. Carter and I need to unearth certain "cogs in the big machine" and get them on the witness stand. And I have a good idea where to find them.

CHAPTER FORTY-FOUR

EUNICE

New York, New York
May 20, 1936

FROM MY EARLIEST days in church, I've been taught that seven is the number of completion, of divine favor. On this seventh day since the beginning of the trial, I pray that this holds true for us today.

From the shocking moment when the bookers changed their pleas and testified about the inner workings of the Combination, to the testimony of two prostitutes who corroborated the men's stories with their own firsthand accounts, we've been making progress. While the defense has poked a few holes—casting aspersions on the credibility of our witnesses, mostly—with each day, we're moving closer to a conviction.

But the woman who now places her trembling hand on the Bible is, I believe, one of our most critical witnesses. Sallow-skinned and sunken-eyed Nancy Presser steps up into the witness stand, a ghost of who she once was. This woman, who arrived in New York chasing dreams (and blessed with the looks) of modeling, became drawn to the underworld after crossing paths with Al Capone. But a life lived too fast—short days, endless nights, too many Gin

Rickeys, and the slow merciless ruin of the needle—ravaged her beauty.

"I do." Her voice is soft as she swears to tell the truth. She sits, her back rigid as if a rod is holding her upright.

Nancy is frail, the toll of the drugs apparent. I take in a slow breath and lift up a silent prayer.

I'm certain Nancy never imagined she'd find herself here, preparing to do the unthinkable—testifying and helping to send Luciano away for a long time. She glances at me, searching for steadiness. And I give her a nearly imperceptible but hopefully encouraging nod.

We rehearsed this moment. I warned her to never look at Luciano. To keep her eyes on Dewey. We discussed every line of questioning from the prosecution and the possible questions that would come from the defense.

I spent just as much time coaching Dewey, another advantage of me being on his team. I explained Nancy's fragility and guided him on how to approach her with authority and grace. He had to treat her with dignity and not pity, and then the jurors would do the same in assessing her testimony.

The chief buttons his jacket as he approaches the stand. "How are you today, Miss Presser?"

"I'm fine." Her voice wavers slightly.

"Thank you for being here."

My breath catches. That's not how I would have opened. I pray Nancy doesn't say she was pressured into being here. When she only nods, I exhale.

Dewey moves swiftly through the opening lines of questioning: her full name, age, place of birth, education, and current residence. Then he moves to the crux of his direct examination.

"Miss Presser, are you acquainted with the defendant, Charles Luciano?"

"Yes."

"How do you know Mr. Luciano?"

She shifts but keeps her eyes on Dewey. "I was one of his . . . uh . . . girls."

"By 'girl,' do you mean prostitute?"

She lowers her eyes and nods. But then she remembers another instruction. "Yes," she says, speaking up and with resolve.

Dewey leads her through the facts she told me: the places she and Luciano met, how much time they spent together, the men who would often join them. "Were there occasions when Mr. Luciano spoke about his business?"

"Yes. Lucky and I often had dinner at this place not too far from Madison Square Garden. And whenever anyone joined us there, they usually ended up talking business."

"Who would join you and Mr. Luciano?"

She says, "The regulars, you know. Lil Davie, Tommy the Bull, Jimmy . . ."

I flinch at her use of the nicknames. I've worked hard to get the girls to use formal names. But the chief clarifies all the names for the court and the jury before he moves to the conversation I told him to draw out.

She says, "There was one evening when Lucky was talking with Lil Davie about some of the houses not paying."

"Objection, hearsay," Luciano's lawyer stands and yells out.

Dewey is prepared for this. Nancy overheard Luciano—and others—make many damaging statements that we need admitted into evidence. Of course, the defense will try to exclude them under the hearsay rule.

But we have our exceptions to that hearsay rule ready to keep hold of Nancy's critical testimony. We know we won't get everything in, but the jury will hear most of it.

"Exception to the hearsay rule," Dewey replies. "Statement of a party opponent."

The judge nods and says, "Objection overruled. You may continue, Miss Presser."

To prompt her along, Dewey asks, "What do you mean by 'the houses'?"

"The brothels. The madams who run them. Some of them weren't paying up, and Lucky told Davie to go in there and smash and crash everything. To destroy the place to make an example."

"Hearsay!" One of Luciano's team jumps up again.

The judge doesn't even bother waiting for Dewey's argument. "Overruled."

She continues, recounting other conversations: "I heard him talking about how he was going to raise the prices, and he talked to the others about when and where the girls were being moved. He talked a lot about expanding the business."

After drawing out everything that Nancy knows about the workings of the Combination, and the statements she overheard Luciano make about running it and wreaking havoc on those who didn't toe the line, Dewey thanks her and steps away. I study the jury. The twelve men have listened closely. Most of them are stone-faced, but the foreman, Edwin Aderer—a dental gold manufacturer—is almost on the edge of his seat.

That's a good sign, but the battle for Nancy Presser's credibility has just begun.

George Morton Levy rises, and I press my hands together. I tried to prepare Nancy for this cross-examination, warning her about the insults and the pure brutality of the questions that would come from Levy. But mostly, I tried to prepare her for *him*. The forty-year-old slick gangster lawyer moves with the confidence and authority of a man who never loses. His booming baritone and sneering tone even rattled me a few times over the last week.

Nancy told me she was ready. All I can do now is hold my breath.

"Miss Presser," Levy begins, addressing her with casual disdain. "You are addicted to drugs, is that correct?"

"I have had difficulty with them in the past, yes. But I am not on anything now."

"And what is your poison?" Before she can respond, he adds, "Or are there too many to count?"

"I have had problems with heroin in the past," she says, her voice steady, as if she's merely stating a fact.

"Ah! Is that why you sell your body? So you can get your next fix?"

"Objection!" Dewey shouts from his chair. "Speculation. Assumes facts not in evidence. And badgering."

"Sustained!"

For the next hour, Levy drags Nancy through the gutter, attempting to reduce her to ruin in the eyes of the court. He asks her to describe her drug addiction: the needles, the dosages, how the high made her feel. He presses her on how many times she fell back into the habit and why she couldn't just stop.

Dewey objects, and most are sustained. But the seed of doubt has been planted and has to be growing in the jurors' minds.

Protectiveness surges through me, and so many times I want to rise, object, and demand that Levy move on. But I cannot, and the man barrels forward, beating Nancy down with every question.

Nancy begins to break. Her chin dips, her shoulders fold, and perspiration glistens on her forehead.

When she begins to sway, Dewey stands. But before he can speak, Judge McCook asks, "Miss Presser, are you all right?"

"No." Her voice is barely audible.

"Would you like a glass of water?" The judge nods to the bailiff.

"I need . . . a moment . . . the bathroom." Before the judge can grant her leave, Nancy bolts from the stand, a hand clamped over her mouth as if she's pressing back a volcano of rising bile in her throat.

The courtroom stirs as Levy strolls back to his chair, his smirk smug and satisfied. I shake my head. More than one of the girls warned me that just talking about their addiction made them nauseous. Levy tried this tactic with the first two girls, but it only worked with Nancy.

When Nancy doesn't immediately return, Judge McCook says, "It's nearly twelve. We'll take this opportunity to take a lunch recess until one o'clock."

He has barely rapped his gavel again before the room erupts. I gather my briefcase, prepared to rush after Nancy. But just as I rise, a blond boy, no older than sixteen, brushes past me. He slips a folded piece of paper into my hand.

I freeze. Before I can think or speak, he's gone.

My hands shake as I stare at the paper. Is this another threat from Luciano and his goons? Would they be so brazen as to actually threaten me in court? I unfold the note and read. Then I scan the room. No eyes are on me. I ease out of the courtroom.

Less than thirty minutes later, I hop out of Mr. Johnson's Buick and bound up the stairs of the New York Public Library. The twin marble lions of Patience and Fortitude majestically flank the entrance, but today I barely notice the statues.

I move quickly through the grand vestibule, weaving past students and scholars, until I reach the sweeping staircase. On the second floor, I find her in the history stacks.

Today, Polly wears heels so high, I hope they were purchased with a parachute. Her black satin dress is a bit too clingy and fancy for daytime. But she scans the shelves as if she's an ordinary patron.

A bit of indignation washes over me. Over all these months, we've been so careful to avoid suspicion and detection. But now? I stride forward, stopping right alongside her, although I do take the precautionary measure of facing the opposite shelves.

"You should not have contacted me this way," I say in a sharp whisper. "You pulled me out of the trial."

"Good afternoon, Mrs. Carter." Her tone is cool and cordial.

"You had your runner slip me a note in open court. Do you know what that could have cost me? Not to mention you?"

"I was not concerned. If anyone asked, you could have said you were receiving a note from an important witness or a colleague."

"Or if they've been watching, someone could have followed your messenger and learned the message came from you. And that would put both of us at risk."

"He wasn't going to come back to me," she says. She gives me a quick sideways glance. "Why are you so skittish? Have you been followed?"

I brush her off with a wave of my hand. "Why did you want to see me, Miss Adler?"

"I've been listening to the radio bulletins on the trial. Your witnesses' credibility's being picked apart."

I huff. When did Polly Adler start practicing law?

"I understand that Nancy Presser is your next witness," she continues.

"She just got off the stand and will go back on again later."

"And she'll be excellent, I'm sure. But just like with the others, many will doubt that she's trustworthy. Those men on the jury will see her only as a drug addict and a two-bit whore."

I flinch at Polly's words. She's never referred to any of the girls that way, but I know it's only to make her point.

"Credibility is the Achilles' heel of your case." She keeps on like she's one of the prosecuting attorneys. "But I have something that can fix that."

The heavy clomp of hard-soled shoes approaching makes her pause, and she waits until the footsteps fade. She pulls a volume from the stacks, opens the pages, and then whispers, "Hotel staff."

"What about them?"

"Lucky spent weeks, sometimes months, living in the Barbizon and the Waldorf."

I stare at the books in front of me. "And?"

"And I'm familiar with his time at the hotels because I sent girls there from time to time. He had the same staff serve him during each of his stays. I know this because I had to get to know them—the managers, doormen, porters, bellhops, attendants, all of them—befriend them, so to speak, so my girls could move freely about the hotel without being harassed."

I drop my arms to my sides, the realization dawning upon me. "And now those same employees could provide useful testimony about him."

"Yes," she says. "The hotel staff would have seen him regularly and come to know him, his habits, and his visitors. I'm sure they can recall an overheard conversation or two."

"They can corroborate what the bookers and the girls have said on the stand," I say, more to myself than Polly.

Polly faces me for just a moment and smiles.

I say, "And they *will be* credible witnesses."

Polly answers with a nod. "I'll be in touch, Mrs. Carter."

"You don't have the names for me?" I'm astounded. Why would she bring me here just for a chat?

"I wanted to see if you'd be amenable to this. You'll hear from me very soon."

I watch as she disappears down the aisle, and then I smile, too. This was worth the risks.

CHAPTER FORTY-FIVE

POLLY

New York, New York
May 20, 1936

STRIKING BLACK MARBLE columns dominating the airy, twenty-foot-high space. Intricate plaster reliefs adorning the ceiling. Rich wood paneling on the walls. Every time I step into the main lobby of the Waldorf-Astoria Hotel, I am struck by its calming, simple elegance, so different than the overwrought crystal-and-gold decor of every other luxury hotel in New York City. Although I know better than most that the same sort of shenanigans go on behind all hotels' closed doors, no matter how they're decorated.

This new iteration of an older hotel is a behemoth. Taking over an entire city block, the hotel begins at Park Avenue and spreads to Lexington, 49th Street, and 50th Street. With thousands of rooms—including multiroom apartments—it's proven to be the toniest hot spot, especially for long-term guests. Like Lucky Luciano.

I cross the lobby and step into Peacock Alley. This corridor that runs off the main lobby is a place to see and be seen. Groupings of club chairs and tables are dotted throughout the marbled space, warmly lit by floor lamps. Several prime seating areas are already taken by what look like society folks and celebrities and dignitaries sipping at tea or cocktails, but I'm not looking for center stage. A dark corner suits my purposes just fine. Perfectly, in fact. It feels good to be taking action.

Spotting a single high-backed chair in a corner, I settle into it and reach for the drinks menu on the end table. The waiter materializes almost instantly.

"May I take your order, ma'am?"

"Yes, I'll have a Gin Fizz, and"—I reach for the sealed envelope in my handbag—"I'd like you to pass this along to Mr. Henry Woelfle, manager of the Towers."

The waiter's facial expression doesn't change; he's ever the perfectly mannered, eager-to-please server. But a single bushy eyebrow lifts at my request. "As you wish, ma'am."

Within minutes, a tidy, compact figure enters Peacock Alley, precisely as I expected. I know the schedule of every supervisor amenable to my line of work at all the luxury hotels in the city, Waldorf-Astoria chief among them, and I'd made sure Mr. Woelfle would be on duty. While the manager of the Waldorf-Astoria Towers—the section of the hotel where the apartments are located—hasn't exactly been welcoming to my business, he does tolerate me and my girls at the request of his tenants.

"Miss Adler," he says as a waiter scoots behind him with a chair. After he sits down, he stares at me with pale blue eyes. "How may I assist you?"

"I'm not here to deliver some of my girls, if that's what you're worried about."

The slightest flush creeps onto his cheeks. "I'm here to serve our guests, Miss Adler, whatever their needs. I do not judge, and I hope you know that."

"I do, Mr. Woelfle. Your guests and their needs are exactly what I am here to discuss." I drop my voice. "I understand that you had a Mr. Charles Ross as a tenant in your apartments last year."

Charles Ross is Lucky's favorite alias. It is also the one that he consistently used at the Waldorf-Astoria and Barbizon Hotels. I know this because Lucky's goons instructed my girls to use it when calling up. When Lucky wasn't entertaining his newest girlfriend, showgirl Gay Orlova, that is.

Mr. Woelfle's eyes dart around Peacock Alley. He's undoubtedly scanning for anyone who might overhear this conversation. It's one thing to chat with Polly Adler in Peacock Alley—not ideal, but a necessary evil of his business. It's quite another to discuss Lucky Luciano with her. Especially during the middle of his trial.

"Yes, you are correct, Miss Adler." His volume matches mine. "Mr. Ross was a tenant in the Towers for over six months last year. From April through October."

"How was that experience for you, Mr. Woelfle?"

"Privacy and service for our guests are the two cornerstones of the Waldorf-Astoria business, Miss Adler. Qualities that you benefited from as well, if I'm not mistaken. So I'm certain you understand why I'm not at liberty to share with you the details of Mr. Ross' stay."

"I'm not here to pry for details. Lord knows I'm privy to too many secrets already. So let me clarify my question. I am asking whether Mr. Ross is a guest you'd like to have stay at the hotel again."

He's quiet for a long moment. Conflicting emotions flicker across his face, from duty to disdain to reluctance. "I do not discuss my tenants, Miss Adler, and I typically make it a practice to refuse such exchanges. But in this particular case, I think I might make an exception. It's fair to say that Mr. Ross presented certain challenges to the hotel staff, his fellow guests, and the building itself, and this makes him a less appealing repeat or long-term guest. Although, if we should host him again, my staff and I would treat him with the same respect, accord, and service for which the Waldorf-Astoria is world-renowned."

As I suspected. I heard from my girls that Lucky and his thugs were running roughshod over the hotel staff and wrecking the luxurious apartment as well as the various hotel bars. *Imagine,* I think, *Lucky striding through this glorious space with mobsters like Vito Genovese, Meyer Lansky, and Frank Costello.* What if they wanted to use this luxurious hotel as the base of operations for some clandestine criminal activity? Would they park in the attached garage, take the private elevator to Lucky's apartment, then vanish into the crowds of the lobby or the city streets as they headed out to whatever bad business they were up to? What must the other hotel guests have thought about the rough manners of his gang? I'm counting on the fact that Mr. Woelfle wouldn't want Lucky and his goons back.

I nod sympathetically. "I figured as much. It pains me to tell you that Mr. Ross recently announced that—as soon as he cleared his name—his first port of call would be the Waldorf."

His Adam's apple moves as he swallows. "He said that?"

"Yes. In fact, he's rumored to have said, 'The Towers is the best-class address in New York and I can't wait to get back to my apartment and celebrate.' Supposedly he's hoping Cole Porter will write him a tune."

The songwriter Cole Porter is one of the long-term guests in Mr. Woelfle's Towers, where he's lived for years in a six-bedroom residence. Mr. Porter adores the Waldorf so much that he referenced it in a song: *You're the top, you're a Waldorf salad.* The fact that he keeps his precious Steinway in that Waldorf Towers apartment is a testament to his love of the establishment.

"I see." Mr. Woelfle falls back in his chair. "But why are you telling me this? I can't conceive how this might matter to you."

"Did you ever think how Mr. Ross' interference in my business hurts me and my girls? And I don't mean financially. Did you ever consider that it might behoove me to not have him return to the Waldorf? Or New York City?" Making this confession is a calculated risk, particularly if this man were ever to repeat these sentiments. But I know it's necessary to soften him for my next request.

"I confess that I didn't, Miss Adler," Mr. Woelfle says in a surprisingly soft tone. "But I can imagine it now, and I'm sorry."

I'm so little used to sympathy that Mr. Woelfle's minuscule show of kindness moves me. A moment passes before I can reassemble myself enough to step back unto the breach. "What if I told you that there's a way to ensure that Mr. Ross won't return?"

"I would tell you I'm listening."

"If you've been keeping tabs on the trial as I have, you've noticed that the prosecution has a credibility problem with its witnesses."

"I'm familiar with the newspaper reports."

"Then you know Dewey needs reliable testimony from average citizens to bolster the statements made by the girls and the bookers. I believe there is a treasure trove of those sorts of witnesses here at the Waldorf."

Mr. Woelfle's brow furrows. "What do you mean?"

"I know a bit about how hotels operate. I'm guessing that the same staff members serviced Mr. Ross' apartment day after day—trustworthy staff members. The same maids cleaned his rooms, the same waiters delivered meals, the same busboys delivered packages and luggage, and so on. Am I right?"

"You are largely correct. Depending on the day of the week, of course, and the shift. We do like to provide a certain continuity of service, and arranging for the same staff members to offer it is the best way to do so. And it helped limit information about Mr. Ross and his associates from spreading."

"As I suspected," I say. "I am also guessing that, on at least a couple of occasions, your staff observed other people in Mr. Ross' apartment, maybe when they were serving meals or delivering items. Perhaps they even overheard conversations while setting up the food or clearing dishes. Those staff members could be invaluable witnesses for the prosecution, because they could verify the crucial testimony offered by the girls and the bookers. This would help Special Prosecutor Dewey's credibility problem immeasurably and help with the success of his case."

The unblinking blue eyes suddenly start blinking quite rapidly. Mr. Woelfle then reaches for my untouched Gin Fizz and downs it in one go. "You want me to ask my staff to be witnesses in"—here he whispers—"Lucky Luciano's trial?"

"I guess that's the long and short of it. They are uniquely situated to help put him behind bars."

He nods, albeit so very slowly it's hard to discern at first. His hand then shoots in the air, and a waiter practically runs to our side. Before the fellow can even ask what we'd like, Mr. Woelfle says, "Another Gin Fizz for my guest, and a whiskey for me. Just about to go off duty."

We don't speak until fresh drinks are in our hands, and I consider it a victory that Mr. Woelfle hasn't run off or banished me from the Waldorf forever. But will he actually agree to encourage his staff to testify at trial? We both know how the Mob treats snitches, even if they aren't of the homegrown variety.

When we've downed half a drink each, Mr. Woelfle sighs and finally says, "Tell me how this would work."

CHAPTER FORTY-SIX

EUNICE

New York, New York
May 21, 1936

At just half past six in the morning, Park Avenue is almost empty. The city is not yet fully awake as I drive past the grandiose entrance of the Waldorf-Astoria Hotel and Towers. On the corner of Park Avenue and East 50th Street, I enter the garage and slowly make my way to the back.

This is the first time I've taken the wheel since our car was vandalized back in March. Now that Luciano is on trial, I believe it's safe—Luciano wouldn't dare threaten or harm us now. That would be too obvious. But Lisle insisted that we keep our arrangement with Mr. Johnson, and I agreed, if only to avoid stirring the waters between us.

This morning's meeting, however, is one that I must attend alone. I rang Mr. Johnson last night and told him I wouldn't need his services until tomorrow. Now I can only pray that Mr. Johnson doesn't mention this to Lisle. My saving grace is that the court is not in session today. So I'll have the car back and be home hours before Lisle walks through the door.

I round the car to the second level, where Polly said she'd be waiting near the elevator. There are a few parked cars, but I don't see her. And then a plume of cigarette smoke circles in the air, and I spot her, hiding in the concrete shadows of the garage.

I park in a space just feet from where Polly stands, next to a Packard that I assume is hers. When I slide out, I nod; she nods. When she spins around, I follow, past the elevator, around a corner. Then we slip into the hotel through an industrial door.

It all feels so clandestine as Polly moves with the confidence of someone familiar with the hidden warren of the Waldorf. This entrance, with the unpolished concrete floors that blend into the walls, is a world apart from the marbled elegance and chandelier-lit lobby I've seen in *Vanity Fair* magazine photographs.

I say a prayer as we move quickly. We cannot encounter anyone. I don't look like staff, and a colored guest in the Waldorf would be met with lifted brow, even if we're far from the hotel's main entrance and the Fifth Avenue set. I blanched last night when I received Polly's note to meet here. But in the end, I couldn't expect potential witnesses to come to me; I had to take this risk.

Finally, Polly stops before a door and knocks. When the door creaks open, I quickly assess the medium-height, fair-haired man. They exchange a few hushed words before he nods, and Polly turns to me.

"They're ready for you. I'll meet you back at the car."

"Thank you," I say before stepping inside. The room is simple, utilitarian in size and structure. A plain wooden table, nicked and worn, with eight chairs around it, is set in the center.

The blond man stands flanked by a taller, dark-haired gentleman and a younger woman, both already dressed in fresh uniforms.

"Good morning. Thank you for meeting with me," I greet them.

He gives a slight bow of his head. "I'm Henry Woelfle, manager of the Towers." His tone is as stiff as starch, and so is his posture.

The other man mirrors his formality. Only the young woman offers a smile brighter than expected so early in the morning, or for the purpose of this gathering.

Mr. Woelfle gestures to the others. "This is Mr. Joseph Weinman, one of our senior waiters, and Miss Marjorie Brown, a chambermaid in the Towers."

I nod again, and my gaze lingers on the woman. She's young—in her early twenties, I would guess—with flame-red hair swept into a roll at the nape of her neck. It's her freckles and her smile that draw me in. She's not at all rattled by this meeting, but instead seems curious.

Mr. Woelfle gestures to the table, and I take an empty chair opposite them. He says, "I understand you're with the prosecutor's office. One of the attorneys on . . . the trial," he says, seeming as if he's avoiding speaking Luciano's name.

"Yes, and—"

Mr. Weinman cuts in. "My wife and I have been listening to the broadcasts every night and reading the *Times* in the morning. But we can't tell what's what. One night, the announcer will say the prosecution had a good day, but then the next morning, the newspapers say the defense ripped the prosecution's witnesses apart."

"The press thrives on this, the spectacle of it all. But we believe the trial is going well." I tell him the truth. "We have a strong case, but any credible testimony could strengthen our case further. That's why I'm here."

Mr. Woelfle clears his throat. "I hope you understand, Mrs. Carter, this is highly irregular. At the Waldorf, we pride ourselves on extending the utmost discretion to our guests. They expect it."

"I understand. And I would not be here if this were not such an extraordinary circumstance. Your accounts could prove vital."

The two men trade uneasy glances, but Miss Brown sits up

straighter, like she's ready for anything. "I'm willing to help if I can."

Her words surprise me. The men seem weighted with caution, but Miss Brown is not. She's unflinching and unshaken.

When I glance at her curiously, she shrugs. "It's not every day someone wants to talk to me about a gangster."

She makes me want to smile. "I have a few questions. Anything you can tell me that would be pertinent to our investigation."

Miss Brown says, "Okay, what do you want to know?"

Before answering, I take a deep breath. "First, I must be clear—if what you tell me proves crucial, you may be called to testify."

"In court?" Mr. Weinman recoils.

I nod. "But—"

He pushes himself away from the table. "Absolutely not. I have a wife and a boy at home. I'll speak with you here, but I'm not putting my family in harm's way."

"Nor will I," Mr. Woelfle adds quickly. "My daughter just turned nine. I'll speak with you here—in confidence—but I will not risk her safety."

"I understand your fears," I say, feeling this opportunity slipping away. "But let me assure you, you will have the support of the special prosecutor's office."

"The special prosecutor will not help us once we leave that courtroom," Mr. Weinman scoffs. "Mr. Dewey won't be there when someone kicks down my front door at midnight."

"We can arrange protection, if that's what you desire. We will keep you and your family safe," I say, trying to calm the current I feel rising in the room. "We just need your help to put Luciano away."

Miss Brown meets my gaze. "I don't have a husband or any children to worry about, Mrs. Carter. But I do have a memory and a conscience. And I remember being in Mr. Ross' suite and hearing things I didn't want to hear and seeing things I can't forget. They treated me like wallpaper, and you know what? I thank the good Lord for that. Because the way they slapped some of those girls around?" She shakes her head. "One day, I had to give a girl a towel because she was slapped so hard, her nose bled like she was shot. And then there were the girls who were passed out on his bed. From drinking? From drugs? I don't know. All I know is that they weren't just sleeping. They weren't lying there completely naked and exposed to the world by choice.

"That's what I remember, and my conscience won't allow me to walk away now that you're asking. Mr. Ross and some of those other men need to be put away for a long time."

"That's what we're hoping, Miss Brown. If we get a conviction, he'll be gone for decades."

"Decades? How many?"

"He could face fifty, even sixty years."

She nods, resolute. "I say we push for seventy." Turning to the men, she says, "Look, I'm not saying we have to be heroes, but we have to be decent. I know what I saw, you know what you saw. Somebody has to stand up. Why can't it be us?"

I want to reach across the table, take her hand, and ask where she finds the courage. How is she so brave when so many are weak?

Mr. Woelfle lowers his eyes. Mr. Weinman shifts in his seat.

She shakes her head. "All right. I understand why Mr. Woelfle and Mr. Weinman won't speak, but I will."

Mr. Woelfle glances up. "No, Miss Brown. We all can." To me, he asks, "What exactly do you need to know?"

I guess what Mama always said is true—nothing moves a man faster than the fear of being shown up by a woman.

CHAPTER FORTY-SEVEN

POLLY

New York, New York
May 21, 1936

I SIT BEHIND the steering wheel of my car, deep in the bowels of the Waldorf parking garage. I'm clutching on to the leather-clad wheel, my hands gripping as tightly as if I were careening down a sinuous highway, a cliff to my left. In a sense, this is my situation.

The overhead garage lights flicker, but I can make out the door to the hotel interior well enough. When I'm not watching that entrance—eager for Mrs. Carter's return—I'm staring at the dashboard clock. Over an hour has passed since I bid her farewell at Mr. Woelfle's door. I didn't have a sense of how long Mrs. Carter would meet with the Waldorf staff, but it feels like an eternity. At least we don't have to worry about getting her back to court, as it's not in session today.

Will they deliver what she needs? What we all need? I'm betting the bank on it here; I've got no more aces up my sleeves.

I've thrown in my lot with Mrs. Carter, no doubt about it. If the prosecution doesn't prevail and Lucky is returned to the streets of New York, I'll need an exit strategy. Because someone, somehow, at some time, will figure out my role in all this. And Lucky will make me pay and my girls along with me, never mind that they've had nothing to do with it. Actually, the more I think about my girls, the more I realize that if Lucky gets off scot-free and runs the Combination again, there's a chance he will learn about the part I've played from Angelica.

I release my grip on the steering wheel and reach for my handbag. A Chesterfield is calling to me, and my nerves calm with the first inhale. As I blow out the smoke through the rolled-down window, I hear a creaking sound. I turn toward the door. Light streams into the garage as it opens and Mrs. Carter returns.

I want to leap from the car and ask her how it went. But we must be cautious. Mrs. Carter and I will only make contact if she's sussed out the setting and deemed it safe.

As she approaches my car, I can't make out her face with the light behind her like some kind of fluorescent halo. When she finally gets close enough to tap on my window, I see that she's smiling. An honest-to-goodness smile. Maybe the first one I've ever seen on her face.

I open the car door from the inside, and she slides into the passenger seat. "You look like the cat that ate the canary."

"I suppose I did. In a manner of speaking," she says, that smile widening.

"What in the name of all that's holy happened in there?"

I was hopeful after my initial conversation with Mr. Woelfle. His experience with "Mr. Ross" had been abominable, and he seemed willing to prevent Lucky's return. But I was too leery to wish for much, particularly his ability to recruit more witnesses. This is a dangerous business, after all. From the look on Mrs. Carter's face, however, I might have underestimated the Waldorf staff.

"They are gems," Mrs. Carter says, her eyes bright. "True gems."

"Tell me," I say.

"Well, Mr. Woelfle is the picture of respectability, a longtime manager in the most luxurious hotel in the world. He'll testify that Mr. Charles Ross resided in the Waldorf-Astoria Towers for six months. That, while Mr. Ross was staying in the Towers, he entertained a steady stream of 'unusual characters' in his apartment, men and women. The sort of 'characters' that drew the attention of other Waldorf guests, such that Mr. Woelfle had to intervene on several occasions in the hotel's public spaces. He'll also say that he heard rumors that Mr. Ross was none other than Mr. Lucky Luciano. Now, this last bit will be speculation or hearsay, of course, but I daresay Dewey will sneak in the whole question before the defense objects, thereby planting the seed in the jury's mind. But even if he doesn't, Mr. Woelfle will be able to identify Luciano in the courtroom—linking Mr. Ross to Mr. Luciano and supporting the testimony of the prostitutes who recounted conversations at the Waldorf."

I let out a low whistle. "Like Nancy Presser."

"Like Nancy Presser," she says, her expression almost gleeful. "That's not even the best part."

"What could be better?"

"The testimony of the maid and the waiter. Mr. Weinman, an upstanding workingman, served Luciano meals in his apartment several times. On at least three occasions, there were other men present. Luciano referred to one of the men as Fredericks."

"That's Jimmy Frederico's nickname!"

"Exactly. The co-defendant that Luciano has repeatedly denied knowing. Luciano's insistence that he has never met the other defendants before is one of the oddest arguments his attorney is making at trial, particularly since they are known compatriots. We now have a reputable witness who can put the two men together, here at the Waldorf."

"And that will shore up other statements on the witness stand about Lucky and Jimmy."

Mrs. Carter puts a gloved finger on her nose and gives me a little grin. "But the real star is Miss Marjorie Brown."

"How so?"

"First of all, she's so darn likable. A decent young woman who travels into the city every day from Union City, New Jersey, to spend long hours cleaning at the Waldorf. She's excelled at her job and has been given a plum position servicing the apartments on the thirty-ninth and fortieth floors. Most importantly, she personally observed the other defendants entering and exiting Luciano's apartments dozens of times—"

"Did you say dozens?" I can't help but interject. Surely I've misheard her.

"I did."

"Miss Brown saw Jimmy Frederico, Little Davie Betillo, Little Abie Wahrman, and Meyer Berkman going in and out dozens of times."

"She did. I showed her their pictures. She even saw girls in Luciano's suite, some of which were drugged up or beaten. And she overheard snippets of conversations about the business. She's fearless. Once I promised her and the others that we'd protect them throughout the trial and afterward. Even moving them if we have to."

"What a find!"

"This is your find, Miss Adler. And your find will not only correct our credibility problem with the other witnesses but add new, important testimony. I am immensely grateful," she says. "You know, in another lifetime, you would have made an excellent lawyer. Such good instincts and such a talent for knitting together a compelling case."

How nice that would have been, I think, warming to her compliment. Yet how little Mrs. Carter knows about my dire origins to even suggest such a thing might have been possible. "Ah, I've told you a bit about my background, so you know that would have required a much easier upbringing, one with more opportunities and supportive parents. Maybe one closer to your own," I say.

All her softness vanishes in a flash, replaced by the guarded woman I first encountered. "I hardly think it's fair to call the life of a colored woman in this country 'easy.'"

"I never said you've had it easy. All I said is that you had it easier than me. I'm sure it was hard to attend law school as a colored woman, but you must have had people that encouraged you along the way. I never had that. My road hasn't been smoother than yours simply because I'm white," I say, feeling a little defensive myself.

"I never said that. In fact, I talked to a lot of girls and madams as I prepared for trial—colored and white—so I know there must have been hardships. And I can understand because I've endured my own. Violent race riots drove my family out of Atlanta to New York, where my parents made it their purpose to fight against racism. True, they gave me opportunities and support for my education, but I've faced hatred for the color of my skin at every turn."

"*All* our stories are hard, but in very different ways. And there is something I didn't tell you about my early years here. Once I was forced out of school into factory work, I was raped by the foreman. When the distant cousin I lived with discovered I'd gotten pregnant from the rape, she threw me out, and vice was the only place that would have me." I blurt out my terrible story.

I'm not exactly sure why I feel a compulsion to tell Mrs. Carter the full, ugly truth. Maybe speaking it aloud to my mother has freed me to share it with others. Once you've told the person you're meant to care about most the very worst thing about you, how bad can it be to share it with others, right?

"I'm sorry, Miss Adler. I didn't know." She sounds contrite, even empathetic. She is indeed the rare sort of woman with compassion for the girls and madams who descend into this sort of work.

"I guess there is no way to tell who fares better in this godforsaken country—a well-educated woman from the middle class whose skin happens to be colored or a poor Jewish immigrant woman who never got past seventh grade and whose skin happens to be white."

"It's a toss-up, Miss Adler. But one thing is for certain. No matter how difficult your beginnings—and they do sound appalling—you have some latitude to reinvent yourself and your history, something I can't do. Because I cannot change the color of my skin."

CHAPTER FORTY-EIGHT

EUNICE

New York, New York
May 21, 1936

"Chief, may I have a moment?" I ask, finally getting my chance to speak with Dewey, who's been behind closed doors most of the day. I'd informed Miss Rosse that I had urgent information for the chief, but only now he's made himself accessible to me. I begin before he can respond. "This morning, I received statements from three employees of the Waldorf Towers. A manager, a waiter, and a chambermaid." As Dewey sits back, I recount my interview with the three. His eyes flicker with surprise when I repeat all the names the trio mentioned—almost every one of Luciano's co-defendants who were regularly in and out of the Waldorf Towers apartment.

"There is one conversation in particular the manager recalls." I glance down at my notepad. "Luciano told Pennochio to 'talk to Becker, let him know that if he wants his cut, he better keep the cops looking the other way. There's a lot of money to be made off these girls the way I have it set up now.'" I hand Dewey my notepad.

He scans the pages and shakes his head in awe as I continue. "For a time, he was running his prostitution racket straight from the Waldorf. How will Luciano explain these men going in and out of his apartment so frequently when he claims to not know any of them? Not to mention, every single one of these statements implicates him even more."

I cannot withhold a smile of satisfaction. These three are near-unassailable witnesses.

"He won't be able to deny this," I say. "The jury will be convinced."

The chief taps the notepad against his palm. "You never know what a jury of twelve men will do, but this is good work, Mrs. Carter. How did you track these people down?"

Without a pause, I say, "You've been concerned about the gaps between testimonies and credibility. I was determined to find more credible sources."

He doesn't seem to notice that I didn't quite answer his question. He only nods, satisfied. "All right. We'll get them prepped for court."

"I've already established a rapport with them. I can help prep them, especially Miss Brown—just like I've prepped the other women."

"We'll need that at once," he says.

I nod. "I'll arrange for the interviews tomorrow."

"And can you prepare a comprehensive examination outline for each? With so little notice, I want a full run of questions, because their testimonies are critical."

"I'll have it first thing in the morning."

As I make my way back to my office, I feel a bit of dread. I won't get the car back to the garage before Lisle comes home. Perhaps I should ring him, but as quickly as I have that thought, I push it aside. The car will be of no matter—unless, of course, he intends to go out tonight. He's certainly used to the hours I work, especially these past weeks of the trial.

Inside my office, I slide my typewriter to the center of my desk and sit for a moment. This day has been long enough to fill a week, and tonight promises to be even longer. But I am not alone. Since the trial began, most of us have worked well past midnight. I've heard that a few attorneys have even spent nights stretched out on their office floors. I'm certain Dewey has done that a couple of times.

Even now, the office hums like it's the middle of the day rather than well into the evening. But the bustle is not from lawyers alone. Wives bring supper to their husbands, and the scent of coffee and stewed meat mingles in the air. Little children who tagged along to get a bedtime hug and good-night kiss from their fathers fill the corridor with laughter. Everyone is here for the duration, and the families have popped in to support them.

For a moment, I imagine glancing up and seeing Lisle and Junior standing in my doorway. But it is just a dream. My husband is busy with his own work, and we've yet to bring Junior home. But the day for his and Mama's return is edging closer.

Just as I set my fingers on the typewriter keys, a light tap on the door makes me look up, and my smile is instant.

"Eva," I say, greeting Murray's wife. "It's good to see you."

"And you as well, Eunice." She gazes at the papers on my desk. "I don't think I'll ever get used to the sheer amount of work all of you are doing. And such long hours."

"All for a worthy cause."

"Certainly." She reaches into the wicker basket she carries and pulls out a wax-paper-wrapped sandwich. "I just brought Murray his supper. You know, he sometimes forgets to eat when he's buried in work. And I suspect the same is true for you." She hands me the bundle. "I hope you like corned beef with mustard."

"I love it," I say, taken by her thoughtfulness. "Thank you."

"It is my pleasure." She pauses for a moment before she adds, "Eunice, what you're doing here makes all of us so proud." She gives me a nod and then leaves.

For a while, I sit, letting her words settle over me. I appreciate her kindness, but it's what she said—that I'm not making a difference for just colored women but for all women—that heartens me the most.

I unwrap the sandwich and close my eyes after the first bite, savoring the tang of the mustard. My conversation with Eva—and the sandwich—have reenergized me, and I turn back to the typewriter with renewed purpose. Perhaps this won't be such a late night after all.

I WOULD HAVE parked my car in the middle of Edgecombe Avenue if I had to. Anything to avoid walking the two blocks from the garage to my apartment alone. But tonight, God is merciful. A space waits for me right in front of my building as if He saved it for me Himself.

And good thing—it's a quarter past two in the morning, and exhaustion clings to my bones. I will not be able to stagger more than a few feet into my building.

The moment I enter the apartment, I kick off my shoes without undoing the T-strap and lean back against the front door. I want just a moment to summon the strength to ready for bed. Quietly, of course, so I won't disturb Lisle.

But as I pass the parlor, something catches my attention. Lisle sits on the sofa in the dark, his gaze straight ahead, fixed on nothing. My heart kicks inside my chest. Something's happened! To Junior? To my mother?

I rush in and click on the lamp on the side table. "Lisle, darling. What's wrong?"

He doesn't flinch. He doesn't blink.

I'm trembling as I ease down beside him. He still won't look at me, and then I notice. The stiff collar of his shirt is undone, but he's dressed formally, in his black tuxedo with the wide silk lapels.

Now I'm even more confused—until I glance down at the cream-colored program resting on the cocktail table. The words on the front are embossed in gold: *The NAACP honors DR. LISLE CARTER.*

I gasp and snatch the program from the table. "Oh my Lord. Was this tonight?"

For the first time, Lisle's eyes meet mine. "Yes."

I press my hand to my chest. "Lisle . . . sweetheart, I'm so sorry. I can't believe . . . I forgot."

He lifts his glass and takes a slow sip. "Of course. You forgot."

"It's the trial," I say. "It's been so consuming . . . and I had it on my calendar," I add, although I wonder if I remembered to write it down. "Why didn't you remind me?"

He tilts his head. "When would I have done that, Eunice? Somewhere between three and four in the morning? Because you've been leaving for work before I'm awake, and you come home long after I fall asleep. I know what's going on with the trial, but I honestly thought this"—he gestures toward the program—"was important to you, too."

"It was. It is. I just thought it was next week," I murmur. "Lisle, please . . ."

He stares at me for a moment, then glances away. And I'm glad he does. Because it was hard to see what's in his eyes. I was used to his anger and weathered even his rage. But this . . . his disappointment is a heartbreaker.

I stay silent, searching for more words to say.

He speaks first. "All through the dinner, I kept looking up, thinking that at any moment you would walk through that door. I told myself you would come flying in there, breathless and filled with apologies. But you *would* be there. For me."

Tears burn behind my eyes.

"Even when I stood and began my speech, I kept looking at the door. I searched for you when I talked about how I came here to America and how difficult it was being an immigrant. But how it all came together once I met you." Finally, he looks straight at me when he says, "And I ended with how proud I am to be your husband."

I blink and try to breathe. "And I'm proud to be your wife."

After a moment, he nods and stands. "I believe that. I just don't think that's enough. It's not enough for you. And finally, I've come to realize, it may not be enough for me."

He disappears down the hall and into our bedroom. I sit there, afraid to move, afraid to think. Because I don't want to face the meaning of his words.

CHAPTER FORTY-NINE

POLLY

New York, New York
June 3, 1936

"ARE YOU SURE going out is good idea, Polly? I mean, madams are all over the news, and you are the most famous one," the Lion says, ever cautious for me, ever worrisome on my behalf. She might be alone in this concern. Certainly, I've seen no indication of my family's interest in my well-being; they've gone silent. "You might be recognized."

"I need to get out of the apartment," I say, slipping one arm into my lightweight cotton coat and then the other. "Just to be around people. Pretend like everything is normal. Pretend like I haven't been stuck here, listening to the radio and waiting for the other shoe to drop."

"You never can stop moving," the Lion says with a *tsk*.

I am restless. Since my last meeting with Mrs. Carter, where we secured the Waldorf witnesses, I have no outlet for my desire to help the case along. And I've been holed up. I've barely left the apartment because of my fixation on the radio trial reports; my only avenue for information is the same available to any Joe on the street. Even the runner I employ to stand by at the courthouse and gather up tidbits returns with the same dross I can hear anywhere, a recounting of the terrible cross-examiner's onslaught against the prostitute and madam witnesses. I yearn for the moment when the Waldorf employees will take the stand and prove out these women's claims. But I will not reach out to Mrs. Carter again to find out when that will happen, as I don't have other evidence to offer at this stage and I don't want to be a bother. Too much is at stake to disturb her.

"You'll be browsing the aisles of Bonwit Teller, looking at scarves or purses, but everyone's eyes will be on the free madam in their midst." The Lion continues, crossing her arms now and bringing home her point. "Practically the only one left in the whole darn city."

"Let them stare. And anyway, I think you overestimate my fame," I reply, staying firm as I button up the coat. "No one will recognize me."

She sniffs. "Are you forgetting how often your face has been plastered on the front of the newspaper? Very recently, in fact." Without mentioning it explicitly, she references the terrible picture and article in the *Daily Mirror* that precipitated the chasm between me and my family.

"I'm always careful to cover my face."

"The reporters were quicker than you when you stepped out of that last paddy wagon." Now she's rubbing salt in the wound in her efforts to keep me home.

When I don't reply and continue buttoning up my coat instead, she asks, "None of the girls going with you?"

"Kit and Rosalie are out on a job, and as for Angelica coming along, I think I'd draw too much attention if I arrived flanked by one of my girls. Might be too bold a statement while vice is on trial." I don't need to mention my ongoing wariness of Angelica, as the Lion understands that implicitly.

"I think clothes shopping at the high-end department stores in the city like you haven't a care in the world when your whole industry is up in flames is too bold a statement." Her arms are now folded in an impossible knot. "But I'll explain it to Angelica when she gets back from the hair salon. She'll be disappointed to be cooped up here for the rest of the afternoon."

I suddenly have an image of all the prostitutes and madams in New York stuck in their houses, waiting for the verdict on Lucky Luciano to be rendered. It's not just a verdict on the mobster; it's a judgment on how prostitution will be conducted and policed in the future. And, in a way, how the world sees us.

Thinking about those other madams, I doubt that anyone else has someone like the Lion on the lookout for them. I lean toward her and buss her cheek.

Her eyes widen in surprise. The Lion knows how I feel about her, but displays of affection aren't exactly our norm. "What's that for?"

"For caring about me when no one else does," I say, then shimmy past her and out the apartment door before she can react.

When I'm down the elevator and out onto the city streets, I feel I can breathe. I need to step back into my old life, the one I led before the raids, the one before Lucky rolled out his Combination, and the one before I snitched to Mrs. Carter. If only for a few hours. Then, I tell myself, I can go back to waiting, refreshed.

The day is warm, and I almost don't need my coat. But I chose the swingy coat and the low-brimmed cloche hat to make me more anonymous. I'd like to be able to slide into department stores drawing as little attention as possible and return home with a spring in my step. And maybe some shopping bags with inexpensive trinkets for the Lion and the girls, since money is too tight for much more.

I hail a cab and head toward Fifth Avenue, where a plethora of delightful stores await. As we drive closer, we pass perfectly turned-out women window-shopping and chatting with each other, and I'm reminded that the world goes on, blissfully unaware and unaffected by the trial of Lucky Luciano. For most, the trial is a sideshow attraction, a headliner in a frenzied media circus and nothing more.

As I step out of the cab on Fifth Avenue, I walk toward Bonwit Teller. *How well the Lion understands me,* I think, *to know that I'd start here.* The store was an early favorite when I finally had money to spend and is a place I return time and again. Nodding at the doormen as they open the doors for me, I step inside, breathing in the heady scent of perfume and money.

I peruse the glass cases of jewelry and the racks of scarves and the rows of hats on bodiless mannequins, but nothing captivates. *Maybe I should have started at Saks,* I think. It's a little pricier, but I never leave there empty-handed.

Passing by the doormen again as I reenter the day, I decide to walk to Saks. The weather is fine, and the air feels good on my skin after so many hours spent in my house. My arms swing, my pace increases, and my mood lifts as I near the vast, classically designed flagship store. Saks Fifth Avenue never disappoints.

Weaving through the steady stream of well-heeled women—and a few sharply dressed men—entering and exiting the famed store, I stride through the doors and into the accessories department. I browse until a fine black leather handbag catches my eye. But when the well-hidden price tag reveals that the pocketbook costs a hefty thirty-five dollars, I carefully replace it on the shelf. Two years ago, I would have picked it up with a snap, but these days, it's too dear.

I stroll into the makeup department next, where glass cases offer the latest powders, lipsticks, rouges, mascaras, and eyebrow pencils. Women of all ages and shapes flock to the counters, eager to take the makeup companies up on their promises that the right makeup purchase will turn them into the next Greta Garbo or Jean Harlow. And even though I know better, I find myself considering a deep pink shade of Elizabeth Arden rouge.

But then the elegant display of the new luxury makeup brand Lancôme lures me in. And I wander over to examine an array of lipsticks in striking gold packaging. There at the center of several bold red lipsticks—the most popular trend in beauty—sits an unusual pale pink shade. Sliding the sample out of the case, I twist the base, and the subtle scent of rose wafts into the air.

"Miss," I say to the brunette salesgirl behind the counter with her back to me. She's busy restocking a drawer, but I'm sure she'd prefer a sale to that sort of work. "I'm interested in this lipstick."

The woman turns to me, the gentle curls of her long, chocolate-brown hair bouncing as she does, and asks, "How may I help you, ma'am?"

In that moment, I have a flash of recognition. Despite the wildly different hair color, the slightly altered arch of her brows, the conservative clothes, and the crimson, bow-shaped lipstick application, I realize who she is. It is Virginia.

She survived—and she got out. This is beyond my greatest dream for her. So few of my girls ever really leave the world of vice. Mabel, of course, completed her studies and should be a teacher now. There's Gigi, who married one of her regular johns, a rarity in this business; Muriel, who became the pampered mistress of a nightclub and radio comedian; and Fran, who finished her college studies and teaches high school in Connecticut, last I heard. But more often than not, they descend in the ranks of prostitution, get hooked on Cadillac, or choose a different, but no less fraught, illegal path. Martha, for example, was rumored to have left my house to work as a high-end pickpocket. Many are too wounded by their past to take advantage of the present I offer them and build a new future.

But not Virginia.

My mouth opens at the sight of a healthy, successful Virginia, and I feel my hands lift as if to reach across the counter and embrace her. But she gives me the subtlest shake of her head, which she then inclines toward an older woman serving a client next to me. That must be her boss.

I would do nothing to jeopardize the hard-won freedom Virginia has managed for herself, especially given the terrible circumstances of her departure from my house. I know she could provide Mrs. Carter with a wealth of information that would help seal Lucky's fate—as could I, for that matter—but I've offered up enough girls and madams as sacrificial lambs to this trial, a fact about which I feel terrible. If I mean what I say—to myself and others—that my girls are my family and that I want the best for them, then I need to let Virginia go and allow her to embrace this life she's fashioned, against all odds.

Our eyes meet, and I smile at her. "Thank you, miss," I say, and hold up the tube of lipstick. "What a beautiful, fresh shade this is, so different from all that red! I'm always so delighted when someone—or some company, in this case—forges a new path. What is this color called?"

Virginia smiles back with such gratitude that it almost brings a tear to my eye. "It's called Rose de France, ma'am."

"Well, that settles it, miss. I've always wanted to go to France, and I sure do like roses. I'll take two, please. One for me, and one for a friend."

CHAPTER FIFTY

EUNICE

New York, New York
June 3, 1936

I STAND AT the threshold of the dining room, waiting, willing Lisle to glance up. Perhaps he hasn't heard me. That's possible. But it's far more likely that he has and he just doesn't care. I wonder if he's noticed my small efforts. Even as the trial proceeds, I've stopped racing out the door before dawn, instead lingering until he wakes up so we can share our morning coffee. It has taken a toll. I've watched Dewey make note of my lateness, although he's kept his silence.

But what choice is there if I hope to hold on to my marriage?

Still, I don't know if it's working. It's been two weeks since I missed the NAACP award dinner. Two weeks of perfunctory kisses and conversations that barely stretch beyond ten words. Always cordial, always polite, always leaving me feeling like a stranger in my own marriage. I've apologized and pleaded for forgiveness more than once, and while he says it's fine, his tone and his manner tell me nothing is right in our world.

Inside the kitchen, I brew our coffee, then return with our cups. I set Lisle's before him, and he thanks me—without a glance once again. I slide into the chair across from him, but his eyes remain locked on *The Amsterdam News*. I stare at this man I've loved for so long and rake my mind. What can I do to shift Lisle and me back to who we used to be?

This is the greatest conundrum. My husband. My work. Two loves pulling me apart.

I take a deep breath and say, "Did you read the letter from my mother?"

Without glancing up, he nods.

I continue. "Junior is happy, but I must admit that I'm delighted at the thought that with the trial soon coming to an end, our son will be on his way home."

All he says is "Yes," then the silence once again stretches like a river of molasses between us. And in a moment, a thought comes to me. "Lisle, why don't you come to the courthouse?" I blurt out. "It's something being in the room with Luciano and all of those men."

Slowly, he lowers the newspaper and looks at me as if he wonders what kind of harebrained idea this is. I understand. I didn't take a moment to think this through, but it makes sense.

"I'm not speaking in court, of course. Dewey's leading the case. But it's my work that has brought us here. The records, the witnesses, all of the charts—you'll be able to see what I've been doing. You'll be able to hear some of my words in Dewey's cross-examinations, especially if Luciano takes the stand. I've worked hard, and I really want to share this with you."

This time, I'm pleased when he's silent. At least he's not scoffing. "My schedule is full," he finally says.

"I understand," I say, refusing to be deterred. "But if you find time . . . even for just an hour, I'd be so grateful. I'll arrange a pass regardless."

He nods, then lifts the newspaper again.

It's not a victory, but it's a step. So I rise and kiss Lisle's cheek. "Have a good day, darling."

Again, he doesn't glance up, but at least he does say "You, too."

It wasn't a conversation or a flicker of forgiveness. But it feels like hope. And I carry that with me on the ride all the way to the New York County Supreme Court building.

When Mr. Johnson drops me at the curb, I have to hasten inside after lingering at home for so long. I settle into my seat just as the bailiff enters; behind him is Judge McCook, who tells Dewey to call his first witness.

Dewey rises. "Your Honor, the prosecution calls Marjorie Brown."

Mr. Woelfle and Mr. Weinman have already taken the stand. While their testimonies spoke to Luciano's status as a Waldorf guest sometimes in the presence of other co-defendants, Marjorie can reveal so much more.

She slips onto the witness chair looking like she's dressed for church in her round, collared, puffy-sleeved floral dress, with a small tilt hat that she pushed away from her forehead. She sits, head high, shoulders squared, with a confidence that belies her twenty-four years. During her intense preparation, she's maintained this same composure, never faltered. In fact, I daresay she's become stronger, sometimes sounding like she's on a singular mission to obtain justice by herself.

After Dewey takes her through the first formal questions, he asks, "Where do you work, Miss Brown?"

"At the Waldorf Towers. On the thirty-ninth and fortieth floors."

"What are your duties there?"

"I'm a bath maid. I clean the bathrooms, mostly. And sometimes the pantries."

"Do you see anyone in this courtroom who was a regular guest at the Waldorf Towers?"

"Yes."

"Would you point him out?"

Without hesitation, Marjorie points directly at Luciano. "That's him. He told us his name was Charlie Ross."

"Thank you, Miss Brown. And did you ever see people inside Mr. Luciano's apartment?"

"Yes, all the time."

"Can you stand up now and point out anyone in this courtroom that you saw visiting Mr. Luciano?"

"Sure," she says with a smile, as if she's waited all her life for this moment. She rises, but then solemnity returns to her expression. Thoughtfully, she glances around. "That man," she finally says, "in the gray suit and polka-dot tie," pointing out Dave Betillo.

"How many times did you see that man inside Mr. Luciano's apartment?"

"Dozens of times. Twenty, thirty times."

"All right. Anyone else?"

Marjorie goes on to point out Abie Wahrman and Meyer Berkman.

That was all Dewey wanted. Marjorie told us she'd seen four or five of the men enough times to identify them in court. Dewey believed that if she made the connection to just three, it would be enough to underscore the message that Luciano was lying about not knowing these men.

"Was there ever a time when you saw Mr. Luciano in the company of women?"

"Yes, sir. Plenty of times."

"And can you describe the women?"

She shrugs. "Sure. They always wore really nice dresses and lots of rouge and lipstick. Oh, and I liked their perfume. Sometimes I smelled that before I even saw them."

Dewey continues. "Was there a particular time of day when these women were there?"

"Mostly at night, when I had to go to Mr. Ross' room with fresh towels and to turn down the bed. Sometimes the girls were still there when I went back in the morning. They'd be all over the place, stretched out on the sofa, the bed . . . even the floor. Sometimes they'd be asleep, but if they were awake, their eyes were glassy, and they seemed hardly able to keep them open. Like they'd been drugged."

Levy rises. "Objection. Move to strike on the grounds of speculation, lack of foundation—"

Luciano's attorney doesn't even have to finish before the judge says "Sustained," as Dewey knew he would. The goal here is to set the tawdry, exploitative scene for the jury, even if they can't actually consider "drugging" in evidence.

"Was there anything else you observed?"

"Yeah, Mr. Ross and the other men would slap those girls around plenty. There were times when I had to give them towels to cover up their bloody noses or give them ice for their bruises."

"Thank you, Miss Brown."

When Dewey turns over the questioning to the defense, this time, it's Jimmy Frederico's attorney who stands for the cross-examination.

"Miss Brown," the attorney begins, "when you identified the men who were in the company of Mr. Luciano, did you look at every row in this courtroom?"

"Yes."

"Did you look at every man carefully?"

"Yes, I did."

"And the three that you identified are the *only* men you ever saw with Mr. Luciano. Is that correct?"

"Yes, those three, and that other man. The one there in the green suit," she says, pointing to Frederico. "He was there so much, there were times when I wondered if he had moved in with Mr. Ross."

The courtroom erupts in a roar of laughter. Even the bailiff cracks a smile, and I join in, too. With all the money they make, it's baffling that the Mob doesn't retain lawyers with greater legal acumen. Frederico's lawyer is as bad as Levy—he just had his client identified in front of everyone.

Now Levy stands. "Your Honor, there are so many people in the courtroom, there's no reasonable way Miss Brown's testimony can be correct. It has to be confusing for Miss Brown with all of these people here," Levy argues. "Her identifications cannot be accepted by this court."

The attorneys go back and forth until Dewey redirects Marjorie. "Would you be willing to step from the witness stand and put your hand on the shoulder of each man you recognize?"

"Yes, I would," she says, and rises. She moves slowly, but with her head high, she angles past the defense table, where Luciano sits, and then places her hand on the shoulders of Betillo, Wahrman, Berkman, and finally, Frederico.

I am beaming when Marjorie finally steps from the stand. Then I laugh to myself when she glances at me and winks.

Once Marjorie leaves the courtroom, Dewey says, "Your Honor, the prosecution rests."

THE OFFICE IS jubilant. The trial isn't over, of course, but the chief has put on a masterful display. I've learned as much in the first three weeks of this trial as I did in my years of law school. The skillful way he weaved this case together with a medley of witnesses—some of them with questionable credibility—was breathtaking.

Dewey orchestrated a symphony, a new arrangement every day that kept the jury's attention from wandering.

We may have rested today, but this will still be a long night. All of the district attorneys have been given different assignments. I, along with Murray and several others, have been tasked with creating the framework for the closing argument.

My telephone rings, and I reach for it, thinking, hoping it might be Lisle. "Eunice Carter speaking."

"Mrs. Carter, it's Polly."

A beat passes. "This is . . . unexpected," I say, and wonder what name she gave to the switchboard operator. I notice she doesn't use her last name in identifying herself.

"I know you don't need any more from me, especially since it seems as though some of our plans are working well. But I do have something you might want to hear all the same. I found out what happened to Virginia."

It takes a moment for her words to register. For just a second, I'm afraid to ask. "Is she all right?"

"She got out, Mrs. Carter," she says, and I hear more than her relief through the line. She's elated. "I found her at Saks. Working at the cosmetics counter. She looks different, but she looks good."

"Did you speak with her?"

"Not how you mean. She was working, and she's out of the life. I didn't want to do anything to rattle her or bring attention to her. But I did say a few words when I purchased a couple of lipsticks. One for me . . . and one for you."

The gesture surprises and disarms me. "Thank you." And then, because I want to soften the moment, I add, "You always wear such lovely shades. I can only hope it will look as good on me as it does you."

We share a chuckle, and I think this has to be the first time we've had such an unguarded moment. It's not easy, but it's not forced either.

The phone line grows silent as our laughter fades, and she says, "I just heard on the radio that the prosecution has wrapped its case. Congratulations."

"There's still a lot more to come: the defense's case, closing arguments, and of course, the jury's deliberation. We can never predict how long that will take. But we have come a long way," I say, thinking back to that day fourteen months ago when I went to the 30th Street Precinct and asked to speak to Polly Adler. "Together."

"We certainly have," she says. "We make quite a pair."

I smile. "We certainly do."

"Yup. A pair of aces, that's what we are, Mrs. Carter."

"Miss Adler"—I pause for a moment—"after all we've been through, I think it's appropriate for you to call me Eunice."

"Only if you call me Polly."

I can feel her smile through the telephone and imagine that if Polly and I were in the same room, we'd shake hands. We don't yet know the trial's outcome, but we've forged an alliance, not of affection but of necessity. Still, I pray that though the deck is stacked against us, this pair of aces holds the winning hand.

CHAPTER FIFTY-ONE

EUNICE

New York, New York
June 7, 1936

Although the courtroom has been jammed to capacity since the beginning of the trial, today *The People of the State of New York v. Charles Luciano, et al.* is different. Throngs of New Yorkers have flocked to this grand chamber to get a glimpse of the infamous defendant, the last person on the stand. And the room overflows with family and friends, lawyers, politicians, and journalists. Last night, every newspaper headline led with this story—the mobster versus the prosecutor.

The defense informed the court that there would be one last witness: Charles "Lucky" Luciano would take the stand. Everyone in the city was anticipating a showdown between Dewey and Luciano worthy of the Mob's infamous shoot-outs.

Glancing over my shoulder, I inhale. My hope was that Lisle would join me, especially after all the press reports of what was coming today.

"Are you searching for someone?" Murray's voice cuts through the din.

Turning, I smile at my friend. Today, for the first time, all twenty of us assistant district attorneys fill the seats behind the prosecution table.

"No. I'm just taking it all in. The air in here . . ."

"It crackles," he finishes for me just as the bailiff comes in.

When Justice McCook enters, he moves with an air of solemn authority that is more intense today than any other day. I take in the gravity of this moment as the judge settles behind the bench.

"Mr. Levy, are you prepared to call your first witness?"

"Yes, Your Honor. Mr. Charles Luciano will take the stand in his own defense."

The judge turns to Luciano. "Mr. Luciano, are you aware you have the right to remain silent?"

"Yes, Your Honor."

"And if you testify you will be cross-examined by the prosecution?"

Luciano's lips spread into a slow, sinister grin. "I'm ready for Mr. Dewey."

A collective gasp sweeps through the courtroom, forcing Judge McCook to bang his gavel.

The courtroom stills as Luciano rises from the defense table, lifting his cuffed wrists. The closest guard unlocks the irons. Luciano rubs his hands together before, with a measured stride, he approaches the stand. He walks like a man in control, not a man who's been confined for months and faces decades in prison.

The bailiff administers the oath, and Luciano solemnly says "I do," professing that he will tell the whole truth. I tense. This will be the crux of Dewey's cross-examination. We will prove that Luciano has never uttered a truthful word in his life.

The defense's questioning moves swiftly. Mr. Levy asks his client about his early years, attending school on Manhattan's Lower East Side, quitting in the sixth grade to work in a hat factory, and then living on his own and surviving on gambling and dice games. Then Mr. Levy broaches Luciano's criminal record—a decade-old narcotics conviction.

Luciano bows his head. "I regret that," he says, softening his voice, an attempt at showing remorse.

Mr. Levy has prepared his client well. It seems Luciano is not only a liar, he's an actor, too.

"Since that time, I've had no other narcotics arrests, and no convictions except for a gambling fine in Miami. I've done everything I can to live on the right side of the law."

"So you've never sold narcotics again?"

"That is correct."

"Now, Mr. Luciano, I want to speak with you about the other co-defendants. Are you familiar with any of the men?"

He shakes his head. "I've never met any of these men in my life, with the exception of Davie Betillo. And that was just once. But I told him I didn't want to do any business with him."

"Do you know Nancy Presser?"

"No, never met her. Saw her for the first time in this courtroom."

"What about Mildred Balitzer?"

"Never met her. Saw her for the first time in this courtroom."

I hold my breath as Luciano gives the same response for every one of the long list of witnesses and parties. At the end, he adds, "I swear to you and the court, with the exception of the hotel staff from the Waldorf Towers, there is not a witness that Mr. Dewey has called that I've ever met in my life."

"Thank you, Mr. Luciano." Levy turns, and with a quick glance at Dewey, says, "Your witness."

My heart thumps.

Dewey rises, buttoning his suit jacket. At once, I feel a collective intake of breath. Luciano glares at Dewey, his stare cold and steely.

"Good morning, Mr. Luciano," the chief says, his tone polite but sharp.

Luciano gives him a curt nod.

"I want to begin by reviewing the gambling conviction you and Mr. Levy just discussed. You said that was your only other conviction, is that correct?"

"Yeah."

"Isn't it true, Mr. Luciano, that you were also convicted of a gun charge?"

"Mr. Levy didn't mention no gun, and it's not illegal to carry a gun in Miami."

Dewey frowns as if he is confused. "Well, if it's not against the law, why were you convicted of carrying a concealed weapon? In Miami? Which, by the way, I never mentioned in my question."

Luciano sits straight up in his chair, looks the chief straight in his eyes, and says, "I was never convicted."

When the chief pulls out a record of the conviction and shows it to Luciano, he concedes, "I guess I forgot about that."

For the next hour, the chief questions Luciano about how his criminal career began. It is a gripping portrayal of how Luciano started by selling drugs. Of course, Luciano denies it all, but it sets the stage for Luciano's criminal activities. Next, Dewey takes Luciano through a record of his other arrests and convictions—for traffic violations. These are minor offenses, of course, but the chief is able to make the weight of these offenses feel greater because Luciano has once again lied.

More lies follow as Dewey runs through the various professions Luciano has described to arresting officers—a real estate agent, a chauffeur, even a salesman.

"I don't recall telling anyone I was any of these things," Luciano says. "I don't remember any of those arrests."

"Mr. Luciano," Dewey says, "you don't seem to recall too much of anything. Are you telling this court the truth?"

"I would never lie under oath," he says. Judge McCook has to bang the gavel after snickers and chuckles roll through the courtroom. Luciano continues as if half of the spectators didn't just laugh at him. "I wouldn't perjure myself."

This time, I am the one who has to press my hand over half of my face to hide my snicker. I glance at the jury, and while most of the men sit stone-faced, several shake their heads.

Now Dewey turns to Luciano's testimony that he doesn't know any of the other defendants. Luciano again maintains that while he was acquainted with Dave Betillo, he has never worked with him. The names Jimmy Frederico, Ralph Liguori, and Tommy Pennochio are all unfamiliar to him.

"Mr. Luciano, do you recall our witness Marjorie Brown, the bath maid at the Waldorf Towers?"

"Yeah."

"And do you recall ever seeing Miss Brown before?"

"Yeah, at the Waldorf."

"And do you recall Miss Brown's testimony that she'd seen Mr. Betillo in your apartment at least twenty times?"

"I heard her say that, but she was mistaken."

"And do you recall her saying that Jimmy Frederico was in your apartment most of the time?"

"I heard her say that, but there ain't a bit of truth to it."

For every question Dewey asks, it's no longer necessary for Luciano to speak. Everyone in the courtroom can answer for him:

"I don't recall."

"I don't know any of them."

"I've never been there in my life."

It is becoming laughable, especially when Dewey produces telephone slips to prove Luciano's calls to Nancy Presser, Mildred Balitzer, and other witnesses. All of whom he claimed to have never met or been acquainted with.

"I didn't make those telephone calls."

"Everyone in this courtroom has lied about you, Mr. Luciano, is that correct?"

"You said it, I didn't."

The courtroom ripples with more laughter, and the triumph that Dewey feels is evident in his smirk. This is what we wanted to linger in the jurors' minds. He says, "That is all."

After four hours, my shoulders sag with relief. Even as a spectator, it's been grueling, witnessing this duel between the prosecutor and the mobster.

When Luciano finally steps down from the stand, Levy says, "The defense rests."

The courtroom buzzes, and this time Judge McCook struggles to restore order. But once he does, he announces, "We will take a one-hour break, and then the summations will begin."

I rise, and as I reach for my briefcase, my breath catches. I see him. Standing in the back, tucked in a corner. With his hat in hand and an unsure smile, it is Lisle.

Pushing past the other assistant district attorneys and then through the courtroom throng, I rush to him, moving faster than I ever have in my stacked-heel oxfords. When I reach him, I pause for the briefest moment, then whisper, "You're here," the only words that matter right now.

He nods, and I do something I've never done, certainly not in a courtroom in front of my colleagues, court officers, and reporters. I throw my arms around Lisle. When he squeezes me tight, I exhale for the first time today. Or perhaps it's been far longer since I've truly breathed. But with Lisle here now, I can.

Finally, he draws back. "I'm so glad I came."

"Me, too."

"I'm very proud of you."

"Why? I wasn't the one up there questioning Luciano."

"You may not have been standing before him, but I heard your thoughts and your words behind Dewey's questions." He shakes his head as if in awe. "So this is the case you put together."

"I didn't do it alone," I say.

He nods. "Of course, I haven't forgotten about the other nineteen, but today, I saw *my* wife, Attorney Eunice Carter."

I stand before Lisle, beaming. There is one part of his statement that I want to correct. When I said that I didn't do this alone, I wasn't speaking about my colleagues. Maybe one day I will tell Lisle about the other woman on this team.

When Lisle says "I understand, sweetheart. Now I truly understand," I have to brush away a tear, pressing in the corner of my eye.

"I'm going to stay until the end," he says. "I want to be here every day, until the verdict. I want to be here for you."

I respond by taking his hand, gripping him as though I'll never let go. As we stride from the courtroom, joy swells inside me, something I feared was stretching beyond my grasp.

The corridor is as alive as the courtroom, filled with the murmur of reporters and the hum of spectators. The chatter is all the same, the question on every tongue: Will Luciano be found guilty?

I have worked long and hard for the right ending to this case. But whatever the jury decides, I have already won.

I glance at Lisle, his hand so warm in mine, and I know: *This* is the greatest victory.

CHAPTER FIFTY-TWO

POLLY

New York, New York
June 7, 1936

DEWEY TAKES HIS place at the front of the courtroom again, and the packed space becomes eerily silent. He opens his arms expansively, as if to welcome the jurors, the judge, and all of us spectators into his inner circle. It's an invitation to climb onto the great scales of justice alongside him and tip the balance in favor of the prosecution. How glad I am that I took the dangerous gamble of being identified and decided to attend the last day of Lucky's trial. I don't think I'd miss Dewey's closing argument for the world.

"May it please Your Honor, Mr. Foreman, and gentlemen of the jury, my summation begins. . . ."

Even though Dewey has spoken only a few words, I find his voice mellifluous, bordering on hypnotic. Like with the most captivating actors on Broadway, no boundary exists between us and him, between the story he's spinning and our reality. Jaded as I am, I find myself caught up in his sway.

". . . There were sixty-six witnesses called for the People in this case. Each one of those sixty-six witnesses, with the exception of a very few, were professional criminals of one kind or another. Every one of those witnesses had been given immunity before he or she came to testify before you in this courtroom, something the defense has criticized. However, without immunity, I wouldn't have been able to call those witnesses to testify, because a man or a woman can't be forced to testify against himself or herself. As soon as they received that immunity, they could have safely said anything they liked in this courtroom. They could have denied that Lucky Luciano was the head of the Combination. But they didn't. Instead, what have those witnesses established—in both testimony and corroboration?"

I sneak a glance at Mrs. Carter as we reach this critical moment in the prosecution's closing argument, seated unfairly in the seats behind the lead trial attorneys' table. *A paltry acknowledgment of her efforts,* I think.

Is she feeling what I'm feeling? Nervous, yes, but excited as well? Wondering whether our efforts will bear fruit? Whether the jurors will be persuaded by his rhetoric? Mrs. Carter is visible only in profile; I can't catch her eye. While she appears as prim and impervious as always, do I detect an anxious tilt to her head?

My attention shifts from Mrs. Carter as Dewey launches into the more scintillating snippets of the statements from Mildred Balitzer, Nancy Presser, Red Sadie, numerous other girls and madams, Pete Harris, Dave Miller, Al Weiner, and even the defendants' confessions on cross-examination. He weaves them together until he creates a hideous tapestry of exploitation and vice. As I listen, the people around me nod along, and I can feel certainty descend upon the observers and jurors alike. Certainty of Lucky's guilt, it seems to me.

Dewey continues. "This has put the lie to Lucky Luciano's statements that he doesn't know any of the other defendants, all men who've been well-established bookers and enforcers in a large scheme of prostitution called the Combination. Instead, the testimony of the many prosecution witnesses—including upstanding citizens who are employed by the Waldorf-Astoria Hotel—has proven that Lucky Luciano is indeed the Mob boss for the Combination."

In my peripheral vision, I perceive a softening in the erectness of Mrs. Carter's posture. Her shoulders have become less square, and I swear I see her sigh. Is this done in relief at the power of Dewey's testimony? Or is he performing less perfectly than she'd hoped and, layperson that I am, I cannot tell how Dewey is doing? Mrs. Carter has become my bellwether for the success of the trial, but I wonder if she's really the right gauge. She might know too much, and at the same time too little. As might I.

"Much has been made about the credibility of these witnesses," Dewey continues, attempting to eviscerate in advance the argument the defense will undoubtedly make. "It would have been nice to have clergymen and bankers and doctors as our witnesses in this case instead of prostitutes and pimps and madams and bookers and mobsters, but I ask you this: How can you bring a case against a booker of women without the testimony of the women he booked or witnesses who observe the booking? How can you bring a case against the leader of a scheme like the Combination without the statements of those who know about it and very likely participated in it, like the leader's associates? In order to bring this sort of case, we needed to put prostitutes and madams and bookers and enforcers on the stand."

I try not to be offended by the ongoing slurs about the credibility of girls and madams. I try not to let it rankle that the girls were raked over the coals and forced to describe their humiliations while on the stand as part of these machinations. I try not to let anger take hold that only men—twelve *male* jurors—will be deciding the fate of a nefarious Mob organization that exploits women. Instead, I try to remember that my own motives have not always been beyond reproach and that I'm trying to make amends by helping end Lucky's destructive empire.

"But we did have the gift of Marjorie Brown, didn't we? This chambermaid from the Waldorf supported the prosecution theory to the letter," Dewey says, and my heart beats excitedly.

Oh, how this brainchild of mine has really taken flight in the hands of Mrs. Carter and Dewey, I think. Not that anyone will ever know about the hand I played.

"A steadier, more compelling, more trustworthy witness you will never encounter than that bath maid. Her sort of testimony is indisputable."

Thrilled at this recap of the Waldorf employees' contribution, I swivel toward Mrs. Carter. I'm too quick and excitable in my movements, and my wig shifts uncomfortably. I quickly tug it back into place and refocus on Dewey.

Dewey's tone lifts, and I sense that he's reaching the crescendo of his argument. I hope so; it's been hours. "It is time to put behind us the defense's ludicrous theories and convict the Boss in charge of this Combination. The proof establishes each and every element in this case beyond a reasonable doubt. Convict Charles 'Lucky' Luciano, gentlemen of the jury."

At the judge's instruction, the spectators rise for a break, as do the jurors. I glance around the room, studying the men and few women who stretch after being seated for so long and chatter as the defense readies for its closing argument. I note the enthusiastic nods and compliments over Dewey's speech and evidence, and cannot help but believe that the jurors will feel the same and vote to convict. Hope buoys within me.

A strange satisfaction also courses through me at the role I played, and I feel an emotion foreign to me. Could it be pride? I cannot recall the last time I felt proud of my actions, and a tear wells up in the corner of my eye. *How much real change can be wrought from the shadows,* I think. From both me and Mrs. Carter.

Court reconvenes soon thereafter for the defense's closing argument, a flimsy thing even by my inexpert standards. And then the lawyers, parties, and courtroom audience have to wait as the jurors retire to deliberate. No one really thinks that a decision will be rendered today, even though the right verdict seems clear, but still, many linger. So I stay quiet and small in the corner, hoping no one notices me as I wait on the off chance that the jury makes their decision quickly. Because I won't risk coming here again.

Just before the enormous ticking clock that looms over the judge's bench strikes four o'clock, the foreman leads the jurors out of their room and into the courtroom. The space fills with expectant chatter; even the judge looks surprised at the rapidity of their return. Once they settle in the jury box, the judge asks, "Mr. Foreman, has the jury rendered a verdict in the case against Charles Luciano?"

"We have, Your Honor."

"You may proceed with reading your verdict."

The foreman glances back at the eleven men sitting behind him, who nod at him. He then consults his notes and says, "On the sixty-one counts of compulsory prostitution, we the jury find Charles Luciano, also known as 'Lucky' Luciano, guilty as charged." The foreman then goes on to list those charges and also announce that the jury finds nine of Lucky's co-defendants, Thomas Pennochio, Dave Betillo, James Frederico, Abraham Wahrman, Jesse Jacobs, Benny Spiller, Meyer Berkman, and Ralph Liguori, guilty of the charges against them as well.

The courtroom erupts. The defendants stand, some slamming

their cuffed fists on the table. Dewey rises and shakes the hands of his team, including Mrs. Carter. And the reporters hurl questions and comments around the overheated space.

The press is everywhere. Cameras flash and click. Reporters wave their notepads in the air. A barrage of questions is shouted out and merges together, rising through the air and sounding like a hymn.

Dewey holds up his hand, quieting the press as the twenty assistant district attorneys fall into place alongside him, surrounding the man they call the chief. "This is a great day for New York!" someone screams.

Dewey says, "I want to thank the jury for returning the indictment. And the brave witnesses who've testified, along with law enforcement who have worked tirelessly with us on this investigation. And most importantly, every New Yorker who had the courage to speak up. This verdict belongs to all of you, and my gratitude belongs to the assistant district attorneys who aided me on this case." He gestures to the line of his assistants, and I smile at Mrs. Carter. This recognition is far, far less than she deserves but more than I expected. I hope that her contributions will become better known and that this enormous accomplishment will become her legacy.

What will be mine? Running a house like no other? Protecting the Lion and the steady stream of girls who've come through my doors? It would be enough, given where I started, but could there be something more?

Then I remember something Robert Benchley said to me in Hawaii, and I wonder. My role in bringing down Lucky and the Combination will never be known, but perhaps I could leave behind a different legacy. What if I wrote the rest of my story and shared it with the world? On one level, it could be the sometimes-painful, sometimes-exultant tale of a young Jewish immigrant from Yanow who made the astonishing ascent to the top of the heap in the skirt trade, a success story only because she operated efficiently and boldly outside the bounds of the law and expectations for women. On quite another level, that same story could lift the veil on this business and show the world how and why girls really become part of it—rarely by choice, but often by practical necessity—and how many different types of people reap the benefits of the girls, much more so than the girls themselves. Perhaps, if *I* am the lucky one, such a book could transform the way in which prostitution is viewed overall, not as so-called sin or a woman's crime or a failure of will but as a product of our culture and society. I feel buoyant and even hopeful at the thought of this new chapter.

The judge slams his gavel—not once but twice—bringing me back to the present. Everyone simmers down, and he yells, "Order in the court! Court is adjourned for today, and the journalists are instructed to leave the courtroom and wait outside with their questions. We will set the date for sentencing tomorrow morning, and in the meantime, you may take all this ruckus outside to the courtroom steps. I want to thank the jury for serving on this incredibly difficult trial, and good evening to you all."

As the judge sweeps out of the courtroom, the defendants are hauled off by police officers, and the attorneys and reporters ready for their press conference outside, I feel eyes upon me. I turn to discover Eunice staring at me. Our gazes meet, and a deep understanding passes between us. Our road together has not always been easy or pleasant, and we will never be friends. But in some peculiar way, we are much more. Her mouth curves into a shy smile, and I give her a cautious grin in return. The trial has transformed us both in unexpected ways, and I know that, whether or not we ever lay eyes on one another again, we will forever stand in solidarity, hand in hand.

Two women, not friends but allies.

Two women who did the impossible.

An unlikely, winning pair of aces.

MARIE BENEDICT'S AUTHOR'S NOTE

A few years back, if someone had told me that I'd tackle a story that involved the law, I would have answered with a resounding *no*. After eleven years as a commercial litigator at major law firms in New York City and discovering that my mission lay elsewhere, I had no desire to return to the case-building, witness interviews, court appearances, legal procedures, argument crafting, and legal briefs that had filled those days—not to mention the stress and sleepless nights! But with the passage of time—unbelievably, I've been a writer longer than I was a lawyer—when I came across the incredible contributions of Eunice Hunton Carter, my interest was piqued.

At first, just the very notion of a Black woman lawyer in the 1930s—an assistant district attorney no less—drew me in. I myself had entered the legal profession when women were scant compared to today and female partners few and far between, so I knew something of that difficulty—but nothing compared to what Eunice must have experienced in an era of segregation. Then, when I discovered more about the groundbreaking case against the fearsome mobster Lucky Luciano that Eunice built—quite against the mandate of her boss, Special Prosecutor Thomas Dewey, who had no interest in a case founded on prostitution—I felt compelled to dig in.

In learning how Eunice dove headlong into understanding the secret workings of prostitution and the extent to which the Mob's tentacles were wrapped around every aspect of it—and then how she unearthed evidence to support that secret racket—I couldn't help but be amazed. And, given Eunice's access to the information necessary to build the case, I also couldn't help but wonder, Did she have anyone on the inside assisting her? From experience, I know how hard it would be for her to access the sort of evidence necessary to build an unassailable case. Not that this help would in any way detract from Eunice's own brilliance and tenacity in conceiving and building this airtight case; perhaps it would instead support the case from the shadows, since no one in law enforcement would step forward to aid her.

As I delved into the shadow world that Eunice investigated, I became intrigued by this singular historical woman, and Victoria and I had a notion: What if the person who helped Eunice was on the opposite side of the law; a person who shared her desire to bring down the men who were exploiting women; a person who had overcome her own hurdles and prejudice against her to rise up, albeit in the underworld; a person who would never be Eunice's friend, but perhaps could be a comrade in arms against the Mob? A person like Polly Adler, the most famous madam of the age, a Russian Jewish immigrant whose own ascent from poverty and marginalization in the streets of New York was nothing short of breathtaking?

From this, *A Pair of Aces* was born. This story of two unlikely partners who together brought down the Mob allowed Victoria and me to explore yet another aspect of the relationships between Black and white women, one different than those we addressed in *The*

Personal Librarian and *The First Ladies* and one we wanted to address. Here, in a question that is as timely now as it was then, we invite readers to consider whether two people who are not friends—who indeed have a vast divide between them—can come together for the common good. Eunice and Polly seemed to us an inspiring example of what is possible when we put our differences aside and place the common welfare of *all* people front and center.

The process of writing *A Pair of Aces* presented its own challenges—in part because Victoria and I *are* indeed dear friends and sisters! We had to envision how two women from very different backgrounds would tackle challenging problems and strive for the betterment of all *without* the sorts of honest, difficult conversations that we have had during the writing of *The Personal Librarian* and *The First Ladies* and beyond. Sometimes, we had to hold back from having those kinds of discussions for the purpose of the book! By imagining how Eunice and Polly might find their way across the chasm between the lawless and the law enforcer, the underground realm and the establishment, and the worlds of Black and white women in the 1930s, we pushed ourselves to build a different sort of bridge than the ones we've created in our past work—one that maybe, just maybe, might serve as an inspiration for others.

What is fact and what is fiction in *A Pair of Aces*? Well, Eunice Hunton Carter did indeed fashion the case against Lucky Luciano on the basis of organized prostitution that Dewey deployed to bring the infamous mobster down—even though Dewey did not want to base his case on vice. While we may have adjusted certain dates and details around Eunice's work for the purposes of the story, she was the originator of the case and the impetus pushing it forward against the odds. Might she have had someone on the inside to help her with information? Possibly, although we don't really have any firm data on this, and so we invented her relationship with Polly Adler. That is the biggest piece of fiction in this fictional tale, though it may be hard to believe, since Polly herself was larger-than-life.

Much of the depiction of Polly and her "house" in *A Pair of Aces* is based on the facts as Polly herself represented them in her autobiography, *A House Is Not a Home*, and as described in articles and accounts from the time. The decor (yes, she had a King Tut bar), the people who frequented her house (celebrities and mobsters alike), and the different sort of house she aspired to run all come from this material. Although, one must keep in mind that Polly could sometimes be a teller of tall tales. Even her origin story—her Russian Jewish background, her forced immigration to America at twelve years of age despite the academic scholarship she'd been offered, her living situations upon arrival, her schooling (or lack thereof) and her work, the rape and ostracization she endured—comes from her own telling.

The Lion is indeed based on a real person (although she would have passed away during this time frame), but the girls depicted in the novel, particularly Virginia and her plight, are amalgamations of girls Polly details in her book. That said, the story of Polly stumbling across Virginia as a salesgirl in a department store is indeed based on Polly's own account of discovering the fate of one of her girls. Where we really deviate, aside from some alteration of dates and activities for the purposes of the plot—for example, the timing of Polly's family's arrival in America, her own brothers' criminal involvement, and her ultimate showdown with them, as well as the dates of the activities involving Vincent Coll and Polly's awareness of them—is in Polly's account of her knowledge of and involvement in the Mob's mounting control over prostitution. She always professed innocence in that regard, although it behooved her to be oblivious to this. And, of course, her secret support of the prosecution's case against Mob leaders is entirely fictional—but one *we* could envision.

Polly was famous, or infamous, in her day, and Eunice was well-known, so research materials and original source material were available, even if imperfect. That research inspired the fictional tale and characters we created in *A Pair of Aces*. Imagining the intersection of these two women (who never met, to the best of our knowledge) was indeed a challenge and involved understanding both of their lives, their time, the actual case, and their behavior, real and imagined. For readers interested in learning more about Polly Adler, while other sources exist (including some fascinating newspaper articles), I can certainly recommend the terrific biography *Madam: The Biography of Polly Adler, Icon of the Jazz Age* by Debby Applegate, but to truly conjure *my* Polly, I found her own irresistible autobiography, *A House Is Not a Home*, to be instrumental in understanding her, her world, and the era in which she lived. And for those intrigued by the trial, outside the archived original case files themselves, I'd suggest Thomas Dewey's out-of-print autobiography, *Twenty Against the Underworld*, in which Eunice's role is depicted through Dewey's very specific lens. This time period and the mobsters that tyrannized it continue to fascinate—for better or worse—and there is an abundance of materials for even further reading, much of which we perused, along with endless newspaper accounts about these events. We also made visits to the places mentioned in the story.

Not fictional is the enormous legacy Polly left behind with her autobiography, *A House Is Not a Home*. It was much more than a bestseller (that actually became a movie). The book was a completely new kind of immigration narrative, an insider's glimpse into the Mob underworld from the rare perspective of a *woman* (an effort which not only writes women back into this narrative but also deromanticizes the violent Mob life), and a fresh, no-nonsense, singular look at prostitution as a business while not stinting on the endemic exploitation. In fact, Polly's autobiography has become an important historical document in its own right.

We hope this fictional tale of two women from very different realms who come together for the common good inspires readers to come together with those like and unlike themselves for the betterment of us all.

VICTORIA CHRISTOPHER MURRAY'S AUTHOR'S NOTE

My first thought when Marie told me about Eunice Hunton Carter was, *Here is another hidden figure*. But when I began my preliminary search on Google (and Google is not how I truly research), Eunice seemed more overlooked than hidden. The first result under "Eunice Carter" was an entry from the Mob Museum. Really! I had never heard of Mrs. Carter, yet here was the Mob Museum acknowledging her. I felt a bit of pride for Eunice as I read about how the Mob paid homage to the prosecutor who was primarily responsible for taking down one of their own.

But at the same time, I was a little confused. The Mob hadn't erased her from their history, but she barely registered as a footnote in American history. Why hadn't Eunice Carter been given the credit she was due?

Like with my other historical novels, I dove right into that research rabbit hole. I began with the biographies; I read two: *Eunice Hunton Carter: A Lifelong Fight for Social Justice* by Marilyn S. Greenwald and Yun Li, and then what I consider the definitive biography on Eunice—*Invisible*, written by Eunice's grandson, Stephen

L. Carter. If you recognize his name, it's because Stephen Carter is the renowned law professor and prolific writer probably best known for his bestselling novel *The Emperor of Ocean Park.*

What made *Invisible* so compelling is that unlike in many biographies, the personal connection between Mr. Carter and his grandmother allowed for a richer, deeper insight into Eunice as a person. Additionally, I watched an enlightening video of Mr. Carter and his daughter, Leah N. Carter (who collaborated with her father on *Invisible*) speaking at Smith College, Eunice's alma mater. This interview provided me with even more valuable insight into his grandmother.

While Marie and I stayed as close to the historical record as possible with regard to Eunice and the trial against Lucky Luciano, we took a few liberties. First, we have no record that Eunice's mother, Addie Waites Hunton, ever lived with Eunice and her husband. We chose to include Addie in *A Pair of Aces* not only to offer a fuller portrait of Eunice's background but to spotlight and celebrate Addie's own life. She was a towering figure, often listed as one of the most powerful Black women of her time. She was a suffragist and activist who fought for equal rights for women through her work with the YWCA and the NAACP. From her travels through the South, visiting towns terrorized by the KKK where she established NAACP offices, to her trip to France during World War I, where she assisted Black soldiers and documented their experiences, Addie Hunton was a woman determined to have an impact and leave a legacy.

Of course, Eunice learned many lessons from her mother, including, I believe, that it was acceptable to send one's children away as long as it was done for the greater good.

This is another point where we took some liberty. Eunice and her husband did send their son, Lisle Carter Jr., to Barbados, and many accounts attribute this to the rising threats from Eunice's work with the special prosecutor. However, according to her grandson, Eunice sent her son away a year *before* she started working for Thomas Dewey.

One of my favorite scenes in the book is when Eunice uncovers evidence (with the help of Polly) that will be useful in the trial, and she bargains with Dewey for a seat on the trial team. In reality, Dewey chose three trial prosecutors—and Eunice was not one of them. Despite compiling much of the evidentiary groundwork for the case, she was excluded from the trial team and only spent a few days in the courtroom.

Why wasn't she included? No reason was ever stated, but given the context, one could extrapolate: She was a Black woman who would have been presenting before twelve white men. (Although it was technically legal for women and Black men to serve on juries in New York at that time, it was rarely practiced.) It's heartbreaking that after all of her work, Eunice wasn't the one to stand in that courtroom and confront Lucky Luciano. Giving her that scene in the novel was one of our small victories for Eunice.

A few times, we noted that Eunice was the first Black woman to graduate from Fordham University School of Law. This was widely believed at the time; however, Ruth Whitehead Whaley graduated in 1924, eight years before Eunice in 1932. For many years, Fordham did not keep records by race, and Ruth Whitehead Whaley was only officially recognized as the first Black woman to graduate from Fordham University School of Law in the mid-2000s. Technology and better access to records and archives make it possible for us to correct these historical oversights. But writing from the character's point of view means that we must inhabit their belief. At the time, Eunice believed she was the first.

Regarding the threats Eunice received—the letter about her son in Barbados, the doll in the mail, the paint on the car—these were all fictionalized. We do know that the prosecutors were *constantly* threatened, probably far more than we depict in the novel. Thomas Dewey, in his autobiography *Twenty Against the Underworld* (a fascinating book that includes so many details of the trial and witnesses and even transcripts of some of the testimony), refers to the many threats he and his colleagues received, including a harrowing call made to his wife to come to the morgue to identify his body. She was nine months pregnant at the time.

Stephen Carter also referred to the constant threats the prosecutors received in one of his interviews. While we know the special prosecutor and his team faced danger, we do not know the exact nature of these threats. One victory for Dewey's team was that despite the threats, all twenty prosecutors remained on the case until Luciano was convicted.

This case, the second largest in the history of New York at the time, launched the careers of many of the assistant district attorneys. They went on to become judges and political leaders. And Thomas Dewey ascended to national prominence as the three-term governor of New York and a two-time presidential candidate. He was never elected president, losing first to Franklin D. Roosevelt and then to Harry Truman. (Fun fact: Every poll showed that in the 1948 presidential election, Thomas Dewey would defeat Harry Truman. The *Chicago Daily Tribune* didn't even wait for the polls to close. They printed a headline—*Dewey Defeats Truman*—and there's an infamous photograph of Harry Truman holding up that newspaper right before he gave his victory speech.) But even without winning the presidency, Dewey had an illustrious career and remains firmly etched in history.

The same cannot be said of Eunice Hunton Carter. After the Luciano verdict, Eunice continued working in the New York prosecutor's office with Dewey. He appointed her chief of the Special

Sessions Bureau, where Eunice led the department that prosecuted thousands of misdemeanor cases each year. In addition, she continued her work in politics, assisting Dewey with both of his presidential campaigns.

But Eunice's greatest desire was to become a judge. With friends like Thomas Dewey and Fiorello LaGuardia, the mayor of New York, it seemed entirely possible that she could have been appointed the first Black female judge in the country.

Yet that never came to pass. Many believe it was because of her race and gender. However, another factor could have been at play—her brother, Alphaeus Hunton. Alphaeus was a Howard University and Harvard University graduate before he became a professor at Howard. In the early 1940s, he was accused of being a Communist, and according to Stephen L. Carter, the accusation was correct—Alphaeus was a member of the Communist party. Not only was he subjugated to the tactics of having his telephone tapped and his mail confiscated, he also spent six months in jail before he eventually moved to Africa.

Some have speculated that his affiliation with the Communist party was the greatest obstacle to Eunice's judicial aspirations. And there is evidence that Eunice may have believed the same.

As Marie explained in her author's note, we have no evidence that Polly and Eunice conspired to bring down Luciano. But Eunice had to have had some help. And who better than the most notorious madam of that time?

I loved these women and could just imagine them together. Both were fierce in their own way. They stood up to everything and everyone, including each other. It was a joy to bring them to life, but writing this novel was such a different experience for Marie and me, primarily because these two women were not friends. In fact, I'm certain there were moments when each wished the other would simply disappear. Writing about women whose relationship didn't come from a place of love presented more challenges than I expected. With our past novels, especially *The First Ladies*, Marie and I drew heavily on our own friendship to convey how Black and white women could work together toward a common goal. It was almost too easy to show Eleanor Roosevelt and Mary McLeod Bethune laughing together, plotting together, challenging each other, and even becoming angry for a moment. All we had to do was pull from our own experiences.

Writing *A Pair of Aces*, however, was new terrain. It was ground that often felt foreign to both of us. But it was important to us to bring to light two more women who have been hidden deep in the folds of history and to explore a fictional relationship between two women who stood side by side not as friends, but as women who respected each other.

For many of us, the world feels topsy-turvy right now, and we may discover that the best way to survive—and even thrive—through these times is to join forces with people of different races, backgrounds, and experiences. People who may not initially feel like allies yet who stand on our side nonetheless.

The alliance between Eunice and Polly was never destined to blossom into a lifelong friendship. Instead, the two recognized they were on a mission—just for a season, and for a vital reason. They understood that their common goal couldn't be achieved without both of them. So they stood beside each other with mutual respect, proving that friendship is not a prerequisite for alliance.

I hope this message echoes through the pages of our novel. Motives and methods may differ, but women can still join forces to achieve a common goal. Unity and collaboration—and eventually victory—are more important than personal affinity. May these two women, this unlikely pair of aces, serve as inspiration.

MARIE BENEDICT'S ACKNOWLEDGMENTS

Bringing *A Pair of Aces* to life—which has, at its core, the unlikely, world-changing partnership of Eunice Hunton Carter and Polly Adler—took a leap of faith only possible because of my trusting relationship with the generous and talented Victoria Christopher Murray, for which I am immensely grateful. I am also indebted to Laura Dail, my tireless, kind, and brilliant agent, who fosters my mission *always*, along with Katie Gisondi, who handles translation rights. An enormous thanks also goes to Kate Seaver, our insightful guide and editor, and executive editor for Berkley, who, from the start, has championed us every step of the way.

There are many, many other folks at Berkley and Penguin Random House who deserve enormous thanks: the president of Penguin, Allison Dobson; the president of Putnam, Dutton, and Berkley, Ivan Held; the executive vice president and publisher at Berkley, Christine Ball; the senior vice president and editor in chief of Berkley, Claire Zion; the vice president, deputy publisher, and director of marketing at Berkley, Jeanne-Marie Hudson; the vice president, associate publisher, and publicity director at Berkley,

Craig Burke; the senior vice president and executive creative director at Penguin, Anthony Ramondo; the associate director of art and design at Penguin, Vikki Chu; the deputy director of marketing at Berkley, Jin Yu; Berkley marketing associate Hillary Tacuri; the assistant director of publicity at Berkley, Lauren Burnstein; publicist Ariana Abad; executive managing editor Christine Legon; senior designer Katy Riegel; production director Kellie Schirmer; senior production editor Lindsey Tulloch; and assistant editor Amanda Maurer. We are also so grateful to vice president and group sales director Andrew Dudley, director of imprint sales Rachel Obenschain, and the amazing Penguin Publishing Group sales team.

As always, I am most thankful for the love and support of Jim, Jack, and Ben. Not to mention my kind and generous network of family members and friends—and, of course, readers, librarians, and booksellers everywhere.

VICTORIA CHRISTOPHER MURRAY'S ACKNOWLEDGMENTS

Whenever I speak with aspiring authors, I always tell them that it takes a village to write and publish a book. And that is certainly the case with *A Pair of Aces*. I could not have written this novel with anyone other than Marie Benedict, and it has been a joy writing with her since our first collaboration.

My agent, Liza Dawson, and I have been together for fifteen years now, and these have been the best years of my career. She's opened so many doors so that I could live my dream, and for her unwavering belief and never-ending support, I am thankful.

I have been fortunate to work with some of the best editors in the business, but Kate Seaver has raised the bar. I've said this before: An editor who believes in you, challenges you, and pushes you toward your very best self makes all the difference. I have all of that with Kate, but what matters most is this—Kate is my advocate and champion. I am here because of her.

Then, there is the A-team, the people who make all the publishing magic happen: the president of Penguin, Allison Dobson; the CEO of Penguin Random House, Nihar Malaviya; the president of Putnam, Dutton, and Berkley, Ivan Held; the executive vice president and publisher at Berkley, Christine Ball; the senior vice president and editor in chief of Berkley, Claire Zion; the vice president, deputy publisher, and director of marketing at Berkley, Jeanne-Marie Hudson; the vice president, associate publisher, and publicity director at Berkley, Craig Burke; the senior vice president and executive creative director at Penguin, Anthony Ramondo; the associate director of art and design at Penguin, Vikki Chu; the deputy director of marketing at Berkley, Jin Yu; Berkley marketing associate Hillary Tacuri; the assistant director of publicity at Berkley, Lauren Burnstein; publicist Ariana Abad; executive managing editor Christine Legon; senior designer Katy Riegel; production director Kellie Schirmer; senior production editor Lindsey Tulloch; and assistant editor Amanda Maurer. And of course, the entire incredible Penguin sales team. I told you it takes a village, and this one stands above all the others.

To all the booksellers, especially the independent bookstores who hand-sell our books, and the librarians who constantly recommend us to readers—no one would know our stories without you.

And now, the people listed last but who always come first . . . the readers. The readers who show up book after book, who read and share our stories. I wish I could name every reader and every book club, but that would take volumes. I do want to shout out a few: the Personal Librarians (who were inspired to come together by our first novel), Tabahani Book Circle, and Go On Girl Book Club. These book clubs, like hundreds of others, have chosen us, supported us, and cheered us on.

I must also thank the members of Delta Sigma Theta Sorority, Inc. My Sorors rally around every book of mine as if it were a global mission. They don't play about me!

My heart is so full when I think of all the readers who have been with me over these twenty-five years. Please know that you are the reason I write and will continue to do so. As I've told so many of you, a history untold is a history erased. Together, we are keeping history alive.